Praise for

The Good
at Heart

"With skillful eloquence, Ursula Werner weaves a compelling tale of ordinary people living in extraordinarily complex and character-defining times. Poignant and moving, this World War II story paints a fresh perspective on what we are willing to surrender for the greater good."

—Susan Meissner, author of
Secrets of a Charmed Life

"Inspired by her great-grandfather's experience, Werner has written an engaging story about good people and their wartime struggle to stay true to their convictions while protecting those they love. The vignette-style writing, reminiscent of Maeve Binchy, and the rich character development, makes for an evocative narrative that provides a snapshot into the lives of ordinary Germans during World War II."

—*Library Journal*

"The author does a wonderful job of presenting the moral dilemmas the family faced as a whole, and as individuals, as well as the conflicts of belief between family members. . . . Many were 'good at heart'—caught up in an evil from which they could not escape without deadly consequences."

—*Historical Novels Review*

The Good at Heart

URSULA WERNER

TOUCHSTONE

New York   London   Toronto   Sydney   New Delhi

Touchstone
An Imprint of Simon & Schuster, Inc.
1230 Avenue of the Americas
New York, NY 10020

First Touchstone trade paperback edition February 2018

TOUCHSTONE and colophon are registered trademarks of Simon & Schuster, Inc.

For information about special discounts for bulk purchases, please contact Simon & Schuster Special Sales at 1-866-506-1949 or business@simonandschuster.com.

The Simon & Schuster Speakers Bureau can bring authors to your live event. For more information or to book an event, contact the Simon & Schuster Speakers Bureau at 1-866-248-3049 or visit our website at www.simonspeakers.com.

Interior design by Jill Putorti

Manufactured in the United States of America

10 9 8 7 6 5 4 3 2 1

The Library of Congress has cataloged the hardcover edition as follows:

Names: Werner, Ursula, 1964– author.
Title: The good at heart / Ursula Werner.
Description: First Touchstone hardcover edition. | New York : Touchstone, 2017.
Identifiers: LCCN 2016023467 (print) | LCCN 2016028853 (ebook) | ISBN 9781501147579 (hardcover) | ISBN 9781501147586 (trade pbk.) | ISBN 9781501147593 (eBook)
Subjects: LCSH: World War, 1939–1945—Fiction. | World War, 1939–1945—Refugees—Fiction. | Families—Germany—Fiction. | GSAFD: Domestic fiction | Historical fiction
Classification: LCC PS3623.E767 G66 2017 (print) | LCC PS3623.E767 (ebook) | DDC 813/.6—dc23
LC record available at https://lccn.loc.gov/2016023467

ISBN 978-1-5011-4757-9
ISBN 978-1-5011-4758-6 (pbk)
ISBN 978-1-5011-4759-3 (ebook)

To Geoffrey

In spite of everything I still believe that people are really good at heart. I simply can't build up my hopes on a foundation consisting of confusion, misery, and death. I see the world gradually being turned into a wilderness, I hear the ever approaching thunder, which will destroy us too, I can feel the sufferings of millions and yet, if I look up into the heavens, I think that it will all come right, that this cruelty too will end, and that peace and tranquillity will return again.

—Anne Frank,
translated by Barbara Mooyart-Doubleday

– Prologue –

1938

The daisies won her over. Hundreds of miniature daisies, *gänse-blümchen*, raised their heads over the blades of grass and waved to her in the light breeze blowing across the lake. Little else was growing on the property—a young apple tree, a large chestnut just off the road, a cherry tree in the middle of the lawn, a tall willow down near the lake. The rest was grass strewn with daisies.

From a distance, the lot had looked inhospitable. Edith had already begun to set her mind against it as they approached. The dilapidated wooden fence that surrounded the property and the cloud of dust that followed their car along the dirt road did not convey welcome. More disheartening were the train tracks that paralleled the road not fifty yards from the property line. Edith had no idea what the local train schedule was like, but even one train a day barreling past would be one too many for her nerves.

But when she saw the daisies, she forgave the property its faults. She took off her shoes and woolen stockings and grazed her bare feet across the delicate daisy petals before stepping gently into the green velvet blanket of their leaves. Oskar took her hand, and together they walked across the length of the lawn to the edge of the lake. A narrow beach of small gray pebbles met the water in a thick border of willow reeds. They looked for swans, and saw instead a pair of small black grebes nesting near the shore. Across the lake, the coastline was blue-green forests dotted with white towns. Beyond that rose the pearl-gray outlines of the Swiss Alps.

This was it, Edith knew.

When Oskar first shared his dream of a vacation home with Edith, back in their earliest years in Berlin, it had been just that—a dream. Oskar's government job paid hardly enough to cover the rent for their small apartment. Still, in the darkness of night, long after the last oil lamp had been extinguished and the front door bolted, Oskar and Edith lay under the feathers of their down comforter and built their house. In quiet whispers they built it, stone by stone, tile by tile, window by window, year after year.

They were just imagining the interior when the Black Hand killed Archduke Franz Ferdinand and his wife, Sophie, on their fourteenth wedding anniversary, catapulting Europe into war. In the few months before Oskar was called away to the front, they lay in bed and worked on the entrance hall: a thick mahogany front door carved with foxes and cats, ivy and lilies; an Italian marble floor, pale pink with streaks of cream and light brown; three antique ebony tables set with fresh flowers, no matter the season. While Oskar was commanding foot soldiers in France, they worked on the kitchen, planning most of it through heavily censored letters: the heavy oak bench spanning the northeast corner and surrounding the breakfast table, large and ponderous for baking projects and boiled eggs in hand-painted eggcups; the south wall lined with cabinets, one of which—the one on the far right, where they would keep the liqueurs and chocolate—would be locked, out of the children's reach; the cast-iron stove, coal-burning. They would keep the unsightly coal pile in some out-of-the-way place, perhaps a cellar.

On their daughter Marina's fifth birthday, they added a skylight to the roof of the master bedroom, for midnight stargazing and daytime raindrop races. When their son, Peter, died of pneumonia before his third birthday, their grief sowed an entire garden of roses and red currant bushes, daffodils and dahlias, carpets of purple and black pansies dotted with pale-blue forget-me-nots. Slowly, over the years, as Marina outgrew her dirndls and her braids and then moved to an apartment of her own with her new husband, the house took shape room by room, carpeted with deep crimson Persian rugs, shaded with Belgian lace curtains, each detail painstakingly considered, no expense spared.

Oskar was promoted.

They began to look at properties. Oskar focused on the countryside surrounding Berlin, so they could be near Marina's family and see their grandchildren. But Edith increasingly wished herself and her family as far away from Berlin as possible. The city was changing in dangerous ways; she feared its effect upon her family. She was silent when Oskar took her to see the various lots he had surveyed. He did not press. She would speak, as always, when she was ready. And indeed, one night, under the feathers, she whispered, "Wouldn't it be lovely to have a view of the Alps?"

Oskar was an accommodating man. He began looking south. And now they were surveying this property on a large lake, the Bodensee. Oskar turned to Edith. "It is a good piece of land with a good view of the mountains."

Edith smiled at him. "I like the daisies."

They began construction immediately. They started with the garage, which was to be right by the road, near the train tracks— the house would be closer to the lake. They had just completed the roof over the cement walls that would enclose their car when another war broke out.

Day One

July 18, 1944

– One –

The day the German army opened fire on its own citizens in Blumental was the day of Pimpanella's miracle. It was a cool summer morning, with the first promise of sun after four drizzly, cold days. Rosie woke early, hopped out of bed, and ran downstairs. Ever since she turned five, she had been allowed to check for eggs in the henhouse. She loved crawling into the small plywood hutch that housed the four chickens, reaching into each nest, and gently wiggling her fingers between the straw and the burlap, feeling around for that small, smooth oval, still warm from being under the hen's puffed chest, the shell slightly soft.

Rosie also loved the hens, Pimpanella especially. Spindly little Pimpanella was the closest thing Rosie had to a pet; she was the only chicken who did not peck at Rosie's feet in the outhouse. And Rosie protected Pimpanella against her grandfather. The last time Opa was home from Berlin, he declared Pimpanella useless because she had never been able to produce an egg. "A poor excuse for a fowl," he called her. He chased Pimpanella around the yard with a stewpot lid, yelling at her to pull herself together and do her part for the war effort.

This morning, Rosie crawled up the short ladder and crept into the dusty coop. She made her way around the circle of nests: first Nina (one egg), then Rosamunde (also one), then Hanni (none, but she had a habit of laying her eggs any old place), and finally Pimpanella. Rosie's older sisters, Lara and Sofia, didn't even check Pimpanella's nest anymore because in the entire year they'd had her, they had never found anything. But Rosie had faith in Pimpanella, even if no one else did. You had to believe, Rosie thought. You had to believe in good things because there were too many bad things to scare you if you didn't. Like when you saw soldiers with only half a face at the bakery in Berlin. Or when you saw the soldiers missing an arm or a leg. Or both.

Rosie gently patted Pimpanella's entire nest, starting at the side nearest to her. Nothing. Undiscouraged, she started over, this time digging down a bit deeper with her fingers. Halfway through, on the edge of the tamped-down hay where Pimpanella usually sat, there it was—an egg, buried under about three centimeters of straw. Then, to Rosie's surprise and delight, she found another, right next to the first one. *Two* eggs! Twins!

It was a glorious day. Rosie would have to remember to bring Pimpanella some carrot tops as a special treat. For now, she gathered all the eggs up carefully in her pajama top and walked back uphill to the house. The small square building stood at the northern end of their property, right by the road that ran along the train tracks into town. Its stucco walls held layers of ivy and honeysuckle, which wound their way around the blackened oak window frames up to a clay tile roof. Given the green cloak of these vines, and how tiny the house was compared to the vast garden surrounding it, anyone passing by the property along the lake path to the south might overlook the structure altogether.

For the Eberhardt family, however, the house was enough. Though cramped, it could hold five people, sometimes six or seven if Rosie's father came home from the eastern front, or if her grandfather came south from his job in Berlin. The last time Rosie's father was home, he was so skinny he looked like a ghost, and he woke up every night screaming. He didn't stay long. The war wanted him back.

When Rosie entered the kitchen, it was empty except for the smell of warm bread. She deposited the eggs in the basket on the table. From the big hand on the clock, she knew she was late.

Rosie ran outside to the front of the house, where Sofia was waiting for her. The 8:00 a.m. train whistled in the distance. The girls didn't have much time. Their daily race to see who would be first to the underpass would have to start right now.

Sofia looked at Rosie. "You're not even dressed yet."

"There wasn't time," Rosie said. "Quick, the train is coming!"

"All right, but you don't get a head start just because you're barefoot. Ready . . . set . . . go!"

It did not take more than several seconds for Sofia, two years older and at least a head taller than Rosie, to pull out in front, blond braids flapping against her shoulders. Racing just a few steps behind her sister, Rosie balled her fingers into fists. Her grandfather had told her that helped your speed. She was almost at Sofia's feet.

"Coming to get you, coming to get you," Rosie taunted. Sofia took a quick glance backward, stuck her tongue out, and sped up for the final few meters. She rounded the corner at the base of the bridge a few steps before Rosie, just as the three-car train shook the steel girders over their heads. The girls stood there, bent over and breathing heavily.

"Look, Rosie," Sofia said. "The barricade is gone!"

Two mornings ago, at the end of their race, Rosie and Sofia had almost crashed into an enormous pile of tree trunks that had been piled under the bridge. Someone had chopped down all the trees from a nearby thicket and stacked them on top of one another. Even today, the copse of trees that had yielded them still looked naked and embarrassed. Their leftover stumps stared blankly up at the stark sunlight, as if in shock from the trauma of decapitation.

For the past two days, that makeshift wall had blocked all traffic on the narrow road that ran along the Bodensee between the towns of Blumental and Meerfeld. Everyone knew the barricade was Captain Rodemann's doing, and the smoldering hatred they already bore him for disrupting their lives grew to a blaze.

Captain Heinrich Rodemann, the seventeen-year-old leader of the Twenty-Sixth Battalion of the Hohenfeld foot patrol, had high expectations for his own military fame. He had always imagined he would make his name on a battlefield, even though he had entered the war only eight months earlier. Like the Führer whom he so proudly served, Heinrich Rodemann was not at all concerned about the recent Allied invasion of Normandy. He had great faith in the German military machine, for he shared with the Führer that intensity of ego that urged him to fight with greater strength and resistance the closer the end appeared to be.

In late June, when Berlin sent Rodemann south to investigate rumors of a possible French incursion on German soil, the overeager captain took the assignment very seriously. He decided to establish headquarters in a small town on the west end of the Bodensee. Blumental was ideally located for his purposes. No one seemed to know exactly if or when French troops would appear, but Captain Rodemann was committed to the engagement, eager to exercise his pubescent military muscle. His foot soldiers set up camp in the vineyards around the Catholic church of Birnau, to the east of town, while he took the best room in the town's only inn, the Gasthof zum Löwen. Twice a day, the captain sent out scouting teams to ascertain whether there was any sign of the French; twice a day, his hopes were dashed with negative reports. To pass the time, he marched his troops around the marketplace. They stomped past the pigeon-stained bronze statue of Albrecht Munter, first mayor of Blumental. They paraded through the small commercial district distinguished by one newsstand, one jeweler, a clothing store, a pharmacy, a butcher, and the bakery of the three Mecklen sisters. They strutted down the lake promenade, where the metal chairs and tables of outdoor cafés rested wearily against one another, resigned to the rust that claimed more of their frames with each summer storm.

To ease the pain of his frustrated ambitions, Captain Rodemann commandeered chickens, fresh milk, and local produce from the farmers, and he practically emptied the vintner's wine cellar. But not even these amenities could assuage his growing impatience and mounting irritation. He sent daily telegrams to Berlin, describing in exaggerated detail the reconnaissance efforts undertaken in the previous twenty-four hours and bemoaning the continued absence of signs of a French offensive. After three weeks, Berlin had had enough, and Rodemann was ordered to move his troops out. On his own initiative, Rodemann decided to erect an impediment that would hinder the French, should they ever arrive. He ordered his men to set up a barricade. They filled the underpass with headless tree trunks.

Nobody dared to move them, at least not immediately, and not in daylight. Deliveries that usually arrived via the southeast road were rerouted along a smaller dirt path intended for the farmers and shepherds who used the grass fields near the Birnau forest. By the end of the barricade's first day, a hay wagon had collided with a meat van, two oversize trucks were stuck in the mud next to the sheep pastures, and the bewildered sheep had been introduced to an entirely new vocabulary of epithets. Grumbling about the situation began quietly, in conversations between two or three people, then spread through flocks of women at Mecklen's Bakery and six-packs of men at the town tavern. By the end of the second day, everyone had run out of patience, and a resolute group of Blumental citizens, fortified by several pints of beer, dismantled the pile of logs under cover of darkness.

Marina Thiessen was outside in the yard, talking to her neighbor across the fence, when Rosie ran up the gravel driveway.

"Mutti, Mutti! They unblocked the road!"

"Rosie, hush." Marina held up her hand and gave her daughter a stern look. "I'm speaking with Frau Breckenmüller about it."

Rosie liked Frau Breckenmüller. She lived next door and had the pink cheeks of a fairy-tale grandmother. Rosie also liked Herr Breckenmüller—even though he was a fisherman and often smelled like fish—because he had helped her grandfather hang a swing in the apple tree. Last summer, after Rosie pestered her opa all morning about the swing, Opa had marched over to the Breckenmüllers' to borrow some rope. Rosie remembered Herr Breckenmüller leaning on the fence next to her, puffing quietly on his cigar, a half smile creeping up his cheek, while Opa threw the ropes over the apple tree branch to secure the wooden board.

"Sure those knots are tight, Oskar?" Herr Breckenmüller had asked.

"Stop yammering at me, old man," Opa had growled. "Don't you think I know how to tie a knot?" Herr Breckenmüller had smiled and winked at Rosie. He knew something he wasn't telling.

"Okay, then," Opa had said, grabbing the two ropes on each side of the swing. "Let me just try it once, Rosie, and then it's all yours." He took a few steps back, the seat of the swing dangling beneath him, then kicked up his feet and briefly pulled himself into the air before firmly depositing his bottom on the wooden plank. The knot in the rope unraveled immediately, landing Opa in the dirt with a loud thud.

"*Scheisse und verdammt nochmal!*"

Rosie had never seen her grandfather get so angry, and for an instant she had been afraid. He stood up slowly, still cursing loudly and rubbing his backside. But when he turned and saw Rosie, his face changed immediately. She saw the skin that had been fixed in tight ripples around his mouth and eyes become smooth and relax back into the sheepish smile of the Opa she knew.

Herr Breckenmüller tried hard not to laugh. Then he stamped out his cigar and walked slowly over to the apple tree. "It takes a fisherman to know his way around ropes," he had said, winking at Rosie conspiratorially.

This morning, Rosie ran over to the apple tree so she could swing while her mother was talking.

"Yes, Karl helped them take down the barricade early this morning, before he went out in his boat," Frau Breckenmüller said. "I tried to talk him out of it. I didn't want him involved."

"The authority of Captain Heinrich Rodemann is *so* sacrosanct." Her mother clenched her fists and pushed them into the pockets of her apron. "Of course we should be careful not to disturb the grand military edifice of dead trees erected by that great officer, never mind that he is nothing more than a *pig!*" Marina spat out the word. Frau Breckenmüller gasped and quickly reached across the fence to cover Marina's mouth with her hand. Rosie slowed the swing.

"You're not immune, you know," Frau Breckenmüller cautioned, "just because your father works for the Führer. Remember the Rosenbergs. People can disappear overnight."

Marina nodded and removed Frau Breckenmüller's fingers from her lips. "Come, Rosie. Let's get you some breakfast." She looked at Rosie's bare feet and frowned. "Even better, let's get you dressed."

"Oooh, yes!" Rosie suddenly remembered Pimpanella's eggs. "Come see the big surprise!"

Her grandmother was talking on the phone as Rosie and Marina walked into the kitchen. Any other day, Rosie would have run over to Oma and demanded to talk to whoever was on the line (usually her opa), because the telephone was still a novelty. Very few families in Blumental had one in their house, and most people had to use the telephone at the post office if they wanted to make a call. But her opa was an important person in Berlin, so they got one. Mostly they used it to call him.

Rosie wished Opa did not have to stay in Berlin to work while the rest of the family lived in Blumental, but as Oma often reminded her, everyone had to make sacrifices for the war. Long ago, when she was very little, they had all lived in Berlin. Then Sofia and Oma had almost died the night the bombs fell, and they moved to Blumental. Rosie didn't remember anything about that night. Apparently Sofia didn't either, because whenever Rosie asked about it, Sofia curled up into a little ball and whispered, "I don't remember."

Pulling her mother past the telephone room, Rosie stopped at the kitchen table.

"Look, Mutti." She pointed at the basket. "Eggs!"

Marina smiled hesitantly. "One, two, three . . . four eggs. That's wonderful, Rosie. Nina, Rosamunde, and Hanni are working very hard."

"No, no, only two of the eggs are from Nina and Rosamunde," Rosie interrupted. "The other two are from Pimpanella. They were right in her nest under the straw. Both of them."

"She probably stole them from the other chickens when they weren't looking," Lara said, shuffling into the kitchen in her slippers.

"She did not! She laid those eggs all by herself." Rosie ran over to her older sister and pummeled her in the stomach. Lara laughed and easily pushed Rosie away. Just then, Edith walked into the kitchen, her telephone conversation with Oskar ended.

"What does Oskar say?" Marina asked. She placed a pot of milk on the stove. "What's the news from Berlin?"

"Oskar is in Fürchtesgaden, not Berlin," Edith said. "Apparently the Führer felt the need for mountain air and asked the cabinet to join him for its weekly meeting."

"Hm. Sounds like our Führer, uprooting everyone from their normal lives because he 'felt the need,'" Marina said with a sniff, just as the porch door flew open and Sofia dashed into the kitchen.

"Irene Nagel's cat had kittens!" she said.

"Kittens!" Rosie thrust the basket of eggs into Edith's hands. Kittens were fluffy and warm and bouncy. Like a ball made out of feathers. "Can we go see them, Mutti? Oma? Please, can we?" Rosie ran over to her mother and put on her saddest, most plead- ing face.

"Actually, Rosie, your opa told me he needs your help with a special project this morning." Edith put her arms on Rosie's shoul- ders and addressed all three girls. "Everyone can help. We need to make a new flag for our window. A red, white, and blue one."

Marina looked up. So did Lara, who had been examining the fingernails on her right hand.

"Those are the colors of France," Lara said.

It turned out that the French army's approach was not a complete fabrication of Captain Rodemann's mind. One German intelli- gence dispatch reported sighting a small French battalion march- ing southeast to the German border, toward the lake. In their telephone conversation, Oskar told Edith that it was still many days away and probably not something to be overly concerned about. Nevertheless, he urged her to take precautions. Change the flag, he advised.

The flag flying from the second-floor window of the Eber- hardt home was, like every other flag displayed outside Blumental homes, the national flag of the Third Reich. One of the Führer's earliest laws required all German homes to display that flag in a prominent location. In Blumental, unanimous compliance with this decree was less a demonstration of the town's civic loyalty and unerring faith in the nation than a triumph of the efforts of the *bürgermeister* to safeguard his person.

On the day the law went into effect, long before the war began, the mayor of Blumental, Bürgermeister Hans Munter, al- most choked on the soft-boiled egg he had been enjoying with his morning newspaper. The government, he read, would hold the mayor of every city and town accountable for *any* transgression by *any* citizen. This was a shock to Munter, whose own mayoral approach to civic governance was laissez-faire, rooted in his conviction that everyone should be left alone and confrontation should be avoided at all costs. But could all of his citizens be trusted to comply with this law without his intervention? He didn't know, and he didn't want to find out.

Through expeditious use of the municipality's emergency fund, Munter soon ensured that full-size replicas of the national flag of the Third Reich were distributed to each Blumental family and hung prominently in front of every home. What Oskar feared, and what he shared with Edith over the phone, was that an invading French battalion might not feel generously inclined toward a town where swastikas flapped outside every window. Would it not be more prudent to substitute a French flag, or, if one could not be found, a white flag of surrender? Weighing strict compliance with the Führer's edicts against concern for public safety—primarily the safety of his family—Oskar thought the balance tipped in favor of changing the flags.

Edith agreed. After breakfast, she hurried over to the home of the Duponts, who had relatives in Paris, to share Oskar's news and request their help. Digging into the supply of French flags they had saved from Bastille Day celebrations, the Dupont family generously donated them to many of their neighbors. Families that did not receive French flags borrowed white cloth diapers from families with babies. By lunchtime, Blumental had successfully transformed itself into an apparent Francophile oasis, and everyone awaited the possibility of French occupation with trepidation.

When Captain Rodemann, marching east from Blumental with his battalion, received a telegram containing the same report that prompted Oskar's telephone call, he was so elated, he almost fell off his horse. The French army was finally marching toward the northern shore of the lake! Of course, if they were still in France, as the report indicated, it would be at least a week before they reached the Bodensee. They might head through the Black Forest or follow the Rhine along the Swiss border until it reached the lake. Either way, Rodemann was determined to intercept them and thus, as he imagined the consequences, to solidify his place in military history—first for restoring and holding the southern front and then for turning the tide of the war inexorably toward German victory. Veering west, the captain ordered his men to march at double time.

Captain Rodemann and his troops reentered Blumental poised for battle. In fact, Rodemann was so intent upon his upcoming victory that he did not immediately notice the red, white, and blue stripes hanging on each building the battalion passed on its way down the main street. Nevertheless, the flags wove in and out of his consciousness with steady regularity, slowly but firmly knitting a pernicious banner of dissension and rebellion, a banner of popular support for the enemy. Captain Rodemann turned the corner to where he had built the perfect roadblock, where he had constructed out of tree trunks alone an impregnable barrier, and where now stood . . . nothing. He turned around and looked up the street he had just marched down. Flags flapped at him, mocked him, laughed at him in white, blue, and red. Captain Rodemann exploded in anger.

Rosie and Sofia had spent the morning staining a white cloth diaper with red currant and blackberry juices, trying to make a French flag for the upstairs window. They had just hung the finished product outside the second-floor dormer when their grandmother called them down to lunch.

It was a quiet meal of fish with small yellow potatoes from Edith's garden. Rosie sat next to Sofia on the oak bench, opposite Lara, who insisted on sitting in her own chair. Rosie had eaten very quickly today because she wanted to get to Irene Nagel's kittens. Irene had told Sofia there were five. Certainly no house needed that many cats. Sooner or later, Irene's mother would be giving away some of those kittens, and Rosie and Sofia wanted to be first in line to claim one. Rosie fiddled with the lace curtains and plucked one of the African violets from the little potted plants on the windowsill. She pulled off its petals one by one and looked around the table.

Her mother and grandmother were silent, but that often happened after Opa called. Sometimes he told them news about Rosie's father, who was away fighting in France. He used to be away fighting in Russia, but then he got stuck in that Russian city, and every time Opa called, her mother grabbed the phone, and when she was done talking to Opa, she would bite her lip. She bit her lip all winter.

Rosie looked to see if her mother was biting her lip now. But today, her mother was only pressing her lips together. Rosie jiggled her legs impatiently. Sofia's plate still had two potatoes and a lot of fish on it. She kicked Sofia under the table. "Eat faster," she urged.

Noticing Rosie's impatience, Edith stood up from her chair and walked over to the chocolate cabinet. "Tell you what, Rosie," she said. "Why don't you have a peppermint while you wait?"

Rosie loved peppermints. She unwrapped this one from its crinkly pink paper and held it between her thumb and forefinger and licked it slowly to make it last longer. She only put the whole thing in her mouth later, when lunch was finally over and she needed her hands to dry the dishes. Sofia washed and Rosie dried, sweeping the dish towel over the wet plate at the same time that she swirled her tongue around the peppermint.

Pecka pecka pecka. Rosie looked up when she heard the noise. It sounded like a woodpecker. A loud one, and very close. She usually only heard woodpeckers during walks through the Birnau forest with her mother. But there it was again. Rosie went to the kitchen window to try to see it, but at that moment, three things happened simultaneously: one of the empty milk bottles that was sitting on the front door stoop shattered, Sofia dropped a pot that she had been washing, and Marina came thundering down the stairs and through the kitchen, shouting, "Into the reeds! Now! Into the reeds!"

The Eberhardt family response to air raids and other military dangers was the same as that of every family living along the lakefront: leave the house immediately and hide in the thicket of willow reeds on the shore. Though air raids were rare this far south, there had been a few bombings in nearby Friedrichshafen that had required them to put this escape plan into effect. The girls hated hiding in the reeds. It was wet and scary and uncomfortable to stand in the water motionless for up to an hour and a half. In the summer, the water was warm and home to leeches; in the winter, it was unbearably cold.

In less than a minute, Edith and Lara were already outside the French doors and running down the lawn toward the lake. Neighbors all around were doing the same, shrieking and shouting and scrambling as quickly as possible to get to the relative safety of the thick, camouflaging reeds. Sofia was still near the sink, curling herself into a ball next to the pile of pots Rosie had just dried. Rosie knew that Sofia was trying to make herself as small as possible so that the danger would overlook her and move on. It had worked for her in Berlin.

But Marina knew where to find her. "Out! Out!" Marina screamed, grabbing Sofia's arm and pulling her up from the stone floor where she was cowering. She pushed Sofia's stiff form out of the house, and then—awkwardly, because Sofia was getting too big for Marina to carry—gathered her up and ran haltingly down to the lake.

Rosie recognized the look of panic on her mother's face when she ran through the kitchen. The look said, *Run! Now!* For an instant, Rosie was confused because she did not understand why a woodpecker would be dangerous, but now there were other sounds coming up the street, sounds that Rosie had heard in Berlin at night, before they moved. Guns. Yes, Rosie concluded as her feet began to run, it must be gunfire that was peppering the stone houses. Rosie knew that machine guns meant follow the exit drill, and Rosie was very good at the exit drill.

She had just reached the French doors heading to the backyard when she remembered Hans-Jürg. He was still upstairs in her bed. Hans-Jürg the bear had always been with Rosie. She was devoted to him, in part because he was the only other member of the family with brown eyes, just like hers. Rosie could not leave Hans-Jürg alone with gunfire going off all around him. So as Marina was running out of the house dragging Sofia behind her, Rosie ran through the living room to the staircase.

Rosie knew, with each step upward, that she should not let herself feel scared or listen to the increasing volume of the machine-gun sounds, which meant that the soldiers, whoever they were, were now on *their* street, getting closer to *their* house. She should not, *could* not, let any of that into her mind. Instead, she thought about Hans-Jürg. Hans-Jürg. *Hans*, putting her right foot on one step, *Jürg*, her left foot on the next one. *Hans*, right, *Jürg*, left. *Hans, Jürg. Hans, Jürg.* At the top of the staircase, she half tripped over the old throw rug, put her hand down briefly to catch her balance, and ran to the left into her room. She could tell immediately that Hans-Jürg was grateful to her for coming back. He sat on the faded pink quilt, smiling at her with his thick-threaded, slightly crooked black mouth.

Wrapping Hans-Jürg in her arms to protect him, Rosie ran back down through the house and yard, so quickly she did not have time to feel scared. She ran straight through her grandmother's pansies, past the ripening cherry tree—where just yesterday she and Sofia had practiced spitting pits into the Breckenmüllers' yard—over the molehills and through the back fence gate. It did not matter this time that she left it open.

Rosie ran from the bullets, across the pebbles of the shallow beach, into the tall willow reeds, through the water, the mud sucking at her sandals. Unable to pull up her foot, she stopped, panting. She had ignored her terror until now. Now it clamped onto her rib cage and paralyzed her lungs. She had to fight to suck in air. Finally she began to sob and clutched her bear to her heaving chest.

"Rosie!" her mother called out. Marina brushed aside willow stalks and thrust her way through the defiant sludge and water of the lake. "Shh, shh! I'm here, Rosie, I'm here." Rosie felt her mother's arms wrap around her and hold her tightly. She pressed her head into her mother's body, burrowing her face into the coarse wool of her mother's skirt. Gradually, the air Rosie breathed in became warm and minty, a reminder of her peppermint.

"This is crazy," Frau Dachmaier said as Marina and Rosie waded over to the group. "I thought the French were civilized. Why would they shoot at civilians?"

The older Dachmaier boys, Boris and Jan, had broken off two of the longer reeds and were engaged in a mock machine-gun shootout, splashing about in the shallow sections of the beach. "Stop it!" Lara hissed at them. "Keep quiet!" She reached over, grabbed Boris's reed, and snapped it in half. The boys glared at her in fury.

"I . . . don't . . . think . . . it's . . . the . . . French . . . who . . . are . . . shooting." Old Herr Schmidt spoke in a measured, ruminative way, as if he were one of the clocks that he had spent his lifetime fixing and could issue only one word per second. He shook his graying head for a moment, then looked over at Edith and raised his eyebrows, inviting her speculation.

"Well, it can't be the Russians, can it?" Frau Dachmaier continued. "They've never gotten this far south. Or west, for that matter."

Rosie watched her grandmother study Herr Schmidt's face. "No," Edith said finally. "It's not the Russians either. There's only one army battalion nearby, and it doesn't belong to the enemy. It's us. It's Rodemann."

The neighbors fell silent and let Edith's words float among the reeds.

Captain Rodemann was furious. The removal of the barricade constituted flagrant contempt for his authority, criminal disrespect for a military officer. There was no question that removal of this barrier aided and abetted the enemy in its incursion onto German soil. And there were all those French flags too, flapping from the town's windows like derisive tongues taunting him as he passed by. The more the captain considered the situation, the more the whole thing looked like treason. It appeared that Blumental was a hitherto undiscovered haven for the Resistance. Someone would have to answer for this, someone visible to the entire community. The *bürgermeister*.

On his way to the *bürgermeister*'s home, Rodemann allowed his men to fire their rifles and machine guns into rose gardens and playgrounds and living rooms, chasing everyone into hiding. If their weapons were somewhat indiscriminately discharged, Rodemann did not worry about it, for the residents of Blumental needed a lesson in the consequences of disloyalty. Eventually he found his target, for poor Hans Munter's fringe of dwindling blond curls was not dense enough to camouflage him in the middle of his neighbor's herd of sheep.

Captain Rodemann marched Hans Munter at riflepoint through the town and up the hill to the Catholic church. It was a steep hill, and Hans found that he could do little better than stumble his way up—years of sausages and strawberry schnapps had taken their toll, and he seemed to have lost complete control of his legs.

Hans Munter had spent his entire life successfully avoiding his country's wars—too young for the first and exempted from the second because, as *bürgermeister*, he was in charge of sending a roster of military-eligible Blumental men to Berlin, and he conveniently forgot to add his own name. He had read with sorrow and heartache many of those same names on monthly casualty lists sent to the town, and personally visited each family that had lost a young son or father to offer his condolences. Each spring, on Remembrance Day, he lit candles for those lost men. Thus did Hans try to give to the war effort without actually offering his life.

But the war could not be fooled, he realized now. It had come to extract payment, in the form of a rifle butt that kept prodding him to move forward. He was no more ready to give up his life today than he'd been four years ago. Only one small glimmer of hope flickered amid the panic that had seized his brain: negotiation through abject apology.

Hans could tell that Captain Rodemann was angry. He could also tell that he himself was, in some way that he didn't understand, at fault. He decided that he must look for an opportunity to apologize to the captain for whatever it was that was irking him. Surely if Hans took responsibility for whatever this transgression was, if he was contrite and sincere and offered the captain whatever amends might be demanded, surely—possibly—everything could be straightened out.

Hans shuffled on, willing his feet to keep moving. Why the apology had to take place on top of the highest hill in the village, in front of the church, he didn't know. Perhaps the captain was religious.

The machine guns had been quiet for some time. Rosie waited with her sisters while the adults pushed their way through the reeds and looked up and down the lake path, listening for danger.

After several minutes, Marina came back through the water and waved them to shore. The children stood still while their parents checked them for leeches.

Rosie was too impatient to wait for her mother, so she lifted her pants leg herself. She was neither surprised nor upset to find a small leech attached to her calf. She plucked it off and threw it back into the reeds, then grabbed Sofia's hand.

"Come on, Sofia, Mutti and Oma are going to the marketplace to make sure everyone else is okay," Rosie said, pulling her sister forward and stomping her feet to get the mud off her shoes.

By the time they all arrived at the town center, most of the residents had come out of hiding. They emerged from linen closets and bathtubs. They threw off potato sacks in cellars. They left haylofts and chicken coops, picking bits of dried grass and feathers from their shirts. They climbed down from apple trees. And they walked over to the marketplace. The instinct to establish contact with friends and neighbors, to take stock, to shake hands, slap shoulders, and hug children, was universal. It appeared that everyone was safe.

The only two who were unaccounted for were Hans Munter and young Max Fuchs. And just as Johann Wiessmeyer, the Protestant minister, was comforting and reassuring Max's mother, Max himself came running back into town from the Birnau forest, where he had been hiding. "They're going to hang the *bürgermeister!*" he shouted. "Come quickly, they're going to hang him!"

Hans Munter kept waiting for his opportunity to clarify the situation. When Captain Rodemann stopped underneath the old yew tree on the perimeter of the graveyard, Hans tried to speak, despite the fact that he could scarcely control his bladder and that his arms were forcefully held by two burly soldiers.

"Pardon, Herr Captain, if I could just have a—" he began.

"Silence!" screamed Rodemann. He pointed to a soldier behind the *bürgermeister*. "You there, get a rope. Throw it around that tree branch." As the lanky blond boy ran back down the hill, Rodemann sighed with irritation, then took a knife from the sheath on his hip and began cleaning his fingernails.

"Captain, I think—" Hans tried again.

Rodemann turned on the *bürgermeister*, knifepoint extended menacingly. "Did I not tell you to be quiet? Did I not ask for silence? Must I stuff a potato in your mouth?" Rodemann could not abide these interruptions. He needed to keep his anger alive. From the time he had discovered the dismantled barricade to the moment his men had located Munter, his fury had been reliably constant. He had a plan that had come to him at the height of his rage, and he required rage to carry it out. But this interminable march up the hill, and now the delay in finding a strong piece of rope—all this had deflected his anger, allowed it to subside. His anger was like a wave that had swelled and risen, promising to crest and crash, but now instead it was emptying slowly onto the shore and threatening to creep back to the ocean. Rodemann wanted his anger to crash; he needed a collision, a catharsis of some kind. He was determined not to let his anger go, not until he had completed his plan.

By the time his soldier returned with a long section of hemp—stolen, in the end, from a pair of horses tied to an untended plow—Max's urgent report had brought the townspeople of Blumental from the marketplace to the foot of the Birnau hill. Rodemann saw them coming and didn't stop them. In fact, he was pleased that they'd come of their own accord. It was better to have an audience for things like this.

Rosie wanted to go to Birnau with Marina and the Breckenmüllers. So did Lara. But Marina told the girls to go home with Edith, and Edith said that it was no spectacle for children, not even—she looked pointedly at Marina—for adults. Sofia had been silent.

It took Rosie less than fifteen minutes to sneak back out of the house. Lara had stomped up to the girls' bedroom in a huff the moment the front door shut behind them, despite Edith's suggestion that the girls all join her in the living room for cookies and tea and a story from the illustrated *Adventures of Kasperle* that she kept next to the sofa. Sofia happily agreed, but Rosie said she was tired. "Hans-Jürg and I need a little quiet time," she said, turning toward the stairs. To allay suspicion, she warned Sofia, "But don't eat all the cookies! We'll come down later."

At the top of the stairs, Rosie waited for what seemed like hours while her grandmother heated water on the cast-iron stove. When she finally heard the familiar singsong of Edith's gentle storytelling voice, she tiptoed into Oma and Opa's bedroom, climbed onto the big bed under the skylight, reached up to unlatch it, and pulled herself through the window onto the sloping roof. She left Hans-Jürg behind. He was afraid of heights.

Rosie knew the route well, since she and Sofia had used it countless times to make naptime pass more quickly. Across the roof tiles, down the unused attic ladder, with a short drop onto the back porch. Then she had to keep her head down as she crept past the French doors and around the kitchen side of the house. She unlatched the iron gate to the street and let it swing back into the anemones while she ran to the hill that led to Birnau.

Weaving her way among all the people, Rosie slowed as she approached the small group where her mother was standing next to Frau and Herr Breckenmüller. Marina and Myra were tightly grasping each other's hands. Just below them on the hill, near the vineyard, stood a wheelbarrow piled high with grapevines. Rosie quickly ran behind it so she could see and hear everything that happened without herself being seen.

Three soldiers were securing a thick rope to one of the lower branches of the old yew tree at the top of the hill, leaving a long loop hanging down in a makeshift noose. Rosie had seen nooses in newspaper photographs, but this one looked different. It hung crookedly and the coil did not look very tight. The soldiers exchanged curses as they tried to secure one of the rope ends. Rosie saw Karl Breckenmüller lean over to his wife. "Bad knot," he said, in a whisper heavy with condescension and relief.

Captain Rodemann ordered his men to bring the *bürgermeister* over to the tree. Hans Munter had been dutifully holding his tongue, but he had nothing more to lose.

"Please, Herr Captain, this is unnecessary," he pleaded. Rodemann ignored him. "It was all a mistake," the *bürgermeister* continued, his voice breaking. A soldier pushed him over to a milking stool that the others had placed under the noose and motioned for him to climb up on it. "I apologize for whatever it is that has angered you. I apologize. I am so, so sorry," Herr Munter begged while the noose was placed over his head. A trickle of liquid ran down his exposed ankle. Captain Rodemann watched it drip onto the ground and then slowly walked over to him. "Apology accepted," he said, and kicked the stool out from under the *bürgermeister*'s feet.

Hans Munter never had a moment to feel the rope tighten around his neck. The noose unraveled almost immediately upon bearing his weight, and he fell to the ground with a heavy thud. He lay there quietly, breathing in the dirt. He did not feel like moving; he hoped that if he lay still enough, everyone might think he was dead. Sudden heart attack or stroke caused by the stress of the situation—surely that was possible. In any case, there was no need to call attention to himself.

Captain Rodemann rediscovered his anger. "Fools!" he barked at his soldiers. "Can none of you make a proper noose?" Rodemann spat in the direction of his battalion and strode over to the townspeople, now gathered at the top of the path. He leaned into Gerhard Mainz, the butcher, and hissed, "Is there *no one* here who knows how to tie a knot?" Rosie saw Myra Breckenmüller tug on her husband's arm, pulling him farther back into the crowd. "Well?" Rodemann's eyes fastened onto the butcher's and would not let go.

"Th-the f-fisherman," the butcher whispered.

"The fisherman!" Rodemann crooned, and scanned the crowd. "Where, oh where is the fisherman?"

Rosie held her breath, hoping no one would identify her friend. But, though some of the Blumentalers managed to look down at their feet in response to the question, many of them instinctively turned their heads in Herr Breckenmüller's direction. Rosie watched with fear and horror as he pried his wife's fingers from his arm, kissed her on the cheek, and quietly pushed his way through the crowd. *No, don't go!* Rosie screamed in her head. She saw her mother put her arms around Myra Breckenmüller's shoulders. "Nothing will happen to him," her mother said. "He will be fine."

Myra shook her head. "If he has to tie the noose that hangs and kills Hans Munter, he will not be fine."

Rosie watched as Karl Breckenmüller slowly made his way up the hill to the old yew tree. He picked up the loose end of the swinging rope, made a large loop, and began winding it tightly around itself. By the time he finished tying the knots that would hold the loop in place, the entire thing looked to Rosie like a coiled snake with a wide-open mouth. The *bürgermeister* was huddled underneath it. He did not look happy. He did not even look to Rosie as if he was fully awake. He swayed from side to side, his hands tied behind his back. Two soldiers kept prodding him to stay upright. Another was yelling at them and at the *bürgermeister*. Then, just as the mouth of the snake-coil rope was being positioned over the *bürgermeister*'s head, she saw the approaching horse.

It came from the opposite side of the church plaza, its hooves clacking across the cobblestones. There was a tall soldier sitting on it. A general, Rosie knew, because he wore a uniform just like the kind her opa had hanging in his closet. The horse had been galloping, but the general slowed it to a walk as he neared the yew tree. His gaze was fixed on Captain Rodemann. As he came closer, Rosie saw that the general had dark hair, and as he came closer still, she recognized his dark eyes and thick eyebrows, those wonderful fuzzy brows that she loved to stroke.

General Erich Wolf rode his horse right up to Captain Rodemann and did not dismount. He was grateful now that he was still wearing the uniform he'd had on for his meeting with the Führer in Fürchtesgaden that morning. Erich did not like wearing his uniform any more than he absolutely had to, but he had been in a hurry, so he had not taken the time to change. Sitting comfortably up on the horse, he appreciated the poetic justice of being able literally to look down on a captain who thought so highly of himself. He was pleased when he saw Rodemann flinch.

Captain Rodemann was already acquainted with General Wolf. He did not like to remember the brief time he had spent working in the general's office in Berlin, before he was assigned to field duty. The general had had an extremely attractive secretary, a woman who rejected Rodemann's advances (unthinkable; she was probably a Sapphist) and tried thereafter to tarnish his good reputation with the general by blaming Rodemann for oversights that were undoubtedly her own responsibility. Despite all subsequent efforts by Rodemann to ingratiate himself with the general, he was fairly certain that the man had a poor opinion of him.

Raising a hand, Captain Rodemann gestured to one of his men to suspend the hanging for the moment. Freed from the restraining hold of the soldiers, Hans Munter slumped to the ground again. General Wolf glanced briefly at the *bürgermeister*, then positioned his horse broadside between the captain and his subordinates, so that, should the man dare to give another command, they would not be able to see him.

"Captain Rodemann," General Wolf barked. "What *exactly* is going on here?"

The captain looked stricken, and for a brief moment was speechless. Then, inhaling deeply, he squared his shoulders and shouted out, in as imperious a voice as he could manage, "Insurrection, sir! I have discovered, singlehandedly, that the town of Blumental is a hotbed of resistance and—"

"Stop!" The general cut Rodemann off. He moved his horse one step closer and leaned down to stare the captain in the eye. "Do you wonder why the Third Reich is struggling to win this war when commanders such as yourself disobey direct orders? When they stray from their duties and try to lighten their boredom by mixing themselves in the affairs of the very people *they should be trying to protect?*" He held the captain's gaze for a long moment, then slowly straightened back up. "I am not concerned with this town or its people. Nor is it clear to me why you should be, given that you have strict orders from the Führer to intercept the French army, which is approaching this town *as we speak!*"

At this, General Wolf reached into his jacket and pulled out a piece of paper. He slapped it open with a quick snap of his wrist and waved it before Rodemann's stunned face. "This is a telegram from Berlin, containing an order that was reiterated to me by the Führer in Fürchtesgaden this morning. Do you know what it says?" Rodemann opened his mouth, but nothing came out. The general did not wait for him. "It instructs you and your men to repel the French incursion. Not that I understand either Berlin's or the Führer's confidence in your ability to accomplish this. Nothing I have seen in you, either today or in the past, suggests that you possess an iota of competence." He refolded the telegram. "Nevertheless, it is not my place to second-guess the Führer, who has given you a direct order. And I daresay—no, I am *certain*—that he would not approve of this . . ." He leaned down again, to within a handbreadth of the captain, as if his snarling teeth might take a bite out of him. "This *digression*."

Captain Rodemann was shocked. It was true, he had completely forgotten about the French. How could he have let that happen? The French army was his instrument of triumph, his weapon of glory, his catalyst to fame, and he had lost sight of his grand objective because of some petty little villagers? He called himself to attention. Looking to the soldiers who were still standing next to Munter's now-prostrate and apparently unconscious body, he swept his hand through the air and announced, "Yes, sir, General! We will engage the enemy immediately!" Then, in a tempest of loud commands and clattering boots, Captain Rodemann and his regiment were gone, marching west toward the enemy.

Rosie ran over to Erich Wolf's horse. "Erich! Erich! Will you let me sit up there with you?"

"Rosie!" Though surprised to see her, Erich Wolf dismounted and picked her up, kissing her mop of brown curls as he placed her on top of the horse. "Does your mother know you're here?"

"No, but she's here somewhere, and now she'll see that I'm with you. Oooh! I'm so tall up here! I can see everything!" Rosie looked over to the yew tree, where Dr. Schufeldt was bent over Hans Munter, checking his breathing and heart rate. Frau Breckenmüller was helping him, cradling the *bürgermeister*'s head in her lap and murmuring reassuring words. Rosie was not certain, but she thought she heard Frau Breckenmüller naming various kinds of sausages and meats. Turning her head downhill to where the crowd was gathered, Rosie saw Marina striding toward them. Fortunately, she did not look angry.

"Erich, how wonderful that you're here!" Her mother seemed not to notice Rosie at all. She looked at Erich as if she hadn't seen him in many, many years, when actually they had seen each other in Meerfeld just last summer. Rosie knew because she had been there too, with Sofia, and they'd fed bread crusts to the swans. Lara had stayed home with Oma, who said she wasn't ready to see Erich. Rosie did not understand that. What would Oma need to do to be ready to see him?

Back when they lived in Berlin, Erich used to come to the playground near Lara's school to push Rosie in the swings. He was there every weekday, standing next to the swing set in his ribboned uniform, waiting for Marina and Sofia and Rosie after they dropped Lara off. Marina referred to him as "Onkel Erich," but she said that he wasn't really an uncle because he wasn't Oma and Opa's son. He had just lived in their house, before her mother got married. All of that was too confusing for Rosie, so she simply referred to him as Erich. And he was a great swing pusher. He pushed her as hard as she asked him to, so Rosie could swing higher and higher. After swinging, Marina usually let Rosie and Sofia play in the sandbox while she and Erich sat on a bench nearby.

Now Rosie looked down from the horse at her mother and Erich. They were facing each other, Erich with his hands on Marina's arms.

"I was heading this way anyway," he was saying. "Though I had no idea when I left Fürchtesgaden this morning that Rodemann was marching about. As I got closer, I heard rumors about a German attack on one of the towns on the lake. So I stepped up my pace." He smiled. "My car broke down back in Schwanfeld. But I was able to borrow a horse. My preferred means of transportation, as you know."

"Well, it's a miracle, really. Who knows what would have happened if you hadn't intervened," Marina said. "You must have galloped over here at full speed. It's a good thing you're in shape, or you'd be in a hospital bed right next to Hans Munter, recovering from a heart attack or exhaustion."

"Yes, if nothing else, the Third Reich keeps me fit." Erich patted the horse on its side. "This mare did her best, poor thing. I imagine she hasn't had such a workout in a long time."

Rosie perked up. "Then she deserves a reward! We can give her some of our carrots."

"Yes, Rosie, I'm certain she would love that," Erich said.

"And the French, Erich?" Marina was looking out toward the lake, as if searching for signs of men marching in the distance. Rosie followed her gaze, but she saw nothing.

Erich shrugged. "We're getting conflicting reports. This morning, they were definitely heading toward the southeast border, but the telegram I picked up in Schwanfeld had them reversing course. Perhaps they heard that Captain Rodemann had been sent to engage them." He smiled. "I wouldn't worry too much about the French, Marina. Oskar regrets alarming everyone. He's en route and should be here tomorrow."

"Opa's coming?" Rosie gleefully bounced up and down on the horse's back. "We need to tell Oma! Erich, will you ride me to my house? Can he, Mutti? And can he stay for dinner? Please?"

"Rosie, I would be honored to accompany you to your destination. But about dinner . . ." He hesitated and glanced at Marina. "I'm not sure I should stay. I don't know how Edith would feel about it."

Rosie readied a harsh glare and protest, but Marina was nodding. "It's been long enough, don't you think?"

Rosie's happiness was complete. She was riding a horse, a real horse, with her favorite uncle and her Mutti walking next to her. And Sofia would see her on the horse when they got home. And Erich would stay for dinner. And he could have Pimpanella's last egg.

"Mutti, can Erich have one of Pimpanella's eggs?" she asked.

"Pimpanella's *eggs*?" Erich looked amazed. "That suggests she laid more than one."

"Two! It's another miracle." Marina laughed. "Probably all she has in her, but don't tell Oskar that."

They made their way home. The horse's hooves kicked up puffs of fine gray dust that swirled behind them in eddies of haze. Rosie took a moment on her high perch to look back at the yew tree. She had to squint through the small atmospheric tempests of dirt to see the dangling rope. It was still there, swinging slowly back and forth, a reminder of how suddenly things could change.

– Two –

Edith decided to start dinner. It had been hours since Marina and the Breckenmüllers had headed up to Birnau, and she was going to keep herself busy rather than worry. If anything bad had happened up on that hill, she would have heard by now. Max Fuchs was good at spreading news throughout town. She was going to assume all was well.

She took a deep breath and closed her eyes momentarily, gathering comfort from her kitchen. She loved this house. Of course, it was nothing like what she and Oskar had imagined; they'd had no time to construct anything grand when they made the decision to move the family south permanently, away from the air raids up north. Initially, the only structure they had been able to erect on the property was the garage. The war precluded any more extensive construction. They were able to make do for their summer visits by outfitting the garage space with basic furniture. Two years ago, when the family moved in year-round, they expanded by enlisting local workmen to add a small second story and a cellar.

Edith knew that once the war was over, Oskar would suggest they build a larger house, the one they had created so vividly in their minds. But she didn't want to abandon this makeshift little home, with its whistling lead windows and chatty pine staircase. In any case, she had no idea where they might build a new structure. Although the property was large, the garden was already so thoroughly planted that Edith couldn't imagine uprooting any of it. There was simply no space to rebuild. No, there would be no new house when the war was over.

When the war was over. That was hard to imagine, for this war was relentless. And unpredictable, like a rabid animal. Your best chances of survival were to gather your family around you, get everyone as far away from the war as possible, and take shelter. Edith knew she had been lucky so far, but the events of today reminded her that, no matter how protected she might tell herself they were, the war was still out there. The crazy Captain Rodemanns of the world were still firing machine guns directly at the people she loved. And then there was Sofia. Edith sighed. Sofia's psychic trauma from that night of bombing in Berlin was a constant concern.

Edith heard laughter outside. Rosie's laughter. She had thought Rosie was still upstairs. But of course that imp had probably gone out to play in the yard at some point during the afternoon. Edith was just heading across the kitchen to the porch doors to call her back inside when Marina stepped into the house from the porch. Her smiling face told Edith everything she needed to know about whether Hans Munter was safe. Edith let out a deep sigh of relief. "So, you're back. And all is well, I take it?"

"Well, Hans is not *dead*, at least. He seems mostly all right." Marina shook her head in disbelief at all that the *bürgermeister* had endured that day. "The doctor is keeping him overnight, just to be safe."

"Thank God." Edith reached for the checkered apron hanging on a wall hook and pulled it over her head. "Absolutely insane, that captain, shooting randomly into the town. I feared he might not come to his senses."

"I wouldn't say he came to his senses, exactly," Marina started. "He was *reminded* of his true objectives. He's off now, marching again to find the elusive French."

"Now, that's a blessing." Edith fumbled with the strings of her apron. "But what restored our dear captain to sanity?"

Marina looked over at the door that led from the kitchen to the living room and opened her mouth to say something, then stopped. Edith was too busy with the apron to notice. She had the right string in her right hand, but the left one eluded her. She was reaching back, fingers outstretched, grasping for it, when she felt two large hands clasp her own.

"Edith." It was a voice she knew very well, a voice she had once heard daily in their home in Berlin. A deep bass, like a slow wave rising from the bottom of the sea, almost as familiar to her as Oskar's own tenor. She had not heard the low resonance of that voice in five years, and the sound of it again, unexpectedly here in her kitchen, made her reach for the counter to steady herself.

Erich. Edith had always thought of him as God's atonement for her precious Peter, the baby He had taken from her. She had always felt that fate brought Erich to her—he was in need of a mother; she was missing a son.

She stood still, her eyes moistening with tears. That day before the war, when she'd realized what Erich had done, she had been so angry with him, she spent the next five years refusing to see him. Marina and the girls had met with him in Berlin, and even once or twice in Meerfeld after they moved, but she hadn't gone. Initially, she had felt so profoundly betrayed, interpreting his transgression as disrespect for everything she and Oskar had done for him. But it was more than that. She had loved him deeply, loved him like a son—yes, that was it, she thought of him as her son. But of course he wasn't. She had to keep reminding herself of that.

Edith had held on to her hurt for a long time, longer than she needed to. Meanwhile, the war dragged on and battles were waged that she knew Erich was a part of, and she could not help but fear for him. As she feared for Marina's husband, Franz. And if she was completely honest with herself, hadn't she feared for Erich more? Hadn't she cooked him more breakfasts? Hadn't she lived with him in the same house, washed his clothes, cleaned his room? After Stalingrad, when Franz came home a shattered shell of himself, Edith almost screamed. If this could happen to Franz, what about Erich? She had felt desperate to see him. And that desperation slowly dissipated her anger.

Erich's grasp of her hand was tentative—of course, she had made him unsure of her—but he did not let go, and she did not try to wrest her hand free. After a long silence, she turned around and looked up. He had not changed at all, those deep brown eyes of his still calm and steady. "My, my, is it possible you have gotten taller, Erich?" She was going to stay in safe territory.

Erich laughed. "Taller? No. Definitely much grayer, but not taller."

"Well, I must be shrinking into a crone, then."

"Who's turning into a crow?" Rosie interrupted, skipping into the kitchen and jumping onto Erich's back. He let out a small "Oof!" of surprise, then clamped her shins against his torso with his arms, held her feet in his hands, and twirled her around upside down. Edith heard someone giggle in the doorway. Sofia had come downstairs at last.

"You get the next turn, Sofia," Erich assured her, slowing his turns and easing Rosie onto the floor so that she could crawl forward between his legs.

Rosie immediately scrambled over to her sister and began pulling on her arm. "Sofia, Sofia! Come see the horse! There's a horse in the yard and I rode her. And you can ride her too!"

"A *horse?*" Edith thought she had misheard.

"Yes, Mutti, a real horse," Marina said. "I believe it is mowing our clover at this very moment. But don't worry, Erich will return it right away."

"Oh no! Not right away," Rosie whined. "Can't we play with it for a while? At least until dinner? *Please?*" She elbowed Sofia lightly and whispered in her sister's ear. Sofia nodded, suddenly animated.

"Please, Oma?" Sofia chimed in.

Edith could not resist Sofia. She suspected that Rosie knew it. It was not the first time that she admired the slyness of her youngest granddaughter. "Okay, fine. But she's not spending the night here, is that understood?"

Rosie and Sofia danced in celebration, then ran outside. Two seconds later, Rosie ran back in. "Oma, can I have the carrots you set aside for me today?"

"I thought these carrots were for Pimpanella," she said, picking them up from the counter.

"Pimpanella won't mind," Rosie said, grabbing them from Edith's hand. "She's excited about the horse too."

"I highly doubt that," Edith said to Marina and Erich as Rosie ran back outside. "You two might want to go out to make sure the girls don't try to put any of the chickens on top of that horse. And try to let Erich be seen by the neighbors. Maybe it will stop all the gossip about Pastor Wiessmeyer."

Erich stopped at the threshold. "The minister?" he asked.

"Stop it, Mutti," Marina said. "Let's not get into that again." She turned to Erich. "There's nothing. I'm married. Everyone knows that."

"Of course they do, my dear." Edith pulled out the heavy iron stewpot and banged it onto the stove. "But your husband has been away for a long while, and everyone wonders at the extraordinary amount of time you spend having tea with the minister."

"Surely," Erich offered, "sharing a cup of tea with a man of the cloth is a safe activity."

"He's not Catholic," Marina said, pursing her lips. "So no, he's not safe, not as far as Blumental is concerned."

Edith pictured Johann Wiessmeyer, envisioning his gentle eyes widening at the implication that there might be something dangerous about him. "It's a bit silly, really. The man himself is lovely—you would like him, Erich. It's just that Marina refuses to adjust to the difference in attitudes down here. She acts as if she's still in Berlin."

"Mutti, we drink tea, for heaven's sake. In a *public* café. If people find that objectionable, then so be it." Marina grabbed Erich's arm. "Come on, General. Let's go out and be *seen*."

Edith swallowed the rebuke she was readying. She had been fighting Marina's rebelliousness for years. Before the war, it was a question of propriety, of Marina not calling undue attention to herself. These days, it was more often a question of survival. Marina was headstrong, always would be, and there was, Edith had learned, very little she could do about it.

Best to accept the things you cannot control, she thought, looking at the potatoes and leeks lying before her on the counter, and exercise control where you can. Soup was entirely controllable. She grabbed a potato and picked up a paring knife.

– Three –

The bells of Birnau were chiming seven o'clock when Pastor Johann Wiessmeyer arrived at the foot of the Stahlberg hill. Though he was already late, Johann took a moment to listen to the four E major notes leaping over each other. Tireless chimes, Johann thought, sounding every quarter hour, day and night. Steady, inexhaustible. The Birnau bells could be heard even beyond the surrounding fields, well into town, where they competed with the more modest bells of Johann's Protestant church. Their call was bright and cheerful, open and inviting, like the church they inhabited.

Johann looked over the lake to the Swiss border. The first time he saw that slate expanse of water—years ago, with his sister Sonja and her Jewish husband, Berthold, in the car—the mental and moral struggle he now knew so well had just begun. Sonja and Berthold had left Berlin early. "They're only boycotting Jewish businesses and firing Jewish professors now," Berthold had said. "Later, who knows?"

Johann remembered clearly the first day of that 1933 boycott. He was still in the seminary then, and had just stepped out of the underground station at Alexanderplatz. Walking toward Kaiserstrasse, he saw storm troopers blocking an elderly woman who was trying to enter a butcher's shop emblazoned with a white chalk Star of David. The woman must have been at least eighty, possibly ninety years old, judging from the deep curve of her back and her skeleton-white hair. She was irate and undaunted by the uniforms in front of her. "I will shop where I shop! I will buy meat from whomever I choose to buy meat from!" she shouted, raising her straw shopping basket and shaking it at the men. Her defiance and outrage should have been widespread, but weren't.

Those early days in Berlin seemed so distant now. Was it fear of losing their own jobs or latent anti-Semitism that had kept his university colleagues from signing those very early petitions protesting the government's increasingly oppressive actions in the name of racial purity? Johann thought of himself as a man who tried to live God's truth in every aspect of his life, but looking back now, he realized how insignificant his actions had been. Writing and delivering carefully worded treatises and essays, affirming the presence of God in every man, regardless of race . . . such mild slaps to the lily-livered evangelical community. Over time his statements became bolder—the true Church must embrace both German and Jew—and he sought audiences outside academia. But he succeeded only in drawing attention to himself, and spent more than one night in jail, released only to the care of his cousin Gottfried Schrumm, an attorney in the Defense Ministry.

It took the emigration of his beloved sister to truly awaken Johann's spiritual imperative. Sonja, only eleven months younger than he, practically his twin and certainly his best friend throughout childhood. She was his partner in four-handed piano back when Johann thought he might be a musician. Later, when he decided to study theology, and the rest of their academically minded, agnostic family questioned that decision, it was she who defended his choice. "He has talked to me about God every night since we were babies," she told them. "No one knows more about God than Johann."

At the University of Berlin, Johann dated the raven-haired, ravishing Beate, while Sonja, unwilling to be left behind, fell in love with Beate's brother, Berthold. But impetuous and romantic

Beate was bored with Johann's quiet philosophies, and she ran off to Spain with an artist. The only union between the two families would be Sonja and Berthold's.

By Kristallnacht, in 1938, Sonja and Berthold had been married for five years. Even though Johann had baptized Berthold as a Christian, the young couple did not feel safe. So while Jewish shop owners swept up the splintered glass of storefronts, Sonja tearfully began packing up her home. Johann was too worried for her safety to try to dissuade her. Eight months after Berthold's conversion, Johann found himself driving them to the Swiss border late at night, with fabricated credentials that Gottfried had provided. This very border, just on the other side of the lake.

Watching Sonja and Berthold disappear into a blanket of fog that night, Johann saw an opening, an opportunity to act in a manner consistent with his beliefs. The border here was porous: a large lake, dense forests, small towns and roads. What was required was a guide, a shepherd who knew his way around. A pastor. And to Johann's good fortune, two years later, a vacancy arose in a small parish here in Blumental.

A loud "Oof!" interrupted Johann's reverie. A boy's voice. Johann looked over to the East Blumental station, the small satellite train depot that had stopped serving passengers since the war began. "*Verdammt nochmal!*" cursed the voice from somewhere behind the wooden building. Johann followed the trail of profanity-peppered grunts to the back of the station, where he saw a familiar dusty-haired, scrap-clad boy trying to position a boulder underneath one of the windows.

"Need some help with that?" Johann decided not to say anything about the curses. Shame and remorse already colored Max Fuchs's face. He surveyed the enormous rock and marveled that scrawny Max had enough strength to move it any distance at all.

"Pastor Johann! Oh, well, yes, but, yes, thank you, sir," Max stuttered, uncertain whether he had been caught in a transgression.

"And what exactly am I helping you with?" Johann asked as he rolled up his sleeves and squatted next to the boulder.

"Well, Willie was helping me earlier today, but we couldn't move it all the way to the window, it was just so heavy." Max's words poured forth in a torrent while Johann put all of his strength and weight into moving the massive block of stone. The boy spoke like a rain-swollen brook, ideas splashing over banks and running every which way. "Oh, uh, that way, Pastor Johann, to the right, that's it, yes. So I didn't really want Willie's help because I didn't want to share the glory of catching the spies. I want to catch the spies all by myself. Yes, up against the window, there. I haven't seen any yet but I'm sure it's just a matter of time. I mean, isn't this a perfect spot? And I know Willie will want some credit, who wouldn't? Yes, perfect. Thank you so much, sir."

"Spies?" Johann gave the large rock one final heave, so that it rested directly under the window. He mopped his brow with his forearm. "I haven't heard about any spies."

"Well, you wouldn't, would you?" Max said, quickly climbing onto the rock and standing on his tiptoes to look through the hazy glass. "But if you were a spy trying to infiltrate from the south, this would be the perfect place to hide, don't you think? Especially since no one really uses it anymore. It's out of the way. *And* on a train line. And only two trains ever stop here. One in the afternoon, and the other"—Max lowered his voice to a hoarse whisper—"at *midnight*."

"Hmm." Johann pretended to mull this thought over, trying not to betray the concern he felt at Max's unwitting insight. "I can see that, I suppose." Max was surveying the inside of the station from his perch, scanning the room from left to right. Johann decided to keep his tone light. "Well, any signs of infiltration?"

"No, not yet. But they may have come and gone. They might still be out spying," Max said, face pressed to the glass. "They could come back any minute. Must be vigilant!"

"Indeed." Johann walked over to the window and put a hand

on the boy's shoulder. Max was a tenacious and imaginative young man, and if he'd taken an interest in spies, it was not one he would abandon lightly. But the semiabandoned East Blumental station played a major role in Johann's movement of packages from the east to Switzerland, and Max's innocent curiosity had the potential to greatly complicate that operation. Johann would have to find ways to keep Max otherwise engaged when deliveries were in transit, or find a new safe house. For now, it was enough to send the boy home.

"You know, Max, I certainly commend you for the service you are doing for the community, trying to keep us all safe. But after all you put your dear mother through earlier this afternoon, I think it might be best if you went home for dinner."

There was no room for dispute in Johann's voice. Max understood. He nodded and climbed down to the ground. "Yes, sir." The two of them walked back to the path in silence. Unexpectedly, Max turned to Johann and held out his hand. "Thank you, sir. I greatly appreciate your help. And your . . . your . . ." Max searched in vain for the word *discretion*.

"I won't say a word to anyone, Max," Johann assured him, shaking the hand that was proffered. "And please give your mother my best regards."

The bells chimed the half hour. Johann headed back up the Stahlberg hill. Thirty minutes until choir practice, and there was much to do.

– Four –

If Oskar was coming home tomorrow, Edith thought, she would have to refill the stove. Oskar at home meant plenty of cooking. She had already decided to go to the market in the morning. Retrieving the tin coal pail from behind the stove, she headed to the cellar.

Edith liked the cellar. The gentle embrace of cool damp and almost total darkness tamped her nerves. The pulse of the house beat quietly and steadily down here, somewhere between the mountain of coal and the mountain of potatoes. Food and fuel, all that was necessary to stabilize the family chaos. This was where she kept her preserves: the cherry jam, apple jelly, cucumber relish, and all the other carefully stored products of her garden's harvest.

Normally, Edith would have sent one of the girls down for the coal—most likely Lara, because Rosie was too hard to pin down and Sofia had a pathological fear of underground rooms. Lara did not fear the cellar and its darkness, but she was in that stage of life where every request for help from Edith or Marina required, in her mind, some supreme sacrifice or commitment, and today Edith did not want to wrestle with her.

Edith carried the pail down the narrow stone staircase, poorly illuminated by the bare bulb in the center of the ceiling. She placed the pail on the floor and bent down to fill it with coal. Oskar would be here tomorrow. That knowledge suffused her with a warm flush of expectation and bliss. She stifled the nagging internal voice that told her she should use this visit to confront him, once again, with her questions. Questions about his responsibilities, the actions he took on behalf of the Führer. What he knew and did not know about the Führer's long-term goals. Questions that plagued her when she was alone. But the one time she had voiced her doubts to him, last winter, he lost his temper. They had such limited time together, she reasoned. She did not want to disturb it by bringing up unpleasant and difficult topics.

They had been together . . . thirty-five years this September, Edith counted. And she still loved him as wholly and fiercely as the day they had gotten married. This man whom she thought she knew well. A convivial man fond of *bratkartoffeln* and spaetzle; a courageous and unapologetically patriotic officer whose unremitting sense of duty to his commanders and his soldiers earned him fierce allegiance or reluctant respect; an eager, whimsical grandfather; a warm, generous husband. And, Edith reminded herself with a smile, an extraordinary dancer. Where he had developed that ability, Edith never learned. She decided it must be an innate skill. His favorite dance was the waltz.

Edith herself was not a great waltzer. She had taken the requisite cotillion classes with Frau Winkler only because it was a rite of passage for girls approaching marriageable age in Potsdam. Edith's mother had insisted on it. She said Edith wouldn't be winning any suitors with her looks, so she might as well work on her dancing skills. But Frau Winkler made it clear early on and with embarrassing regularity that Edith had no talent for dancing and that she was one of those rare and lamentable girls for whom practice was futile. So during her first spring ball season in Berlin, at the age of sixteen, her spirits shackled by Frau Winkler's judgment, Edith spent the evenings sipping cider with her aunt at the small café tables set along the edges of ballrooms for spinsters, chaperones, and the elderly.

No one was more surprised than she the night the sandy-haired young soldier strolled purposefully over to her chair. She did not know him, but she had seen him before, at other balls. He was a full head taller than every other man in the room. And if that was not enough to get him noticed, when the music started and he began to move across the floor, his body was pure fluidity in motion, conveying with its dips and turns the lyric grace and swaying strength being sung by the orchestra's strings. He was unforgettable.

Edith didn't expect him to notice her. She had no reason to doubt her mother's assessment of her own attractiveness, especially as the girls around her were whisked off to the parquet floor while she remained seated. Had she and her aunt been at the dance longer than an hour, she would have pretended she had a headache so they might leave. Unfortunately, it was still too early.

But then Oskar asked her to dance. Of all the ladies in the room, he was choosing her. She rose uncertainly, ready to protest until a stern look from her aunt made her bite her tongue, regretting already the fact that her first dance, in the arms of one with such consummate skill, would undoubtedly be her last.

She need not have worried. In Oskar's arms, and guided by his sure feet, Edith's own barely touched the floor. He held her tightly, twirled her round and round the room. The other dancers, musicians, and lights all reeled in a multicolored blur. Later her aunt would tell her that their movement reminded her of a comet as they traversed the enormous ballroom space in wide arcs, spinning between and around the other couples in that waltzing universe, the long glittering train of Edith's dress sweeping through the air behind them like a sparkling tail. For Edith, the dance ended almost as soon as it had begun, and she felt quite dizzy afterward and had to spend several minutes seated quietly, sipping water and looking at the floor.

Never had she felt so completely secure, so completely taken care of, as in this man's arms. And the way he looked at her when the dance ended—it was the first time Edith felt *seen*, truly seen.

What was still more amazing and intoxicating, though even today Edith did not understand it, was what Oskar told her later, what he repeated with wonderful regularity over the years: he thought she was the most beautiful woman he had ever seen.

A few years afterward, when it became clear that Oskar was to be a permanent part of Edith's life, she would take separate instruction from Frau Winkler, who taught her how to hold her head when being spun about, to avoid spells of nausea. Happily, this was a skill for which Frau Winkler determined Edith did have some aptitude, and after several weeks of head-turning lessons, she pronounced Edith an expert.

It had been such a long time since they had danced together, Edith thought, ascending the stairs back to the kitchen. Carrying the coal pail through the foyer, still smiling at the memories of those early dances, she almost bumped into Marina, who was putting on her coat.

"I'll be back late, Mutti, no need to wait up for me," Marina said, tying a scarf over her head.

"Late from what?" Edith felt momentarily confused.

"We're going singing!" Rosie exploded through the kitchen door, dragging her blue overcoat behind her.

"*I'm* going singing, you goose. You are accompanying me on the walk," Marina corrected. She knelt down and guided Rosie's arms into her coat, then fastened it.

"Me and Erich are both 'companying you," Rosie said.

Edith looked around at the empty room. "He's meeting us at the path to Birnau," Marina said, answering Edith's unspoken question and securing the last button on Rosie's coat. "He said not to worry about the horse. He'll take it back as soon as he returns."

"I'm going to kiss it good-bye one last time," Rosie said, running out the door before anyone could stop her.

Marina hesitated at the open door. "Thank you for letting Erich join us for dinner. I know it meant a great deal to him."

"I hope we can all move forward now," Edith said. She thought back to the fear she had experienced five years ago, that the family would splinter. But that had not happened.

Marina gave her mother a hard look. "It's only you who hasn't wanted to move forward."

Edith bristled. "It wasn't a move *forward*, it was—I don't know, sideways, slantways."

"You wanted me to keep away from Erich."

"No, I wanted—" Edith stopped. She didn't know what she had wanted five years ago. To keep the family together, she supposed. To keep people from getting hurt. The war had effectively dispensed with that wish.

"I'm late. I need to go." Marina turned her back and left.

Edith slowly pulled the door shut. Her beautiful oak door, intricately carved with fleurs-de-lis and fantastical creatures. A birthday present to her from Oskar. Somehow he had managed to get it through customs. Perhaps because it came from Turkey, where she imagined some wizened artisan channeling Mesopotamian mysticism into his carvings, Edith felt there was some magic about this door. As if it had secret power, and its wooden striations were infused with hidden strength to protect what lay behind it. She ran her hand over the tail feathers of one of the peacocks. Not a bad door to have during wartime, she thought.

– Five –

Johann still experienced a small moment of pleasant surprise each time he entered the sanctuary of Birnau. This rococo church, dressed everywhere in pink and gold, was playful and flamboyant. Worshipping amid the creamy, rose-swirled marble walls and pillars was like being in a roomful of ice cream. Hundreds of blushing naked cupids danced everywhere, from the filigreed balcony that sheltered the tall golden organ pipes to the ceiling of the nave, where they scampered on a frescoed trompe l'oeil tableau of blue sky and puffy white clouds.

What a contrast to the world outside, he thought, making his way up the main aisle. And what a contrast to the dour churches of Berlin. He passed in front of the altar and stopped at the door that led to the Sunday school room. There, he pulled out the large ring of keys that Father Georg had given him. His custody of these keys was another divine intervention in his life. Newly arrived from Berlin three years earlier, Johann had been sitting at a café on the lake promenade, humming his favorite hymn as he considered how to execute his plan. He did not notice Father Georg sitting nearby. But in the next instant, Father Georg joined him at his table and implored him to take charge of the Birnau choir.

"I am honored you would consider me, sir," Johann said. "You must know, of course, that I am not Catholic."

"Ach, Catholicism has nothing to do with it." Father Georg

brushed the air with his hand. "You have a lovely tenor voice and you can carry a tune."

"But—" Johann began.

"But nothing, my boy. You have a gift. You must share it. And the dairy farmers' wives—whose voices, I must warn you, could pluck the feathers from a rooster—would much rather sing for a beautiful young man than a weathered old goat."

Yes, God worked in such mysterious ways. This choir had turned out to be the cover he needed for his little group. Johann fumbled through the keys. Over his shoulder, he felt the gaze of the *Honigschlecker*, a naked babe statue, all creamy and pink with a solid gold cape. His fleshy little body twisted around the beehive that he cradled in one arm while he sucked on a finger that was dripping pure golden honey. Marina had once told Johann that the *Honigschlecker* reminded her of her baby brother, Peter, and that he smiled at her in merry complicity every time she passed by him. Johann saw his honey-laden finger pointing not toward his mouth, but up to heaven, a reminder that God was always there, that He was present in everything people did.

Until recently, Johann had not doubted God's presence in his actions. He felt he had received a clear message the night that he watched Sonja and Berthold head over to safety in Switzerland, a message that was confirmed when he was appointed to the presbytery in Blumental. And with Father Georg's keys in hand, he had been able, relatively quickly and secretly, to execute his plan. Within weeks of Johann's arrival, Blumental became a haphazard but relatively successful resting stop for refugees fleeing from eastern Europe to Switzerland.

It had been mostly Polish, mostly Jewish families, running from the destruction and extermination of their villages. There was no standard route, and the underground trail to Blumental shifted constantly due to the occasional betrayal by informants and the interception of transports. Over the past three years, Johann and his small circle had been able to deliver ten groups of refugees safely across the border. His cousin Gottfried Schrumm in the Defense Ministry had been instrumental in the effort, supplying Johann with official visa forms and government stamps that he could use to forge the paperwork needed to get his charges to safety. And it was Gottfried who had recently provided Johann with another, far more radical, instrument of political opposition—the briefcase that Johann kept in his clothes closet.

He switched on the lights in the children's reading alcove. Faith is not a light switch, Marina had said to him once. You cannot suddenly turn it on. He agreed—faith was more of a carefully tended fire, slow burning and constant. But the fire of faith had been extinguished in Marina. Johann was not evangelical—he thought everyone should be permitted to believe what he or she wanted. Still, if someone showed an interest in God, as Marina seemed to, he was a ready and compassionate listener.

She had once believed in God, she told him, perhaps as fully as he did. But the war had destroyed her faith. She could not understand how God would allow someone like the Führer to exist, to wield power and influence over so great a portion of the world. Would not God instruct His church, His followers, to rise up against such a man? But the Catholic Church was doing nothing. The Protestant Church was doing nothing. How could God condone this?

Johann had listened to Marina's reasoning silently, with more sympathy than he was willing to disclose. Of the primary question, the existence of God, he had no doubt. Johann had never questioned His existence, for he was lucky enough to experience God personally and on a daily basis. He simply *knew* that God was an incontrovertible presence in his life and in the world, and because of this knowledge, he sought as much as possible to live His Word. Yes, the Führer lived in this world too, and war was tolerated in it, but that was not because God had turned His back— it was because of the timeless and inalterable presence of evil, which, as the Bible made clear, had been with man since Eden.

Shrill laughter pierced Johann's reverie. Käthe Renningen, the seamstress—it was impossible not to recognize that laugh, so similar in pitch to the woman's atonal singing. He quickly pulled forward the necessary chairs and reentered the main church. There he found Käthe and the choirmistress, Gisela Mecklen, putting on their choir robes.

"Good evening, ladies. You're early tonight."

"My twin baby girls are exercising their lungs," Käthe said wearily. "I left as soon as my mother arrived to take over."

"Perhaps they are auditioning for a position in our choir."

"Goodness, I hope not! This is my only refuge. Promise me you won't let them in until they are at least thirteen!"

"No, not thirteen," Gisela cautioned. "There will be entirely different reasons to get away from your daughters when they are thirteen. Twenty would be better."

Käthe dropped her head in dismay. "Please tell me you're kidding."

"Of course she is teasing you." Johann gently put his arm around Käthe's shoulders. "Come downstairs to the kitchen and get a cup of tea while we wait for the rest of the group. And Gisela, I remember now that I asked you to come early because I need a favor."

Gisela's eyes narrowed like those of a cat sizing up a bird. Johann could almost feel the vibrations of her calculating brain. The Mecklens were schemers. Ever since the disappearance of the Rosenberg family, Johann did not entirely trust them. Though he had no actual proof that Gisela and Regina Mecklen had anything to do with the Rosenbergs' swift and sudden departure from Blumental, he knew that the Rosenbergs' presence in town, and their occupation of a prime commercial piece of real estate, had been a thorn in the Mecklens' side. The Rosenbergs were bakers—excellent bakers—and the Mecklens' principal competitors for business. The Rosenberg bakery had been located on the plaza just opposite the Münster, the town's oldest church building.

Johann had always purchased his bread from the Rosenbergs, for they could somehow transform even rye flour into tasty *brötchen*, a feat that the Mecklens decidedly could not accomplish.

Israel and Miriam. Their children, Isaac and Rachel. Johann had added their names to his prayers when, one morning, he found their bakery closed and saw Regina Mecklen inside taking measurements for curtains. Just like that, they were gone.

Johann hated making himself indebted to Gisela Mecklen in any way, but he did need her help tonight. "Could you lead the choir after the break? Father Georg asked me to help him in the rectory, and he doesn't want to stay awake until we are done."

Probably Johann did not even need to use the priest as an excuse, because he knew Gisela would not refuse him. Marina had told him that the Mecklen sisters were great fans of his. According to her, they admired men of God, particularly *single* men of God of the Protestant faith, who were free to wed. Although the older two Mecklen women, Regina and Gisela, were married, the youngest, Sabine, was not. Visitors to the Mecklen household knew that many an evening was spent in discussion about eligible bachelors in the immediate Blumental vicinity and their desirability as mates. Johann had been thoroughly studied and the Mecklens' unanimous conclusion was that although he was a bit aloof and formal and was, regrettably, not a baker, he would do quite well for Sabine.

As Johann expected, Gisela smiled at him. She probably intended to appear ingratiating and modest, but the set of her eyebrows and the crookedness of her mouth made it look like she was sneering. "Certainly, Pastor Wiessmeyer. I am quite happy to do any favor you ask." She paused, then added, "As no doubt you would do for me."

The costs of doing God's work, Johann thought, were often unpredictable. But whatever Gisela had in mind, he felt confident he could protect himself. Tonight, he had other things to worry about.

– Six –

The fading summer light lingered over the lake, reluctant to submit to the shadow of night stealthily approaching from the mountains. Colors were beginning to wash away, gradually flattening and dissolving into a monotone shade of gray. The path leading up to Birnau, crowded and dusty several hours earlier, was now completely deserted, a silent, sinuous ribbon of pebbles and sand crowned with the rose facade of the church. It was easy to forget that this had been the site of an attempted execution less than seven hours ago.

Rosie ran ahead of Marina and Erich, stopping occasionally to examine the snails emerging from their daily slumber in the brush, slithering slowly to the sheep pastures across the path. The one that Rosie eventually picked up was breaking no records for speed. "Can I bring it home, Mutti? Please?" Rosie dangled the snail at arm's length in front of Marina, who took a startled step backward. "I could put it in one of Oma's jelly jars and feed it stuff from the garden."

"Rosie, we've been through this before. Remember last year, when you found that turtle?" Marina knelt down next to her daughter. She did not want to bring up the turtle, which, after its initial novelty wore off, was forgotten by the entire household until the day Marina found its wasted corpse in a cardboard box under Rosie's bed.

Rosie showed no remorse. "Petzi was *sick*, that's why he died.

And this is a *snail*, not a turtle. *And*"—Rosie punctuated the air with her snail-laden fist—"I am *five* now."

Marina looked up at Erich, who had covered the lower half of his face with his hand and whose eyes were squinting with re-strained laughter. *A little help, please?* she mouthed.

"Rosie." Erich put his hand on Rosie's small head. "How about you give me your snail and I'll take care of him for you until we get back home?"

Rosie looked dubious. "Where are you going to put him?"

Erich unbuttoned the large pocket on the front of his canvas jacket. "Right in here, and when we get back to the house, you can find a nice place for him in the garden." Reassured, Rosie was all smiles. She carefully placed her new pet in Erich's pocket, then ran ahead up the path.

"Coward," Marina said, slapping Erich playfully. "Edith is going to kill you."

"We'll see if Rosie even remembers the snail by the time we get back," Erich said.

"Oh, she'll remember." Marina watched her daughter skip back and forth across the path, singing an atonal ditty about a frog and a snail that she was clearly making up as she went along. How she admired Rosie's toughness, a surprise to her after Lara's and Sofia's more mild-mannered and meek responses to the world around them. Of course, all children were different, but Marina was convinced that the war had done much to shape her own. Lara and Sofia knew peacetime and missed it; Rosie did not. A significant consideration in Marina's decision to leave Berlin had been the desire to shield the girls as much as possible, not just from air raids and firestorms but from the daily confrontations with loss and despair. Like the teenage soldier they saw one win-ter afternoon at the café in the Kaiserallee: He had been sitting at a table by the window, presenting only his right profile to pass-ersby because the left side of his face had been shattered by a grenade. Lara flinched at the sight of him, Sofia buried her face in Marina's skirt, but Rosie, just three years old, stood still, looked squarely at him, and smiled. Wartime was everything Rosie knew. An atmosphere of fear was normal for her, and she was a child bent on having a childhood.

Erich interrupted her thoughts. "So how long have you been in this choir? I had absolutely no idea that you could sing." He stopped to look at her. "And I thought I knew everything about you."

Unexpectedly, Marina felt herself blush. Then she laughed, gesturing toward Rosie, whose alternating flat and sharp notes colored the night air. "I sing about as well as my daughter, I'd say. Thankfully, Johann Wiessmeyer isn't too picky. They've tolerated my presence for almost a year. I stand in the back, next to the very loud Elle Benz, who makes sure that I cannot be heard."

"Ah, you and the famous Johann Wiessmeyer. The relationship everyone is talking about, apparently," Erich said. Was he teasing? Or did she detect a note of hurt?

Marina reached for Erich's hand, bent his elbow so she could walk arm-in-arm with him. "We're *friends*," she said, leaning into Erich, his solidity. She relaxed into the warmth of his body. "He's my . . . Well, I suppose you could say he is my spiritual advisor."

Erich raised his eyebrows. "'Spiritual advisor'? I didn't know you needed one."

"I didn't." Marina suddenly felt tired. "But it's difficult here. The atmosphere is very conservative, *very* Catholic. Just because we don't go to church with our neighbors, we are suspect." Marina would never forget the first few months in Blumental, a complete culture shock. She was not used to minute scrutiny of her behavior by people whom she barely knew and who came to troubling conclusions about the family's innocuous—but in hindsight, perhaps ill-considered—activities. The first summer they vacationed in Blumental, for example, before their more permanent move south, Oskar suggested they celebrate Midsummer's Eve by burning a witch. He pulled out an old broom, some balloons and streamers, paper, and—the crowning touch—a few fireworks.

The girls happily crafted an exquisitely misshapen and brightly colored crone whose straw head they adorned with pansies and hollyhock blooms. Right before he lit her Roman candle arms and sparkler hair, Oskar gave the pagan queen a reverent kiss. Then they all stepped back and watched her magnificent explosion. That little stunt, along with Edith's and Marina's failure to appear at mass on Sundays, placed the family, in Blumental's eyes, in a category only slightly above Gypsies. Edith had worked hard since their move to redeem their reputation.

Marina was less concerned with public opinion, but she valued the pastor's friendship. "Johann is a good person to talk to. And I don't have that many choices around here. It was his suggestion that I join the choir. It's supposed to be nondenominational, though as far as I can tell, he and I are the only non-Catholics. But at least this way, we have some presence in the church community. It makes us look slightly less dangerous."

"It's hard to see how anyone could think of your family as dangerous," Erich said. "But I understand what you're saying, Marina. I wish I could help."

"Oh, you helped tremendously today. Your appearance this afternoon, the way you rescued poor Hans Munter . . . Captain Rodemann is so hated by the town, I think everyone wanted to invite you to dinner after that. And you chose us." Marina's good humor was restored as she remembered the look of horror on Rodemann's face. "Our standing has increased a thousandfold. Good sir"—she curtsied deeply and bowed her head—"I feel honored to be in your presence."

Erich reclaimed Marina's hand and pulled her back up. "The honor is all mine." Marina trembled slightly; she would always thrill at this man's touch, this man she had known almost her entire life. Her first impression of Erich, the night Oskar brought him home at the end of the first war, was that he was very quiet. Quiet and gangly, as if he still had to grow into his long arms and legs. Marina was four years old; Erich was nineteen and, she learned

much later, newly orphaned. After the signing of the armistice at
Compiègne, Private Erich Wolf had been making preparations to
return home to Hamburg when he received the news that both
of his parents had died in an outbreak of the Spanish flu. Oskar
had the grim duty of delivering the telegram to him. With Edith's
blessing, Oskar invited Erich to come stay with them in Berlin
until he "found his footing," as they put it. Erich stayed with the
family for twelve years.

Marina rose from her curtsy, not relinquishing the hand Erich
had offered her. They walked together, following Rosie's voice.
Across the lake, the moon rose behind a horizon of treetops, a
massive golden globe peering unhurriedly over the water, surveying the damage of the day. "How long can you stay?"

"A day or two, no more, I think," Erich answered. "There are
matters in Berlin that—"

"Stop," Marina said. "I get enough secrecy from my father. If
you must have secrets from me, I don't want to know they exist."
Everything was secrets and duplicity. Marina wondered whether
by the time the war ended any of them would remember how to
tell the truth.

They reached the railroad crossing near the defunct platform
of East Blumental. For all her willfulness, Rosie still stopped before crossing the tracks and waited for Erich and Marina to catch
up with her. Erich grabbed Rosie's left hand, Marina her right,
and on the count of three, they flew her over the tracks while she
kicked her legs wildly in the air. At the foot of the hill on the opposite side, Rosie groaned. "Can someone carry me? I've already
run up there once today. I don't think . . ." Her voice changed
pitch, and Marina heard Oskar's words uttered in her daughter's
distinctive whine. "I don't think my heart can take it."

"Hmm, five years old and cardiac trouble already?" Erich knelt
down and put his ear to Rosie's chest. "Sounds like your heart
is still beating, but we better not take any chances." He heaved
Rosie onto his shoulders. "You navigate with the ears. Pull on the

left one to go left, right to go right. But *gently*, or else this horse will toss you off quicker than you can say *heinzelmännchen*."

Marina watched the two of them gallop up the hill. By the time she herself reached the top, clouds had moved in and partially obscured the moon. Its weakened light now barely illuminated the cobblestones behind Birnau and cast a faint glow over the vineyard that stretched from the plaza down to the lake. Somewhere in the middle of this vineyard, Marina knew, though she could not see it in the gloom, was the old monastery, long abandoned but still intact enough to offer shelter to the seasonal workers who used to harvest grapes here before the war. Tonight the plaza was quiet and empty; all the choristers who had lingered outside to watch the sun set had already gone into the church.

"Well, this is where I go in," Marina said, stooping to give Rosie a kiss. "You stay with Uncle Erich, right? No running away and hiding, not at night. And into bed the moment you get home."

"The moment I get home? I don't have to brush my teeth?"

"Nice try. You know better."

Erich looked at Marina. "Let me know what time to come back and get you. I don't want you walking home in the dark."

"No, that's very kind, but I'll walk back with Myra. I think I just saw her go in." Marina smiled as Erich grabbed Rosie's hand.

"So, lake or forest for the walk back?" he asked her.

"Oooooo, forest! It's so dark and scary now," Rosie said, her eyes widening. "But you have to tell me a story about a wolf."

"Right, a wolf tale it is." Erich winked at Marina over Rosie's head.

"And when we get home, we can make a bed in the garden for my snail."

Marina stifled her laughter. She knew her child so well.

– Seven –

Erich Wolf did not have far to go to return the mare he had borrowed. The farmer in Schwanfeld had told Erich she could be returned to his cousin, Fritz Nagel, who lived on the eastern edge of Blumental, a short ride from the Eberhardt house. Erich would have been happy to ride all the way back to Schwanfeld just to be able to sit on the back of a horse for longer, but as always, he thought first of the horse's welfare. He did not want to overtire her. But she'd had several hours of rest in the Eberhardt yard and was happily resuscitated with carrots and clover, so he decided to ride her just the short distance to the Nagels' at a comfortably slow gait.

The chestnut mare was a compliant, good-natured animal, certainly not as beautiful as his own Arrakis, but then Arrakis was an Arabian and set a fairly high bar against which farm animals should not be measured. This mare was better than most farm animals, though: she was an Oldenburg. He'd recognized the telltale crown branded on her flank when he passed her grazing in a field of tall grasses. It was the brand that led him to commandeer her in the name of the German army, knowing from his cavalry experience that Oldenburgs were peerless in strength and athleticism. She had met his expectations this afternoon, and he was determined to treat her like the equine queen she was.

Darkness had settled onto the trees and rooftops. No sound but the steady plodding of horseshoes on packed dirt. Erich could not remember the last time he had ridden at night. Could it have been in Stalingrad, a year and a half ago? What a hellish reconnaissance assignment that had been, part of Field Marshal Manstein's effort to break through the Soviet stranglehold and rescue the German army trapped within the city. That horrific night when his cavalry regiment approached the Myshkova River, under the light of a full moon, a snowstorm had risen up, sudden and unpredicted. They had all drawn closer to await its passing, not recognizing that, as they huddled together on dirt that was slowly being transformed into a reflective white landscape, their dark horses made them sitting ducks for the Russian sharpshooters. Of one hundred pairs of men and horses, only fifteen had returned. Erich reached down and patted the mare on her neck.

This was why he had joined the cavalry when he'd first entered the army. Somehow Erich knew, instinctively, that he would need the support of another living creature to face the trauma of war, that the rhythmic rise and fall of a smooth rib cage against his thighs would steady his heart and the slap of a mud-encrusted tail dispersing flies would ease his tension as he stood atop a hill waiting for the order to charge. Loki, his mount in the first war, was such a fine stallion—a huge gray Hanoverian, standing seventeen hands and proud of every centimeter. Though Loki could be as mischievous as the Norse god he was named after, he surpassed all other horses in Erich's experience—before and since—in fearlessness. Nothing terrified that horse, not fire, machine guns, or mortar shells. Loki ran through all of it without hesitation, and his bravado inspired the rest of the regiment.

Indeed, had it not been for Loki, Erich might never have met Oskar. Erich thought back to the march through Belgium in the first war. They had been camped just east of Mons with the Second Army Corps when Loki became restless. For all his very fine qualities, Loki had a wicked sweet tooth along with an uncanny instinct for sugar, and when both of these were activated, the animal completely discarded the niceties of chain of command. Near their encampment, a lucky scouting party from the Third Army Corps led by Oskar found a stash of sugar and a barrel of apples in an abandoned Norman barn. When Oskar ordered the cook to prepare some caramelized apples for the regiment, it was inevitable that Loki would line up with the men, even though the horse had been tethered to a post outside Erich's tent miles away. Oskar later told Erich that he was convinced such an enterprising horse must have an equally intrepid rider, so with conviction and curiosity, Oskar personally rode Loki back to meet Erich. Shortly thereafter, Erich and Loki transferred to Oskar's regiment.

Riding slowly up the dirt road to the Nagel farm, Erich thought the landscape not all that different from Belgium. On his left beckoned the modest houses of Blumental. To his right was farmland interspersed with the occasional gray farmhouse or barn. Rows of cabbages and potatoes snaked eastward, ending abruptly in a wall of fruit trees, beyond which the Birnau forest stretched its limbs.

The town that expanded to his left was dark now, no light daring to shine lest an aerial bomber were to seek it out. Only an occasional candle illuminated the whitewashed cement homes. Erich imagined the interiors: Rooms furnished with sofas, probably somewhat worn by the weight of mothers knitting and children scrambling over them. Rooms flush with paintings, perhaps of ancestors, staring down wistfully from their walls. Rooms safe in their day-to-day routines, with feathered pillows and photographs of insistently smiling families. Rooms that were sheltered and vigilant, especially in the evenings, when the round black knob of the cherry sound-box on the mantelpiece was turned clockwise and news from the outside world marched in on muddy boots.

Erich had not been to Hamburg since he buried his parents twenty-six years ago, but he could still remember the rooms of his childhood. Small but sufficient, cluttered with relics from a different era, memorabilia of an older, slower culture and time: parchment maps of the tribes of Germany before the Franco-Prussian

War, burgundy and gold volumes of Schiller and Hölderlin. His parents' heroes had been Kaiser Wilhelm, Beethoven, and Brahms. Shaped by their quiet, classical values, the Erich Wolf who left Hamburg for the first war was not the same man who returned four years later. That man had died with his parents, with the Germany they had so loved and revered, and with the home they had created for him, burned to the ground by neighbors fearful of the influenza.

When Oskar offered to let him come live with his family in Berlin, Erich had gratefully accepted, yet he had never thought of their house as home. And he'd never quite thought of the Eberhardts as family, though he loved them deeply. He had been too intent on searching for himself between the wars, trying to reestablish his lost identity. Oskar had been extraordinarily helpful in that search. So had Marina.

A loud series of barks brought Erich's attention back to the road. Up ahead, a dark-brown dachshund whose width rivaled its length trundled its way toward the horse, chased by two young boys in makeshift soldier uniforms. The dog's white muzzle and its semiarthritic gait reassured both Erich and the mare that it was not a threat, but he nevertheless pulled his mount up short until the boys could catch up with the dog.

The first boy to reach the dachshund was an unkempt, sinewy lad with short-cropped sandy hair that looked to have at least a week's worth of dirt in it. He grabbed the dog by the collar, choking off another bark. "Puck! Stop it!" Thrown off balance, the hound landed on his back, where he pedaled the air once or twice before relaxing his legs and offering his belly up to the world. The boy let out an exasperated sigh. "You are *such* an annoying animal," he said, crouching down to give the dog the belly rub he wanted.

Erich laughed. "But I can see that you love him anyway."

"Oh yes, sir," said the boy. "Puck is my best friend, next to Willie." He nodded his head toward the second boy, who was now stumbling up, darker haired but about the same age. Both were just shy of adolescence, Erich guessed. Willie was panting and staring intently at Erich's uniform.

"You're a general, aren't you?" Willie asked when he caught his breath. "Max, this is the officer who rescued Bürgermeister Munter today at Birnau!"

"Guilty as charged," Erich said.

"I was glad you came when you did," Max Fuchs said, standing up again.

"So was I," said Willie. "Sort of . . ."

"Sort of?" Erich asked.

"Well, I've never seen a hanging. I kind of wanted to see how it goes."

"Ah." These boys did not know how lucky they were, Erich thought, to be so far from the front. The wonder in their eyes— how very different from what he had seen in the young boys of Warsaw or the small towns of Poland.

"Why is your *waffenfarbe* gold?" Willie asked. "Shouldn't it be red if you're a general?"

Erich reflexively looked down at the gold piping outlining his shoulder patches. "Yes, but gold is for cavalry. And today I'm a cavalryman, as you can see."

"Horses are obsolete," Willie stated importantly. "My father says the next war won't use them at all. He drives a tank. His *waffenfarbe* is rose, for the Panzer Corps."

"Well." Erich shifted in his saddle, suddenly speechless. The idea that another war might follow this one overwhelmed him with exhaustion. Of course these boys might think so. War had permeated their parents' lives and now their own. All of a sudden, the day's events settled heavily on Erich, urging him to rest. He felt the mare's impatience as she lifted first one hoof, then another. She too was ready to call it a day. "I hope your father is right and horses will never again be used in war. But I hope he's wrong that there will be another one."

"There *has* to be another one," Willie said. "Max and I are preparing."

"Boys, I'm sorry," Erich interrupted. "I have to get this lovely lady to a barn. Can one of you direct me to the Nagel farm?"

Max pointed back down the road behind Erich. "You passed it, sir, not far back. The entrance is hidden behind hazelnut bushes, that's probably why you missed it."

Erich tipped his head in thanks and turned the horse around. The boys ran off in the opposite direction, shouts mixing with Puck's barks. Erich neared the dense hedge of hazelnuts Max had indicated and became aware of a rhythmic metallic banging that intensified as he approached the Nagel farm. He guided the horse through the shrubbery and emerged in a large barnyard scattered with farm equipment. In its center, bent over the open hood of an enormous truck, a large gray-haired man clad in overalls was wielding a hammer, trying to secure a flat sheet of some sort of metal inside the bay.

"Hallo!" Erich called out. Startled, the man dropped the sheet of metal and the hammer. Erich guided the horse through a haphazard collection of wheelbarrows, tractors, and carts, as the old man straightened up slowly, one hand on his back. When he turned around, the clearly outlined muscles in his arms and the broad fullness of his chest told Erich that this old man was far from infirm. Noticing Erich's uniform, the man glanced quickly around the barnyard, taking stock of everything that might be lying about.

"Are you Fritz Nagel?" Erich dismounted so he would appear less threatening.

"Yes, yes I am." The man moved in front of the open engine bay. He planted his feet wide apart, taking up the stance of a gladiator. "How can I help you, General . . . ?"

"Wolf. Erich Wolf. I am here to return this fine mare. She belongs to a cousin of yours. I believe his name is Bernard?"

"Ah, Frieda!" The moment he recognized the horse, the old

man's shoulders relaxed slightly, and a chuckle escaped him. He reached into his pocket for a cigarette, lit it, and took a deep, thoughtful drag. "I thought that was Frieda at Birnau today. But it didn't seem possible, so I told myself my eyes must be starting to fail. But here she is after all." Another pocket yielded a cube of sugar that Fritz now offered to the mare. She ate it quickly, then nudged him insistently with her muzzle. Eventually he gave in and patted her with obvious affection. "You old girl. Very impressive performance. Bernie will be so proud."

"Indeed, she is a fine animal. In fact, I would very much like to compensate you and your cousin for allowing me to use her today." Erich opened his shoulder bag for his wallet. "I'm afraid I was in too much of a hurry to properly reward Bernard earlier."

The old man stepped forward and restrained Erich's arm with a grip that defied challenge. "Oh no, certainly not. She did service for the Reich, didn't she? It's our honor that she was chosen." The statement closed the discussion as far as Fritz Nagel was concerned. He took the reins from Erich and led the horse into a somewhat decrepit structure that Erich assumed was the barn. It could use some shoring up, he thought, watching the man carefully swing open a door on its one remaining hinge. Fritz propped the door open with a large rock and disappeared with the horse.

Left alone, Erich approached the truck the old man had been working on. It was a long-nose Volvo, significantly bigger than the ones Erich had seen while in the army, but basically similar in design: a large, flat bed in the back for transporting goods and materials, a smaller cab for the driver and one or two passengers, and a large engine out front, beneath a substantial bifurcated hood. Having spent time doing maintenance on trucks during the first war, Erich preferred these to their snub-nosed cousins. The long-nose sported an engine hood that opened outward from the center, like a bird spreading its wings, and this design made access to its twin engine bays child's play. Here, Fritz Nagel had opened only the left side of the hood, but when Erich peered in-side, expecting to see some machinery or part of the engine, he was confronted with open space. Yet there were no spare pieces of machinery lying about the barnyard to suggest that Herr Nagel was disassembling the truck. Perhaps he had already stored the engine someplace else. A loose sheet of some metal—the material that the man had been working on when Erich interrupted him— was lying on the ground in front of the empty engine bay. Was it asbestos? Erich put his hand on the edge of the bay and crouched down to get a better look.

Suddenly, the truck hood slammed shut. Only Erich's lightning-quick reflexes kept his fingers from getting crushed. Erich looked up to see Fritz Nagel standing before him. His left hand was clamped firmly on the hood cover, and from the tendons straining against the skin of the man's forearm, Erich knew that Herr Nagel intended the hood to remain closed. His half-finished cigarette lay smoldering in the dirt.

"Wonderful old truck," Erich said, patting the hood in ap-preciation. He did not want to exacerbate whatever anxiety the old man was feeling, even though he couldn't imagine what had prompted it. "One doesn't see these big ones very often."

"They're quite common on farms down here," Fritz countered quickly. "Too big and slow for the army, thankfully for us. I've had this one for years. Pinocchio."

"I'm sorry?"

"Pinocchio. The long nose. I couldn't resist."

"Ah." Erich wondered whether all farmers named their trucks. "Are you having engine trouble?"

Fritz stiffened. "No, no trouble. Not really. Just . . ." He seemed to be searching his mind for the right phrase. "Just trying to maxi-mize engine efficiency."

"Really? With asbestos?"

"It's an experiment. Still a work in progress." He picked the sheet of metal up from the ground and grabbed a wrench that was lying nearby. "But I'm done for the day and must be going in. I thank you again on behalf of Bernard for returning the horse."

"Of course," Erich said. Fritz Nagel nodded toward the farm entrance, indicating that it was time for Erich to leave. Erich made his way back through the hazelnuts, then turned south on the road, toward the Gasthof zum Löwen, the inn where he would be staying. Instead of wondering about the farmer and his truck, he decided to focus on the luxury awaiting him: a feather bed. The Führer did not believe in feathers for soldiers. But Erich felt he could benefit from a little softness tonight.

– Eight –

The choir break never lasted more than ten minutes. Marina told Gisela Mecklen that she would be leaving early to help her mother prepare for Oskar's visit the next day. Gisela raised her eyebrows, but Marina ignored her. She had no love for the Mecklens after their takeover of the Rosenberg bakery.

In case anyone was watching, Marina headed down the hill toward town, then looped around the front of the church. Following the dirt path, she stopped at a door just beneath the stained-glass window that depicted the fourth Station of the Cross. It was locked. She knocked twice, paused, then knocked again three times. Someone approached from inside, fumbled with the lock, and opened the door. "I'm so glad you were able to join us," Johann said. "When you told Gisela you had to leave, I wasn't certain whether that was for our benefit or your family's."

"I'm always happy to give Gisela Mecklen something new to ponder," Marina said.

She followed Johann into the children's reading alcove, where the other two members of the group were already sitting somewhat precariously in the too-small chairs: Ludmilla Schenk, the postmistress; and Ernst Rausch, the young owner of the print shop in Meerfeld, who had been spared military service because he was blind in one eye. Marina knew Ludmilla well. Other than Oskar, the postmistress was her primary source of information about Franz, since all letters and telegrams from the front passed through Ludmilla's fingers.

Ludmilla had lost both of her sons and her husband to the war. Marina could not bear to imagine the growing horror and disbelief the postmistress must have felt, sitting in front of the telegraph machine, watching it print out word by word the news of her sons' deaths, one year after it had printed out the same words about her husband. Those tragedies had brought Ludmilla to the group. With her own family beyond salvation, she had nothing to lose, she said, and she couldn't just sit idly by and watch other families be destroyed as hers had been. Johann had offered her an active solution.

Ernst Rausch was a pacifist. Marina knew little more than that fact about him, but she knew his printing expertise was vast. Ernst spoke very little. It was one of the things that Johann valued about him.

Johann took his place next to a small easel, on which a child's abstract pointillist version of the *Honigschlecker* statue had wrinkled. He looked more tired than usual, Marina thought. His thinning blond hair and darkly shadowed eyes under small wire-rimmed glasses made him look much older than his thirty-two years, a stark contrast to the baby roundness of his face.

He stood quietly, waiting. The muted chatter outside was finally interrupted by Gisela Mecklen's muffled but distinctive voice. The choir began its warm-up, and as the scales and arpeggios began to seep through the walls of the children's room, Johann spoke, taking care to talk only while the singing continued.

"Thank you for coming on such short notice. This won't take long. I was informed two days ago that we might be getting a delivery very soon, and though nothing is certain, as it never is, I thought we should try to find a storage location."

"Do you know how many?" Ludmilla asked.

"It is a family," Johann said. "Two adults—" He paused as the choir abruptly stopped, and they again heard a muted Gisela through the stone. After a few minutes, the choir launched into *"Nun ruhen alle Wälder."*

"Two young children and a baby," Johann continued. "Now, do not even attempt to offer, Ludmilla, because your new apartment is just too small, I'm afraid. And I am a bit fearful of sending them to Meerfeld, Ernst, because of Captain Rodemann and his regiment. Does anyone know where they are tonight?"

"The last telegram I saw for him went to the Meerfeld depot," Ludmilla said. "But perhaps they will move on tomorrow."

"Marina, if we have no other alternative—is there any chance?"

Marina hesitated. Her family's home was always only an option of last resort. Oskar was coming tomorrow, his first visit since Christmas. Marina found herself surprisingly happy at the prospect of seeing him, given the tension that had been simmering between her and her father ever since the war began. Their weekly phone conversations were short and perfunctory, a delivery of information, usually about the movements and safety of Franz's battalion. But now, she felt her spirits lift at the thought of his arrival.

It was the same sense of excitement she used to feel as a child, looking out the living room window, watching for Oskar to come home from work. Back then, when she was very young (too young to know any better, she might say now), Marina adored her father. Revered him. Followed him everywhere he went, if she could. "Your vati has a second shadow," Edith used to joke. That bond had never really broken, despite her current suspicions and anger. Marina allowed herself a moment to bask in the comfort of memory: the embrace she gave him each time they reunited, the earthy amber-and-tobacco smell of him, the faint cloud of cigar smoke mixed with Mouchoir de Monsieur cologne that spread through a room when he entered.

"Marina?" Johann was giving her a bemused look.

"What? Oh, I don't know, Johann, Oskar arrives tomorrow," Marina said. "It might be difficult." What an understatement. If Oskar was at home, hiding a family of five in the house was out of the question.

"Well, I hope we will find another solution. Meanwhile, I will try to confirm the exact arrival date and time," Johann said. "Ernst or Ludmilla, let me know the moment Rodemann moves his men out. Maybe the farmers can sour some of their milk for him, hurry him along." Marina imagined that Captain Rodemann might thrive on sour milk, but she did not say so aloud. "Also, Ernst, could you put together a set of travel documents? I have their identifying information here." The young man, who had been thoughtfully shaping the end of his mustache, took the folded piece of paper that Johann handed him. "The sooner you can get this done, the better. I know it's short notice . . ."

"I'll work on it tonight. Where can I find you tomorrow?"

"At the Protestant church. Thank you so much, Ernst, it is good to have that taken care of." But there was no relief in Johann's face, Marina thought as he turned to her. "And Marina, we can talk more tomorrow, yes? Are we still meeting at nine?"

Marina nodded. Oskar would not arrive before lunchtime, at the earliest.

"Johann, tell me," Ludmilla said. "How did it go with our last charge?"

"Oh, I'm sorry, I should have mentioned that in the beginning. Yes, Ludmilla, he arrived quite successfully, I'm pleased to say. Reunited with his aunt in Britain, I'm told." The group breathed a collective sigh of relief. They didn't always get news confirming the successful arrival of travelers.

For Marina, such news assuaged complicated feelings about her participation in this group. When Johann had asked her why she wanted to join, she could not give him a complete answer. Sympathy for the plight of the refugees, of course, and anger at the Führer for his aggression toward other countries and their people. But that wasn't all of it. There was also guilt. For most of her life, Marina hadn't thought much about Oskar's position in the government. She knew he was highly placed, head of the Economics Ministry, with vague responsibilities for wartime transports. The complications in her own life had always overshadowed her curiosity about Oskar's duties and authority. But shortly after Sofia's birth, the world around her shook her out of her self-centered cocoon. The yellow stars that so many of her friends and acquaintances were required to wear. The forced closing, after Kristallnacht, of many of the shops that she had frequented. The disappearance of the Sterns.

Hilde and Martin Stern lived across the hall from her parents' apartment in Berlin. Close neighbors, and closer friends. Marina adored them. Martin was Oskar's smoking buddy, his accomplice in the domestic crime of enjoying imported South American cigars, which Martin was inexplicably able to procure even after the war began. Marina remembered childhood evenings spent hiding under the table while the Sterns and her parents played canasta and drank sherry and pretended they didn't know she was there. When she was older, she occasionally joined Oskar and Martin for a glass of brandy on the fire escape, to which the men were banished because Hilde and Edith claimed they detested the smell of cigar smoke.

Marina didn't even remember that the Sterns were Jewish until Hilde asked for help in sewing stars onto their clothing. Marina had then felt a great wave of fear and nausea for her friends. She asked her father to help them get visas out of the country, but Oskar seemed reluctant. "Don't get involved," he had said. "It's not safe, Marina." It was a tone of resignation and finality that she had heard before, one that indicated the discussion was over.

Marina had refused to give up. She began an exploration of the underground. It was not hard to find the right people, if you knew where to look, and if you were willing to take risks, which Marina was. But it took time to get the necessary papers, and by the time she found the right printer who could forge visas to Palestine, the Sterns had been sent to a Jewish ghetto in Poland.

To this day, Marina didn't forgive herself for her delay. Nor had she forgiven her father for his inertia. Perhaps he was complicit in the actions of the regime. She didn't know, but if so, she was as guilty as he was. Guilt by association. Guilt by blood. Whatever sins he might be committing she needed to do something to expiate. That was why she was here. She sat back in the tiny Sunday school chair and listened to the hymn being sung by the choir outside. It was familiar:

Wo bist du, Sonne, blieben?
Die Nacht hat dich vertrieben,
die Nacht, des Tages Feind . . .

It was Marina's bedtime lullaby, the one she sang to her daughters. "*Where have you gone, dear sun? Night has made you run; night, the foe of day . . .*" Her own mother used to sing it to her. Edith's alto was rich and full; it had been months since Marina had heard it. *Nighttime is casting its shadow*, the choir sang. True enough. But night was not the only shadow casting darkness upon them.

– Nine –

"Oma, can we get one of Irene's kittens?" Sofia lay on her pillow in bed next to Rosie, light woolen blankets tucked around her and her favorite doll, Millie. Her long blond hair swam around the pillow cover like strands of algae in a lake. In a different world, Sofia could be a mermaid, Edith thought. Those intense blue eyes luring sailors off course. Edith herself tried now to resist them.

"Sofia, we can ask Opa when he gets here, okay?" She bent over Rosie to give Sofia a kiss, taking care not to bump her head against the ceiling that slanted over the girls' bed. It was a wonder that Sofia liked sleeping on the inside of this double bed. The bed frame had been pushed as far as possible against the wall, to make space for Marina and Lara's bed on the other side of the room. The descending roof sliced through the air above the pillow closest to the wall, making the space slightly claustrophobic. Edith would have thought that Sofia would feel anxious and enclosed. But Sofia insisted on taking that side of the bed, saying she liked to hear the dormice scratch and scrabble on the other side of the wall when she woke up late at night, that it made her feel less alone.

Rosie had been whispering quietly to Hans-Jürg, but at the mention of the word *Opa*, she popped up, letting the bear fall to the floor. "Is Opa coming tomorrow morning or tomorrow afternoon?"

Edith picked up the bear, gently pushed Rosie's torso back down, and pulled the blanket over her. "Tomorrow lunchtime."

"Is he staying for the night?"

"I think so. But it's bedtime now, sweetheart, so you must go to sleep." Edith gave Rosie a kiss on the forehead and laid Hans-Jürg next to her pillow.

"Is he staying the next day?"

"I don't know. I hope so."

"Where's Lara?"

"She's downstairs reading, I think."

"Why doesn't she have to come to bed?"

Edith sighed. "When you're thirteen, you can stay up longer and read too. But first you have to learn how to read."

"Sofia can read and she's not staying up," Rosie pointed out.

This girl was too smart for her own good. "Enough, Rosie. Quiet now. Good night!"

Edith pulled the door shut on the girls' quiet whispers and crossed the tiny foyer that connected the staircase to the two bedrooms on the second floor. She stepped into the room that she shared with Oskar. It was no bigger than the one the girls shared with Marina, but because it had to accommodate only one double bed, there was also room for a writing desk and a chair, both of which were wedged into the alcove that looked onto the Breckenmüllers' garden. Edith walked over to the chair and draped her sweater over its shoulders.

The desk was a Biedermeier. Oskar's other beloved, Edith thought, running her fingers along its top edge. The secretary had been with them since the early days of their marriage. It had been no small feat, transporting it here from Berlin, but she was glad they'd made the effort. It was an old friend, stunning in its beauty—even after all these years, the infinite gradations of chestnut and bay that danced over the surface of its whorled grain could distract her from her writing if she let her mind stray. It was also wonderfully practical, with its many recessed drawers and hidden compartments that held clips and blotters and pen nibs and a variety of other miscellaneous items like buttons and tobacco.

Whenever the late-morning hour was quiet enough, Edith sat at this desk to write letters. Here, as nowhere else, Oskar was always present. She felt him in the spare smoking pipes that rested inside an empty jam jar; in the collection of well-sharpened pencils lying side by side in a hollow cigar box; in the small silver army knife, "the thinking man's mustache comb," as Oskar called it, tucked into a stack of papers. Edith had her own designated drawer on the left side where she kept her ink and stationery, and she was careful always to put her things away and out of sight when she was done using them, lest she disturb the Oskarness of the entire space.

Now Edith shuffled over to the bed, pulled off her house slippers, and lay down. The claustrophobic roof incline in this room had been offset by the skylight they had always dreamed of, a very large pane of glass, almost as big as the bed itself, and square in shape rather than the customary narrow rectangle. This skylight had caused a big ruckus during construction: The roofer had insisted that, because of its "unprecedented and irresponsible" size, there was no way to ensure "the integrity of its borders." He warned that it might leak over time. Edith had said she'd take that chance, fired the man, and hired his subordinate, who had no issues with installing the window and was grateful for the extra pay. She did keep a tube of bathroom caulk under the bed, though so far she'd had no need for it.

Edith stared through the glass to the darkening indigo blue of the sky. She wondered what her husband was doing. She had never been to the Führer's summer vacation home in Austria, but Oskar was obliged to go to Fürchtesgaden regularly. The Führer had purchased the property shortly after the war began and then undertaken extensive renovations of the main house and grounds with the aim of establishing an alternative seat of government in the bucolic perch high in the Alps. Edith was aware of those renovations only because they coincided in time with the expansion of their own house in Blumental. Knowing that Oskar was engaged in a similar venture, the Führer relentlessly pressed him for opinions on a wide range of questions. Should he install Ionic or Corinthian columns to replace a load-bearing wall in the ballroom? What was the relative heat resistance in a fireplace hearth of marble from Italy versus granite from India? What was the expected life span of a caged singing canary?

The sky above Edith's bed was clear enough now to make the Pleiades visible. A faint and gentle cloud of stars. At dinner that night, Erich had said the Führer was still entertaining at Fürchtesgaden on a regular basis. Despite all military indications to the contrary, he seemed confident of success in the war. This was welcome news, for Edith knew that Oskar's mood was dependent on the Führer's. If, as Erich reported, champagne was still flowing nightly, it meant that the Führer was feeling buoyant, which was far better for his subordinates than when he felt discontent. When their leader was unhappy, disquiet reigned among the cabinet ministers. They all knew from the bitter experience of predecessors who had suddenly disappeared that he held each and every one of them responsible for the smooth operation of all things around him, and they tried valiantly, often in vain, to satisfy his demands.

Tonight Edith was troubled that Oskar had not left Fürchtesgaden with Erich. It implied a closeness to the Führer that she once thought would be anathema to Oskar. But her husband had changed over the past year. He had become quiet, more contemplative, almost secretive, and had spent more time in Berlin. Edith didn't know what to make of it. She had always assumed Oskar was a begrudging and reluctant advisor to the Führer. She'd presumed that Oskar's loyalty to the present administration arose entirely out of his Prussian instinct to serve his country as best he could and not shirk responsibility. He was the only holdover from the prior administration whom the Führer had called upon to remain in his post. There should be continuity of leadership in the Economics Ministry, the Führer had insisted, to secure the nation's economic stability during a volatile political time. Presented in such a way, there was never any question that Oskar would agree, as the Führer well knew.

But one-on-one meetings with the Führer in the private offices of his summer retreat? Those had never been part of Oskar's job description, nor, Edith would have thought before now, did he want them to be. In truth, Edith knew little about Oskar's responsibilities. Since the second war began, the few times she'd broached any topic related to the administration or his office, he closed off discussion peremptorily. Nowadays, he crossed that barrier only to offer her and Marina advance information about military movements that might affect them in the south, and to update them about events in France, especially those that could bear on Franz's safety. Oskar's day-to-day administrative duties in Berlin were largely a mystery.

Edith wondered when she had first begun to doubt her husband. Perhaps it was as early as the darkening of the atmosphere in Berlin. She had watched the growing intolerance of minorities, especially Jews, with bafflement and fear. That fear peaked when people like their friends Hilde and Martin Stern were told to pack up their belongings and report to the train station, where they disappeared on one of countless trains heading east. Why were coal trains being repurposed as human transports? Where were they going? Marina sought information on a daily basis, and shared some of what she heard with Edith. The few facts Marina came across simply raised new and more disturbing questions in Edith's mind. What was Oskar's role in these transports? Did he control those trains? Did he sign the orders sending hundreds of people away from their homes?

Reluctant to acknowledge the terrifying reality suggested by those rumors, Edith didn't confront Oskar until a letter she had written to Hilde Stern returned unopened last winter. They'd been sitting alone in the living room sipping the coffee Oskar had brought from Berlin. Outside, a storm raged, one of those that rattled the glass in their casements. The wind buffeted the chest-nut tree, and the heavy branches of its shadowy bulk knocked and scratched on the windows. Oskar looked up from the newspaper he'd been reading as a bough screeched across one of the glass panes. "When was the last time we had that tree trimmed, Edith?" She ignored the question. The letter that she'd sent to Hilde two weeks earlier had been returned from Lodz that afternoon, com-pletely intact and sealed, with the words FORWARDING ADDRESS UNKNOWN stamped across Hilde's name. *Now*, she thought. She'd been content to embrace ignorance, but she loved Hilde and had to know that she was safe.

"You know, Oskar," she began, "sometimes I sit here wonder-ing what you do in Berlin. I look up at the clock and I think, 'What is he doing right now?'"

Oskar laughed and put his coffee cup down. "Is that why we haven't had the tree trimmed, my dear? Because you are preoc-cupied with my work?"

Edith approached cautiously. "No, not 'preoccupied,' that's overstating it. But I do think about you, you know I do. And I wonder about your day, what meetings you might be in, what decisions you might have to be making."

"Oh, my day is far from exciting," Oskar said, reaching for the sugar bowl, frowning when he discovered it empty. "If I told you ev-erything I did, you'd immediately feel an overwhelming urge to nap."

"No, Oskar, really, I'd like to know a bit more. We used to talk about things all the time."

"Family matters, mostly," Oskar said. "Not dull things like fuel supply depots in Köln."

She knew she was pushing but willed herself to continue. "Is that mostly it? Military support issues?"

Oskar sat up in his chair, his jaw beginning to clench. "Edith, I have told you I cannot speak of these things with you. There are things I am involved in—things that, for your sake and our fam-ily's, I cannot share."

Having started, Edith was not now going to stop. "Is it just coal being transported on those rails, Oskar?" Edith's mind flooded with imagined scenes, and she closed her eyes, trying to block them out. "Marina hears things about the rail lines, you know. Horrible things . . ."

Suddenly Oskar slammed his hand on the table, hard enough to tip the cup in its saucer. His eyes were hard. She had seen caution there in the past when she'd strayed close to dangerous territory. But the look today was harsher—a warning, the kind shouted at someone headed toward a minefield.

"Don't!" Oskar barked. "Do not speculate. You don't have that luxury, Edith, nor does Marina. Given who you are, people mistake your speculations for the truth, and that opens the door to trouble."

Taken aback by his sudden furor, Edith tried to disarm him. "Oskar, Marina and I only speak to each other about these things."

He was not reassured. "It is just. Not. *Safe!*" Oskar almost snarled.

"How, Oskar? How is my talking to my daughter not safe?" Edith demanded.

Oskar picked up the toppled coffee cup and clenched it with such force that Edith feared the china would crack. "Edith." He waited after speaking her name, breathing in and out with his eyes closed. Was there moisture at their corners? She could not tell. "There are rumors everywhere about everything," he finally continued. "Marina shouldn't believe what she hears. And she certainly shouldn't engage in discussions about it. It's not safe. People disappear for less. Certain topics are risky for anyone, and particularly for us."

Now it was Edith's turn to explode. "But it's Hilde and Martin! I need to know they're not hurt. I need to know they're not on those trains packed together with complete strangers, hundreds to a car, heading to some godforsaken place! Please tell me they're not!"

Edith could have mentioned any number of other Jewish

friends that she and Oskar had known in Berlin, but she was most concerned about the Sterns. The last time she had seen Hilde, her friend had offered Edith the small wooden inlaid box that she had found in Turkey on her honeymoon, the one Edith had always admired. Hilde and Martin had been ordered to leave Berlin, Hilde explained, along with thousands of other Jewish families, and they were permitted to bring only two small cardboard boxes of personal belongings. Edith was dumbstruck. Later, Oskar was able to determine that the Sterns had been sent to a settlement established expressly for Jews in Lodz, Poland.

Edith had reassured herself that they were all right. She didn't know much about the settlement at Lodz, but she told herself that Martin was likely to have gotten one of the larger apartments there, given his prominence in the Berlin community. Perhaps Hilde even had a small garden, or at least a window box, where she could plant some flowers. Of course, the settlement would be very crowded, and no doubt there would be food shortages, even worse than those in Berlin. But like Edith and Oskar, Hilde and Martin Stern had endured the horrendous scarcities of the first war. They were not strangers to hunger. They could, Edith reasoned, survive such adversity again. When Edith heard a report that soldiers had shot several Jews on the streets of the Jewish tenement in Minsk, she was sure that those unfortunate youths—she was convinced they must have been young—had foolishly antagonized the officers. There was still no excuse for such excessive force, but if similar events were taking place in Lodz, Edith felt certain that Martin and Hilde, two quiet, retiring people who were very respectful of authority, wouldn't be involved.

These rationalizations began to fray when Marina told Edith about the train transports. Thousands of Jews, Marina said, were being packed into freight trains like cattle and shipped east. Rumors of their ultimate destination abounded. Some said they were being deported to Palestine and other foreign countries; others claimed that they were sent to forced labor camps in eastern Germany and Poland.

That winter evening, Edith's outburst seemed to strike a chord in Oskar. He leaned forward and took her hands. "Edith, I don't know where the Sterns are. I have been keeping an eye on Lodz, and what I can tell you is that many people were relocated. The settlement was vastly overcrowded, but many people remain there. Perhaps our friends are among them."

That evening and again tonight, Edith wanted to believe her husband. Perhaps he was right, she thought, staring up at the sky through her beloved skylight. Perhaps she should not assume anything from an undelivered letter. The stars were twinkling hesitantly, it seemed to her. Perhaps Hilde was growing petunias and Martin was now smoking contraband cigarettes. Perhaps the Führer really did want to talk to Oskar about cold-pressed steel pipes. Perhaps Oskar would return home early tomorrow afternoon and hide her boots in the woodpile as a joke, as he always did. Perhaps.

– Ten –

Despite the darkness, Marina decided to return home through the forest, as Erich and Rosie had. She followed the path into the ink of silver firs and pines. The canopy of trees filtered out all but the most persistent sunbeams during the day and now forbade passage to the hesitant moonlight. A layer of pine needles carpeted the ground between looming sentries of towering tree trunks. This was the kind of wooded environment that inspired the Brothers Grimm in their tales, but Marina didn't find the atmosphere menacing. Rather, she found herself breathing more freely with each step, the musky, loamy air slowing her pulse and relieving the tension in her body. Here, she embraced a sense of expansiveness and possibility, mystery and magic. She could more readily imagine a tribe of golden-haired elves hiding behind the trees than a pack of snarling wolves. If only that were true outside the forest as well.

These woods were wilder and less cultivated than Grosswald, the park Marina so loved in Berlin. In all the time Marina spent exploring Grosswald's sprawling grandeur, she rarely encountered debris of any kind. As a natural extension of Berlin's city limits, the park was carefully maintained—branches and trees felled by wind and storm were quickly cleared away by rangers. In Birnau's forest, by contrast, fallen limbs lay where they dropped, rotting slowly into their surroundings, nature undisturbed and timeless.

Suspended in time. What a blessing that would be. Marina

could not say time had been her friend. Certainly it was not her friend now, as Oskar's impending visit was about to coincide with one of Johann's smuggling enterprises. From the beginning, Oskar's position in Berlin had made the group wary of Marina's involvement, fearful of her motives. Even after Marina had won Johann's confidence, Ludmilla was cautious and begrudging around her. Marina was surprised that Ludmilla had not questioned her tonight about Erich Wolf, had not asked Marina why she appeared to have such a close friendship with a high-ranking military officer. Had she been asked, Marina was not sure what she would have said. That Erich was a family friend, perhaps. Oskar's protégé. Her adopted brother.

But Marina had never thought of him as a brother, though she knew Edith loved him as a son. When he came to live with them in Berlin, Erich took over the small room on the third floor of the apartment. For the young Marina, he was a favorite playmate. He was gentle and kind, and he often smiled slyly at her, as if they were in on a secret no one else knew about. More than any other adult, he was willing to enter Marina's reality. He knelt when he spoke to her and sat on the floor rather than on a chair when they were together.

Over the next decade, Erich became an ideal older friend for Marina. He wasn't young enough that she experienced the embarrassments and annoyances of early manhood that she heard her girlfriends with brothers complain about: the smelly discarded socks on the kitchen floor, the shaven hair stubble circling the bathroom sink. Nor did he tease her, as other brothers mercilessly did, about her body once it began to develop. No, he was always the perfect gentleman, always treated her with respect. And she adored him.

So did her friends, once they all entered adolescence. How could Erich, a cavalryman, not inspire their budding female fantasies? Their girlish love of horses mixed with a burgeoning interest in boys settled naturally on Erich's equestrian grace. Later, fed on Goethe and Schiller in school, the girls debated whether Erich more closely resembled Faust or Don Carlos. Marina did not participate in these discussions, for in her own mind at that time, Erich was still a fraternal figure. Until he left the house.

He spent the years immediately after the first war training cavalry regiments, but the modern military machine had no use for horses. Steel tanks and armored cars sent them all trotting off to pastures. Erich's own beloved Arrakis, Loki's successor, went to a stable in Ludwigsfelde, an hour's drive from Berlin. At thirty-one, Erich found himself militarily obsolete. Urged by his superiors, he applied to the prestigious Prussian Military Academy, whose graduates became officers of the Prussian General Staff, the military's highest rank. To no one's surprise but his own, he was admitted.

The day Erich moved out of Oskar and Edith's home was the day after Marina's sixteenth birthday. He had delayed his departure deliberately, he said, to help Oskar and Edith chaperone the celebration the night before and to ensure that all of Marina's male admirers controlled themselves. Marina came downstairs that morning wearing one of the two new dresses Edith had sewn for her. This one had a fitted lace bodice with puffed cap sleeves that Marina had seen in a Paris fashion magazine. Its light-blue voile skirt flowed, Marina hoped, suggestively but demurely around her hips, and she descended with full self-awareness, swaying her body gently back and forth to create the desired air-sweeping effect.

"Are you all right, dear?" Edith asked, observing her. "You look a bit unsteady."

"Ah, she probably just drank too much champagne last night," Oskar joked. "Takes a while for the center of balance to right itself again."

"I did *not* drink too much champagne, Vati," Marina protested, reaching the first floor. She twirled around the foyer a few times, testing the horizontal reach of her skirt. "I am just trying out my new dress."

Oskar looked skeptical. "Well, try it out any more than that and you won't have to bother wearing it."

Erich stood silently by the front door, his army trunk, rucksack, and assorted books piled next to him. "Well, Erich," Marina said, dancing around him, "what do *you* think?"

"You look beautiful," he said. He caught her in midswirl and held her at arm's length. Marina watched his eyes move over her, slowly wandering upward, from toe to head, resting finally upon her face. She watched his eyes trace the outline of her brow, her nose, her lips, and at last her eyes. There he lingered, and then he quickly dropped his hands and kissed her forehead. "But then you always have," he whispered. Ten minutes later, he was gone.

Marina did not expect to miss him as much as she did. She did not expect his departure to plunge her into a state of loss and longing. She did not expect to wake up each morning, wrapped in her comforter, waiting to hear his footsteps overhead, or to dread the moment every day when she came home from school and walked into the house to find the sofa where he used to sit empty. Though Erich still joined the family for dinner from time to time, these isolated visits proved more painful to Marina than his absence. Each time he came to the house and then left, she was reminded of the fact that not long ago, he had *not* left.

Grosswald alone brought her solace. It was an easy trip on the S-Bahn, and Marina visited the park almost daily. She explored the vast expanse of its endless meandering trails and footpaths, traversing the banks of the Havel River and the Wannsee, hiking around the muddy shrubs of Rechte Lanke and past the tall pines of Schildhorn. Within six months, she had navigated almost every acre of land within Grosswald's boundaries. Then she met Franz.

She was walking along the shore of a small lake, collecting pinecones for Edith, who liked scenting them with cinnamon for her potpourris. Bent over and shuffling slowly forward, eyes fixed on the ground for right-sized cones, Marina did not notice the young man in khaki shorts and suspenders who stood on the trail and watched her approach. Hearing a laugh, she abruptly straightened up. A tall, thin man, or perhaps still a boy, was staring at her out of cornflower-blue eyes.

"What's so funny?" Marina demanded.

"Oh, I'm sorry, miss, nothing all that funny, really." The young man backed away from her.

"No, you were definitely laughing."

He swallowed and wrestled with the muscles around his mouth to stop himself from chuckling. "It's just that you looked like— like a giant anteater." He loudly guffawed. "With your arm hanging down and your torso sweeping from right to left, you could be a giant anteater vacuuming up . . . What are you gathering?"

Marina grasped the canvas satchel that was slung over her shoulder and held it before her defensively. "Pinecones," she answered tersely. "I'm gathering pinecones. Is that a crime?"

"Oh no," he said. His look was sincere and apologetic. "At least I wouldn't think so. Of course, if everyone was allowed to pick up every pinecone they saw, I suppose that might be a problem. Though now that I think about it, I don't know why that would be a problem. It probably wouldn't be. And, you know, definitely not a crime."

Marina listened to his verbal gymnastics with amusement. He was unaware of how comical he sounded and looked, with those suspenders and dark socks, and that tweed cap topping a pair of very protuberant ears. But she did like his smile, shy and hesitant, offered like an invitation he expected to be refused. She extended her hand. "Well, if you're thinking of turning me in to the authorities, I shouldn't be telling you my name, but you seem trustworthy. Marina Eberhardt. Pleased to meet you."

He shuffled toward her quickly, grabbed her hand, and pumped it up and down. "Thiessen. Franz Thiessen. I am honored to make your acquaintance."

"Hello, Franz." Marina gave him the smile she had been practicing in her mirror, the one she copied from Greta Schröder in *Nosferatu*—a combination of warmth and beguilement that required a certain elongation of the neck for maximum effect. Franz stood before her transfixed, still clutching her hand. "So what are you doing in Grosswald?" she asked, gently untangling her hand from his.

"Oh, sorry." Franz shook his arm as if he had been electrified. "I'm, you know, just walking. Walking and watching. Bird-watching."

"*Bird*-watching?" Marina noticed for the first time the small pair of binoculars hanging around his neck. "I've never met a bird-watcher. Fascinating. What sorts of birds do you watch?"

"Oh, whatever's out there. In the air, you know. Or the trees."

"Yes, that makes sense. That's where they usually are. But how do you find them? Do you look at the sky or the trees through those?" Marina pointed at the binoculars.

Franz shook his head earnestly. "No, that wouldn't work. I mean, not that that's a bad idea, you know, it might work for some people, maybe. Certainly you could try that." He paused. He was trying so hard not to offend her.

He went on. "What *I* do is, I listen for bird songs. For ones that I know. And if I recognize one, then I try to locate where it's coming from—you know, a tree nearby, or maybe a lake or the river. And then, when I sort of narrow that down, *then* I use the binoculars." Franz grasped the tubes of his binoculars with both hands and began twisting them back and forth on the central shaft.

"You must know a lot of bird songs."

"Not a lot. The usual amount. Enough." Franz was rotating the binocular tubes back and forth with such vigor, it was possible he might break the apparatus entirely. His anxiety was both painful and amusing to watch. Marina decided to try to make him more comfortable.

"What are your favorites? Birds, I mean."

"Oh, that's a difficult question to answer. I have lots of favorites. I mean, you know, there are just so many. Like the song thrush, this little brown-speckled bird, you know? Very tiny, really, but it has a loud, I mean a *really* loud song for its weight. Like, you know, it's amazing how such a little bird can make so much noise. I'd love to know if it has oversize lungs or something. I should make a note of that." Franz pulled a small notepad from his back pocket and scribbled something with a pencil that had been tucked behind his ear. "And the green woodpecker, that's a beautiful bird. It has a red head and a green body, really very pretty, very lovely. But also, you know, the reason I like the green woodpecker so much is that its call sounds like a laugh. You kind of have to smile when you hear it. And it doesn't migrate. It's a sedentary bird. It likes to stay close to home. I can relate to that." Franz suddenly became quiet and looked down at his feet.

If only Franz had been able to stay close to home, Marina thought now, nearing the edge of the Birnau forest, where the sheep pastures bridged the gap between wilderness and civilization. Franz was a good man, thoroughly honorable and kind. Marina loved his goodness, loved the fact that the world could still produce such a man. Such men should never see war; such decency should be preserved at all costs. Marina wondered where in Normandy her husband was without allowing herself to ask whether he still *was*. If his regiment had been repelling the Allied invasion on the beaches—Oskar could not determine, from the confused information that came to Berlin, which German troops had been stationed where—Marina hoped that he would have been in the rear. She hoped he had crawled behind a dune or found a large clump of grass for cover. She wished him that "pocket of comfort." That was the phrase Franz used to explain how he had survived Stalingrad: by thinking of her and the girls, or of his wanderings in Grosswald. She hoped he could find those pockets now.

Marina walked beneath the railroad underpass and turned onto the little lane that wound around the Eberhardt property, allowing her to enter from the lakefront. She opened the gate and carefully closed it behind her. The house stood at the top of a slight hill that sloped down to the expanse of lawn she stood on. From this distance, it looked very small, like the garage it was originally meant to be, but it was solid and sturdy, and at the moment it sheltered almost everyone dear to her in this world.

Tendrils from the garden brushed Marina's skirt. The scents of honeysuckle and rose invited her into the arbor. Looking around at this horticultural Eden, Marina admired the depth of her mother's dedication and hard work. Finding plants and flowers had been a challenge in those early wartime years, but Edith's calculated admiration of her neighbors' flower beds led to their willing donation of cuttings and bulbs. These she augmented with plants from her garden in Berlin. Now the yard was festooned with spring daffodils, tulips, wind anemones, hyacinths, summer trees laden with cherries, shrubs covered in strawberries and gooseberries and blackberries and red currants, flower beds overflowing with pansies and hydrangeas and roses. The roses were Edith's gardening triumph. She had experimented with rose varieties over the years, hybridizing them in the kitchen, trying to cultivate only the most fragrant blooms. She did not believe a rose deserved its name unless it had a scent. The result was magnificent—her rose garden was a small oasis of perfume: pillows of fragrance rose slowly from each open bloom and drifted through the air, swirling around and through one another in an olfactory kaleidoscope.

Walking through the arbor up to the house, Marina breathed it all in. Pockets of comfort, she thought. She had to take them where she found them.

Day Two

JULY 19, 1944

– Eleven –

The Wednesday-morning market in Blumental always assembled in the Münsterplatz. This large plaza was at the center of town, right next to the defunct church that Hans Munter referred to as "our historic Münster," and that less civically minded individuals disparaged as "that crumbling pile of rocks." Before the war, the *bürgermeister* and his forebears had tried to extricate money from the Blumental citizenry to repair the four-hundred-year-old sanctuary. But the few families with disposable income gravitated toward the more gilt-edged and ornate Catholic faith. And the handful of people who eschewed Catholicism worshipped not at the Münster but at Johann Wiessmeyer's smaller Protestant chapel on the western edge of town. Nevertheless, the Münster remained a sturdy and reliable landmark, with its somber Gothic arches and stained-glass windows.

This Wednesday morning, Hans Munter, still somewhat shaken from his recent near-death experience, ambled toward the modest collection of vegetable crates and sun umbrellas assembled in the shadow of the Münster bell tower. He mourned the prewar markets that had teemed with farmers and trucks, bakers and cakes, butchers and sausages. Back then, the plaza had been in full bloom with food, with farmers arriving before daylight to claim the prime real estate on the plaza's eastern perimeter, where the bell tower's shadow offered a welcome patch of shade in the summer. But with the arrival of war, and the Führer's regular con-

fiscation of local harvests for his armies, the market stalls had
dwindled drastically in number, and those that remained were
now so sparsely stocked that customers arrived early to ensure
first pick of whatever might be available that day, for it would not
be available long.

This morning, because of Captain Rodemann's food-
commandeering over the past few weeks, the market had even
less to offer than usual. By 8:15, when Hans made his way
through the Münsterplatz, several vendors were already packing up. Most of the women who had come to do their weekly
foraging for food had given up, and many of them had gathered
around the Mecklen bakery stall, where they shared the week's
gossip near the vigilant ear of Regina Mecklen.

Hans edged his way around the circle of ladies, all of whom
were abuzz about the previous day's drama. Had the Mecklen pastries not been calling to him, he might have avoided the stall
altogether, for he didn't want to call attention to himself, though
he blissfully couldn't remember much of yesterday. Marina Thiessen, standing nearby with her mother, was about to speak out in
greeting, but he put his finger to his mouth, silently begging her
not to.

"... unconscionable, really! I mean, right during our afternoon
quiet period," Anne Nagel said as Hans approached. "Although I
suppose that was lucky because at least Fritz was inside resting. If
they'd come any other time, he would have been outside clanking
away at that truck of his, a sitting duck for all those bullets."

"At least the children weren't outdoors playing," Regina
Mecklen said, to the earnest nods of several mothers. She took
a basket from one of the women and handed it back to her sister
Gisela, who counted out a dozen rolls from the bushel of rye flour
brötchen that sat at the back of the stall. Beyond the stall, in the
distance, Hans could see Johann Wiessmeyer stepping into the
plaza. The pastor was just starting to head across when a young
man came hurrying up to him. Though the man was not from

Blumental, Hans was sure he had seen him before. He was from Meerfeld, Hans thought, had some sort of job in the writing profession. A printer, perhaps? For a moment, Hans was awash in irrational fear about the man's purpose, but he waved it away. The doctor had warned Hans that he might be subject to sudden bouts of anxiety after his trauma yesterday.

Hans was not the only one to notice the appearance of Johann Wiessmeyer. Gisela turned to whisper something into her sister Sabine's ear. Hans used the opportunity of their private conversation to shuffle forward.

"Herr Munter! You're looking well today!" Sabine's greeting was loud and full of false sincerity.

"And how are you feeling this morning, Herr Bürgermeister?" Regina added.

"I am well, Frau Mecklen, Fräulein Mecklen, very well, thank you," Hans said. Feeling uncomfortable, he cast his eyes downward to the safety of the pastries and baked goods. He had never been good with compliments, especially those so obviously disingenuous. "I believe I shall try one of your pastries here."

"Well, Herr Bürgermeister, you know our pastries better than anyone, of course," Regina reminded him.

"Indeed I do, Frau Mecklen, indeed I do." Hans considered the collection of strudel, *linzerschnitten*, and *mandelbrot* thoughtfully. "While I'm making up my mind, I wonder if you might be able to get a few white *brötchen* for me, Fräulein Mecklen, my dear?"

"White ones?" Sabine glanced over to her older sister.

"I'm so sorry, Herr Bürgermeister," Regina apologized quickly, "but we have no more white *brötchen* this morning. I'm afraid Frau Eberhardt cleaned me out entirely. But do let us get you some of our rye ones while Sabine helps our dear Pastor Wiessmeyer." Hans's face fell. He could not abide *brötchen* made with rye flour, the norm for wartime bread. They were hard and heavy, better used for athletic games than breakfast.

The only woman who had been able to do anything with rye

flour was Miriam Rosenberg. Hans sighed, thinking back on that lovely lady. So much energy in such a petite frame. Her pale, translucent skin and wide brown eyes suggested delicacy, but her wiry arms and ready smile revealed vitality. And such beautiful pastries! Miriam Rosenberg was more than a baker, she was an artist of dough.

When the family left so suddenly, there had been murmurs around town that the Mecklens were somehow involved, that they had complained to the regional Liaison for Enforcement of National Socialism about the presence of a Jewish family, and indeed one day a LENS official had appeared in Hans's office asking for directions to Gisela Mecklen's house. Hans had had no idea why the man was there and was eager to get rid of him. He had pointed him in the direction of the Mecklens' neighborhood. Shortly thereafter, Gisela was seen parading the man around town.

Hans did not want to think ill of people, nor did he believe in connecting dots that needn't be connected, particularly when doing so involved him in business not his own. The flurry of rumors that the Rosenbergs had been taken by storm troopers in the dead of night had never been substantiated. Hans liked to think that the Rosenbergs were happily baking *brötchen* and cakes somewhere in Switzerland, where the baking competition was less keen.

"Good morning, ladies." Johann Wiessmeyer bowed slightly upon his arrival. Sabine giggled, bosom bouncing. "I wonder, Fräulein Mecklen," Johann said, addressing Sabine, whose tittering face was now colored by a deep blush, "whether you might be able to offer a hungry man of the cloth some sustenance?"

"Oh, Herr Pastor, it is so good to see you this morning!" Sabine gushed, smoothing her flour-coated apron over her belly with small, plump hands. She quickly tucked a coil of hair behind her ear, dusting her cheek with flour as she did so. "But you are late today, you almost missed the white *brötchen*," she chided. Though Sabine tried to lower her voice, it was impossible for Hans not to hear the exchange. "I have, however, set aside a few just for you, Father. I know how much you like them." She gave Johann the broadest, winningest smile she knew—Hans thought her face resembled that of a laughing horse—and ducked under her table to retrieve the wrapped bundle. "Here they are," her muffled voice announced, and she popped back up, her belly knocking a large piece of strudel off the counter and into the dirt as she handed the package to Johann. Hans Munter looked at the strudel unraveling in the sun, quickly attracting the attention of ants and flies. He gave Sabine a questioning look. She ignored him.

"Thank you so much, dear lady," Johann said, bowing again, more deeply. "I am so very grateful." He fished through his pocket and handed Sabine several coins. "And though God's work is never a burden, I must say it is much easier to do when His servants are nourished by such excellent food." Sabine's blush and wide smile seemed permanent fixtures, and she nodded her head a bit too wildly in enthusiastic receipt of Johann's compliment. The face, Hans decided, really looked more like a donkey's than a horse's.

"And Marina," Johann said, acknowledging Edith and Marina at the edge of the small crowd, "we have a rendezvous later this morning, do we not?"

In an instant, Sabine Mecklen's smile crumbled, and a low-toned hiss escaped her lips, sending a light spray of spittle over the remaining strudel. Hans decided to avoid the pastries in her vicinity. The hiss caught Gisela Mecklen's attention, and she turned from the customer she was attending just in time to see Johann putting a hand on Marina's shoulder.

"Yes, Johann, I have not forgotten," Marina said. "Café Armbruster at nine."

"Excellent, I will see you then. Farewell, Fräulein Mecklen." Johann waved his hand in departure, but Sabine and Gisela were both too intent on glaring at Marina to notice. As Marina gathered her children, oblivious to their scowls, Gisela put an arm around Sabine and whispered something in her ear. The younger sister nodded emphatically.

Hans watched the young Thiessen girls, Rosie and Sofia, leave the fountain where they had been playing and skip along behind their mother. The lightness of their being made him happy, the way they ran through the world on the balls of their feet instead of plodding as he did, their exuberance at living in the moment instead of reexperiencing the terrors of the past. Perhaps he could learn from them, he thought. He could be grateful that he was here today, in this marvelous market, before these pungent pastries.

He returned to the task at hand and finally made his choice— a slice of *linzerschnitten*. Before Dr. Schufeldt had let Hans leave the clinic this morning, he had warned him to be more judicious in his food choices. More fruits and nuts, the doctor said. More vegetables. Fewer sausages. There were walnuts and hazelnuts in the *linzerschnitten*'s lattice crust, and blackberries in the filling, Hans told himself. Just what the doctor ordered.

– Twelve –

"Stop right there, Old Shatterhand!" Max Fuchs stood on top of a pile of mailbags outside the Blumental post office. He was threatening Willie Schnabel with a long, skinny twig that he had chewed to a rough point. "Go no further or I, Intschu-tschuna, the greatest chief of all the Apache tribes, will pierce your heart with the arrow that my great-great-grandfather crafted from the horn of the sacred bison!"

"I am not afraid of you, Intschu-tschuna," Willie said, pulling from his back pocket a shorter, fatter branch and waving it at his rival. "Your arrow is no match for my revolver!" Willie knelt down in the hard dirt, wrapping both hands around his branch and squinting his right eye as he pointed it straight at Max.

Max threw back his head and tried to laugh menacingly. "You dare to threaten me, Old Shatterhand? Ha ha ha! I scoff at the pride of the white man!"

Suddenly, to both Max's and Willie's surprise, Ralf Winzel's head popped out from between the mailbags. "And I—" Ralf grunted, trying to wriggle his body out from the mass of canvas sacks so he could clamber up next to Max, "I am Winnetou, firstborn son of the great Intschu-tschuna and future leader of all the Apache tribes."

Max sighed. He did not want Ralf in this game, but he knew better than to challenge him directly—he had seen that fist split too many lips. Still, Max owed it to Willie to try to get rid of him. "Um, Ralf. Sorry, Winnetou isn't in this one."

"Well, he is now, because he's here to ambush Old Shatterhand in a surprise attack!" Ralf smirked, using his foot to dislodge several of the larger mailbags at the top of the heap. "A rock slide!" Six or seven heavy sacks tumbled down all at once, lumbering slowly and haphazardly enough to give Willie plenty of time to get out of their way.

"You know nothing about Winnetou, Ralf," Willie taunted. "He's too noble for a sudden ambush. He's virtuous and true."

Max smiled inwardly at Willie's characterization of the Native American hero. Between the two of them, he and Willie had almost every book about Winnetou that their favorite author, Karl May, had ever written. The first, which introduced the cowboy Old Shatterhand, was so worn and tattered from frequent readings that Max had had to tape its spine. In his games with Willie, Max always played one of the Indians, partly because he had gathered enough duck feathers over time to make a passable headdress for Intschu-tschuna, but also because he liked the fact that the Indians remained true to themselves and their beliefs. They knew who they were and stuck with it. Willie preferred the cowboys. He loved guns.

"Ralf Winzel, *what* are you doing?" Ludmilla Schenk's voice was far louder than seemed possible for her petite frame. The boys looked over to the post office, where Frau Schenk made her way down the steps carrying a bundle of envelopes in her hands, stooping over as if they were heavy. Max hurried down to help.

"Here, Frau Schenk, I'll take those for you." As he grabbed the bundle from her arms, he realized they weren't heavy at all.

"Thank you, Max." Frau Schenk leaned on a nearby hitching post and stood quietly for a moment, gathering her breath. Max felt sorry for her. She looked much older than she used to. Max remembered—it wasn't that long ago—when she stood tall on the post office porch, her long brown hair tied in a loose braid. She had always smiled as he passed her on his way to school. These days she put her graying hair up in a bun and looked even more tired than his mother. But the postmistress still had some strength and outrage, as she demonstrated now.

"Ralf, if you do not get down from those mailbags this instant, I will grab your arms and legs, tether them together, and put you in a sack headed to Antarctica." Her voice was low and gravelly, like a bear's growl. "And do not for a moment doubt the unpleasantness of that experience, for you will be tossed and sorted with all the other oversize packages, many of which weigh five times as much as you do, and I truly doubt all your bones would survive intact." Frau Schenk waited while Ralf scrambled down. She turned to Max.

"You might as well hang on to those envelopes, Max," she said. "These invitations were just dropped off by Herr Weber's secretary. She was insistent that they be delivered as soon as possible. Some sort of concert going on at the Weber estate tomorrow night, I gather. Apparently very last-minute."

Max was surprised to hear that Klaus Weber, renowned recluse of Blumental, was having any kind of party. He'd thought the famous composer had settled on the Bodensee because he hated cities and the people in them. Every time Max tried to sneak into the Weber estate, he was shooed away by the guards who patrolled it.

Max flipped through the envelopes Frau Schenk had handed to him. There weren't many, maybe fifteen or twenty. If he worked his way eastward from the west side of town, it might take an hour and a half, maybe less if he could convince Willie to help him. Then he could go over to the East Blumental train station and check for spies again. "Of course, Frau Schenk, no problem."

The postmistress patted Max on the back. "You're a dear boy, Max. I'll pay you a bit extra for today." Max colored and saw Ralf Winzel smirk at the words *dear boy*. He would hear those words again in some future taunt, he knew. Suddenly Frau Schenk turned her head. "Oh, Lara, how lovely you look today." Lara Thiessen was coming up the path.

Lara. Max had been in love with her since he was ten years old, but she was too beautiful to pay any attention to him. Now he was approaching twelve, very close to manhood. Soon, perhaps, he might grow a mustache, and then his prospects with her would be more favorable. In the meantime, he wooed her with gifts. Last winter, it had been a stone that he found on the beach near the boat pier, perfectly flat for skipping across the water. Once cleaned and polished, it was a beautiful gray color that reminded him of November fog. In the spring, he had collected forget-me-nots and pressed them flat, then glued them onto a piece of paper in the shape of a heart. He had left both of these presents on the Eberhardt front doorstep, running away before anyone could see him.

Frau Schenk was right, Lara looked lovely, but then she always did to Max. Today she was wearing a yellow sundress with a short flouncy skirt that showed off her long legs, and a sweater. Her silky blond hair was tied back in a ponytail that swung from side to side, keeping the same rhythm as the sway of her hips. Max was mesmerized and muted, watching her walk toward him.

"Thank you, Frau Schenk. My opa is coming home today. We're preparing a big lunch for him." Lara smiled as she passed Max and climbed the stairs. Her ponytail swished suddenly to the right, brushing his shoulder. "Good morning, Max."

Max could neither speak nor move. It was possible he had stopped breathing. But Ralf Winzel's voice was intact. "Hey, Lara! Bea-uuu-tee-ful Lara! Wanna join our game and be an Indian princess?" Lara paused on the top step and squinted at Ralf, fixing her blue eyes on him for a silent half minute. She snorted with disdain and walked inside.

"Too bad," Ralf said. "She would have made a good Nscho-tschi. She could have begged our father to spare your life, Old Shatterhand. Plus, it would have been even numbers, two against two." He shook his head in mock disappointment. "Tough luck, Willie boy, you'll just have to hope the cavalry sends in reinforcements." Willie, however, had dropped his stick and abandoned the game. Turning his back to Ralf and Max, he started up the road that led to his home. "Well, at least Old Shatterhand knows when he's beaten," Ralf called loudly, trying to goad Willie back. "Come on, Max, let's go chase some ducks from their nests."

Max picked up the canvas bag that he kept under the porch for deliveries and put the envelopes inside. He would have liked to stay a bit longer to wait for Lara, but if he did, it would be harder to get rid of Ralf, and he did not want to sacrifice his entire morning. "I can't, Ralf, I have to go deliver these." Before the other boy could protest or come up with the idea of joining him, Max ran up the same road Willie had taken.

– Thirteen –

The moment Edith arrived back home from the market, Rosie disappeared. Edith had too much to do to worry about what she was up to. Probably gone to look for that pet snail. Edith was zig-zagging through the kitchen, pulling out pans and knives, when she noticed Sofia sitting on the bench, tucked into the corner, staring at the African violets on the windowsill. Her eyes were wide and distant, as if the blue petals had carried her off into some other world.

When Sofia's trances first appeared, after the air raid, Dr. Schnall's diagnosis was that it was a perfectly sound, even healthy, way for Sofia to dissociate herself from her fear. He called them "reveries," as if they were lovely, dreamlike states. To Edith, they felt more like evil spells.

If only they had moved earlier, they could have spared Sofia this lingering pain. But air attacks on Berlin had been rare before that fateful night, with minimal damage, and Marina was adamant about staying—no doubt, in retrospect, because Erich was there. Edith too had been reluctant to admit that the city she grew up in, the most comfortable city in the world to her, was no longer safe.

It had been a Monday evening in November, Oskar's sixtieth birthday. They had gone to dinner at his favorite restaurant, the Hahnen Haus, with Marina and the girls. Oskar had, as was usual on his birthday, ordered an enormous slice of Black Forest cherry torte, and they had, as usual, helped him eat all of it. Marina suggested they walk home, since Oskar and Edith's apartment was less than thirty minutes away on foot and it would give the torte a chance to settle.

The night was cold and clear. Oskar, invigorated by two glasses of *apfelschnaps*, challenged Lara to a skipping contest. He was losing deliberately, careening and swaying dramatically from curb to curb. Sofia was delighted by his antics and asked to challenge him next, but she had a small pebble in her shoe. She knelt beneath a street lamp to get it out, and Edith waited with her. The rest of the family continued on, unaware that they had stopped.

Every time Edith thought back to that night, she remembered the wailing of the air raid sirens as simultaneous with the droning of the incoming British bombers that descended upon them, though surely, in reality, the sirens must have sounded first. They always blared at least five minutes before explosions began.

And yet, as Edith remembered it, there had been no time. The first explosion, a dull thud followed by a spectacular burst of fire and flame, was close enough that the reverberation shattered all the street lamps along the street. Edith looked around for Oskar, Marina, and the other girls, but they had disappeared. She had to get herself and Sofia to safety. The apartment was too far away. Splinters of glass rained down onto the pavement, crunching beneath Edith's feet like freshly fallen sleet. She ran with Sofia toward the train station, to the public air raid shelter there, a steel monstrosity built to keep large numbers of civilians safe.

A second bomb exploded, closer than the first. Then a third and fourth. The sirens wailed on endlessly, assailing Edith and Sofia from all sides, the cries of other pedestrians only slightly muffled by a dense cloud of searing dust and smoke. Flames shot up ahead of them, obliterating the road to the train station. Someone screamed, possibly Sofia. They would need to find an alternative. Gathering Sofia in her arms, Edith turned right onto Maximilianstrasse and ran toward the public playground where she had spent so many hours with Marina when she was young. There was, Edith remembered, a large apartment building facing that playground, and she headed toward it. She yanked open the glass doors, ran through the lobby to the oak door next to the staircase, wrenched it open, and bolted down the stone steps into the cellar.

Forty or fifty people were already gathered in the dark room, some sitting on wooden boxes, others on the dirt floor, backs against the cellar walls. A few families had brought flashlights, which cast gloomy beams of dispersed light upon the ceiling. One boy used his to illuminate a path as Edith and Sofia picked their way through the crowd. Edith squeezed herself into a space on the floor between an older man with a mustache and a heavyset middle-aged woman. Nobody else paid attention to them.

Edith cradled Sofia in her lap and leaned back against the wall. She expected to find the whitewashed stone cold against her skin, and was surprised at the wave of heat that penetrated her woolen coat and silk blouse. Sofia was still, huddled into Edith's embrace. She did not whimper. Her eyes peered over Edith's right shoulder, alert to every movement, blinking occasionally to avoid the fine dust that fell from the ceiling as each bomb dropped.

Edith didn't know how long they waited in that cellar. It might have been an hour, it might have been several. The steady bombing showed no signs of abating. The ceiling began giving up larger and larger chunks of plaster. A feeling of unease spread through the assembled group. Eventually, one young man, his dark wiry hair speckled with bits of dirt and paper, jumped up. He ran to the cellar door, apparently intending to leave. It would not open. He pushed against it with all his strength, to no avail. A few others lent their weight to his effort but were equally unsuccessful.

The young man, now wild-eyed, ran to the wall separating the cellar from the neighboring apartment building and pounded his fist against it. "How long will these walls hold?" he shouted. "How long can we stay here before we are all buried in rubble?!"

An older man with a manicured beard and small round spectacles, who had been sitting with a group of women and young children, tried to calm him and encouraged him to take his seat again. But the fear, once spoken, gained momentum, and soon the cellar was humming with murmurs and whimpers, feigned words of reassurance and sincere prayers for deliverance. When another bomb dislodged some of the bricks in the northeast corner of the room, the young man leaped to his feet again.

"Are we all just going to sit here? Do none of you want to save yourselves?" He grabbed a thick wooden two-by-four that swung from the ceiling and pulled it down in a shower of dust and plaster particles. "This wall," he shouted, ramming the wood against the dividing wall at the far end of the room, "this wall is our only salvation now."

A stocky man in a frayed overcoat stood up. "He's right. We can get out through the building next door. If we break through that wall." He picked up another piece of wood and joined the effort.

Tension and unease now mushroomed into panic as people realized that they might be trapped underground. Soon several others stepped up, holding pieces of wood or empty barrels, or using nothing more than their strong shoulders. All pushed in tandem against the restraining wall. The room pulsed with each collision, the thick gray air heaved to and fro, the walls reverberated and throbbed.

Edith had moved away from the wall she had been leaning against earlier, as the heat emanating from it had become unbearable. She now wondered, watching the scene at the far end of the room unfold, exactly what they would find when that other wall was broken.

"Wait!" The older man with the round glasses stood up hesitantly. "You don't know what's going on in the next building! Shouldn't we—?" But his question was lost. All at once, the plaster from the dividing wall exploded into the adjoining cellar, and a maelstrom of fire and heat sucked everything that was not secured to the ground or walls into the tongues of flame and billows of smoke next door. Cardboard boxes, wooden barrels, an old rolled-up carpet, a discarded broom—all flew into the furnace of the neighboring building. The five men who had been beating against the plaster disappeared in an instant, swept off their feet so suddenly that they had no time to cry out. "Papa!" screamed a young woman to the man with the round glasses. But he was gone.

Instantly, Edith pushed Sofia to the floor and flattened herself on top of the girl's body, pulling her long overcoat as far around both of them as possible. There they lay, immobile.

Edith had developed two important skills during the last war. One was knowing when to keep her eyes shut or avert her gaze—if her daily walk to the bakery happened to take her past the city hospital, she learned to lower her eyes when she got to the brown brick wall of the south gate, where a collection of severed, gangrenous limbs awaited incineration. The second skill was knowing how to erase from her brain those images that had been imprinted there against her will and still occasionally popped up, like the picture of her son Peter's unnaturally small coffin being lowered into a shadowy grave. These skills served Edith well that November night, for she, like Sofia, had a very limited memory of the events following the collapse of the cellar wall.

Edith's instinct now, watching Sofia lost in her daze, was to pull her back from that other world to the present, where there was family, love, kittens, and flowers.

"Sofia, dear, could you do your oma a very big favor?" Sofia either did not hear Edith or chose not to. Edith walked over to the kitchen table and gently shook her granddaughter. "Sofia?"

The girl looked up with blank eyes. Her pupils were almost as large as her irises. Edith held Sofia's hand and stroked her hair until finally Sofia gave her head a little shake and came to. "Oma?"

"I was hoping you could help me this morning, dear." Edith

opened a drawer in the table and pulled out a pair of garden shears. "We need a big festive bouquet for today's luncheon, to welcome Opa back. Could you go cut some flowers from the garden?"

"Flowers?" Sofia looked at her grandmother as if she did not understand the word.

"Yes, flowers. Roses and daisies and some hydrangeas, perhaps. Lots of red and white and pink."

"And blue?"

It was hard for Sofia to let go of her other world. "Well, blue too if you like," Edith said. "You can take some of the delphiniums."

"Okay." Sofia took the shears from Edith and shuffled over to the porch.

"When you're done, bring them back here and we can arrange them together."

"Okay," Sofia repeated, stepping out into the yard. She wasn't wearing shoes, but Edith couldn't blame her for wanting to bare her feet to the garden on a sunny day like this, summer at its height.

– Fourteen –

Johann Wiessmeyer took a seat at one of the outside tables at the Café Armbruster, where he could look out over the promenade and the lake. There was föhn this morning, a dry, warm wind that swept down from the Alps and clarified the air; he could see the entire outline of the mountains beyond the Austrian shoreline. For some reason—perhaps it was the change in atmospheric pressure—Johann always got a headache just behind his eyes when there was föhn. He was hoping a strong cup of tea could knock out the dull pain in his skull.

A stooped waiter dressed in a worn tuxedo and a sagging bow tie hurried over to Johann the moment he sat down. The waiter deposited two small glasses of water on the table and thrust an old cardboard menu at him, more out of routine than any expectation that the minister would be enticed to order from its faded photographs of elaborate ice cream sundaes in ornate crystal dishes.

Johann waved the menu away. "Thank you, Gustav, but I'll have just the usual this morning. Two teas, please. Mine extra strong." Keeping his head down, Gustav nodded and shuffled away. He was used to Johann ordering two teas even though he was the only one seated. Sooner or later, Frau Thiessen would appear.

Johann pulled out the mail that Ludmilla Schenk had handed him when he'd stopped by the post office. There were two envelopes, one with the red, white, and blue border of all airmail missives from America. The other was plain brown and opaque,

preserving the privacy of a telegram. Johann had immediately
recognized his sister Sonja's handwriting on the airmail envelope.
It had been a long while since he had received a letter from her,
and even this one appeared barely to have made it past the Frank-
furt censors, judging from its worn and heavily inked appearance.
He eagerly tore open its top seam. The telegram could wait.

> My dear brother,
>   I trust that this letter finds you well. Perhaps I should say I
> pray that you are well, because I do. I pray each morning and
> night. And at Berthold's suggestion, the entire synagogue now
> prays for the safety of everyone overseas on Saturday mornings.
> So as you can see, we are doing all we can. You must do your
> part as well, dearest brother, for my heart is yours . . .

Johann knew his sister's synagogue. After her move, he had
been able to contrive a six-month teaching fellowship at the
Union Theological Seminary in New York City. He stayed
with Sonja and Berthold in their small apartment in Brooklyn,
with its tiny backyard in which Sonja valiantly tried to grow
vegetables. Every morning, he rose before dawn to walk over
the majestic bridge to the buzzing granite island of Manhat-
tan and headed north toward Harlem for his classes. On his
walk uptown along Broadway, he was captivated by the kaleidoscope of spiritual denominations—Baptists, Episcopalians,
Catholics, but also Muslims, Mormons, Buddhists—and plenty
of nonbelievers, some of whom felt the need to challenge him
on the street; his collar made him a target.

What surprised Johann was his overarching sense of oneness
in the midst of this variety of religious experience. He was struck
not by the differences between beliefs, but by their similarities.
Sonja and Berthold's synagogue on Kane Street, for example. The
same God as his own, expressed through different traditions. The
choir in his church, the cantor in theirs. The Kane Street cantor,

a short, heavyset man, more square than round, more plinth than pillar, his sonorous bass voice, like an instrument of God, surging across the ocean to people of the Jewish faith whose own leaders had been silenced.

And the revelation of gospel music, in the vibrant congregation of the Abyssinian Baptist Church in Harlem. How the God of a community could be perpetuated through the vocal cords of its ancestors, even when those ancestors were faced with ungodly circumstances. What an uplifting feeling of freedom the Harlem congregation had given him. It was the closest thing to pure joy he had experienced in years. Reading on, it was as if his sister had anticipated precisely this reaction:

> . . . *You will be pleased to hear that I have managed to find the music you asked me for. Your friend Reverend Waters in Harlem was most helpful, and he strongly encouraged me to purchase the Selah Jubilee Singers' recording of "Take My Hand, Precious Lord." So now I have it for you. I am hesitant to send it, however, for I fear the album may not survive the ocean crossing. I will keep it here with me, and you can pick it up when you return to us. You are right about that song, Johann, it is very lovely. I listen to it at night and think of you. Then Berthold comes in and tells me to stop worrying and we put on Albert Brumley's "Turn Your Radio On" and dance until the neighbors yell at us to turn the radio off!*

The rest of Sonja's missive resonated with her squeaky-sweet chatter: *I made the most abysmal streuselkuchen the other day, rock hard, almost inedible. . . . Do come back next summer to see the garden we've started, we grew a lovely tomato and next year perhaps we'll have two!* If only he could go visit Sonja again; he missed her so. Perhaps next time he would stay. But the instant that thought entered his head, he shook it back out. Not yet. He still had work to do here.

Johann used his thumbnail to tear open the telegram. The message inside was from Eva Münch. Eva lived near Regensburg, northeast of Dachau, and it was her contacts who had initially sought Johann's help in their fledgling underground movement. Her message was characteristically brief: *2 pkgs. arr. Thu. 10:30.* Thursday. Tomorrow. Sooner than expected, though not impossible. But the reduction in number from five to two . . . Johann pressed on his temples with his forefingers and said a silent prayer.

Gustav arrived with two steaming cups of tea and placed them on the table just as Marina walked up. Bowing slightly, the waiter quickly pulled out a chair for her. She smiled her thanks and sat down, setting her market basket at her feet.

"I was early, as always," Johann explained. "So I ordered for us both."

"Excellent. After all this morning shopping, I need some sort of stimulant before I launch into the cooking phase of the day." She took a generous sip. "There. I feel vastly improved already."

"And I am improved simply by your company," Johann said. It was true; he had felt disheartened after reading the telegram, but Marina's arrival made it easier to bear the news. It was not the first time he had felt better in her presence.

"Now, Johann, you must save your compliments for Sabine," Marina teased.

"On the contrary, I fear I must be quite careful with what I say to Fräulein Mecklen." Johann blushed. He was not oblivious to the Mecklen sisters' hope that he would join their family. Regina and Gisela had invited him to their homes for dinner several times, with Sabine of course always in attendance, dressed in her finest gown and spewing forced laughter across the table at him. It was not that Johann disliked Sabine; he just didn't *like* her. If pressed on this point, he would have said that he didn't really know her, despite all the occasions on which they had been thrown together. Her adoration and overeagerness to win his approval caused her to affect a meek femininity that didn't suit her.

Johann had heard the story of Sabine's engagement, several years earlier, to a journalist who had come to the Bodensee for the summer and managed, in four short weeks, to win her heart and, apparently, her virginity.

"And then, just like that, *poof*! He disappeared," Regina had told him at one of those dinner evenings. She had waited until Sabine was in the kitchen to share this confidence.

"It might be just as well," Gisela opined from another corner of their living room. "He was probably a Communist."

"She was heartbroken," Regina said, her own eyes tearing slightly at the memory. "Standing on the steps of Birnau in Mutti's wedding gown, crying . . ."

"Good riddance, I say," Gisela said.

Right now, Johann didn't have the luxury of seeking a spouse. He did want to get married someday, to share his life with another human being in the most intimate way possible. That was, however, an aspiration for peacetime. Now he was grateful that he was single, for he had to be able to engage in his activities without worrying about anyone else. But if and when he did look for a life partner, he would want someone who was honest in her self-presentation. Someone sure of who she was and what she wanted. Someone, well, like Marina. From the first day he met Marina Thiessen, he had been drawn to her sincerity. She had introduced herself after one of his Sunday services, said she was considering a new approach to God. It was Johann's suggestion that they meet for tea, hers that they do so regularly. He found himself looking forward to these meetings and was hesitant to admit how much he enjoyed her company.

"I truly do not want to give Sabine any false impressions," Johann said.

Marina shook her head. "I fear she will take her impressions as she pleases. But you can't help that."

"Short of being rude or impolite . . ."

" . . . and you could never be that . . ."

" . . . and I could never be that," Johann agreed, smiling at their repartee. He took a sip of tea and relaxed into the thin cushion on his chair, willing his headache to lift. To the southeast, he could see the Insel Hagentau. According to local history, the Swedish prince who owned the island had given up his claim to the throne in order to marry the commoner he was in love with. They had celebrated their union by planting gardens, and now the island, abandoned during the war, was a bower of untended flowers. Just past that, farther south on the Hagentau road, he knew, was Switzerland. Which, with any luck, would soon increase its population by two, at least temporarily. Johann took out the telegram and read its brief contents again, double-checking the number. "I received a message." He glanced up at Marina. "We need to be ready tomorrow at ten thirty."

"Have you found space for them? Five requires some room—" Marina started.

"It's two, not five," Johann interrupted. Better tell her quickly, to get it over with.

"Only two?" Marina's voice cracked.

"Two." They were both silent. Johann thought back to the last time he was in Berlin, in April. His cousin Gottfried had insisted that they meet for coffee on Bendlerstrasse, near his office in the Defense Ministry. The brown leather journal Gottfried had pushed carefully across the tablecloth that day was a meticulous documentation of all the crimes perpetrated by the regime that his office had information about, information it kept highly classified. A written catalogue of evidence compiled by a fledgling resistance organization, of which Gottfried was a member. With Gottfried watching silently, Johann reviewed the pages of the journal. He read slowly and with growing horror its confirmation of rumors heard and fears harbored. Accounts narrated by army soldiers who watched as storm troopers forced hundreds of Polish Jews to dig mass graves, then shot them down with machine guns, covering bodies both dead and halfway alive with mounds of dirt that continued to pulse in the landscape long after the troopers had abandoned their shovels. His face blanched at the strange catalogue: the number of murders, according to psychiatrists, that a soldier could be expected to commit before he was in danger of mental and emotional breakdown; the number of cattle cars required to transport the population of Siedlce to Treblinka; the number of meters in length, width, and depth, required for a pit to accommodate the bodies of all the Jews of Vinnytsya. Johann had not shared any of this information with Marina, as Gottfried had sworn him to secrecy, but he knew she had her own suspicions. "Marina, what is it?" he asked, seeing her wet cheeks. He moved his chair closer to hers.

"Oh, you know, I can't help imagining," she said quietly. "And I don't know if it's worse or better than the truth. And I feel sometimes that I could know so much more, that I *should* know so much more about what's happening. That I should demand to know more from my father." Marina's voice began to rise a bit. "Because he must know more than he tells us, right? But he doesn't tell us *anything*!" She wiped her eyes with a cloth napkin and took a deep, hiccup-laced breath. "But then I wonder, if he did tell us—if he knew what was happening to all the people disappearing from the cities and towns, if he knew anything about the train transports I've heard of—well, what would we do? I mean, what *could* we do?"

Johann checked an impulse to reach across the table and touch Marina, to reassure her. Instead, he pressed his hands together and bowed his head. He too had doubts about her father. "We don't know what Oskar knows," he said finally. "You must remember that he's in the Economics Ministry, not Defense. And from what my cousin tells me, there is practically no communication within the government. Each department is operating largely on its own, in an atmosphere of paranoia and mistrust."

"He's right." Marina straightened the napkin on her lap and refolded it. Another small hiccup escaped. "Oskar says that too."

Johann offered her his glass of water, though she had her own. She leaned forward and took a sip without taking the glass from him.

"Even if Oskar knows *something*," Johann continued, "whatever that something may be, it's entirely possible he is trying to protect you from that information." Johann held up his hand as Marina started to protest. "Perhaps it would be dangerous for you to have such knowledge. Dangerous for you and Edith. Dangerous for your daughters." He paused to let Marina take this in. "Think of your daughters. Think how much you love them. You would do anything to protect them, wouldn't you?" Marina nodded, tears again flowing. "Don't you think Oskar feels that way about you?"

"Yes," she said quietly. "Yes, I know he does."

Johann was not a father, but someday he hoped to be. He longed for a son or daughter. Every once in a while, when he spoke with a young boy in Blumental, he had a moment, just a moment, in which he imagined the boy to be his own. Max Fuchs, for example: spirited but clever, harboring a good heart. "So, the refugees arrive late tomorrow morning," Johann said. "And your home is out because of Oskar."

"Yes," Marina said. "And he usually stays for two or three days, otherwise he wouldn't bother making the trip. Also, we haven't seen him in a while, so he might stay even longer."

"Right. Well, then, Ernst is probably our best option for short-term housing. He printed the travel documents and brought them to me this morning. According to him, there is no sign of Rodemann, which is excellent. This afternoon, I will go to Fritz Nagel's farm to check on the truck."

"Has he finished it? Oh, wouldn't that be wonderful!" Marina looked more hopeful than she had all morning.

"I don't know. Last time I went by, he was still working on the barrier between Pinocchio's engine and the storage space." When Johann first noticed Fritz driving the long-nosed Volvo into Blumental a month earlier, he immediately saw potential in the truck's enormous front hood and in Fritz's regular trips across the Swiss border to deliver crops to Kreuzlingen. With the appropriate financial incentive, Fritz promised to keep his mouth shut, and Johann asked him to modify the engine block to create enough extra space between the engine and the truck body to accommodate the human form. When the truck approached the border loaded with crates of fruits and vegetables, the driver might be stopped by guards searching for contraband goods or refugees. Those guards had been known to use their bayonets to pierce crates and sacks, a malicious test to discourage the smuggling of anything but produce. Whatever was stored in the engine block, however, could pass through unnoticed. Johann had visited Fritz last Friday to check on his progress and was quietly optimistic about the truck's potential for successful deliveries.

"I might even have time to test-drive it," Johann added.

Marina raised an eyebrow in skepticism. "You know how to drive a Volvo truck?"

"God gave me many talents to do His work." Johann smiled. "I will, with Fritz's blessing and produce, drive the truck to Meerfeld, load the two passengers, and then, God willing, cross the border without incident and drop them off at the rendezvous point. But before that, I will need your help. I need someone to bring them to Meerfeld. Can you do that for me? Would you be able to get away unnoticed?"

Marina didn't hesitate. "Count on it, Johann. My father usually retires in the afternoon to nap or read. They'll be at the East Blumental station?"

Johann thought for a moment. They had used the deserted station in the past as a resting place, with great success, but that was before Max Fuchs started watching it for spies. He would have to find a way to keep Max busy. "Yes," he answered finally. "I'll pick them up at the main station and bring them over to the East Blumental station. Then you just need to get them over to Ernst before the four p.m. mail train makes its daily stop there. I'll aim to pick them up shortly after midnight."

Marina placed her napkin back on the table. She had folded it into the shape of a rose. "Fine," she said. "I can do that. There will be so much chaos at our house, no one will notice my absence for an hour." She pushed her chair back and stood up. "And now, I'm afraid I should go. There are potatoes to mash and berries to crush and egg whites to whip to stiff attention."

"Sounds violent." Johann stood up with her.

"It's a good outlet." Marina sighed. "Keeps me out of trouble." She gave Johann a quick kiss on the cheek and headed down the promenade. Johann watched her go. He watched the eyes of everyone she passed follow her along the promenade. It was not Marina's appearance that drew the gaze of other people, for although she was unquestionably attractive, even beautiful, there were other women in Blumental who were more physically stunning. Rather, it was the way she moved through her surroundings. She radiated unbridled strength and courage. Hope too, Johann thought, communicated through her straight posture and confident step, and in the animated swing of the thick light-brown braid across her back. People wanted to hold on to the sight of her calm conviction, her assurance. She was so certain in everything she did. It was intoxicating.

Johann had worked hard to attain that kind of certainty for himself. The day he read through Gottfried's secret journal, forcing himself through one page after another, his stomach had involuntarily heaved. The evidence he was confronting, actions inconceivable in a civilized society that was heir to Goethe and Bach, manifested a degree of malevolence and evil that had, until then, been unfathomable to him. Gottfried had watched his cousin's face carefully that day. "Now," Gottfried had said, "will you join us?"

Thus the moral question took a new twist for Johann. It was one thing to affirm an obligation to help the victims of a treacherous regime; that was fairly easy to reconcile with God's Word. Far more difficult was the question of whether, and to what extent, he should engage in the overthrow of such a government. Everyone in the Resistance agreed that the Führer had to be removed. It was clear that removal meant killing the man. Marina had once asked Johann if God could forgive his followers for remaining idle before the evil of the Führer. But the spiritual question that Johann wrestled with now was how to justify murder. Would a God who gave Moses the Ten Commandments condone assassination? Johann had spent countless hours in contemplation of this question. A brown leather briefcase sat in his coat closet awaiting his answer.

– Fifteen –

In the back corner of Edith's garden stood a copper birdbath, part of Edith's plan to make her home as welcoming as possible to all manner of creatures. She had planted blackberry bushes a few meters away, and over the years they began to circumnavigate their way around the bath, eventually growing tall enough that the entire basin was obscured from view. Edith was immensely pleased. Now the birds had their privacy, she said, and she told the girls not to disturb them. But it was too tempting a space to be limited by a grandmother's prohibitions. The blackberry bushes, now at their peak, had entwined themselves completely around one another, and their leafy vines, seeking to annex more territory, had reached across the lawn to the birdbath itself. The resulting plot of grass, shaded and shielded by their canopy of leaves and berries, was the perfect hideout for a teenage girl.

Lara could not believe it when the postmistress handed her the magazine that morning. She had been waiting for so long. Ever since Opa told her, back in April, that he had heard that Princess Elizabeth of England was on the cover of *Life* magazine, she had been *desperate* to have a copy. He'd promised to try to find one, and here it was. She laid the magazine carefully on the dish towel she had placed on the ground next to the birdbath, for she did not want any dirt on the princess's beautiful face.

The cover was a perfect photograph of Elizabeth. She looked absolutely radiant, Lara thought. Her hair was excellently coiffed,

swept off her forehead to the left and pinned back, dark curls falling to her shoulder. Her eyes were sparkling, and she was gazing
at something beyond the camera, her family perhaps, everyone
making faces to get her to smile. She was smiling, but not too
strongly, not too happily, because of course England was at war.
Lara thought it was the best photo she had seen of Elizabeth so far,
and she had seen many pictures of Elizabeth.

She opened the magazine carefully, with the reverence befit-
ting a publication featuring photographs of the most famous princess in the world. Turning to the table of contents, she saw a small
photograph of the British royal family and examined it carefully
for clues to Elizabeth's life. The princess was looking over the
king's shoulder while he was reading some important state papers.
Of course she had to be introduced to the business of government,
as she would be eligible to be queen in three years.

If she and Elizabeth lived near each other and were not on
opposite sides of this stupid war, Lara imagined that they could
be best friends. They could share stories about the difficulties of
growing up in a household with an important official personage.
How that personage, king or cabinet secretary, was not necessarily available when you wanted him to be. How he was often
called away from family lunches by telegrams. Or if he stayed
through lunch, he went upstairs afterward for a nap and was not
to be disturbed. How you came to be an expert in reading military
uniforms. Lara wondered whether the princess would trust her
enough to share government information. Lara would assure her
that she considered the bonds of friendship sacred and that she
would never reveal anything the princess told her. Unfortunately,
she would not be able to reciprocate with any information of her
own, for her opa never told her anything about his work in Berlin.
But she didn't really want to know. She'd stifled any curiosity she
felt about what her grandfather did for the Führer years ago, after
her mother had that big fight with him.

It started when Lara's friends Adelaide and Berit had asked her to join them in the Führer Youth Corps program in Berlin. She had been only eight, and when she asked her mother if she could go to evening meetings at her school, Marina adamantly refused. There was no need for Lara to get involved in politics at such a young age, Marina insisted. She had far more important things to learn about in school. No amount of protest from Lara could change Marina's mind, and her opa would not get involved. Oskar told Lara that if she wanted to join the group, she would have to convince her mother herself. That was, Lara knew, an impossible task.

A year later, membership in the Sorority of Aryan Sisters and its sibling group, the Fraternity for the Führer, was made mandatory for all children between the ages of eight and eighteen. Rosalie Mohn, a girl from the seventh class, came into Lara's classroom one spring morning, wearing the summer uniform of the Sorority and carrying a small pile of papers, which she gave to Lara's teacher. Frau Finkel took a quick glance at them and stood before her desk.

"Girls," she said, tapping authoritatively on the desk with a ruler warped by frequent contact with students' knuckles. Lara kept her hands in her lap whenever possible, for she never knew what might anger Frau Finkel. "Today I will be giving you a form that you must return to me tomorrow. It is an order form for a uniform like the one Fräulein Mohn is wearing." Rosalie stepped forward and did a pirouette, trying to make the uniform swing around her but thwarted by the stiffness of its long navy skirt.

Lara adored the uniform, especially the crisp, pristine white blouse with its short blue tie. It all looked very smart, very polished. She could hardly wait to wear one. Adelaide had cautiously raised her hand. "What if we already—"

"If you already have a uniform," Frau Finkel interrupted her, waving the ruler in the air menacingly and causing Adelaide to lower her hand quickly, "then you should check that it still fits you. Some of you have grown like fungi over the past year." She glared with distaste and accusation at Sarah Schwartzmann, who was on the front end of the bell curve of puberty and now hung her head in shame. "So I want everyone to take a form and have her parents fill it out and sign it at the bottom." Frau Finkel slammed the ruler on the desk for emphasis.

Lara ran all the way home that day and burst through the front door yelling for Marina. "Mutti! Mutti!"

"Hush!" Her mother came out of the kitchen, drying her hands on her apron skirt. "Opa is still resting before he has to go back to work." But her opa was standing at the top of the staircase.

"Too late," he said. "The old geezer has awakened." He descended slowly, groaning in exaggeration. "Come, dear child, share some of that youthful energy with an old man." Lara ran over to kiss Oskar, then ran back to her schoolbag, pulled out the order form, and handed it to Marina.

"You have to fill that out today and sign it," she said with authority, "so I can get a new uniform. Every girl has to have one. They are so pretty, Mutti, like sailors' suits but with skirts!"

Marina looked at the paper and frowned. She shook her head. "No, Lara, we've been through this already. You are not joining the Sorority of Aryan Sisters. End of story."

"But I *have* to join!" Lara protested. "I have to! Frau Finkel says everyone has to. And I *want* to join, I've wanted to for so long. Why won't you let me?" Lara tried not to cry. She had cried the last time she pleaded with her mother to let her join, and it had not worked at all. Marina had only become more resolute.

"I don't care if you want to join, Lara, it's not something I want you to be a part of." Marina folded up the paper into a small rectangle and held it out to Lara. "If I need to go talk to Frau Finkel about this, I will."

Oskar made a throat-clearing noise. Lara looked over to him, eager for an ally. He had pulled his handkerchief out of his jacket pocket and was cleaning his glasses with it. When he put them back on, he raised his eyebrows, as if trying to stretch his eyes wide open. She sidled over to stand closer to him.

"Marina, my dear, you don't have as much latitude on this question as you did earlier," he said. Lara had no idea what the word *latitude* meant, but Opa was using his slow, serious voice, and that was promising.

Marina bristled, her body stiffening, bracing for some sort of fight. "What do you mean, I don't have 'latitude'? Lara is still my daughter, isn't she?" She grabbed Lara's backpack from the floor as if arming herself with a weapon. "And my opinion of these youth organizations has not improved with time. On the contrary. Honestly, Vati, all this marching around and singing songs in praise of the Führer"—Marina stomped around the sofa in mock imitation, waving the backpack over her head—"what is that supposed to teach them? How is that *useful*"—she slammed the backpack on the floor—"except as a form of indoctrination?"

When Opa spoke again, his voice was still calm and steady. Lara noticed that the angrier her mother got, the quieter he did, or maybe it was just that he seemed to be quieter because her mother was so loud. "I have no doubt, Marina, that the children could be given more useful civic responsibilities. But the fact remains"—he walked over to the open window and pulled it down—"that you have no choice in the matter."

"No *choice*?!" Lara was impressed with how well her opa had anticipated her mother's screaming. "This is my daughter! Since when does the Führer come into my house and tell me what I can and cannot do with my daughter?!" Marina reached forward and tried to grab Lara, but Lara slipped away and ran to the sofa, against which Oskar was leaning. She grabbed one of the pillows and hugged it for protection. "Am I required to submit my daughter to brainwashing about her duty as a German *woman*? I can only imagine how many little bastards have already been born to teenage girls who took their duty to procreate seriously!"

Marina's words were getting way beyond Lara's comprehension now, but Opa's face suggested that he was not enjoying this rant. "Marina, you are overreacting."

"Am I? Am I overreacting because I want Lara to come to her own beliefs? To have her own opinions? Why should I let someone else tell my daughter what to believe?"

Oskar took a deep breath. "This is not about belief. It's about the *law*."

"It is absolutely about belief! It's about the government using law to compel belief! Can't you see that? Don't you want to protect your granddaughter from that? Unless . . ." In her tirade, Marina had been striding toward the sofa, toward Lara and Opa, then away again from both of them. But now she stopped. It was strange—it felt to Lara as if something new had entered the living room. Something heavy, and perhaps slightly dangerous, had blown into the air right in front of where she sat, right between her mother and her grandfather. Opa had been patting his pockets, looking, Lara knew, for his pipe and tobacco, but when Marina suddenly quieted, he looked up. "Unless you don't want Lara to start questioning things." The words came out slowly from her mouth, as if she were feeling them out with her tongue before she spoke. "Because then she might come to question *you*. Like her mother does." This was no longer a conversation about the Führer Youth, but Lara did not know what it had become. Her mother's eyes were brimming with tears. Her opa stared at her for a long time.

"I had to stay in my position," he said.

"You had a choice. You *chose* to stay."

Oskar walked over to the hat rack by the front door and took his tweed fedora off the top hook. He smoothed the small brown feather on its right side and placed the hat on his head. "You're right, Marina, I did have a choice, or at least it appeared so at the time." He opened the front door. "But our choices are not always what they seem to others." Then he stepped out and closed the door behind him.

That wasn't the last time her mother and Opa had fought. Lara usually left the room when it looked like they were getting angry with each other. After that day, however, Marina stopped calling Opa "Vati"; she called him "Oskar" instead. Also after that day, Lara got her uniform. Once the weather became cooler, she received a jacket, a light-brown tailored blazer fitted close to the body, the most stylish piece of clothing she owned. She wore it whenever possible, though technically she was only supposed to wear it to Sorority meetings.

Lara sighed into the blackberry foliage, remembering that jacket. It was impossibly small now, and there was no reason to buy a new one because they had moved away from Berlin. She knew Meerfeld used to have a Sorority chapter that some of the Blumental girls attended earlier in the war, but she didn't know if they still met, and it all seemed less important than it used to.

She turned her attention back to the magazine, flipping the pages slowly, taking her time. Finally, Lara arrived at page eighty-one, where the article about Princess Elizabeth began on the right-hand side of the centerfold. Glancing briefly at the facing left-hand page, Lara inhaled sharply, appalled. There, directly across from a half-page photograph of Elizabeth playing the piano in an ornate music room, was a full-page advertisement for Modess sanitary napkins. What disrespect for royalty, what flagrant disregard for Elizabeth's innocence and sensitivity! Lara quickly folded back the magazine along its spine so that Elizabeth would not have to look at the ad. Only then could she comfortably read the article.

Her nickname was "Betts," and because she was being groomed for queendom, she had her own private tutor, Crawfie, who taught her every subject from English literature to world history, including (and this was apparently a first for an English monarch) American history after 1776. Her birthday was April 21, which meant that she had been eighteen for almost three months now. Her father gave her a pearl each year for her birthday. Plus, this year, since she was coming of age, she would get her own lady-in-waiting. Lara imagined the luxury: having someone whose job it was to do what you asked them to. She could put the lady-in-waiting in charge of hanging the laundry or cleaning out the henhouse.

Much to Lara's disappointment, the princess was said to have no sense of fashion. She was probably just too sheltered, Lara thought. What she needed was a *close friend* to go shopping with. Lara could easily help the princess make good use of her large annual income to spruce up her clothing. And at eighteen, Lara remembered from the various English fashion magazines she had read, Elizabeth should be having a debutante ball this year. Lara fantasized about helping the princess find the perfect ball gown, like Cinderella's fairy godmother. Silver-sequined bodices, lace sleeves, long alabaster-white satin trains—these images wafted through Lara's mind until she read, in the next paragraph, that there would be no ball this year because of the war. Instead, the princess would entertain guests at a small dance at her country house. Lara felt anguished on the princess's behalf.

"Lara!" Sofia was calling from the back porch. "Lara, come have lunch, Opa's here!" Lara's heart leaped. Lunch she could wait for, but her opa? No. She closed the magazine, returned it to its envelope, and crawled out of the blackberries as quickly as she could. Running uphill through grass that definitely needed to be cut (something else Lara could assign to her lady-in-waiting), she thought of all the things she had to tell her opa: about Elizabeth's studies, the sacrifice of her debutante ball, and her preparations to be queen. It did not matter to her where Opa had been or who he had been with or what he had done. What mattered was that he was home.

– Sixteen –

Edith looked out the French doors to the backyard, where Oskar was standing on the stone terrace with Sofia, who was running in circles around him and dodging his tickles. Lara was sprinting up the hill, her blond hair freed from its ponytail and swinging wildly around her. She arrived panting, and Oskar caught her in a giant hug. Edith watched Lara bury her face in Oskar's woolen vest, pushing herself into his body, confirming his solidity.

Edith had had a similar instinct when Oskar put his arms around her in the kitchen an hour ago. Having wished him near her so many times in the past six months, she found it hard to believe that his embrace was not a fantasy that would evaporate at any minute.

"I'm so sorry," he had whispered into her hair. "What happened yesterday, the flags, it was all my fault." He gripped her more tightly. "I'm so grateful nothing happened to anyone. To you." Edith didn't say anything. Not because she was angry. She didn't blame Oskar for Captain Rodemann's outburst. Rather, she too was grateful. To have him back, to have him holding her, to have him declare that he still needed her. When he let go and stood back to look at her, Edith could see that his hair, which used to be somewhat gray, had gone completely white, and his eyes were set in even deeper, darker hollows. Otherwise, he looked just as handsome and well-dressed as always, his rectangular spectacles perched on the bump in his nose, his pipe stem peeking out from behind the carefully triangulated white handkerchief in his jacket pocket, and his brown socks bridging the gap between cuffed trousers and laced black leather shoes.

Now on the porch, Oskar took a long look at Lara. "Ho ho, young lady, where have you been? Let's see, from the purple stain on your dress, I'm going to guess . . . the blackberries! Are they ripe yet? Did you bring me any to eat?" Lara shook her head, smiling. Oskar noticed the envelope she was clutching in her right hand. "Ah, I see you got my package! Was it the right issue? I assumed so, from the cover."

Lara nodded, and her words gushed forth as if he had opened a spigot. "Oh, Opa! It is *so* perfect! Even better than perfect, it's perfect-plus! Pluperfect! I've never seen so many pictures of Elizabeth in one place at a time, and such a long story too. It tells me so much about her life. Do you know she plays piano? And she sings. Not very well, apparently, but that's okay, because she's a princess. And she gets pearls for her birthday, on a necklace, one pearl each year, from her father. Of course he can give her pearls, he's the king of England, so he has lots of them. Probably he could give her rubies or emeralds if she wanted them, but I suppose she likes pearls best. I like pearls too, they're smooth and creamy, like her skin—"

Oskar turned to the house and, seeing Edith, put a large hand over Lara's mouth, muffling her midsentence. "Whoa there, Lara, here's your oma, come with important news from the kitchen." Edith had been waiting for a break in Lara's monologue. As she lingered, she'd worked to remove her apron. "Here, my dear, let me rid you of those shackles of domesticity and perfect your transformation into the queen we all know you to be." Oskar untied the bow at the back, folded the apron into a neat square, and handed it to his wife. "Lara has been telling me how royalty lives in England, but I sense we are about to experience a princely luncheon right here on the Continent!"

"Ah yes," Edith said, recognizing the shift in Oskar's tone. Her husband was so good at deflecting reality with fairy tales and fantasies, just as they had during the last war, building their dream home in their letters, partly to solidify their connection to each other, partly to avoid the grim truths of the day.

"The chef serves only princely meals in this kitchen," Edith announced. "Today's highlights are princely potatoes from the royal garden and princely trout from the royal fisherfolk who live next door, and who have kindly agreed to join the royal family for this afternoon feast."

"Trout *again*?" Lara and Sofia groaned simultaneously.

"Not just any trout," Oskar said in a low, conspiratorial voice. The girls perked up; a story was imminent. "These are *rainbow* trout. And do you know why they call them rainbow trout?" Lara and Sofia shook their heads.

Edith waved them all inside before Oskar could continue. "Brother Grimm, could you tell your story in the dining room, where, I'm sure you'll be glad to hear, a much larger audience awaits?"

The living and dining areas of the Eberhardt home shared a single large room downstairs that had been designed to accommodate two or three Mercedes sedans. Edith had domesticated this cavernous space through judicious placement of sofas, armchairs, throw rugs, and lamps. She had hung a low candlelight chandelier over the mahogany dining room table, more for atmosphere than illumination. Today, even though it was midday, Edith had lit all its yellow beeswax candles, and the faces of the family and their guests were now gathered in the glow. She had set the table with her wedding china, the cream-colored Rosenthal that she had dragged south, fearing the vicissitudes of Allied bombings over Berlin. A large vase in the center of the table held the bouquet that Sofia had gathered from half a dozen different garden flowers: leafy fuchsia and dark red roses, shoots of pale pink hydrangeas and tall blue delphiniums.

Edith was glad that Erich had decided to stay on for an extra day, and that he had accepted her invitation to join them. One more stitch toward mending the rift between them. Erich was sitting across from Marina, who sat next to Myra Breckenmüller in front of the tile oven that provided heat for the room. She noticed that her daughter had chosen to wear her hair down today. No doubt it was Erich's presence, not Oskar's, that inspired this change. Edith bit her tongue on a comment from that familiar space of fear and anger, a place she had firmly decided not to revisit. She took her place at the head of the table, opposite Oskar, while Lara quickly took the chair next to Rosie, leaving Sofia to sit between Karl and Myra Breckenmüller.

"Is Opa telling a story? What is it about?" Rosie asked.

"Yes, Oskar, tell your story while we start passing around the food," Edith said. Though his stories tended to ramble, today she was happy to indulge him. Oskar in storytelling mode was Oskar at his best.

"Karl, would you do the honors of serving the fish?" She passed a steaming oval platter to her guest.

Oskar snapped his folded napkin in the air and placed it in his lap with a flourish. "Well, it's the story of how the rainbow trout got its name, a story you too must know, right, Karl?"

Recognizing that his was a supporting role, Karl kept his head down as he meticulously placed fish fillets on the plates passed over to him. "Oh no, Oskar, I don't know any fish stories. The fish never talk to me, you see," he said. "Given our respective roles, we're not really on speaking terms."

"Opa, Herr Breckenmüller is a *fisherman*!" Sofia reminded Oskar.

"Right, right, stupid me," Oskar said, shoveling potatoes onto his plate. "So, I was explaining about the rainbow trout, which we have the distinct honor of tasting today. You all know how when it rains and there's still some sunshine around, sometimes we get a rainbow, right?" There were nods all around the table. Pleased with everyone's full attention, Oskar continued. "But"—

he pierced the air with his knife—"this was not always so. Long ago, there was no such thing as color. There was just black and white." He paused to let the magnitude of a colorless world sink in, then he picked up a forkful of carrots and held them before his face as if admiring their complete and unequivocal orangeness before putting them in his mouth. "It was pretty dull. One day a fish—a trout, to be exact—just happened to be jumping around the water for fun during a rainstorm. And just as he finished making the arc of his jump, leaving behind a spray of water droplets"—Oskar swung the potato impaled on his fork through the air to illustrate—"a flash of lightning came down from the sky and hit all those little drops of water! Guess what happened?"

"Ka-pow!" Rosie shouted, smashing her fork into the carrots on her plate. Edith frowned.

"Right! An explosion! And right over our very own lake, it began to rain down colors of every kind—red, blue, yellow, green, orange, purple . . ."

"Pink!" Rosie shouted, jumping up.

"Yes, pink, of course, and turquoise and brown—in fact, every color imaginable, and all of a sudden the world was transformed by colors. And from that day forward all the trout like the one hit by lightning were known as rainbow trout."

"And everyone celebrated all the colors as equally beautiful," Marina added.

"But pink was the best," Rosie said.

"No, blue!" Sofia insisted.

"There wasn't a best color," Marina told them. "They were all just different."

Oskar looked up at Marina, amusement from his storytelling success still lighting his eyes. "I did not know this story had a moral, my dear," he said.

In an instant, Marina bristled at the nerve Oskar unwittingly touched. "Don't you believe in morals anymore?" she asked pointedly. Total quiet descended upon the table. Edith saw Oskar flinch, from either anger or hurt. Marina looked down at her plate as if regretting her words, but Edith knew her daughter was too proud to apologize. Fortunately, Lara came to the rescue.

"Mutti learns all about morals from Pastor Johann," Lara said. "They have tea together almost every day." It was the perfect statement. It deflected her mother's barb, setting it in a more innocuous context. Edith wondered when her eldest granddaughter had become a diplomat, but then Lara was as eager as Edith to prevent arguments between Marina and Oskar. She was old enough to remember the fractious meals around the dinner table in Berlin before Oskar and Marina achieved their fragile détente.

"Is that right?" Oskar asked. "Daily conversations with the local pastor?" He fumbled with the napkin on his lap as he spoke. From the tone of forced curiosity in his voice, Edith could tell he was trying to put Marina's comment behind him. Clearing his throat, he placed his napkin on the table and stood up. "Well, then, a toast." He raised his water glass toward Marina. "To Pastor Johann, for keeping us on the straight and narrow." Marina heard the forgiveness in her father's voice and looked up at him. Whatever had risen between them was put to rest. "To the rainbow trout, for being so tasty with hollandaise sauce," Oskar continued. "To my extraordinary neighbors, Myra and Karl; my cherished friend and son, Erich; and of course, my beloved family of women, who reinvent beauty with each generation." Edith blushed while Lara beamed. "And to the miracle that permits everyone dear to me in life to sit around one table at one time for one moment." Oskar paused and shut his eyes. "May it be one of many."

"*Prost!*" Glasses clinked all around the table. Although the candles in the chandelier were getting quite low, they seemed to be emitting more light. Edith looked around at the faces of everyone surrounding the table, faces on which shadows had been softened and creases of worry smoothed by the buttery glow of the burning beeswax. Their outlines blurred and shimmered, holding them in this moment, fusing them more permanently together in some enduring space.

"So tell me," Oskar demanded, breaking her reverie. "What's new in Blumental?"

"They almost killed the *bürgermeister* yesterday!" Rosie announced. "And he peed his pants!" She looked at Sofia and they both giggled.

"Rosie!" Marina chided. "Don't repeat that."

"But it's true!"

"Yes, it's true, but it's embarrassing to Herr Munter, and you know, he was very scared," Marina said.

"I'm sure I would pee my pants if I thought I was going to be hanged," Karl said.

"Well, issues of incontinence aside," Edith said, "Erich was the hero and saved the day. He even rode in on a horse."

"A horse? Didn't you leave Fürchtesgaden in a car?" Oskar asked.

"I did, but modern transportation failed me. I had to commandeer a more reliable means of transit, which thankfully was nibbling on a patch of clover right next to the road."

"It was the beautifulest horse ever, Opa!" Rosie pronounced.

"And I haven't had a chance to thank you, General," Myra Breckenmüller said, reaching across Sofia for her husband's hand. "I'm not sure what Karl would have done if . . ."

"Karl?" Confused, Oskar looked at his friend, who was staring into the napkin on his lap.

"It was my knot around Hans Munter's neck," Karl said.

"Captain Rodemann thought the *bürgermeister* was a traitor," Myra explained. "I suppose it was all based on orders from the Führer about civilian disobedience."

Marina, who had been helping Edith clear the table, came into the room carrying two steaming bowls. "That Captain Rodemann can go to hell, with his damn barricades and machine-gun fire in the streets. It's a miracle no one was killed," she said, setting the bowls on the table with more force than was necessary. Grimacing, Myra passed them down to Sofia and Karl. "Such arrogance and idiocy! He's like a little boy who drowns kittens for fun."

At the mention of the word *kitten*, Sofia scrambled out of her seat, stepped over Karl, and stood on the bench next to Oskar's chair. She cupped his chin in her two small hands and turned his face toward hers. "Opa, Irene has kittens. Can we have one?"

Setting a bowl of creamed wheat down before Oskar, Edith watched his features soften. A slow, wistful smile moved the corners of his mustache, and for a moment, he looked far away. Then, placing his hands on the top of Sofia's head, he leaned forward and kissed her forehead. "Of course you can. Of course," he said. "You get the best mouse eater in the bunch and bring it here, and we will call it Munter."

"Oooh, *griessbrei*!" cried Rosie, eyeing the hot creamed wheat.

"With raspberry coulis. The blackberries aren't ripe enough yet," Edith apologized. She knew Oskar loved blackberries. After serving everyone, she took her own seat and picked up her spoon. There were murmurs of appreciation from both sides of the table as the raspberries mixed with the warmed wheat on everyone's tongues.

Marina was the first to break the rapturous silence. "So the last we heard, Captain Rodemann had left Meerfeld. Please tell me he's been reassigned elsewhere and is marching his troops away as we speak."

Oskar shook his head slowly. "For your sake, Marina, I wish I could tell you that. But there has been a new development that requires Captain Rodemann and his troops to return to the vicinity, at least for a day or two." Oskar paused. All eyes turned to him. He met the collective gaze, but he was waiting a long time to speak, Edith thought.

"The Führer is coming for a visit," Oskar said.

It felt to Edith as if the air had been sucked out of the room all at once. She gasped. "What? Here? To Blumental? Why on earth would he come here?"

"Technically, he is visiting Blumental to see his good friend, the composer Klaus Weber." Klaus Weber. Famed recluse of Blumental. Edith hated Weber's music. All of his compositions were loud and bombastic, but their martial, noisily Teutonic nature had been adopted by the Third Reich as inspirational marching songs. Toward the man himself Edith had no particular feelings of any kind, for he made himself as scarce as possible. The Weber estate was situated south of the lakeshore path into Blumental, the huge property shielded from public curiosity by dense hedges. Herr Weber himself was notoriously monastic.

"Apparently, Herr Weber has just completed a new march," Oskar continued. "He wants to dedicate it to the Führer in a private performance at his home. But fear not, only I must attend." Edith relaxed slightly. A private performance on the Weber estate was perhaps tolerable, especially if she didn't have to go. Her peace did not last long. "However," Oskar said, watching her carefully, "the Führer told me yesterday that, since he was going to be in the neighborhood, he would like to meet all of you. He is going to join us at our house for tea."

"*Tea?!*" Edith and Marina cried out simultaneously.

"I told him we would be greatly honored to serve him."

Edith closed her eyes and pressed on the bridge of her nose with her thumb and forefinger, trying to center herself in a sudden whirl of vertigo. The Führer. That dark man with the dark hair and dark eyes. Edith's instinctive reaction to him, when she first saw him in Berlin—thankfully from a great distance—had been to shrink away, to keep him from seeing her. Somehow, long before Kristallnacht and his policies of racial oppression, she had sensed the danger he posed to the world order. His black brows and upturned mustache (this was before he trimmed it) reminded her of that terrorizing tailor in the children's book *Struwwelpeter*, the one who ran after thumb-sucking children with giant shears and cut their thumbs off.

Now the Führer was coming here. To this house, her *home*.

The home that she and Oskar had created and populated with children and grandchildren. The home whose threshold had been crossed only by friends. The home that she had enclosed in beauty, deliberately planting layer upon layer of blooming plants and scented flowers around it, so that everyone inside, looking out, would be reminded how wondrous the world was. Or how wondrous it *could be*, if carefully tended.

And Oskar proposed to allow the Führer into this sanctuary. The Führer, a man whose philosophy was based on destruction and conquest, who proclaimed to love beauty but knew nothing about it. Because beauty was—wasn't it?—based on truth, and he lived in lies.

"When?" Marina asked.

"Tomorrow afternoon."

Edith didn't notice Erich standing up. His *griessbrei* was untouched. Rosie quickly reached for his bowl and continued shoveling spoonfuls of the sweet wheat porridge into her mouth.

"I'm so sorry, Edith," Erich said, placing his napkin on the table. "If the Führer is arriving tomorrow, people have no doubt been trying to reach me to arrange security, and I have not been to the inn to pick up my messages all morning. Would you forgive me for making a premature departure?" He walked over to Edith, took her hand, and kissed it. "Sir," he added with a nod to Oskar.

Edith was still reeling from Oskar's announcement, wondering desperately if there was any way to rescind the invitation. Her mouth felt strangely unresponsive, her tongue thick and sluggish. She finally managed to say, "Dear Erich," and patted his hand.

"I'll walk you out." Marina pushed her chair back. "Mutti, you stay and talk your husband out of this madness."

The Breckenmüllers exchanged a knowing look. Karl Breckenmüller patted his belly and sighed. "Well, if you feed the Führer as well as you've fed me, you might have to cart him over to the Weber place afterward. This meal has quite done me in. I'm not sure I can get up anymore." Edith heard Oskar's strained laugh, but she refused to join. She knew he was hoping to lighten the atmosphere, but its heaviness was his own doing. He should feel her anger, she thought. He should bear the weight of what he had told them. Fortunately for Oskar, Rosie was still at the table. Her single-minded pursuit of every last grain of raspberry-flavored wheat had led her finally to hold her bowl up to her face and lick the inside of it. The persistent clanking of her teeth against china caught Myra Breckenmüller's attention.

"Rosie," she called, leaning over the table and tapping her forefinger on the wood in front of the little girl. Her voice held no tone of recrimination, just amusement. Rosie lowered the bowl from her face. A thin pink crust of *griessbrei* and coulis circled her mouth and dotted her nose, and her hair, hands, and clothing were all caked with patches of dried grain. Oskar's laugh now was deep and genuine, and, looking at Rosie, even Edith had to smile.

"Lara, would you please take Rosie and help her get washed up?" she asked. Making a face, Lara grabbed Rosie's sticky hand and headed out of the room to the washbasin beyond the kitchen. Seeing her sisters depart, Sofia, who had remained silent all this time, leaped to her feet. She turned her big blue eyes to Edith and pleaded, "Can I go to Irene's?"

"Yes, you may go."

"And . . . ?"

"And since I don't believe in contradicting your opa's promises, even if he doesn't consult me about them"—Edith gave Oskar a glare—"you may choose a kitten." Sofia ran to Edith and hugged her, then went to Oskar and kissed him on the cheek. She disappeared out the porch door.

"We should be going too," Myra said, standing up with Karl. "But let me help you first with the dishes, Edith. We can catch up on gossip."

"Oh, no need." It was rare that Edith turned down an opportunity to chat with Myra, but she felt too overwhelmed at the moment to engage with anyone. She needed to process what was going to happen in the next twenty-four hours and how she would manage it with grace rather than resentment. And she needed to talk to Oskar. "You take care of the indigestion that Karl looks like he's having." Edith walked her friends out to the foyer. Oskar followed, keeping his distance. At the front door, Edith stopped and kissed her friend on both cheeks. "I'll stop by later, perhaps."

"Do," Myra said, ushering Karl out the door. "Please do. I can help you plan tomorrow, if you need help." Edith nodded. She stood on the threshold and watched the Breckenmüllers walk hand in hand over to their house. Myra was a lucky woman. Karl was a sweet man, and straightforward. There was nothing hidden or complicated about a fisherman.

When they disappeared from view, Edith closed the front door. "Oskar, we need to discuss this." But Oskar had gone.

– Seventeen –

Erich Wolf berated himself for not taking the field telegraph. When he had gone back to Schwanfeld this morning to arrange for his broken-down car to be hauled to the military depot in Friedrichshafen, he had considered pulling the telegraph kit out of the trunk. But he had left it where it was, thinking he wouldn't need it in the next day or two. Now he was unprepared. Short-sightedness, he thought. He should have known better.

Oskar and Edith had a telephone in their home, but Erich couldn't use it without raising all sorts of questions. Nor would it have felt right to send *this* telegram from Oskar's home. His only way to communicate with Gottfried Schrumm was to send a telegram from the post office. He would have to trust the postmistress to be discreet. Hopefully the Führer's impending visit would occasion a flurry of telegrams to and from Berlin, and his wouldn't attract attention.

At least he would be able to see Marina again later. He had hoped to spend the entire afternoon with her, but when Oskar announced that the Führer would be visiting the next day, Erich realized that an opportunity he couldn't ignore was presenting itself, and he had to notify Berlin as soon as possible. Before he left the house, he asked Marina to meet him in the garden after the girls were in bed. She understood that he had pressing business now. "Go. Do what needs to be done," she said. Little did she understand the true meaning of those words.

Until now, the plan had been almost entirely theoretical, but he was about to take the first step to actualize it. The agitation he felt was familiar. He had experienced it countless times during cavalry missions in the first war: overlooking the enemy's battalion, his horse, Loki, nervously picking up first one foot, then the other, poised to fly the instant their commander gave the order. Now too Erich felt poised to fly, like a hawk perched on a falconer's glove, quivering in anticipation of the quick upward thrust of the gauntlet that would send it into motion. But now he didn't have a horse to soothe him. He was alone in this venture.

His heavy boots crunched loudly on the gravel-strewn dirt of the lake footpath, sending the more skittish waterbirds up into the air. Thickets of aquatic reed alternated with small pebbled beaches all along the lakeshore, up to the Weber estate, where the shoreline was arrested by a five-foot concrete wall. It was an incongruous boundary in a town whose property lines were usually marked by hollyhock rows and lightweight crumbling fences. At the time of its construction, twenty years earlier, some pockets of Blumental citizens had grumbled, in the name of urban aesthetic integrity. Weber had quieted all opposition with a timely offer to finance the restoration of the Münster bell tower, which was on the verge of collapse.

Passing by the iron gate to the front driveway, Erich stopped to peer inside the grounds. A squadron of tall, closely planted hornbeams lined the long drive up to the Weber house and effectively reduced the view of the estate to what lay between them, which in this case was little more than tamped-down dirt. Erich hadn't expected to see more, and he didn't need to. This wasn't a reconnaissance mission. He would have time to survey the grounds tomorrow afternoon. He felt a measure of relief. Finally, months of planning were about to culminate in one decisive, tangible action. He grimaced ever so slightly at the thought of how the world might change in the next week, and at the idea that he might have a hand in that change.

The man his father had raised him to be wouldn't have contemplated the role Erich was about to play. That younger, prewar boy had watched with awe and reverence as his father polished the medal on the mantelpiece every Sunday: the cherished Blue Max, four golden eagles perched between the arms of a blue Maltese cross. That boy had enlisted in the army, eager to follow the path of heroism and glory blazed by his father almost half a century earlier in the Franco-Prussian War, which created a unified country out of a handful of bickering states. Through ritual and behavior, Erich's parents instilled in him everything they believed in. Honor for the family name, for example, was located in the black leather Bible and its rote recitation before Sunday lunch. Reverence for family and ancestors hung in every word his father read from that heavy tome, its flyleaf inscribed with the names of generations of Wolfs—their births, baptisms, marriages, deaths—scrolling through the centuries in painstakingly beautiful ink scripts. That volume was permeated with the glory of Martin Luther and Carl Hildebrand von Canstein, who brought the word of God to the German people. The significance of the fact that, of all the languages in the world, God's word should first be translated into German was not lost on Erich's father.

His mother too did her part in showing him the beauty of his native tongue, lulling Erich to sleep every night with her soft soprano. Through his mother's voice, the music of Schiller gently swept through Erich's darkened room: *O schlinge dich, du sanfte Quelle / Ein breiter Strom um uns herum / Und drohend mit empörter Welle / Verteidige dies Heiligtum.*

Armed with this conviction in the strength and grandeur of his culture, Erich had entered the German army in time for the first great war. When he met Oskar Eberhardt, his sense of devotion to his country was still unbounded and unwavering. Over the next two muddy, bloody years, Oskar taught the young soldier a supplementary but indispensable principle: the unquestioning allegiance of a soldier to his commander. Years later, when Erich entered the Führer's General Staff and took the oath of loyalty, he believed wholeheartedly in the military tenet of devotion to the commander in chief, absolute obedience to orders. He had, for many years, no reason to doubt that axiom.

Until the invasion of Poland. After conquering Warsaw to help satisfy the Führer's insatiable appetite for territory, the Twenty-Fifth Panzer Division was ordered to head east to secure the out-lying towns and head off the Soviet army marching westward. Erich was detailed from the Führer's General Staff to support the army's Nineteenth Division, which remained critical in Warsaw. Their duty was to maintain order before the arrival of the *einsatzgruppen*, elite security forces being trained for occupation. Erich understood the ultimate military mission in Poland to be annexation. He did not then comprehend that the Führer's real purpose was to raze the entire Polish civilization.

Stuck in Warsaw, Erich chafed at his assignment. He wanted to be in charge of the military action to the east. Not because he enjoyed the task of overpowering foreign citizens, but because one particular place east of Warsaw beckoned to him: Niebiosa Podlaski. Every true cavalryman knew of it. An expanse of lush meadows and dense forests, Niebiosa Podlaski was a renowned stud farm, famous for its incomparable Arabians, especially the great stallion Witrez, a grand black-and-bay male whose athleti-cism and beauty reportedly left onlookers speechless. The farm was tantalizingly close. It felt impossible that Erich should not see it. So, leaving Captain Rutger Moritz in charge of Warsaw one overcast afternoon, Erich ventured out to see the fabled estate.

It took two hours by car to reach the turnoff to Niebiosa Pod-laski. Erich had been surprised to see dust swirling over the dirt driveway that veered from the main roadway, as if there had been recent visitors. He shut off the car's engine and waited at the turnoff, listening, not sure what he expected to hear. The sounds that came to him once the engine no longer drowned them out almost stopped his heart.

The air was cleaved by high-pitched screams, spluttering whinnies, and agonized screeches. Horses in pain. Their cries pierced his ears and lashed his soul. Erich turned his car into the long driveway and sped past rows of dense Norway maples bleeding yellow leaves onto the ground. When he reached the long thatched residence building, he saw tracks from what must have been a fleet of jeeps and squad cars. Mounds of moist earth had been spun out of carefully tended beds and spit onto the macadam walkway, speckled with the severed heads of multicolored zinnias. Erich leaped out of his car and ran in the direction of the stables. In the five minutes it took him to get there, the screaming stopped. He ran quickly up an incline of grass, desperate to move faster, though his feet kept sinking into the fertile sod. Finally he crested the hill and stood still, looking over the meadow, the horse stables, and beyond.

In every direction lay dead horses, their heads pierced by bullets, their bodies slashed open by bayonets. Soft velvety muzzles lay lifeless in patches of clover, unresponsive to the flies settling in their nostrils. Not a single majestic rib cage rose and fell. The only movement came from the insects and a light wind.

The carnage was complete, no animal spared. The senselessness of the slaughter enraged him. There was absolutely no reason to murder these magnificent creatures. There was nothing whatsoever to be gained by eliminating them. Erich slowly walked over to a silver mare whose body lay next to that of her foal. He knelt before her head and reached forward to close her eyes. He had known a few Arabian horses in the first war, had marveled at their grace and fluidity, their intelligence and vitality, their courage. But it was the eyes, he thought. Large, dark, lustrous eyes that followed every move you made, drew you in as you approached them, reached your spirit and invited it to dance. That light in hundreds of pairs of eyes had been cruelly extinguished.

There was no doubt in Erich's mind who was responsible for this slaughter. For the first time since he'd joined the German army, he felt ashamed. There was nothing admirable about sharing a uniform with these butchers.

That was the first crack in the foundation of Erich's loyalty. The men who had done this were men with whom he shared a country and a culture. Presumably, these men had been raised to love Goethe and Bach and had learned the same histories of Prussia and Bismarck, war and triumph. Yet they were rogues, contemptible and vile, unworthy of serving a nation that, in Erich's mind, should champion beauty, grace, strength, and intelligence—the same qualities embodied by the senselessly murdered horses scattered before him. Erich's subsequent report to Berlin summarizing the incident and recommending that the officers involved be stripped of their ranks was ignored completely. Later that winter, at a cocktail party in Warsaw, Erich confronted Field Marshal Brommer about the matter. Brommer looked at him in disbelief. "Erich, those were *Polish* horses. I'll grant that they might have been better than the Polish people, which, as we all know, is not saying very much. But the fact remains that they were *Polish*. Expendable."

Three and a half years later, when Erich was approached by Gottfried Schrumm with a secret journal documenting German war crimes, his belief in Oskar's ideal of unconditional fidelity to one's military commander evaporated. By then, Erich had seen with his own eyes much of the inhumanity chronicled in those pages, and he had heard too many racist diatribes by the Führer to doubt that such actions were officially sanctioned, even ordered, at the highest level. According to Gottfried, the small resistance movement headquartered in the Defense Ministry was in search of a military man, preferably one with direct access to the Führer. The military disaster at Stalingrad had made it clearer than ever that something had to be done. The German push toward the Soviet city should never have been initiated

late in the year, and certainly not by an army so woefully under-
supplied and inadequately reinforced. In the eyes of Gottfried
and the Resistance, the Führer's single-minded pursuit of Stalingrad, a goal his advisors considered unattainable, was nothing
less than megalomania, resulting in almost half a million unnecessary German deaths. After reciting this information, Gottfried
had leaned over his desk in Berlin. "Originally, our goal was to
divest him of authority, to make him step down. We have people
inside and outside the administration who are poised to step
into the power vacuum that would be left in his wake. Good
people, people who know how to govern. Of course, he would
never step down willingly. Removing him requires more than
unseating him."

Erich sat upright. He was fairly sure he already knew the answer to his next question. "And what, precisely, does it require?"

"Killing him." Erich did not flinch. "We have already had a
few attempts," Gottfried said, leaning back again in his chair.
"Obviously unsuccessful. The man has an uncanny sixth sense
for danger or he is remarkably lucky. Or both. In any case, we've
come to the conclusion that our principal stumbling block has
been inadequate access. We have in place various men who can
deliver the means to kill him. The instrument, so to speak. They
are located around the country."

"But how do you know the Führer will go to these locations?"
Erich asked.

"We don't," Gottfried admitted. "We have pinpointed several
venues, some highly likely, some less so, in which to place our
weapons. What we lack now is the ability to bring the instrument
right up to the Führer's person. If he should come near one of
these venues, we need a man on the inside, ideally someone on
the General Staff, who could have direct contact with the Führer
without being questioned."

"Someone like me," Erich said.

"That's why you're here, isn't it?" At the time, Gottfried

Schrumm's proposal seemed to Erich the logical culmination of three years of self-examination, three years of struggle with the boundaries of honor and loyalty. Erich was troubled more by the idea of betraying his father and Oskar than by breaking his oath to the Führer. Just as the golden eagles on his father's beloved Blue Max shimmered brightly in the sun, their claws clinging tenaciously to the sides of the Maltese cross, so did his father's ideals of military discipline and allegiance grip Erich's psyche.

And Oskar. Oskar had essentially shaped Erich into the man he was. Every strategy Erich mapped out, every decision on the battlefield, every order to his troops was informed by the years that Erich had served under his first real commander, listening to and executing his directions with growing respect. Then too, after his parents' death, the twelve years that Erich spent at Oskar's home, living in that strange capacity—part son, part compatriot, part friend—had transformed his feelings of gratitude, need, and reverence into something approaching awe. Erich knew Oskar was indelibly Prussian in his understanding of authority. The law was the law, orders were orders, and both were to be followed without hesitation or second-guessing. Oskar believed this essential to civilized society. In Berlin, Oskar had introduced Erich to the writings of Thomas Aquinas and the cardinal virtues of prudence, temperance, justice, and fortitude, by which Oskar measured his own actions.

Ironically, it was Aquinas's insistence on man being true to virtue that offered Erich the answer to his dilemma. What would the saint make of the Führer's orders? Weren't they merely exhortations to commit actions that were contrary to the virtue of the German people and the German culture? Some of the acts the Führer initiated were so heinous, so egregiously sinful, that Erich could imagine Aquinas stepping forward to assassinate the Führer himself. Would Oskar agree? Erich didn't know.

Now he opened the door to the post office and was relieved to see no one inside other than Ludmilla Schenk, the postmistress. "Good afternoon, ma'am," Erich said. "I need to send a telegram to Berlin. It's urgent."

"Of course." Ludmilla reached under the counter and pulled out a slip of paper. "If you fill this out, I will transmit it immediately."

Erich took the pencil she offered and filled in all the requisite formalities—Gottfried's name, title, office, and room number, then the message that he had worked out in his head: *Send info re instrument pickup. Will deliver tomorrow 18:00–20:00 at Weber's. Wolf*

Erich pushed the paper across the counter. "Thank you for expediting this."

Ludmilla Schenk smiled politely. "It is no problem, General. As you can see, I am somewhat at leisure. But I imagine things will get a bit more hectic in the next twenty-four hours." She turned and disappeared into a small room adjoining the main office.

Erich was surprised that the postmistress seemed already to know of the Führer's visit. But she had likely received a few early telegrams from Berlin and drawn the obvious conclusion. The point of his own telegram was not to tell Gottfried that the Führer would be in Blumental, a fact Gottfried most likely knew already. What Gottfried did *not* know was that *Erich* was in Blumental too, and, more important, that he saw an opportunity. Erich heard the light tapping of telegraph keys as he departed the post office. Now he had to wait.

Too restless to return to his inn, he headed toward the town center. He was not certain when, or even if, he would receive an answer from Berlin. The plan that Gottfried had outlined involved explosives entrusted to an unidentified carrier. For safety reasons, Gottfried explained, everyone participating must remain unknown to the others; all Erich knew of the plan was his own role. How the carrier would transport the explosives to a rendezvous location hadn't been specified. Presumably Gottfried counted on a window of opportunity for attack that would last a few days at least. But the opportunity here in Blumental would be available no more than twenty-four hours. It was a very narrow window, a veritable balistraria. The arrow Erich was about to let loose might not reach its target in time.

– Eighteen –

The bowl of shelled walnuts in front of Edith was almost halfway full. One or two more batches of nuts and she could begin grinding. She adjusted the pillow behind her back and sat up straighter in the kitchen chair. It was a tedious job, shelling nuts, but she had never minded it, even as a child. It took practice to cradle the hard outer shell of a walnut in the palm of one hand and apply just enough pressure with the nutcracker so that you did not break the treasure inside. Of course, with a Linzer torte, where the walnuts were ground before they went into the dough, it did not matter if the nut was whole. But it was still worth cracking the hull with care, to avoid crushing the membrane that surrounded and separated the two halves of the kernel inside. She took another walnut from the canvas bag lying on the table, cradled it in her left palm, and positioned the nutcracker over its central seam. She had just emptied its perfect golden kernel into her bowl when Marina walked into the kitchen.

"Have you seen Oskar?"

"Ah, the question of the hour—where has Oskar gone?" Edith tried not to sound annoyed. "No, my dear, your father was in his study after lunch, sending telegrams to who knows where, but when I went up to talk to him, he'd disappeared. He may have gone on a walk with Sofia. I think she wanted to show him the kitten she chose." She cracked the walnut she had been holding with a bit too much violence and placed it to one side.

"Do you want to talk to him about what happened at lunch? Because I think he's quite forgotten the incident. It might be best to let it go."

"No, that comment about morals just slipped out," Marina said. "Too many things on my mind, I suppose. I'm glad he's not dwelling on it." She sat down in front of the grinder that Edith had attached to the edge of the table and began absent-mindedly turning the handle. "I was hoping to ask him about tomorrow."

"What about tomorrow?" Another broken nut. Edith pushed it aside.

"I wanted to find out when the Führer is expected for tea. I have some errands to do in the morning, but I want to help you prepare. And then too"—Marina inhaled deeply—"there is the matter of *mental* preparation."

"I'm not sure there's enough time in the world to mentally prepare," Edith said. "But Oskar told me that the scheduled tea hour is four o'clock. So you do whatever you need to do in the morning. I might need some help as we get closer to the tea." She looked up at Marina. Her daughter's eyes were dark, and there was a familiar pain behind them. Edith pushed the bowl of shelled walnuts across the table. "Here. If you're going to turn that handle, you might as well make it worthwhile."

The two women were silent, taking comfort in the mesmerizing and calming predictability of their tasks. After a while, Edith dared to broach the subject that had been on her mind for two days. "The things you need to do tomorrow, Marina. Do they involve Erich?"

Marina tightened her grip on the grinder, keeping her gaze on the slow, steady gyration of its handle. "I don't want to talk about him, Mutti. I don't want to argue."

"Talking about him doesn't mean we have to argue."

"It always has in the past," Marina said.

"But I've forgiven him now," Edith offered.

"*Forgiven* him?" Marina bristled. She could not keep the disdain out of her voice. "Because he committed such a sin?"

Edith laid the nutcracker down on the table and tried to choose her words carefully. "Look, I know that in the past I have been unsympathetic to your relationship with him. But I want to speak with you now about the future. I know his presence here affects you, makes you restless." Marina opened her mouth for another retort, but Edith held up her hand. "Please, just hear me out before you say anything." Reluctantly, Marina closed her lips, folding her hands onto her lap with measured patience. "When I first confronted you with my suspicions about you and Erich," Edith continued, "and you told me you were in love with him, I'm afraid I didn't react well." Marina raised her eyebrows—a mocking gesture, Edith knew. "I was shocked, of course. Because you were my daughter, and he was practically my son, or at least it felt like that to me, and that made it feel, well, wrong."

"But he's *not* your son," Marina interjected. "Just because he feels like your son to you doesn't mean he felt like a brother to me."

"I know, dear, I know. And I was able to get past that with time. The bigger problem for me, though, was fear of what your love would do to our household, fear of the threat it posed to our family. I put that fear ahead of trying to understand your needs and your feelings, and I want you to know that I'm sorry about that." She paused to let Marina speak, but her daughter was too surprised by this unexpected apology to respond. Sighing, Edith continued. "I don't know what you and Erich spoke about in Berlin before the war. I don't know if the two of you contemplated leaving together. Back then I tried, for my own reasons, to convince you of the importance of maintaining an intact family, of staying for the girls, for Franz, even for your father. And then the war came, and the possibility of running away was taken from you." A tear escaped Marina's left eye and slowly slid down her cheek. Edith reached over and wrapped her fingers around her daughter's hands. "Now he's here, and I imagine that the past has been hurtling back at you, with all its emotions and passions. And you may be facing the same situation and questions you were confronting back then, yes?" Although Marina remained silent, her tears answered for her. Edith squeezed her hands tightly. "Erich is a good man, but so is Franz."

"I know! I *know* Franz is good." Marina's wail was filled with anguish, guilt, shame, love, and a touch of anger. "And I do love him. I've never stopped loving him. But my love for Franz isn't like my love for Erich. The way Erich makes me feel . . ." Marina looked out the window, caught by the memory. "Alive, yes, but also truly cherished for who I am. And safe, protected, always." She turned back to Edith. "Oh, it would be so much easier if Franz were awful. If he beat me, if he were a drunk or had other women. But he's good." Marina's voice became quiet. "Or at least he was."

Edith knew what her daughter meant. The last time Franz came home, after Stalingrad, he was unrecognizable: a skeletal, broken frame of a man, ghostly. Initially, Edith and Marina considered it lucky that he had survived the three-month siege by the Soviet army in the bitter cold of a Russian winter, when 95 percent of his comrades had perished. But the man who returned was not really alive, not as he had been. During the month Franz was home, the tension in the house was a living, wounded, snarling animal that curled up in a corner and attacked if you came too near. Franz spent most of his days napping, but it was nightmarish sleep, and he often awoke screaming. Once, when Edith had stayed with Franz so that Marina could take a short, much-needed nap, he had popped up in bed, eyes wide open but clearly not seeing. "Don't pet the dogs!" Franz cried out. "They have bombs strapped to their bellies! No, don't! *Don't!*" The only thing that soothed him, Edith remembered, was Marina's voice, reading aloud to him from his library of ornithological treatises, tales about the migration of the bar-tailed godwit and the nesting habits of the fan-tailed warbler.

"I have been lucky in love," Edith said at last. "Very, very lucky, to marry a man who makes my heart beat faster every time he comes near, to share my life with someone I fall for over and over again every time I see him." She smiled at her own romantic confession. "Well, almost every time. The point is, I never felt that I had to settle in my marriage, to accept something that was less than what I wanted because it was all that was offered or available at the time, or because . . ." She gently patted Marina's hands. "Because I had to. The truth is, Marina, if I had the opportunity to choose again, to pick a man to build a life with, I would make the same choice." Edith paused for an instant, trying to assess the truth of this statement in light of all her current fears and doubts about her husband, and she imagined Oskar's eyes, gray and green, with slivers of teal and ice blue near the pupils, radiating warmth and love and twinkling lightly with mischief. "Yes, I would choose Oskar."

"Despite everything?" Marina's look was full of judgment.

"I'm not certain there is an 'everything,' Marina."

"Oh, come now, Mutti. He must know something about what's going on."

"But we don't know what exactly *is* going on," Edith reminded her daughter. "All we know is what we hear, and none of that is particularly reliable."

"Still, what we do know is already pretty horrible. Innocent people being thrown out of their homes, sent to work camps . . ."

"Stop, Marina." Edith hit the table with the palm of her hand to interrupt. "This is not about Oskar. What the Führer does, what he requires his subordinates to do for him, none of that will change how I feel about your father. Because I love him unconditionally." Marina stared at her mother in silence, as if trying to understand such a love. "As for Franz," Edith continued, "remember that the two of you have built a family together, a family that means more to you than I think you understand. And if you leave now, if you are thinking of leaving, you know you would be leaving alone. Without the girls. There is no way they could come with you during wartime, and you would not risk their safety."

Marina appeared shocked at this suggestion. "No, of course not! You know I wouldn't do that. But . . ." She picked an intact walnut out of the pile in front of Edith and rolled it between her palms. "They may not need me as much as you think they do. They could survive without me for a time, couldn't they?" Now it was Edith's turn to look shocked. Before her mother could object, Marina backtracked. "In any case, it won't *always* be unsafe. The war has to end sometime."

"Yes, it does," Edith said, feeling relief wash over her. "And that is my point, dear. Wait. Don't make any decisions now. Wait until the war is over. And then . . ."

"And then?" Marina asked.

Unexpectedly, Edith felt her daughter's hope. Marina did not need Edith's approval or blessing for the things she did, as she'd made quite clear. But did she perhaps prefer having them to not having them? If so, Edith resolved to nurture that hope. "Marina, I don't want to see you married all your life to someone who doesn't make you happy. You wouldn't want that for your own girls either, would you? And Franz," Edith added, thinking of her son-in-law's quiet sensitivity. "He too deserves to be married to someone who wants to be married to him, who truly loves him. You do Franz no favors by staying in this marriage if you don't love him."

Marina stared at the wall behind the kitchen table where Edith had taped various artistic creations that Lara, Sofia, and Rosie had given her over the years: Lara's lion, its mane made of pasted bits of ribbons; Sofia's abstract study of shades of blue in various shapes; Rosie's drawing of a girl in a sailboat feeding a cookie to a shark. Suddenly she pushed back her chair and stood up. "I'm going to check on Rosie and Sofia," she said. "But I'll be right back to help."

"Take your time, I'll be here for a while," Edith said.

Marina paused in the doorway. "Do you really love Oskar that much?" Edith reached for one of the walnuts that she had crushed too violently earlier. She found herself in a more patient mood now, ready to pick out tiny bits of membrane and shell from its nutmeat.

"Yes, Marina. I really do."

– Nineteen –

Johann Wiessmeyer did not have many parishioners; only a small circle of citizens ever attended his Sunday-morning services at the Protestant church. But his job as spiritual shepherd reached beyond his tiny flock to the larger Blumental community. In furtherance of that role, he spent weekday mornings making social rounds about town, checking on residents who were unwell and calling upon anyone who had sought his ear the day before. By the time the lunch hour arrived, he was happy to return to the rectory he called home, where he routinely ate a modest meal alone, reviewing his morning activities and contemplating his obligations.

After lunch, Johann usually spent an hour or two in meditation and prayer. Today he felt particularly in need of that solitude. So many concerns vied for attention in his head—the impending arrival of the two refugees tomorrow morning, the complicating presence of Oskar Eberhardt, the potentially dangerous spy games of Max Fuchs, the questionable discretion of Fritz Nagel—but he had resolved to focus on only one this afternoon: the briefcase. Gottfried had given it to him before they parted in Berlin. He might never have to use it, Gottfried had said. There were other briefcases in other locations, for the Resistance never knew when or where an opportunity might present itself. "In the scheme of possible venues, your position on the Bodensee is fairly unlikely," he had reassured Johann. "But it is on the route from Fürchtesgaden back to Berlin, so it's not entirely out of the question."

Johann walked past the mossy headstones of the graveyard toward the church building. Opening its heavy oak door, he stepped into a long nave flanked by smooth walls of gray sandstone. Faintly colored light filtered through narrow glass windows, bathing the interior of the church in subdued shadows of cobalt blue and emerald green. Johann had fallen in love with this church the first time he laid eyes on it. It was so different from Birnau. Johann liked Birnau too, but his appreciation was grounded in amusement at Birnau's gold filigrees and chubby pink dancing babes. He found it hard to take religion seriously in the Catholic basilica, as if it were a kind of playground where God let off steam and enjoyed Himself. But this small church on the edge of the forest was different. It welcomed contemplation, inviting Johann to rest on its pale brown flotilla of wooden benches, rocking gently on waves of muted blue and green.

More often than not, the church was empty, which suited Johann. Today, a tall figure sat in the pews. A man, Johann saw as he came nearer, dressed in the gray woolen uniform of the German army, his head not bowed in prayer but staring straight forward, and so deep in thought that he didn't appear to notice the pastor approaching. "Are you seeking solitude, or may I join you?" Johann asked.

"Ah, well, my solitude is proving far too noisy," the man replied, tapping the side of his head in explanation and sliding to the left to make room on the bench. "I welcome some change in focus."

Taking a seat in the pew, Johann suddenly recognized the man as the general who had rescued Hans Munter the day before. What was his name? Wolf. "Excuse me, General Wolf," Johann began apologetically, again not wanting to intrude, "but I feel I must thank you on behalf of Blumental for your intervention with Captain Rodemann yesterday. We were all a bit paralyzed with fear, I believe, at the suddenness of the events that unfolded."

The general raised his right hand in dismissal. "No need to

thank me. Captain Rodemann lost sight of his responsibilities as an officer. Fortunately, I was there to correct him."

"His responsibilities as an officer?"

"Protection of the civilian population and adherence to the orders of superiors. He was commanded to secure the area against a possible invasion by the French, not to terrorize local inhabitants and exact vengeance for some perceived insult to his authority."

Johann nodded, impressed by the accuracy of this man's analysis of the incident. "Of course, he is very young, and it was perhaps more difficult for him to keep his emotions under control."

General Wolf shook his head emphatically. "No excuse. Captain Rodemann acted like a boy playing a game, with no understanding of the true consequences of killing someone."

The word *killing* echoed through the church and settled uneasily in Johann's heart. "And what do you understand to be the consequences of killing someone in wartime?"

The general seemed to consider the question carefully. He looked over to the windows, as if he might discern his response in the overlapping blue and green light shafts. "Early in the first war, the only way I could go into any battle was to dehumanize my opponent." He looked back to Johann. "You have to reach a mental state of indiscriminate shooting, you see. And I could only achieve that state by thinking of my targets as abstract entities armed with deadly weapons trained upon me and my comrades."

"So the moral consequences of killing . . . ?"

General Wolf let the unfinished question hang in the air before answering thoughtfully. "The *moral* consequences of killing, Father, don't really factor into battle. Not for me, at least not until after the fighting is over. And even then, if the sight of a field of corpses lying facedown in the mud transforms itself in your mind into a field of individual bodies, dead sons who will soon be mourned by grieving mothers and wives, young fathers who will never see their children grow to adulthood—well, then you have our great military code of loyalty and duty, which steps in to help you compartmentalize. If you've been ordered to kill the enemy, you are required to kill the enemy. You kill the enemy so that he can't kill you or your men." He stopped abruptly and turned his gaze back to the window. Johann decided not to say anything. He had clearly touched upon a subject that the general was wrestling with in some way. Strange that they should both be in similar positions. Or perhaps not, Johann thought. After all, there was a war going on. When the general turned back to Johann, he seemed to have arrived at some conclusion. "Necessity," he said.

"Necessity? I'm sorry, I don't follow."

"Necessity is an exception to the moral imperative against killing. 'Thou shalt not kill' is certainly a precept to be followed, unless killing is necessary. In wartime, unfortunately, it is."

"Ah." Johann had not expected the conversation to take this turn. When he first saw the general in the church, he was vexed that today of all days, there should be someone to distract him. But he was beginning to see that perhaps there was a reason for General Wolf's presence here.

"You don't agree, I suppose," General Wolf said. "The Church says the Ten Commandments are sacrosanct, and we are not to violate them under any circumstances, I imagine you'd say." Perhaps the general was not here to seek guidance. Perhaps he was, unwittingly, here to give it. Johann too looked over to the windows and watched the colors flowing through them. He had a strange and growing sensation of fullness in his lungs, as if he were breathing in something richer than oxygen.

The general was waiting for him to respond. "No," Johann began cautiously, trying to feel out his thoughts as he spoke. "No, I am not certain I would say that."

General Wolf looked surprised. "Really, Father? So you agree with me?"

There was a clarity to these colors floating toward Johann, and he tried to open his mind, to allow it in. He did not close his eyes.

He was being told to look. When he eventually spoke, he felt a certainty that he had not experienced in a long time. "What I am saying is this: We cannot follow the Ten Commandments simply because we are afraid of making a mistake. We cannot be afraid of incurring guilt for our behavior. Because to be human is to be imperfect." And there it was. The answer was completely visible before him. "To live freely, as a human being, it is impossible to avoid doing wrong. Of course!" Johann was amazed that he had not seen it before. "It is the redeeming mystery of Jesus Christ."

The general shook his head. "I'm afraid you've lost me, Father. How does Christ figure into this calculation?"

Johann turned to the general eagerly. "Because Christ was human. And therefore Christ could understand sin, *truly* understand it, because he felt the possibility of being sinful firsthand. Being human, Christ could feel the same guilt that we bear when we sin. Yet God allowed him to be redeemed nevertheless. Do you see?" General Wolf's face showed that he did not. Johann tried again. "God chose to make himself human through Christ to show us that there could be redemption in sin, that guilt is a necessary aspect of being human."

"So we might violate the Ten Commandments and still be close to God? Closer to God than we were before?" The general smiled. "That will make a lot of criminals and sinners very happy."

Johann shook his head emphatically. "No, no, it is not a blanket invitation for wrongdoing. The underlying motive must be well-intentioned, there must be a desire for responsible action. I am only recognizing that, in certain situations . . ." Like the one he was facing. Suddenly Johann knew.

The general prodded him on. "Yes? In certain situations?"

"Responsible action must include a readiness to accept guilt. In some situations, if we wish to live responsibly and fully, we must be willing to incur the guilt that arises out of our wrongdoing."

"And killing someone could be one of those situations?"

The church door was pushed open suddenly and loudly. General Wolf and Johann both looked back to see Max Fuchs trotting up the aisle with a pair of brown envelopes.

"Pastor Johann! Pastor Johann!" he called. "I'm so glad I found you. An urgent telegram for you. From Berlin!"

"Well, well," Johann said. "Come, Max, sit, you look like you need a rest." As he patted the bench he had been sitting on, he noticed General Wolf looking at him with some astonishment.

"Ah! Of course—you are Johann Wiessmeyer. Of course," Erich repeated.

"I'm sorry, General, I should have introduced myself earlier."

"No, it's quite all right, I should have known it was you." The general shook his head. "I have heard so much about you, you see." To the pastor's quizzical look, he replied, "Marina Thiessen thinks very highly of you."

"Ah, Marina . . ." Johann's voice trailed off.

Max Fuchs had been leaning against the church pew, panting heavily. He glanced at the envelopes he was carrying and thrust one of them at Johann. "Here you go, sir, that one's for you," he said. Then he reached into his back pocket and pulled out a folded piece of paper. "And this too, this was just given to me by—" Max looked at General Wolf and leaned forward to whisper in Johann's ear. "This is a private message for you, Pastor, from Frau Thiessen. She asked me to bring it to you as soon as possible."

Johann opened the folded paper, recognized Marina's handwriting, and closed it again without reading it. He slipped it into his shirt pocket. The telegram rested precariously on his lap, unbalanced. "Sit, Max. Your breathing is making me feel winded."

"But I can't. I can't stop right now. Frau Schenk told me I couldn't stop until both telegrams were delivered. I have to find General Wolf right away." The boy was waving a second brown envelope in the air. The general raised his hand in the air.

"I'm General Wolf, young man," he said. "You can indeed rest now, your job is done."

"Oh, that's lucky!" Max happily handed over the second telegram. Then he jumped to attention. "But I'm not tired at all. I
could run another ten kilometers if I had to."

"I'm quite certain you could," the general said. He searched his
pocket for a coin, and finding one with enough size and weight
not to be an insult, he gave it to Max. Max examined the coin
carefully, a smile spreading across his face.

"Thank you, General!" Before either man could engage him
in further conversation, Max turned and ran toward the exit.
"Thank you too, Pastor Johann!"

"I'm not sure what I did to deserve thanks," Johann said as
the oak door swung closed behind Max. "Other than to keep you
here in conversation and facilitate the most efficient delivery of
his telegrams."

"Well, I was very grateful for the conversation," the general
said somewhat absentmindedly. He ran a finger along the edge
of the envelope and stared at his name, carefully written in el-
egant cursive. Putting the envelope in his coat pocket, he stood.
"I should be going now. I have some matters to organize, and I
should leave you to your news from Berlin."

"It was a pleasure sitting with you, General. If you don't mind,
I will let you see yourself out," Johann said, taking a seat on the
bench again. He watched General Wolf head down the narrow
nave. The church had grown silent and gray as clouds outside
cloaked the sun. Once the general had left, Johann placed his
own telegram flat in the palms of his hands, as if by feeling its
weight he could divine its content. A telegram from Berlin could
mean only one thing: an opportunity to use the briefcase. Was
he ready to take this step? Johann took a deep breath and ripped
open the envelope.

– Twenty –

Before the war, trains had passed through Blumental regularly, but the war had reduced their frequency. Now there was one in the morning for passengers, one in midafternoon for mail, and a final one at midnight for freight. So after the four o'clock train there was absolutely no danger in walking along the tracks that ran from west Blumental, where Max had delivered his last telegram, to east Blumental, where Lara lived.

Max's mother had forbidden him to walk along the rails, but Max felt no remorse in ignoring this prohibition. His mother was always imposing unnecessary restraints on his life. Differentiating between the valid and invalid demands she made was, Max felt, part of growing up. Thus his conscience was entirely clear as he alternately strode and hopped from one rail tie to the next, occasionally stopping to examine the grass between the iron rails when he thought he saw something glint in the early-evening sun. You never knew where you might find a spent artillery casing or cartridge shell, or, even better, a grenade safety pin. All of these were valuable in the Meerfeld and Blumental community of boys, who jockeyed for recognition and influence in a world where military distinction was paramount. Since, in their minds, they had been cruelly excluded from the war arena, these boys eagerly collected any remnants affiliated with combat and channeled all their frustrated military fervor into the parade and trade of these items. Max was collecting grenade pins and rings, which were far more difficult to find than artillery or mortar shell casings, as they were smaller and thinner and more easily hidden on the ground when they fell. So far this summer, he had gathered eighteen, all of them rings from German M39s that he had found on or near the train tracks, where Rodemann and his men had practiced military maneuvers. Two weeks ago, he had traded ten of his M39 rings for four of Freddi Klein's Soviet RG42 rings, which were copper-colored. When Max saw how nicely the RG42s shone when polished, he went back to Freddi for one more, but Freddi, sensing his advantage, had demanded an unreasonable four M39s in exchange. Max was irate, but ultimately he was going to have little choice if he wanted the necklace he was making to be symmetrical. Five gray M39s interspersed with five sparkly copper RG42s; the combination would look perfect on Lara's porcelain skin.

From the length of his shadow strolling ahead of him along the tracks, Max knew it was getting close to dinnertime. Passing the deserted East Blumental station, he calculated that he had just enough time to check for spies and still be able to make a quick stop at the Eberhardt property if he jogged the rest of the way. Max scrambled down the embankment toward the station building, scattering pebbles. Keeping his head low, he crawled through the dirt on his stomach to the cement building. It would have been faster to run, but what if today there really *was* a spy watching through the window? They had never had a spy in Blumental, but there were all sorts of stories about Allied spies up north, and one or two spies, perhaps French or, better yet, Russian, may have drifted south.

The window that Max approached was easily accessible now that the boulder was in place. Standing on top of his rock, he placed his fingers on the windowsill, then slowly pulled his head up just far enough to look through the glass. The room inside was shadowed, save for the space around the opposite window, which was illuminated by the crouching sun. One end of the room was spanned by three long wooden benches, wide enough to accommodate a sleeping body, if a spy decided to spend the night. But the benches were empty in the settling darkness, no one visible on or beneath them. Max quickly scanned the room, his gaze sweeping past the stained yellow train schedule, the unoccupied ticket counter with its shutters, the open doors of the vacant baggage lockers. Nothing. Nobody. He was only mildly disappointed, jumping off the rock and starting back to the tracks at a trot. He wouldn't have had time to discover a spy today, not if he wanted to stop by Lara's house before dinner. Five minutes later, panting slightly, Max saw the curved clay roof tiles of the Eberhardt home and the large chestnut tree he was aiming for. Skilled climber that he was, Max had no trouble finding footholds in the tree's massive, deeply ridged trunk. He pulled himself up through the thicket of branches to his favorite perch. The dense foliage on this limb was perfect camouflage, and the spot offered a good, if obstructed, view of the bedroom that Lara shared with her sisters and mother.

The door of the closet near the bedroom window stood ajar. Two dresses were slung over the top edge. That was Lara's closet, Max knew from prior visits to the tree. The other one was shared by Sofia and Rosie. Lara was standing in front of the half mirror that was nailed to the inside of the closet door, wearing a third dress and swinging its skirt back and forth while watching herself from different angles. When she stopped briefly, her back was to Max and he saw—with great delight, some fear, and a skip of his heart—that the dress was unzipped. He had a view of a part of Lara's body that he had never seen before, from her shoulder blades to her midback. It took his breath away. This path of skin and flesh—beautiful, smooth, creamy white, unblemished, pure—epitomized everything Lara was for Max. He knew he should avert his gaze, but he couldn't. He longed to reach forward and touch that skin, stroke it, feel its warmth. He didn't want to kiss it—that was too strange a concept—but he did want to make contact with it. Unconsciously, Max leaned forward, and because of that slight shift, he almost fell out of the tree when Lara did what she did next.

She took off the dress. Lara simply brushed the sleeves off her shoulders, let the dress fall to the floor, and stepped out of it. Shocked, Max inhaled sharply and grabbed on to a nearby branch for support. His heart sped up and his palms began to sweat. It was too much—the camisole, the glimpse of corset, the hint of some other cotton eyelet-trimmed garment beneath the half-slip. Max shut his eyes. He hadn't expected this, wasn't ready for it, but he opened his eyes again and looked, more insistently this time, without shame. She was so beautiful. She was like a dream. She was— "Max Fuchs!" a voice boomed from below. "Are you look-ing for chestnuts?"

Startled, Max scrambled farther back into the surrounding fo-liage. A flutter of leaves rained down on the face of Oskar Eber-hardt. Lara's opa. Max had delivered a telegram to him once, and to his great surprise, Herr Eberhardt had given him a tip, a silver five-mark coin, a unique gift because of the eagle on the back of it. On every other five-mark coin Max had ever seen, the eagle held a wreath inscribed with a swastika in its talons, but on this coin, the eagle had its talons outstretched, free of that burden. Initially, Max was not sure whether the coin was real money, but even if it was, its difference made it too special to use, and he hid it in his sock drawer. Max was in awe of Oskar Eberhardt. Not because he was Lara's opa—a fact he found difficult to believe because Herr Eberhardt was so very unlike Max's own opa, who was stout and grizzled and constantly napping. Herr Eberhardt, by contrast, was tall, had a carefully trimmed mustache, and seemed always to be wearing a three-piece tweed suit. It was impossible to imagine him taking a nap. More impressively, Herr Eberhardt lived in Berlin, and his work was essential to the Third Reich, ac-cording to Max's mother. Max wanted to ask Lara what "essential to the Third Reich" meant, but in two years, he had yet to build up the courage. Nobody in Max's circle of friends knew precisely what Herr Eberhardt did, but they knew he worked directly with the Führer, and that made him a figure of reverence and fear.

"Well, young man?" Herr Eberhardt called again. "Come on down, chestnuts won't be ripe for some time." He waved at Max and pointed to the ground. Max had no choice. After creeping backward along his branch, he reached the trunk and shimmied down, then reluctantly shuffled over to where Herr Eberhardt was waiting for him. "So, Max," the man said. He opened his jacket and reached into the inside pocket for his pipe and a small silver lighter. Finding them, he took a moment to light the tobacco; then he took several deep puffs on the pipe, relit it, and settled into a more contemplative smoking rhythm, all while looking down at the top of Max's head. Max felt he should say something, apologize, though he did not know what Herr Eberhardt had seen, whether he knew Max was there to gaze at Lara, knew what Max had seen through the window. If he didn't know, then surely it would be better if Max just kept quiet. Because what was wrong with Max sitting in the chestnut tree? Well, technically, Max was trespassing, but nobody in Blumental took that seriously, except Herr Weber. Boys were constantly climbing trees all over the place. It was expected. Still, Herr Eberhardt was from Berlin, and he worked for the Führer. It might be prudent to say something about the trespassing.

Max took a deep breath and then spewed forth his apology. "I'm so sorry, Herr Eberhardt, I didn't mean to trespass on your property. I mean, I did mean to, because I was in your tree and I knew it was your tree, but what I mean is, I didn't mean to *trespass* because, well, everybody does it, climb trees, that is, especially if they're big and their branches are good, as your tree is, sir. You have a most excellent climbing tree. The branches are spaced just right. Do you do that yourself in the spring, sir? Because I know how to prune trees, my opa showed me once, and I could help if you need someone—"

"No, thank you," Herr Eberhardt interrupted. "We are well situated on the tree-trimming front." He sucked deeply on his pipe, and as Max looked on in awe, blew a series of smoke rings into the air. The two watched the rings expand and rise in silence. "So," Herr Eberhardt spoke again. "I was a boy once, you know." Max didn't say anything. Herr Eberhardt's statement seemed both obvious and impossible. "I used to love climbing trees, so I know what you mean about a good climbing tree. And believe me, I understand the attraction of this chestnut. *All* of the attractions of this chestnut." He looked closely at Max. Expecting an expression of harsh rebuke, Max was startled to find compassion in the older man's gaze. "I'm not telling you to stay away from the chestnut, Max. I'm asking you to be respectful. You must be careful in this chestnut tree. There is a line somewhere up in those leaves and branches, a line that separates admiration and adoration from violation. Beware of that line, Max." He took the pipe out of his mouth, looked into the bowl, and frowned. "Damn Italian pipe, just can't get used to it." He relit the tobacco. "English pipes, Max," he said, starting again to puff on the stem. "English pipes, if you ever take up tobacco, are the gold standard."

"Yes, sir," Max answered.

"Right. And on this matter of the chestnut tree, you understand me, don't you?" Herr Eberhardt asked.

"Yes, sir, I do," Max said, though he was not entirely certain he did.

"Good," Herr Eberhardt said. He stepped forward and put his hand on Max's shoulder. "Well, then, you should be getting home for dinner, shouldn't you? Your mother will be worried."

"Yes, sir, thank you, sir." Max turned and began trotting back to the train embankment. He felt lucky, like he had come close to something exciting but dangerous and had been spared the encounter. Herr Eberhardt was not what he had expected; he was neither terrifying nor ferocious. Max found it difficult to reconcile his experience of this kind, grandfatherly gentleman with the image of an angry, intimidating Führer he saw in newspapers. In Max's world, everyone was what he appeared and was expected to be. Max's father was a soldier, strong and brave and protective of his family, or at least that's how Max remembered him. And Max's mother was what a mother should be, a good cook and housekeeper who doled out love and discipline in equal measure. Max's friends were loyal and occasionally annoying but always ready for adventure, as friends should be. This possibility that Herr Eberhardt had just presented—that people might not actually be what Max thought they were—well, it was unexpected and strange. He would have to think on the question some more after dinner, when his grumbling stomach did not distract him.

Max followed the train tracks for another half kilometer before turning onto Himmelstrasse. The narrow, winding street marked the eastern limit of residential settlement in Blumental, and as Max headed up a hill that plateaued before the Birnau forest, he looked quickly to his right to see if Fritz Nagel might be out working. Max could see Fritz's tractors parked just outside the entrance to the hayloft, and beyond the barn doors stood the large Volvo truck with its hood open. Fritz's thick torso swelled over the engine block, and Max heard the clangs of a hammer on steel as he ran over. "Hey, Fritz," he called. "How's Pinocchio? Can I try it out yet?"

A loud thud and a flurry of curses issued from the hood. "Who is that?" Fritz grumbled, pulling his head out of the steel automotive cave. "Is that Max?" A face smeared with engine oil glared at Max. "Have I not told you to hush about this? You pepper me with questions about the truck day after day and I finally tell you, but under oath, remember, Max? You *swore* you would not talk about the truck."

"I swore I wouldn't tell *anyone else* about the truck," Max said, his voice breaking slightly with confusion, apology, and righteous indignation. "You never said I couldn't talk to *you* about it anymore."

Fritz growled and stood up straight, dropping the hammer into the dirt and wiping his palms forcefully against his upper thighs. "So now you're a wordsmith?"

Max stepped past Fritz's towering bulk and, climbing onto the truck's runner, peered into the open hood. The scent of diesel fuel and motor oil swept into his nostrils as he canvassed the engine block and the tunnel of space surrounding it. It looked cavernous. "Wow!" Max exhaled in wonder. "That's a lot of room! You could probably fit a lot of extra cargo in here, Fritz. Like bags of potatoes and cabbages. *Big* bags, I mean, if you wanted to hide them from customs."

"*Ja, ja,* that's the plan," Fritz said, striding over and lifting Max up and out of the hood by his waistband. He slammed the truck hood shut. "Too many greedy *schweinehunde* in Switzerland, damn those customs officers."

"And what the *schweinehunde* don't see won't hurt them," Max announced, repeating one of Fritz's favorite phrases.

"More importantly, what they don't see won't hurt *me,*" Fritz added. He pummeled Max about the shoulders playfully. "So have you eaten? Or should we go inside and see what's for dinner?"

"No thanks, my mom is expecting me," Max said. "But can I come back again and play inside Pinocchio?"

Fritz frowned. "Not in the next few days, Max, I promised Jo—" Fritz checked himself and cleared his throat. "I'll be busy with some transports to the south. But if you stop by early next week, Pinocchio might be free." Fritz bent down and glared intently into Max's eyes. "In the meantime, not a word about this to *anyone.* Right?"

"Right." Max nodded. "Don't worry, Fritz, I'd never say anything that might get you into trouble."

"Well, you might not know what sorts of things would get me into trouble, so the best thing is just not to say anything, okay?"

"Okay. Don't worry." Waving his right arm through the air in farewell as he ran, Max headed back up the Himmelstrasse hill. His home was not far now. He could see his mother's clothesline swaying in the light evening breeze, his own trousers gently kicking themselves dry between two checkered dish towels. Beneath the drying laundry, his dachshund rested his gray muzzle on a towel that had fallen into the dirt. When Max lifted the metal latch of the front gate, its slow squeal recalled some long-abandoned responsibility in the dog's memory to alert and defend, and, barking weakly at a dream rabbit to stay put, Puck raised himself and wagged himself over to Max.

The front door to the house, Max noticed, stood ajar, and someone had left a basket of bread on the threshold. "So, Puck, who's visiting today?" he asked, giving the dog's speckled ears a quick scratch before heading to the front entrance. Too late, Max knew the answer, for her high-pitched laugh pierced his eardrums as her round stomach plowed through the doorway and pinned him against the house wall.

"Oh, Max!" Sabine Mecklen cried in surprise. "Just the boy I was looking for, right, Katrine?" Max's mother, following a step or two behind her, acknowledged this with a silent nod. "Yes, Max, it is so good that you arrived! Your mother told me she didn't know where you were. Really, you ought not to worry her like that, Max. She has enough to do without worrying about you. Having to raise you all alone while your father is away, not that she's the *only* mother who has to do that, God knows there are plenty in this town, and everywhere, really. But that doesn't make the job easy, does it, Katrine?" Because Sabine's question was rhetorical, she did not have to look at Max's mother for an answer, so only Max noticed his mother rolling her eyes in response.

Max tried to listen to Fräulein Mecklen, because he knew it was polite to listen to grown-ups, even if you did not like them, but somehow his ears instinctively closed off to her voice after about thirty seconds, which allowed his brain to travel elsewhere. So he was just going back to the problem of how he might get that copper RG42 out of Freddi Klein for a reasonable trade when Fräulein Mecklen poked her finger in his face. "Yes, Max,

you," she said. She tried to bend toward him, in a gesture perhaps of camaraderie or of authority, but leaning her head over
her torso unexpectedly compromised her balance, so she quickly
righted herself. Max's mother covered her mouth with her right
hand, her eyes twinkling. "I am here to ask you for a favor, a
big favor. Well, actually it's quite a small thing, and something
I'll pay you for, of course, since you are a messenger and you get
paid for that, don't you? No, no, Katrine, don't object, there's
no question, absolutely *no question* that Max should be paid."
Max did not see what Fräulein Mecklen was fussing about, since
as far as he could tell, his mother had made no move to object.
"After all, I am proposing to utilize your services like Ludmilla
does, and *she* pays you. As she should, though I would need you
to deliver the message tonight. That's possible, isn't it, Katrine?"
Fräulein Mecklen turned to Max's mother. "He doesn't have to
do it before dinner, but it does need to get to Pastor Wiessmeyer
before tomorrow—I mean, the poor man needs a *little* notice.
What if he wants to dress up a bit? Or otherwise prepare? Not
that I would expect him to prepare anything, of course not, what
could he have to prepare? A simple after-dinner tea, that's all.
Perhaps a pastry or two for dessert."

Max looked at his mother, confused.

"Fräulein Mecklen would like you to deliver an invitation to
Pastor Wiessmeyer, Max," his mother explained, giving Max her
stern *keep quiet* look. "I told her you'd be happy to run over to the
rectory tonight, after dinner, and that you would do it as a favor to
a good and kind neighbor." Max frowned. He'd just been at Pastor
Johann's church! Obediently, however, he said nothing.

Sabine smiled and looked around for her basket. Noticing it
on the doorstep, she reached for it and put her hand on her lower
back, emitting a small "*Oof!*" of effort. Max's mother quickly bent
down and retrieved the basket, from which Sabine, after much
fumbling and fussing with rolls and a flowered dish towel, pro-
duced a perfumed cream-colored envelope and handed it to Max.

The scent of rosewater was overpowering, and Max had to hold the envelope at arm's length to keep from coughing. He sucked in his lips and cheeks, trying to tighten his nostrils, to close them. The note felt slightly damp, and he wondered whether Fräulein Mecklen had soaked the paper in a bath of eau de cologne. "Well, that's done, then," Sabine said, apparently satisfied. "You will be sure to deliver it tonight, won't you, Max?" Max tried to move around her right side to escape into the house and rid himself of the offensive note. He hoped its redolence would evaporate before he had to deliver it. Was one dinner hour enough time? Max doubted it.

"He'll do it tonight," Max's mother said, putting a firm hand on Max's shoulder and pinning him between the two women. "Won't you, Max?" Now Max had no choice but to speak, if he wanted to get away. He wondered if he could do so without breathing in.

"*Hja*, Fräuleid, I'd do id," Max gasped, then squirmed through the doorway. Still holding his breath, he threw the note onto the hallway table and ran upstairs to the bathroom, where he exhaled thoroughly before splashing cold water on his face. He grabbed the towel hanging on the wall and buried his nose in its wind-hardened cotton pile, inhaling deeply, trying to cleanse his nose hairs of the lingering sickly sweet residue. He was relieved to hear Fräulein Mecklen taking her leave.

"Boys will be boys, I suppose. I don't know how you do it, Katrine. Oh, before I go, do please take these rolls. They are just day-old, practically fresh, and I took the time to reheat them before turning off the oven when I left. You can have them with dinner."

"That's very kind, Sabine, thank you," Max heard his mother say. "Max will be pleased." But Max only liked the white *brötchen* the Mecklens made. The rye flour ones were awful. Going downstairs, Max entered the kitchen, where his mother was dishing out lentil soup for the two of them. He took a seat at the small table.

"Well, what were you up to today?" she asked, handing him his cloth napkin while he grabbed his spoon. "Did you hear any good gossip from town?"

"Mmph, nope," Max mumbled through slurps of soup. "Not really. But there were two telegrams from Berlin today. *And*—"

"From Berlin?" Max's mother interrupted.

"—Captain Rodemann is back!"

"What? Why?"

"I don't know," Max said. "But there were lots of jeeps and trucks going in and out of the Weber property tonight. Lots of soldiers, and storm troopers too, I could see it all from the train tracks." The moment he said it, Max was sorry.

"Max, did you go over to Lara's house again today? Is that why you're late for dinner?" His mother was gentle in her chiding.

"No," Max started, then gave in to her tilted head and knowing look. "Well, yes, but only to see if she was in the yard, and she wasn't." Boy, he would make a terrible spy, he thought. Wasn't the first lesson not to reveal incriminating evidence? Or was that for detectives?

"I'm not going to tell you to stay away from her, Max, because that would be pointless," his mother said, offering him one of Sabine's *brötchen*, which he was happy to see was white, not rye. "The heart goes where it wants to go, and nothing can stop it. But I do want you to be respectful of the Eberhardts, is that understood?"

"Yes, Mutti." Max was about to bite into the *brötchen* he had taken, but just when it was in front of his mouth, he smelled it, and the rosewater mixed with yeast invaded his nose as surely as if Fräulein Mecklen had stuck her forefinger in his nostril. He dropped the bread and stood up suddenly. "Can I go now?"

"The dishes, Max," his mother reminded him.

Max was already in the hallway, wrapping the repulsive envelope in layers of old newspaper to suppress its stench. "I'll do them when I get home!" He stuffed the package in the back of his waistband and ran out the door.

– Twenty-One –

Marina didn't often smoke cigarettes, but tonight she felt the need for one. Something that would make her breathe in deeply, rhythmically, calm herself down. Because in the past twenty-four hours, her mind had become overwhelmed with questions. Where would she and Johann hide their Polish family until Fritz's truck was ready? Meerfeld was no longer an option, given all the security precautions near the Weber estate and beyond. Storm troopers in black boots and red armbands were buzzing around the lakefront road between Meerfeld and Blumental. She wouldn't want to steer a pair of nervous refugees through those hornets. Thankfully, Marina had almost tripped over Max Fuchs this afternoon, when she walked up to the house after looking for Oskar and Sofia. She had written a quick note to Johann, and Max agreed to deliver it immediately. Hopefully, Johann would be able to meet her tomorrow morning before he went to pick up his charges. In the meantime, all she could do was wait. Wait for Johann tomorrow and for Erich tonight.

Marina decided to smoke in the arbor, where she couldn't be seen from the house. The arbor had originally been intended as a venue for afternoon coffee. Summer weekends, as Edith had imagined them before the war, would be filled with visits from Berlin friends, who would bring their children. They would spend mornings exploring the lake, perhaps wandering the kaleidoscopic gardens of Insel Hagentau or peering down into the

seventh-century dungeon of the old castle in Seeburg. Then
they'd gather at the house for a grand midday meal and a post-
prandial rest. In the afternoons, an avalanche of children would
cascade down the hill after naptime, ready to splash and paddle
in the lake, no matter how cold the water. Of course, the parents
would need some sort of refuge, some hidden oasis of peace and
quiet where they could sip their coffee at leisure, so that first summer in Blumental, Edith had asked Oskar to construct a simple
lattice above the arbor, over which grape vines could spread their
shade and protect women from the sun's freckling powers. Where
women sought refuge, Edith knew, men would soon follow. She
purchased a wrought-iron table and a set of chairs and yards of
colorful fabric from which she began to sew a platoon of pillows
to complement her pansies. As a surprise to Edith, Oskar had enlisted the help of a local plumber, who installed a small well and
fountain. Oskar presented it to his wife on the eve of their thirti-
eth wedding anniversary, wrapping a dish towel around her eyes
and leading her into the garden, where a thin stream of water
trickled from an open faucet into a marble basin. Marina could
not resist following them to observe the grand unveiling. "Now,
you'll need to choose a statue to complete this," Oskar had said,
taking the blindfold off.

"Oh, Oskar!" Edith had beamed. She'd bent toward the small
pool of water, resting one hand on its lightly rippling surface. "It's
so lovely."

"I wasn't sure what kind of statue you might want, my dear,"
Oskar elaborated. "There are so many to choose from—fish and
frogs, bears and lions, elephants, if you like. Angels of all kinds.
Even Greek gods and goddesses."

"Daphne?" Edith turned her head.

When Oskar looked confused, Marina explained, "The wood
nymph who bewitched Apollo."

"Ach, 'bewitched'!" Edith interjected. "She narrowly escaped
being raped by that lout."

"Lout?" Oskar mused. "Wasn't Apollo a god?"

"God of the sun," Marina said.

"Seems to me like she might have felt honored by his attentions."

"Really, Oskar?" Edith turned to face him. "That solar Casanova? He just wanted another notch on his Olympian sash. And she wasn't about to give up her virginity for anything less than true and lasting love. So her father turned her into a laurel tree."

"Hmm," Oskar said. "Seems like a drastic solution."

Edith ignored his sarcasm. "She's the original earth mother. Human maternal instincts merged with arboreal sensitivities."

Eventually, Edith did manage to find a statue of Daphne, but because of the war, her dreams of afternoon coffee gatherings never materialized. The grapevines grew unimpeded and over the years formed a dense mass of leaves and branches, as did the hazelnut bushes that Edith planted along the arbor's perimeters. On warm summer nights such as this one, the moisture from the fountain created a perfectly humidified playground for fireflies, and a small band of them were now flitting around Daphne's outstretched arms.

Marina sat down on the pillow-upholstered bench tucked into the hazelnuts. She patted the pillows and leaned back, closing her eyes and trying to let the sound of the running water soothe her. Was it her mind that needed quieting or her heart? Both. She felt fidgety and crossed her legs, right over left, then left over right. She took a cigarette out of the silver case she kept in her skirt pocket, lit it, and inhaled. Much better, she thought, feeling her shoulder blades relax and drop. Her exhalation was long and slow. She watched the smoke curl upward, a soft gray ribbon spiraling into the still air. Away from her current world, where families fled from machine guns and mayors were terrorized, where sanity and order depended on the fortuitous arrival of an army general. Would Erich's appearance in her life always be sudden and unexpected? Would she always have to let him go and wait for him to return, without any certainty as to when, or if, he would come back? The words her mother had spoken in the kitchen earlier weighed heavily on Marina. Edith had asked her to wait, without acknowledging that Marina had been doing just that ever since the war began. She was tired of waiting. Wasn't she allowed, for once, to make the choice *she* wanted?

But she didn't want to leave her girls behind. That, of course, was what made the choice so unthinkable. And Franz—where was Franz at this moment? She thought of his gentle blue eyes, now distant and lost, their blue haunted by dark shadows like a sea beset by tempests. These were not the eyes that she had met in Grosswald, not the eyes that had taken her in with such appreciation the night they went to see *The Blue Angel*.

Marina took another drag of her cigarette, thinking back on that night, which was, in so many ways, fateful. The movie had not been their first date. They had imbibed countless cups of coffee together and attended several matinee films. Franz would have continued taking Marina out for afternoon coffee indefinitely had she not insisted on an evening rendezvous. Franz in the daytime was just the tiniest bit dull, and Marina had hoped that the mystery of nighttime might draw out a wilder side of him.

She remembered him watching her come down the stairs that night, remembered feeling his discomfort as he stood there in the living room with Oskar, even as he savored her appearance. Marina had chosen not to wear a dress but rather a flowered silk blouse and an ivory linen skirt that she had hemmed just that afternoon so that it showed off her calves to better effect, which didn't escape Franz's notice. He was the perfect gentleman, standing up quickly the moment she entered the room, staring at her with awe. Oskar rose too, more slowly but equally cognizant of his daughter's beauty. "You look almost too lovely to release upon the world outside that front door, my dear," Oskar said, winking. He glanced at Franz. "Are you prepared, young man, to facilitate the assimilation of my daughter into the society of Philistines out there? To smooth the passage of her beauty through their pockets of pollution? To defend her virtue against all physical and moral onslaught?"

Franz looked confused. In his distress, he turned his gaze to the chenille pillows on the sofa and studied them. Marina stepped forward and grabbed Franz by the hand. "Vati, please. Enough with the speeches. We'll be back by midnight." She steered Franz toward the front entrance.

Oskar held up two fingers. "Eleven o'clock, please, no later than eleven. Not," he said, cutting off Marina's protest, "because you are too young to stay out later—though in my opinion you are, your mother has convinced me to relent—but because it is safer. Berlin is far too restless these days. Can we agree on this?"

"I'll have her back precisely at eleven o'clock, sir, if not before," Franz said eagerly. He helped Marina with her coat, then offered her the crook of his left arm as Oskar held the door open for them.

The night had been crisp and clear, ideal for walking. There was still plenty of time before the movie, so they decided to forgo a cab and stroll over to the theater. As they headed toward Unter den Linden, the city's cultural boulevard, Marina caught sight of the moon, a glowing pale globe rising above the horizon. She stopped and grabbed hold of Franz's arm. "Look at the moon, Franz!"

Franz followed her gaze and smiled. "Ah, the moon illusion. Fascinating, isn't it? I love the way our brains can trick us." Marina had expected some sort of appreciative murmur about the moon's size or color. She had even dared to hope for a snippet of poetry praising the moon's general appearance. But this response took her completely by surprise.

"The moon illusion?" she repeated.

"Yes, the way we think the moon is bigger when it's coming up on the horizon than when it's directly overhead, that's what I mean," Franz explained. Marina recognized the musing tilt of his head that meant he was about to lapse into science-teacher mode. She was not in the mood for a lesson but didn't know how to stop him without appearing rude. "Tell me," he continued, eager to make the point, "don't you think the moon looks bigger at this moment? Bigger than the last time you saw it in the sky?"

"Of course," Marina said. "It's *huge*."

Franz pressed on. "Why do you think it looks bigger now?"

"Well," Marina said carefully, "I don't *really* know, but I imagine it might have something to do with distortion from the atmosphere, maybe. Or the distance to the horizon as opposed to the distance to outer space."

"No. And kind of." Franz was pleased that the way was open for further instruction. "The moon isn't really any larger now than when it's overhead later at night, it's just our brains that make us think so. It's because we think of the sky as having the shape of a hemisphere above us, but we *perceive* it differently, as a flattened bowl." Franz stopped, evidently satisfied with his explanation, and nodded to himself. They turned onto the grand boulevard, its daytime buzz of shoppers and office workers replaced with nighttime activity. In front of the State Opera house, cabs lined up, discharging passengers for an evening performance.

Marina did not really care about Franz's moon illusion, nor why it existed. She cared about the moon's beauty, inscrutability, romance; about the emotions the moon stirred within her, a complex mixture of passion and fear, desire and loss. But this precise, methodical analysis ignored all of those feelings. She was becoming irritated, and distracted herself by looking over to the opera house to see what was playing.

A nearby poster announced the current performance: THE MAGIC FLUTE: PLAYING TONIGHT! Marina sighed. She loved this Mozart piece. It was the first opera she'd ever been to—ages ago, it seemed, when she was ten. Oskar bought tickets for the family, and Erich introduced her to the music weeks beforehand, explaining the story and outlining the characters. Tamino, the

noble prince. Pamina, the beautiful princess. Sarastro, the sor-
cerer whose goodness is hidden, and the Queen of the Night, who
masks her evil. Best was Papageno, the bird-clown who celebrates
life. Marina remembered Papageno as he appeared onstage, be-
decked in vibrant, multicolored feathers that fluttered loose
from him as he flapped and sang his way around the set. She had
laughed uproariously at his antics. At the end of the performance,
Erich had gone up to the stage and retrieved for Marina one perfect, bright turquoise plume.

Now Marina looked across the boulevard to the opera house,
where women in long gowns were ascending the stone staircases,
pursued by men in tuxedos and dark suits. Bright, colorful banners
hung suspended between the marble columns, and the illuminated
entranceway beckoned everyone over. Suddenly, she caught her
breath. There, going up the steps at the right side of the building—
was that Erich? She squinted her eyes to focus more closely. The
man turned to offer his arm to a woman just one step below him,
and Marina saw his face in the reflected light. It *was* Erich. But
who was he with? All Marina could see was the woman's long dark
hair and her emerald skirt sweeping the ground. The woman put
her hand on Erich's forearm and they disappeared behind a banner
advertising *Der Rosenkavalier*, an upcoming attraction.

Marina felt numb. She had never before seen Erich with a
woman, and the sight unnerved her. She chided herself for the
reaction. It was perfectly natural that Erich should invite a
woman to the opera, and if he was looking for female companion-
ship, he might as well ask a woman who was attractive, as this
woman appeared to be, at least from a distance. She wondered
who the woman was and how they knew each other. At the Military Academy, Erich would not have had occasion to meet many
women, would he? Marina imagined that there were women who
frequented the sidewalks outside the academy, predators waiting
to catch an unsuspecting officer with a good salary. Probably this
woman belonged in that category. But why would Erich take her

to this opera, *their* opera? If he really wanted to see this performance, he could have invited Marina. She would have been more than happy to go on a date with him. But Erich would not think of her as a date. She was likely still a child in his eyes. Marina bit her lip in frustration and anger. She felt betrayed.

"Two, please," Franz said to the woman in the ticket booth at the movie house. Marina pulled out the elastic band holding her hair and shook it free. She wasn't a child. She took Franz's hand as they entered the darkened theater. Franz headed toward the front, but she steered him to the back row. "Tonight," she whispered, "I want more privacy."

In the arbor, Marina exhaled another cloud of smoke at a cluster of fireflies. One day she would have to see *The Blue Angel* again. The first talking movie she had ever seen, yet she remembered very little of it, just snippets. The maid tossing a dead canary into the furnace ("It stopped singing long ago"), Marlene Dietrich dropping her bloomers from the top of a staircase onto Professor Rath's shoulder. At the same time, Marina had been taking off her own panties and, emboldened by the certainty of her outrage and hurt, she had undone Franz's trousers.

Some people might have seen her behavior as reckless. They would also have considered Lara's arrival nine months later just penance for Marina and Franz's indiscretion. Thankfully, Edith was not among this group. Instead, when Marina confirmed her mother's suspicions about her sudden inability to tolerate breakfast, Edith was too pragmatic to engage in recrimination and despair. What was done was done, and Edith jumped straight to wedding preparations. She saw no reason to inform Oskar, who was preoccupied with the country's looming economic collapse, about the precipitating event in their daughter's change of status. As for Franz, he didn't hesitate in doing the right thing, for responsibility and propriety were embedded in him, and he loved Marina. Franz told her on their wedding night that he'd never dreamed he would be lucky enough to have her as his wife. He stood before the bed she was sitting on and thanked her for marrying him. He promised always to love her and their baby, to take care of them, to provide them with a home and the amenities of life. "All the comforts I can afford," he had said, "for as long as I can afford them."

And Marina loved Franz as well. It was impossible not to love him—his insistent curiosity about the world around him; his quiet sensitivity to all living creatures, human and animal; his kindness and generosity toward everyone who asked for his help. When Marina thought about her love for Franz, she realized that she had loved him even before she took that bold sexual step that ultimately bound them. Franz was someone she could count on, and that was a significant asset at a time when so much felt unsettled. If she had to describe her love for her husband, Marina would have said that it was measured and steady, free from intense emotions or unbridled ardor.

It was a love that Marina had thought she could live with, especially after Lara appeared and upended everything in her world. Flush with her new sense of maternal purpose, Marina was not even aware that she had a passionate nature, nor, as time went on, that she was stifling it. Seven years later, when Erich finally kindled that flame in Ludwigsfelde, the result was an inferno that Marina could not extinguish. Nor, she discovered, did she want to, for she relished how it made her feel: alive and awake, more sharply defined. The surrounding world shed its muted shadows and acquired crisp edges. It was as if, having spent a lifetime underwater, looking at the world through scratched and clouded glass, she'd suddenly surfaced and removed her goggles.

Perhaps that was what had attracted her to Johann's enterprise, Marina thought now. Danger could mimic passion in reducing life to its essence. She rolled the cigarette between her fingers, wondering about the family arriving tomorrow. At the beginning of their journey they had been five, and now they were two. She could imagine all too well how that reduction might have occurred. She had seen it firsthand in Berlin, back when the city was "cleansing" itself of Jews by shipping them off to God only knew where. She wondered whether it was the children or the parents who had survived, or perhaps it was one of each. The cigarette ember reached Marina's fingers, and the sudden heat made her drop the butt into the dirt. Smoking was a dangerous pastime for the distracted, she thought, and looked over at Daphne.

"Will we ever be free of this constant feeling of danger?" she asked aloud. Daphne, of course, did not answer.

– Twenty-Two –

The day's cooking and baking activities had taken their toll on Edith. She let her hands rest in the warm dishwater to soothe her aching knuckles. Oskar was upstairs putting the younger girls to bed. Lara had retreated to the living room to read. And Marina had gone to the garden after dinner, telling Edith to leave the dishes for later. Edith, however, was ready for bed, and she couldn't go upstairs until the kitchen was clean. Wouldn't life be easier if she could just walk away from dirty dishes or dusty bookshelves or untidy bedrooms? she thought. But she knew she couldn't. It was hard for her to let things go, in all facets of her life. After emptying the sink and drying her hands, she walked into the living room to kiss Lara good night. There sat her eldest granddaughter, in Oskar's favorite chair, legs curled under her dress, buried in her *Life* magazine. All that was visible of Lara's head were waves of golden hair above the cover photograph of Princess Elizabeth. "So how are you enjoying your princess, my dear?" Edith asked.

Lara looked up, beaming. "Oh, Oma, her life is magical! Of course, it has its difficulties too, mostly because of the war, and fewer parties than there should be, but all in all, I would say it's just glorious."

"Well, I'll be very curious to read about it when you're done," Edith said. "If I may."

"Of course, Oma!" Lara looked overjoyed at the idea of sharing her love for Elizabeth. "I'll bring you the magazine when I've finished reading it." Whatever her occasional adolescent faults, Edith thought, kissing Lara on her forehead, she was still a lovely child, polite and generous. And in her fondness for reading, so much like Franz. One person's plovers were another's princesses.

Edith could hear Oskar's low murmur and the occasional giggle from Sofia or Rosie as she climbed the stairs. She went into her bedroom, leaving the door open so that she could continue listening to those happy bedtime sounds, notes of peace and contentment, a kind of lullaby.

How her body ached. A fitting companion to her mind, she thought, for inside her head, the thoughts were spinning around so quickly it was hard for her to grasp any one of them in order to make sense of it. The Führer's visit tomorrow. A nightmare. How could Oskar have permitted it? He knew how she felt about that man. Did her husband not have any choice? She would ask him about it when he came to bed. Not that it really mattered, because what was done was done, but it might open the door for a larger discussion about Oskar's relationship with the Führer. Edith put on her nightgown and lay down in bed to wait for her husband. At least she had finally seen Erich again, two days in a row. It was healing, having him back in her world. Edith was grateful that she felt absolutely no remnant of anger toward him. Five years ago, she had been furious. She had come downstairs from the makeshift nursery in their apartment in Berlin, and there Erich was, standing in the living room. He was wearing his cavalry uniform, his favorite finery, and gripping his riding gloves in his left hand. Marina had stood next to him showing off the newly born Rosie. Erich's strong right hand, its large bare fingers splayed and slightly curved, tenderly cradled Rosie's tiny head, and his face radiated wonder and awe.

In that moment, Edith had known nothing but rage and hurt. The war had not yet taught her that it was critically important to forgive sooner rather than later. Erich had looked up dream-

ily when she entered the room, and that had infuriated her even
more, that this man should experience any moment of rapture in
her home, when he had, in her mind, undermined its foundation.
She had walked briskly over to Erich and slapped him hard. He
hadn't said a word, but looked at Edith with grief-stricken eyes.
He let go of the baby and put his gloves back on. Then he bent
gently to kiss Rosie's head, turned, and walked out the door. So
much pain in that moment, Edith thought. So much pain since
then. But perhaps the only way to forgiveness was through pain.
If so, war was a great teacher of forgiveness. Though for some
people, the pain it inflicted was insurmountable. Edith thought
of Franz. Certainly that man had experienced far more pain in
his lifetime than he ever deserved. Unfortunately, he was likely
to experience even more. Edith settled into her pillow and closed
her eyes. She pulled the down comforter more tightly around her
body. She was not cold, but she wanted its protection. A swad-
dling of feathers, to hold her until Oskar came to bed.

There he was, tall, golden-haired, reaching for her hand, holding her tightly as they waltzed over the smoothly polished floor and
he swirled her through the music, through the spinning chandelier
lights, the walls reeling and the ceiling sparkling with light and
then dark and then darker, the lights exploding into thousands
of shards, and still Oskar gripped her hand, not letting go as she
spun around and around through the bullets and bombs and clods
of dirt and mud heaving up, and shovels digging down and down,
dropping a coffin so small, and she followed it, felt herself falling
into its grave, a bottomless hole . . . but no, his hand pulled her
back, fingers entwining around hers and pulling her up toward his
body. His arms, thick, muscular, sure, reaching over her waist and
under her shoulder. Oskar's body, settling against her back, closing
the distance between them. His form enveloping her completely,
keeping them together. She settled into a deep sleep.

– Twenty-Three –

A quiet click at the back garden gate broke the hypnotic gurgle of the fountain. From her perch on the bench, Marina had a clear view of the approach to the arbor over the back lawn. Looking past the rose-draped trellis arch that informally marked the garden's lower entrance, she saw Erich striding his way toward the arbor, a sense of purpose and urgency in each step. His white shirt reflected just enough of the fading evening light that she could see his face: mouth set in a firm line, eyes serious, slightly sad.

Although Marina was partially concealed by the hazelnuts, Erich walked directly to her. She stood up at his approach and, wordlessly, he wrapped her into him. Marina could barely breathe, but she did not move, pressed against Erich's chest and feeling the steady thud of his heart against her cheekbone. "You found me," she whispered into the crisp cotton of his shirt, "even though I was hiding in the bushes."

"You can't hide from me," Erich said. He kissed Marina's hair. "I always know where you are."

Marina looked up at him, careful not to dislodge his arms. "No, you don't," she said. "Much as I'd like to believe you."

"Ah, such a lack of faith in one so young," Erich said. He released her and took a step back. "And so beautiful."

Marina blushed and frowned at the same time. She loved the way Erich looked at her: like a cinematographer trying to capture his subject on film. But she wasn't accustomed to compliments about her beauty in her daily world, so she changed the subject. "You and faith," she admonished. "Faith is a luxury of peacetime. There is no place for it in war."

"On the contrary," Erich insisted, "faith is a *necessity* of war." His tone was serious. "But I'd rather discuss your undeniable, infinite beauty. How is it that you grow more beautiful as you age, while the rest of us wither over time?"

"If I am beautiful to you, you are besotted." Marina smiled.

"Besotted with love for you? Yes, to that I will always plead guilty," Erich said. He placed his forefinger on her mouth to stop further protests, then drew it gently down her chin and under her jawbone to tip her head back slightly for a kiss. Erich's lips were soft and warm, and Marina felt, not for the first time, her entire being melting into his mouth and tongue. It was a blessing to dissolve like this, however briefly, to let go of the anxieties and fears that inhabited her, to relinquish the feeling of wariness and dread that had hung over her since the war began. It was a gift to be able to inhabit this moment fully, without thoughts of before or after. It was a relief, just for a short time, to trust that things would be all right without her. Being with Erich was as close as she came to faith.

They sat down on the bench, and Marina intertwined her fingers with his. Twenty minutes earlier, she'd had so many questions, about his sudden departure from lunch, the uneasiness she saw in his eyes. But now, as they sat together in silence, listening to the fountain, she wanted nothing more than to extend this moment of peace and comfort for as long as possible. The war was there, right there outside the gate, sending bullets across the yard and coming for tea in her living room tomorrow, but it was not in this garden right now, and she was not going to invite it in. Marina laid her head against Erich's shoulder and looked at the statue of Daphne. The lower half of her bluish-gray marble body was already partially transformed into the tree trunk dictated by myth, and the water for the fountain ran from those roots. The upper half of her body, still human, was twisted clockwise, and the statue had been placed in such a manner that Daphne's head was looking back toward the house.

"A look of regret," Oskar had said the day the statue was installed in the garden. "It makes perfect sense. The moment Daphne realized she would spend eternity as a laurel tree, of *course* she regretted her decision, especially when the alternative was one night with a handsome god." Edith had given Oskar a gentle slap on the back of the head and admonished him for making light of Daphne's principles. But there was more than regret in that look, Marina thought. There was anguish. Daphne had been torn, not just between two loves, for Apollo and for her father, but between the passion she felt and her sense of responsibility and loyalty, her dedication to virtue and family. Marina understood the anguish of loving two men simultaneously, in different ways. Hearts were expansive organs, capable of holding more than she had imagined. And Daphne's position here, looking back to the house beyond the garden, reminded Marina of the torment she felt when she abandoned her own heart, every time she saw Erich and had to let him go again. And the torment she might feel if she made a different choice than the one she was living now.

Six years ago, Marina had come very close to choosing Erich. At the time, she had been married to Franz for seven years. They had two children together. She wouldn't have said that her marriage was unhappy. She had never thought about its happiness, preoccupied as she was with the births around her: first of Lara and Sofia, and then of the Third Reich. For seven years, the demands of those creatures consumed her. She fulfilled their needs and lost sight of her own. On her twenty-fourth birthday, because Franz had been called to military training and could not celebrate with her, Erich invited Marina to go horseback riding with him. Edith encouraged her to go, insisting that Marina take a break from the girls, get some exercise and fresh country air. They went to Ludwigsfelde. Erich took Arrakis, his majestic Arabian; she chose Sakina, a gentle bay partial to peppermints. They rode bareback. Marina felt the smooth movement of the mare's back and shoulder muscles against her legs, and the unexpected early-spring sun on her face. She was amazed by the chocolate ganache birthday torte Erich had managed to pack into a saddlebag. When they returned their horses to the barn, Erich had looked directly at her and rubbed a trace of ganache from the corner of her mouth. Offered his finger to her lips. Leaned in to kiss her. It happened quickly and slowly. Time metamorphosed into something unpredictable. In that afternoon in the Ludwigsfelde barn with Erich, and in the stolen afternoons that followed over the next few months, Marina experienced the expansion of time. Each hour they lay together in the hayloft was not an hour. Each hour chafed insistently against the strictures of its sixty-minute barrier, while they took off their clothes and took each other in. Erich's hands traced her skin, dipped into her curves, sculpted every inch of her body, for days, not minutes. And the shifts in her breathing took weeks, not seconds: first slow and deep, drawing in oxygen, letting her lungs fill completely, and holding it as if she might never breathe again, then short, quick, sudden gulps, grasping at air again and again, while time pulsed and pounded and throbbed against its limits until at last it exploded its dimensional boundary, leaving her and Erich floating, suspended.

Eventually, however, the boundaries of time always reestablished themselves. One such afternoon, lying on the woolen blanket Erich had spread over the hay, Marina looked out the hayloft window at the sky and saw the sunlight waning, a signal that it was time to return home. She wasn't ready to leave, to return to the relative asceticism of her marriage. She loved Franz, but she didn't long for him with hunger and desire. Flush with the experience of acting on a love she had long buried without knowing it, Marina wasn't ready to give it up. Not now. But could she leave Franz? How could she not? "I will leave him." Perhaps saying it aloud would make it feel more real, more plausible.

Erich was propped on one elbow beside her, picking bits of hay out of her hair. "Think carefully, Marina," he cautioned. "God knows, I would love to have you in my life for good. But it would be complicated. Your parents. Your children. I know how you love your children. Leaving Franz might mean losing Lara and Sofia." Erich tossed the hay he had gathered over the edge of the loft. "If you were to divorce . . . The law doesn't favor the adulteress."

Marina cringed at Erich's choice of words, though she knew it was deliberate. "But Franz will understand. He understands true love," Marina answered, feeling desperate. "He knows it from firsthand experience."

"He knows it by loving *you*," Erich reminded her. "And his love for you has a tenacious hold on his heart. I have seen the way he looks at you. He won't let you go easily. He'll make you choose."

"But I *have* chosen," Marina said. "I *will* choose. I choose you. I'm sorry he will be hurt, I really am, but—"

"No," Erich interrupted. He turned her face toward him so that she couldn't avoid the truth of what he was saying. "The choice won't be between *him* and me. It will be between *them* and me. Franz, Lara, Sofia. Oskar. Maybe even Edith. Marina, if you do this, you must do it knowingly. You must be clear about who you'd be giving up."

In the end, the choice was taken from Marina before she could make it. First, she learned she was pregnant with Rosie. Then, several months after Rosie was born, their country was back at war. The outbreak of war preempted everything. The Führer's indefatigable ego, his insatiable desire for power and land, forced Germans to return to a mentality of belligerence that so many had gladly cast off twenty years earlier. Marina's instinct, like that of her fellow citizens, was to keep her family close. In the end, with the onset of war, with both Erich and Franz away fighting, there was no choice but to stay with her family.

It had been five years since then. And the fact was that now the Allies *had* invaded Normandy, and French troops *were* marching around southern Germany somewhere. Wasn't it possible that the war would be over soon? Here in the arbor, Marina felt that possibility. She was ready to reconsider.

Erich's shoulder pressed against her cheek as he took a deep breath. "It is so peaceful here," he said, holding her hands more tightly.

"I imagine there is quite a hub of activity down the road," Marina said, "in preparation for tomorrow evening's concert. Will you be going? Are you invited?"

"I'm not sure I would use the word 'invited,' but yes, I am going. I have been assigned to the Führer's protective detail."

Something in Erich's tone made Marina look up at his face. She didn't know how to interpret the look she saw there, some combination of pensiveness and agitation. "Is there a reason to expect trouble?"

"No more than usual," he said quickly. "You know enough about the Führer, Marina, to know that he considers himself under threat at all times. And I suppose one has to admit that his paranoia about being the target of countless assassins is partially justified, in light of the attempts that have been made on his life."

Marina thought back to the previous fall, when the Führer's chauffeur discovered a bomb in the engine of a car scheduled to take the Führer from Munich to Fürchtesgaden. Erich was to have been a passenger in that vehicle. Had the chauffeur not investigated a strange noise coming from the fan belt as he was retrieving the car from the garage, they would all have been blown to bits before they reached the Austrian border. She closed her eyes and nodded. "He is lucky to have such men as you looking out for his safety," she said.

"We aren't the ones keeping him safe, not in his mind," Erich corrected her. "According to the Führer, he is the anointed one. He is under the direct watch of the Divine."

Marina laughed aloud at this inconsistency. "I thought the man didn't believe in God! Doesn't he dismiss religion as the crutch of the weak and infirm? And if his life is divinely protected, why worry about assassins? Won't they all be hit by lightning bolts before they get to him?"

To her surprise, Erich didn't even smile at this. He appeared to be weighed down by something heavier. "Marina," he began. "I must tell you, though I know I have told you countless times before, how I feel. My heart is yours entirely. If anything were to happen to me . . ."

"Nothing will happen to you." Marina put her hand on his mouth to cut him off. She refused to consider a world without him.

Erich nodded slowly. "Of course not. I am indestructible." He hesitated and closed his eyes. "If only we had peace."

Perhaps he was seeing peace in his mind's eye. Perhaps he could still remember what that looked like. Marina couldn't. She occasionally tried to envision peacetime—and her future life after Franz's return—but her efforts were unsatisfying. She found that when she imagined her future, all she saw was what she consciously forced upon a blank canvas: a picture of Edith; visions of Lara, Sofia, and Rosie; rooms in a house. Even these were only fleeting shadows. Perhaps the future was too uncertain to reveal itself. Perhaps its uncertainty was a product of her own indecision. In this moment, incited possibly by Erich's words, or by Daphne's look of regret, or by the way the fireflies blinked intermittently but inevitably, offering tiny beacons of light against the descending night curtain, Marina realized that whatever shape her future took, she wanted Erich in it. "Erich, what will you do when the war is over?"

Erich sighed deeply. Marina saw him blinking back tears gathering at the corners of his eyes. She reached up with the back of her hand and gently wiped them aside.

"The moment we are done with this war, my love, I will return to Ludwigsfelde, and I will ride Arrakis for hours and hours until we are both exhausted and fall down in a lush green meadow."

He smiled at the thought. "And then I will return to Niebiosa Podlaski."

"The horse farm in Poland?"

"Exactly. Because that's where the knowledge is, and the history. And possibly even a champion or two, hidden during the massacre, spared from the slaughter I saw. And I will ask them how to do this, how to start a line of thoroughbreds." Erich stared beyond Marina at the lawn, as if he could see horses grazing there already.

Marina looked across the lawn with him. "The girls would love that! Yesterday, I thought I would never be able to get Rosie off that horse."

"Ah, Rosie. She changed the balance of everything, didn't she? She's such a force."

"Yes," Marina agreed, picturing her daughter's small, determined form barreling toward some person, place, or thing that she had set her mind on. "She *is* a force. A force of life. It's odd too, in a way. She's a child of war, and yet she has such spirit."

"She is the future. Our future," Erich offered tentatively, as if by articulating their future together, he might jeopardize it. "It is nice to think of our lives being guided by Rosie's spirit."

"I wonder how that spirit will respond to the Führer at tomorrow's tea. I fear it will be like a cosmic collision. You should come watch." Almost immediately, Marina regretted her words, for Erich suddenly sobered. "I take it you can't."

"No. I wish I could, but—" He hesitated. "I have preparations I must make for tomorrow evening's event at the Weber house."

"Preparations?"

"Security matters."

"Ah." Marina took Erich's hand and traced the lines on his palm. "Well, if you hear an enormous explosion, you'll know what happened!" She laughed, trying to recapture the lightness of the previous moment. To her surprise, he winced and pulled his hand away. "Erich?" she asked.

His face was stern. "Marina, there is a chance I may have to leave very quickly tomorrow night. Will you meet me again before I go? After the concert?"

"Tomorrow night? But why would you have to leave?"

"I can't say. I just may need to get to Berlin very quickly. And I would like to see you before I go." He wasn't pleading; his tone was calm but serious. Marina felt she was at a turning point. She remembered something Oskar had told her when she was a young girl. He had just come back from a dinner celebrating a German physicist. Oskar had been fortunate enough to be seated next to the man, who regaled him with theories about time travel and parallel universes. Knowing his daughter loved fantasy, Oskar shared the ideas with Marina. Identical worlds on alternative planes of time, possibly overlapping in certain places, maybe through some time loop or kink. She had been fascinated. Thinking on those ideas now, she wondered: Was it not possible that an alternate world was overlapping with her own, right now, right here in this garden, some corner of it intruding on the present reality? That she could, if she chose to, step into this other space? All that was necessary was a leap of faith. "Will you come to me one last time? At the edge of the Birnau forest, after the concert?" Erich was searching her eyes. His question was a springboard, wasn't it? A bridge, a ladder, call it whatever she might, she saw the step wide and clear.

"Of course," she said. "Of course I'll come to you."

Marina pressed herself against Erich's rib cage, ignoring the weight of the atmosphere around her. Fear still gnawed at her, but she fought it back and listened to Erich's heartbeat. Here with him she was safe, she reminded herself. There, in the house, were her girls and her parents, safe. Nearby, the fountain murmured on, and Daphne stood still, and the cooling air blanketed the perfume of the roses, and there was no other sound or smell. When Marina finally looked up, the last firefly was blinking its way toward the lake.

Day Three

July 20, 1944

– Twenty-Four –

Sofia loved Irene Nagel's barn. Sunlight flowed in through the grand double doors and illuminated everything in a slow, gentle way, even the stall of Bertha the cow way in the back, even the crevices between the rolled hay bundles stacked in piles under the loft where Sofia now lay. Passing through the barn air, the light seemed to pick up tiny pieces of hay dust and cracked seed that slowed its movement, weighed it down so it hovered over things and outlined them in a soft, chalky silhouette. Sofia loved the density of this light, the way it approached things slowly and rested on them cautiously, as if waiting for permission to reveal them. She loved the quiet of the barn too. The voice of Herr Nagel muttering as he looked for his hammer or the moos of Bertha asking if he had brought her an apple—those sounds were hushed by the time they reached Sofia's ears, as if the air were fine sandpaper rubbing off the sharp edges of all noise as it traveled past.

This morning, the only sound Sofia could hear was the soft suckling of the kittens snuggling up to their mother, Mathilde, for breakfast. There were five of them, one black and four black-and-white. Since Mathilde was black, Sofia thought the kittens' vati must be white, because how else could Mathilde have had babies that had white in their fur? Of course, she did not know who the vati cat was. The vati was not around. Vatis were not often around. Her own vati had not been home for years, and she

missed him, but at least she had her opa. Sofia loved Opa very
much, maybe even more than she loved her vati. Poor kittens.
They didn't have an opa. Sofia wanted to take her kitten in her
arms and cuddle her close to make up for her missing vati, and
her nonexistent opa, but right now her kitten was eating, so Sofia
had to wait.

She lay on her stomach in the warm hay, crisscrossing her
feet in the air behind her. Waiting felt as natural as breathing.
She *liked* waiting, because she could close her eyes and go to the
watery blue space in her mind, and no one would chide her for
daydreaming.

Sofia didn't remember anything about the night in the cellar
in Berlin other than a fear so deep that it felt attached to the
inside of her bones. For a long time after that night, Sofia had
the same nightmare, in which she was floating above the floor
of a cellar in a cloud of dust and dirt and bits of debris, while all
around her, the walls collapsed one by one. Each time a wall fell,
it revealed a terrifying black emptiness, a chasm of nothingness
that sucked things into its powerful vacuum. In her nightmare, a
pair of round glasses floated in the cloud right next to her, but she
couldn't reach them, though she felt desperate to keep the glasses
from being sucked away into the blackness. She pushed with all
her might against the walls to keep them from collapsing. But
still they fell, one by one, and the glasses got closer and closer to
the void, and Sofia always woke up screaming just at the moment
when the last wall was about to fall and the glasses were about
to disappear forever. After the night in the cellar, Sofia stayed
with Oma and Opa for a while, because Oma made her feel safe
But Oma had trouble sleeping too, and her doctor gave her some
medicine that made her sleep so deeply that she didn't wake up
until after breakfast sometimes. So it was always Opa who came
to Sofia's bed and held her in his arms and asked her to tell him
about the nightmare. One night, he suggested she stop trying to
support the wall. "You mean I should let it fall?" Sofia was aghast.

"But I'll get sucked away like all the others, I'll be pulled into the blackness!"

"But you don't know for sure what's behind that last wall," Opa said, stroking her hair and speaking softly. "Maybe it's different. Maybe it's another color." Sofia had never considered that there might be something different behind the last wall. Several weeks later, back in her own home, the nightmare woke Sofia again. This time Opa wasn't around. She let herself return to the dream, and instead of bracing herself against the last wall, she stretched forward to secure the glasses, and just as she grabbed their frame, the last wall crumbled—and suddenly everything was blue: a breathtakingly beautiful blue, a deep, dark indigo, magically luminescent. With the last wall down, the blue in her dream washed over Sofia like a great tide. It held her tenderly, securely, like the water in the lake held her when she went swimming and dove underwater. There was no fear in that buoyant blue, just a sense of security and peace. And an invitation. When she woke in the morning, Sofia felt that the blue had welcomed her to return anytime. All she had to do was close her eyes and make her mind blank, think of nothing, and within moments, she would be suspended in the world of blue, free to leave her body behind and wander in its limitless expanse.

A slow creak interrupted Sofia's thoughts. Someone was pushing open the gate that led to the stalls where the barn animals were kept. Sofia couldn't see who it was, but if she crawled forward on her belly just a few meters, she'd reach the spot in the hayloft where the removable wood knot Irene had showed her last year was located. Sofia quietly brushed the straw away from the area and felt around to lift the knot up. She pressed her cheek against the plank and looked through the opening. Nothing. The person, whoever it was, was too far away.

A moment later, the gate squealed more loudly, and she saw Pastor Johann stride by beneath her. Sofia knew Irene's family was Protestant, but why would the pastor come to the barn instead of the house? Sofia heard the other person whisper to Pastor Johann. A woman's voice! She moved her head slightly around the knothole so that her ear was flush with it.

"Meerfeld is out of the question now," Pastor Johann said.

"Yes, I haven't seen Captain Rodemann yet, thank God, but I'm sure he's marching around somewhere." Sofia inhaled sharply; it was her mother!

"We can't risk bringing the refugees to Ernst."

"I know, I know," Marina said. "How will you even get them from the train station, with Rodemann's men patrolling all the roads?"

Sofia was now completely confused. Years ago, when they lived in Berlin, her mother had taken some of her and Rosie's old clothes, the ones they had outgrown, and put them in a box. She told Sofia that these clothes would be donated to "refugees," children who had to leave their homes because of the war, and who needed any kind of clothing they could get. But Blumental didn't have refugees; as far as Sofia knew, none of the children in Blumental were going to leave their homes. So where were these refugees coming from? And why were they coming here?

" . . . along the old city wall and then down from the Birnau forest," Pastor Johann was saying.

"I wish I could help you, but I promised Edith I'd help her with this damn tea."

"Tea?"

"Oh, you don't know." Marina's voice had a pinched tone. "The Führer will be gracing our house as well as Herr Weber's today." She paused. "He is coming to tea."

"Oh, no." Pastor Johann was suddenly very quiet. Was he crying? Sofia pressed her ear closer to the floor. If Pastor Johann *was* crying, her mother would pat him on the back to make him feel better. But she could hear no patting, sobbing, or sniffling. "I had hoped you'd be able to take them, just for a very short time. I was going to push up my departure from Fritz's. But if the Führer is coming to your house . . . no. They'll just have to stay at the train station. I'll tell Max to wash all the church windows, not just the ones in the nave."

"Max?"

"Max Fuchs has taken to checking our train station these days. He thinks he might find spies. So I've given him a window-washing project at my church to keep him busy."

Sofia thought of the windows at Pastor Johann's church: they were the most beautiful blue. A blue that flowed through the glass like water, swirling around all the other colors, surrounding them and turning them into undulating flowers swimming in a stream. Suddenly, Sofia remembered the blue dress she used to have, the one with tiny multicolored flowers. She had loved that dress, but Mutti made her give it to the refugees in Berlin, because she said it was too small. Maybe one of the refugees in the train station would be wearing that dress. What would it look like on her? Sofia would so love to see her dress again. But which train station would the refugees be at? East Blumental or the main one? She'd check both later. Sofia was too scared to go alone. Maybe she could get Rosie to go with her.

"I wish I could take them to the rectory, but another urgent matter needs my attention," Pastor Johann said. "And they need to be on the east side anyway, near here." He was pacing now. Sofia could hear hay crunching beneath his feet. "On top of everything else, last night I received an invitation from Sabine Mecklen to join her for dessert at her home! Of course I won't go . . ."

Sofia heard her mother laugh quietly. "No, you should. Absolutely. With all the other fuss in town, it might be a good idea to have someone who can attest to your whereabouts." The barn was silent except for the sound of Bertha sniffing through her hay feeder for stray pieces of fruit. Sofia felt something soft at her ankle, and she looked up from her peephole. One of the male kittens had wandered over to her and was testing her leg with his paw, considering the best approach for climbing on top of it.

Gently, she picked him up and cradled him in her palms, then returned to her listening.

"The best hiding place for the refugees might be right under his nose," Mutti was saying.

Sofia was again confused. Whose nose were the refugees going to be hidden under? And how would that person not see that they were there? Dislodged slightly from the knothole, Sofia could hear only snatches of the conversation.

" . . . unexpected location, and the cellar is so dark . . ."

" . . . already been searched . . ."

" . . . the cellar . . . coal . . ."

Something mewed right next to Sofia. It was her own kitten, the little black one, come to introduce herself! "*Kuschi, kusch, kusch,*" Sofia clucked in a reassuring motherly tone. Very slowly, she moved her left arm around her kitten, sweeping it up with some hay, and in one continuous motion, she sat up, carefully depositing the kitten into the skirt of her dress. She scooted her body over to a hay bale and leaned back.

Sofia was tired of listening to conversations she couldn't understand. She stroked the kitten's tiny ears, and it purred and pushed its head against the palm of her hand. Then it stretched its back and yawned, curling itself into a puffy ball. Sofia arranged the fabric of her dress snugly around it, creating a little nest—a small blue world above all the ruckus of hammering and machine guns and bombs, away from refugees wearing donated clothes and hiding in train stations under people's noses, a simple world that smelled of hay and warm milk, that was blanketed in filtered light and bits of downy fur and seed, a world that was safe to sleep in.

– Twenty-Five –

The large iron clock suspended in the main hall of the Blumental train station read 10:20 as Johann Wiessmeyer hurried toward the doors that led to the train tracks. Before leaving the rectory for the station, he had fastened his clerical collar, which he usually didn't bother with. Even though the Third Reich officially denounced religion, Johann knew that many of its constituents had been raised in religious households by religious parents. And the young southern constituents of the Reich, like the soldiers in Captain Rodemann's regiment, had probably grown up in Catholic towns not too far from here. It was impossible to undo years of Catholic upbringing with just a few weeks of military training. Johann trusted that these boys would instinctively treat a man of the cloth with deference and respect.

Indeed, nobody stopped him on his way to Track 2, and he headed to the end of the platform, where he knew the last second-class car would come to a stop. There he waited, buttoning his overcoat. The weather had worsened overnight. What had started out this morning as a cool, overcast sky was now deteriorating into a cold mist that saturated everything. Not a desirable development for those planning the Weber concert, but Johann himself welcomed the drifting shrouds of wet fog. The more pairs of eyes that stayed inside while he transported these refugees across town, the better. Yesterday, when Johann received the telegram from Gottfried directing him to deliver the briefcase by two today, he very nearly sent a response saying he couldn't do it. The timing was impossible: he had refugees coming, they had to be smuggled out that night, and an assassination attempt was out of the question. Johann wasn't certain that the bomb would be utilized at the Weber concert that evening, but it seemed likely. Then he decided that the confluence of events was fortuitous. If the bomb did go off during the concert, the chaos that ensued would be a window of opportunity, as long as he moved the refugees out quickly. He only wished he could be as confident as Marina that the Eberhardt house would be a safe place to hide them in the interim.

"Don't you see, Johann?" she had said in the barn. "It's because it's such an unexpected location that it'll be safe. The house will already have been searched in advance by the Führer's men. I just need to get them inside, and then I can bring them down to the cellar to hide behind the coal pile. No one will look down there, I guarantee it. And even if they do look, they won't be able to see anything. I'll take out the light."

"I suppose we have no other choice, do we?" Johann agreed reluctantly. "But I hate putting you in any kind of danger."

Marina had ignored his concern. "You want them at Fritz's by midnight, right?"

Johann realized that midnight would be too late. All the roads leading out of Blumental would surely be blocked by then, whatever the result at the concert. They'd have to leave long before midnight. "No, it will have to be earlier, but still after dark."

"What time?" Marina had looked confused, but he could not tell her more, not without jeopardizing her further.

"I can't give you an exact time, Marina, but you'll know. It will be clear to you when to move them, I promise. There will be a sign at the concert. You'll hear it." Marina opened her mouth and closed it without speaking. Johann watched her stifle her curiosity. The taste of unanswered questions was, he knew, quite bitter. It was a taste familiar to the entire country, an acid tang of self-imposed ignorance. But everyone tolerated it, Johann thought, because the knowledge they so deliberately ignored was poisonous and terrifying. The collective mind and belly of the Third Reich was filled with ulcerous questions.

A shrill squeal of brakes announced the arrival of a train. Johann watched as the cars slid past him, each more slowly, until at last the entire train came to a full stop with a heavy sigh. The doors of the second-class compartment before him opened. He looked for Eva Münch, his point of contact for the last two transfers, and soon her distinctive maroon bowler hat appeared. Eva quickly descended the metal stairs to the platform, then turned to help her charges navigate the steep drop. One girl, probably about twelve, though it was hard to judge from her small, undernourished frame, and then another, much younger, maybe five years old. "Good morning, Eva," Johann said as he walked up to them. "So good of you to bring my nieces down south. Did you have a comfortable trip?" Although there were no soldiers nearby that Johann could see, the pretense was best initiated immediately, for the benefit of anyone within earshot.

"Very comfortable, Pastor Wiessmeyer, perfectly fine. No trouble at all," Eva replied. The older girl gripped Eva's left hand tightly, and the younger girl hid behind her sister. The only thing visible about the younger one was a yarn-haired cloth doll that dangled from her hand. "Nadzia, Pola, do you remember Uncle Johann?"

Cautiously, the older girl, Nadzia, extended her free left hand to Johann. "Hallo, Uncle," she said shyly, obviously uncomfortable with the foreign language.

Johann took her hand gently and patted it. Then he knelt down so he would appear less threatening. "You are even more beautiful than I remember, Nadzia. And I'm sure Pola is too, if only I could get a good look at her." The compliment and kind tone weren't enough to entice the little girl out from behind her sister's long skirt. "But I can wait." He stood back up. "Come, girls, we should be going. The train will be pulling out again soon, and Eva needs to get back on." He gave Eva a quick embrace and whispered, "Parents?"

"Mother, father, and baby brother killed somewhere en route. I don't know how." Johann grimaced as Eva reached into her purse and handed him two documents. "Here are their identification papers. You have the necessary exit visas?"

"Yes, all is ready here. Thank you, Eva. I'll let you know how it goes."

"Please do." Eva straightened her hat and turned to the two girls. "*Być grzeczne.*" In a different situation, Johann might have laughed at Eva's telling these girls to be good. They looked far too scared to do anything other than what they were told.

Now he had to confront the first hurdle: getting the girls past the security checkpoint at the station exit. He took a moment to survey the station hall and was glad to see more commotion than usual, due to the convergence of out-of-town guests arriving for the Weber concert and merchants arranging for its smooth execution. Travelers crisscrossed the stone floor, suitcases and hatboxes in hand, slaloming around trolleys. All paths merged at a tall arched entranceway, beneath which four soldiers armed with machine guns stopped everyone to check papers. Johann herded the girls into a line of people shuffling toward the exit and folded down the lapels of his coat so that his clerical collar was more visible. The older girl, Nadzia, stood in front of him, with her younger sister pressed against her. Johann put his hand on Nadzia's shoulder, trying to channel reassurance and comfort to her through his touch. It would be helpful if the girls didn't appear nervous and frightened as they passed through the checkpoint, though if they did, he was ready to attribute any negative reaction to their exhaustion from a long train trip.

"Papers!" A young private with the posture of a broomstick ejected one arm from his body, while his partner kept a machine gun level with Johann's chest. The two girls immediately moved

behind Johann's coat. Johann offered the soldier the papers Eva
had given him, and the man flipped through them, glancing at
the photographs and then resting his attention on the page with
their biographical specifics. "These girls are from Dresden?"

"Yes, my sister lives there," Johann lied. "They are my nieces."

"Lots of bombing going on up north," the private said, looking around Johann's back. "Isn't that right, little girls? Bombs!
Fire!" He bent over so that his face was level with Nadzia's. "*Ka-
POOF!*" he shouted, splaying his hands outward into their faces
and making both girls shriek and duck underneath Johann's coat.
The travelers in line behind Johann glared at the soldier with
disapproval, but no one dared say a word.

If Johann's teeth had been more tightly clenched, they would
have cracked and splintered. "Are we free to go?" he asked, measuring his words deliberately.

"Of course, of course, go!" The young man chuckled, handing
back the papers and waving them past. "Always fun to play with
the little ones, right, Metz?" He looked to his partner with the
machine gun. Metz did not appear amused by the prank. At least
not everyone's humanity was straitjacketed by a uniform, Johann
thought.

News of the Führer's visit had succeeded in drawing the attention of most of Blumental toward the Meerfeld road, so Johann's
trip through the town's northern neighborhoods went largely unnoticed. Thick banks of fog drifted from the Birnau forest over
the road to the East Blumental station, allowing Johann to take
that leg of their journey a little more slowly, camouflaged by the
gray mist. Midway through town, the younger girl, Pola, began to
stumble as she was pulled along by her older sister. Johann picked
her up and carried her in his arms. Too exhausted to maintain her
fear of him, Pola wrapped her arms around his neck and rested her
head against his chest. By the time they reached the small train
station, she was fast asleep. Johann quickly looked behind the
building to make sure Max wasn't around. There was no sign of

him. Johann carefully laid Pola down on one of the long wooden benches in the silent, empty waiting room, then took the doll he had been carrying inside his coat and placed it under her right arm. Smiling shyly, Nadzia lay down too, curling up her body so that her feet touched Pola's. Johann took off his coat and draped it over both girls as a blanket. He felt a small measure of relief. "You will be safe here, I promise," he told Nadzia. The girl nodded, but whether it was because she understood or just because she was grateful that they could rest, he didn't know. In the distance, the bells of Birnau chimed twelve o'clock. He kissed the top of Nadzia's head and left the station.

It was time to deal with the briefcase.

– Twenty-Six –

Rosie couldn't believe her luck. After lunch, Mutti had completely forgotten about Rosie's nap. Everything was off schedule: breakfast was early; lunch was late, and not even warm. Instead, Oma had hard-boiled the few eggs that Lara found in the chicken coop and set them out on the dining room table with berries and carrots and cold potatoes and other leftovers from yesterday and told everyone to take what they wanted but not to bother her in the kitchen while she and Mutti were baking. Taking one of the eggs, Rosie had gone upstairs to see if Opa wanted to play hide-and-seek, but he was busy sending telegrams.

Rosie was about to take Hans-Jürg down to the lake to check for swan nests when Sofia asked her if she wanted to go look for refugees at the train station. When Rosie said she didn't know what refugees looked like, Sofia told her to look for children who were wearing *their* old clothes, the ones that Mutti had given away. That made Rosie excited, because maybe whoever was wearing Rosie's pink polka-dot shirt would give it back if Rosie asked nicely. She still missed that shirt and she knew it wasn't too small, no matter what Mutti said.

Sofia decided they should go to the main train station first, since there were more trains there. The main station was swarming with German soldiers. They looked like large gray ants with helmets. They were stopping people before the people went in or out the doors. Travelers were pulling out papers and handing them over—identification papers, Sofia told Rosie. It was because the Führer was coming to Blumental, she explained. Everyone looked angry to Rosie. A very bad mood was hanging in the air, something dark and short-tempered, something that had infected all the people around her.

Sofia pulled Rosie over to the side of the station. "We don't have any papers, so we can't go in." She pointed to the pile of wood stacked into a neat and convenient staircase under a nearby window. "But we can still look." Rosie nodded. She started climbing up the pile. "Do you see anything?" Sofia made her way to the top of the woodpile and stood next to her sister.

"No," Rosie said, peering through the panes. "Just lots and lots of people with suitcases."

"I wonder where they would be hidden," Sofia mused, pressing her face close to the window.

"Are they hidden? Why?" Rosie didn't understand why a refugee would have to hide.

"I don't know, but Pastor Johann said they needed a hiding place, and Mutti said something about hiding things under people's noses," Sofia said. Rosie frowned at Sofia. Now her sister just wasn't making sense. But that happened sometimes with Sofia. She saw things that other people didn't, like her blue space. Sofia had tried to describe it to Rosie once, something about swimming and floating and being in a watery cocoon in a world of blue. Rosie had no idea what she was talking about. The only thing Rosie saw when she closed her eyes was blackness. And sometimes reddish streaks, if she closed them tightly while looking up at the sun.

Many of the people in the train station were dressed in uniforms, some with lots of colored ribbons. Her opa's uniform had a lot of colored ribbons on it, plus some pretty metal pins. Rosie once asked him if she could have them when he didn't need them anymore, and he said that she could. Then he said he might have to give some of them to Lara and Sofia too, if they wanted any. That was only fair, he reminded her. Opa was big on being fair.

"You two, on the woodpile! Get down from there, now!" an angry voice shouted.

Startled, Rosie almost fell off the logs. She turned her head to see a German soldier motioning at them with his rifle. Rosie was not afraid of soldiers—there were too many of them around to be afraid of all of them. This one was short and round, and the helmet on his head made him look like a turtle walking upright. "He looks like a turtle," Rosie said to Sofia, not moving. But Sofia was already hurrying down.

"Well, he's a turtle with a *gun*, Rosie, so come on," Sofia urged. Reluctantly, Rosie turned away from the window.

"You shouldn't be wandering around the station without your parents!" the soldier barked. "Go back to your parents! Go!" He waved his rifle through the air as if to herd them toward a pair of imaginary parents. Nodding earnestly, Sofia pulled Rosie off the woodpile and rushed her along, away from the swinging rifle.

"Maybe we can wait until he goes away and then look some more," Rosie said, not ready to give up on the refugees quite yet. Sofia shook her head.

"No, I'm pretty sure they're not in there," Sofia mused. "They must be in East Blumental."

The two girls began running east along Hauptstrasse, past Herr Roch's jewelry shop, past Fräulein Beck's dress store, and more quickly past Herr Eigen's pharmacy, because he was grumpy with children and gave off waves of formaldehyde whenever he moved. As they neared the Mecklen bakery at the next corner, they both slowed, partly to catch their breath, partly to savor the aroma.

"Let's go in and see if Frau Mecklen will give us a cookie," Rosie suggested hopefully.

"She doesn't give me cookies anymore," Sofia said. "I'm too old."

"But she might give *me* one, because I'm not old," Rosie said. "And I'll split it with you."

Sofia smiled. "Okay, but I'll wait out here. You go in and choose." Rosie skipped inside as a bracelet of little bells announced her entrance. Rosie loved the Mecklen bakery. It was her favorite store in Blumental, because it was warm and yeasty, and it had big glass display cases. Back when the Rosenbergs had this bakery, the cases were filled with marzipan animals and chocolate ladybugs wrapped in brightly colored tinfoil. Frau Rosenberg always let her and Sofia choose a marzipan animal when they came over to play with Rachel. Frau Rosenberg could make almost any animal out of marzipan: pigs and cows and mice and sheep, and once she even made a giraffe. The only animals the Mecklens ever made, back when there was enough sugar to make marzipan, were pigs. Another thing about the bakery was that there was always somebody there whom Rosie knew. Rosie liked most people, even the ones who constantly expressed surprise about how fast she was growing. As long as they didn't try to pat her on the head or pinch her cheek.

Regina Mecklen was a pincher, but today she was standing behind the display case, too far away to reach Rosie's face. She was chatting with Frau Schmiede, bending forward over the counter and laughing at something Frau Schmiede had just said. Sofia and Rosie had decided long ago that nobody could really find so many things as funny as Frau Mecklen seemed to, and they began to gauge the sincerity of her laughter by the degree of squinting in her right eye. Today, it was clear to Rosie that Frau Mecklen wasn't really amused by Frau Schmiede's gossip, because her right eye was still open enough to wink at Rosie as she approached.

"*Ja, ja*, he was just here this morning, picking up an order of bread for the evening's festivities," Frau Mecklen said.

Frau Schmiede clucked sympathetically. "Such an enormous amount of work for you and your sisters, dear Regina. But all to the good, all to the good. When does the Führer arrive, do you suppose?" Rosie was only half listening, her face pressed to the display glass. She was gazing intently at the coconut macaroons and the buttery *schweineöhrchen*, flaky pastries curled in the shape of pigs' ears. The macaroon was her favorite, but Sofia didn't like macaroons. The word *Führer* reminded Rosie of her purpose, and the fact that Sofia was waiting, and that they still had to get to East Blumental before it was too late.

"I'm going to see the Führer," she blurted out. "The Führer is coming to our house this afternoon! And pretty please, may I please have a cookie?" At Rosie's announcement, Frau Mecklen's head snapped in the girl's direction. In an instant, the baker abandoned Frau Schmiede.

"Oh, my dear sweet child! Of course you can have a cookie, of course!" She hurried over to the end of the display case and motioned for Rosie to come to the other side. Frau Mecklen's mouth now expanded to its maximum width, stretching her entire face around an array of yellowing teeth. If she could see anything out of those slit eyes now, Rosie thought, it was a miracle. "Help yourself, dear, help yourself to any cookie you want. You are a lucky, lucky girl, to have the Führer at your house, you know. When is he coming?"

Rosie reached into the display case for one of the *schweineöhrchen*, one with its tips dipped in chocolate. "We're supposed to be back in time for afternoon coffee," she said, waving her arm at the door to indicate Sofia's presence outside.

"Oh, afternoon coffee! Of course, that's very civilized. I'm sure your entire family is very excited," Frau Mecklen said. Rosie watched her, fascinated that Frau Mecklen was able to speak without relaxing her mouth. "But what time, my dear?"

"Sometime this afternoon," Rosie said, heading quickly toward the exit. Bells jingled as Rosie called out, "Thank you, Frau Mecklen!" And just like that, she was back outside, with the door closing heavily on Frau Mecklen's plaintive cry.

Rosie glanced around for Sofia. Her sister was not on the street corner. Rosie looked longingly at the *schweineöhrchen* and carefully pressed her thumb and forefinger into the base of its buttery spirals, then shifted it from her right hand to her left to lick the melted chocolate from her coated fingers. "Rosie!" Sofia's voice called to her from down the street, near the marketplace. "Rosie, come help me!" Rosie turned her head to the right, where the voice was coming from. There, in front of the fountain in the Blumental marketplace, she saw Sofia struggling with what looked like a brown suitcase. She ran down the street to join her.

"What are you doing?" she asked.

Sofia put down the case she had been dragging across the cobblestones. "I found Pastor Johann's briefcase."

Rosie looked more closely at the object Sofia was wrestling with. It was just like the little bag Opa used to take with him each morning when they lived in Berlin. He said he kept important papers in it, but all Rosie ever saw come out of it were the lollipops he used to bring home for the girls. "Where did you get that briefcase? What's in it? And how do you know it belongs to Pastor Johann?"

Sofia sighed and sat down on the closure flap at the top of the case. "I don't know what's in it, Rosie. I was waiting for you outside the bakery, and I was looking up the street and saw Pastor Johann walking over to this bench here, next to the fountain. He was looking around, like maybe he was waiting for someone, but then he sat down on the bench. He kept checking the briefcase lock. And then after a bit he stood up again and walked away. Without the briefcase."

"Maybe he forgot about it," Rosie said. "Grown-ups are always forgetting things."

"Well, then, we should try to get it back to him," Sofia said.

"But our cookie is melting and we need to eat it soon," Rosie stated, trying to focus Sofia on more important issues.

"You eat it," Sofia said. "I'm going to get this back to Pastor Johann." She stood and picked up the briefcase with both hands. "*Oof!*" She exhaled as the briefcase thumped against her right thigh. Rosie took a seat on the wooden bench nearby, and she put the tip of the *schweineöhrchen* into her mouth, closing her lips around the edge of the chocolate and sucking on it while she watched her sister. Sofia had made it almost all the way across the marketplace with the briefcase when a familiar voice boomed out behind Rosie.

"Oho! What are you up to?" Rosie turned around a moment before Erich lifted her up off the bench and held her dangling in the air above him. She kicked her legs at him and pretended to be cross, though it was hard not to giggle.

"Put me down! I'm busy, Uncle Erich."

Erich held Rosie in the air for a moment longer and studied her face. "Busy? Hmm, yes, judging from the extensive map of chocolate around your lips, you have been hard at work on that cookie. What are you doing here all alone, Rosie?"

"I'm not alone, I'm with Sofia. She's over there somewhere." Erich looked in the direction that Rosie waved her cookie. All of a sudden, he let go of Rosie and started running.

"*Stop!* Sofia, stop! Wait! *Put that down!*" When Erich reached Sofia, he picked her up with one swoop of his right arm and held her tightly while he wrested the briefcase away from her. She cried out in protest and tried to reach for it, but Erich prevented her. After a moment, he placed the briefcase on the stones behind him, beyond her reach. Then he knelt before Sofia, holding both of her hands in his own and talking to her, too softly for Rosie to hear. Though Erich's back was to Rosie, she could see his rib cage moving in and out quickly. Erich kissed Sofia on top of her head, picked up the briefcase, gave Rosie a wave, and walked away. Sofia ran back to Rosie.

"What did he say to you?" Rosie asked. "Is Erich bringing the briefcase back to Pastor Johann?"

"I don't know," Sofia answered. "He told me not to worry about it anymore." Sofia looked off in the direction Erich had disappeared. "He said he would take care of it."

Rosie slid off the bench. "So should we go to East Blumental now?"

The Münster bell tower chimed two o'clock. "No," Sofia said. "We should probably go home. We have to be home for that stupid tea."

"But what about our clothes?"

"Our clothes?"

"The ones the refugees will be wearing," Rosie reminded her. "I want to see if they're wearing my pink shirt."

"I know, me too, but we don't have time," Sofia said. "I wanted to look for my blue dress. The one with the flowers."

"I remember that one. You used to wear it all the time."

Sofia looked into the distance dreamily as they started walking east toward home. "I loved that dress. I could stare at its skirt for hours." Rosie giggled at the idea of looking at a piece of fabric for hours. Sofia was so strange sometimes. It was almost like she was from a different planet.

– Twenty-Seven –

The Führer's men searched the house shortly after two o'clock. When the first fist rammed their front door, Edith was still in the kitchen assembling the Linzer torte, her hands caked in dough. Marina headed to the foyer. The moment she lifted the bolt on the door, it was pushed open, and four military guards stormed into the front hall. The leader, a squat, stern-looking man with a large bulbous nose, resembled the garden dwarf from their home in Berlin. He introduced himself as Commander Pilzer.

"Madam," Pilzer said in an unctuous tone, bowing with self-important precision, "we must secure the house. For the safety of the Führer and all inhabitants." He looked around and huffed with disdain. "This should take only a few minutes." Pilzer clicked his boots together and barked at the two men closest to the staircase, "You two! Up! Miesvol and I will take the ground floor." As abruptly as they had appeared, the soldiers vanished, trailed by echoes of their stomping boots. A succession of light shudders in the wooden floor and rafters above allowed Marina to follow the soldiers' progress through the bedrooms. Either because they had become expert in assessing danger at a glance or, more likely, because they did not really expect to find anything threatening in so insignificant and modest a structure as this little house, the search upstairs was swift. Downstairs, Miesvol and Pilzer swept through the kitchen and living room in an equally brief matter of minutes, slamming doors with violence. The last room they checked was the cellar, and it fell to Miesvol to climb down the narrow steps into the darkness. Marina had removed the light-bulb that morning.

Three minutes later, Miesvol reappeared, rubbing his shin and brushing cobwebs off his shoulder pads. "Pitch dark down there," he reported. "But all clear."

"Good." Pilzer waved the two upstairs soldiers out to the porch. "You two monitor access from the back. Miesvol and I will guard the front."

Marina had not expected them to post guards at the house entrances. She felt dread settle on her shoulders like a leaden cloak. Offering to hide the refugees in their cellar had been an impetuous idea this morning, but Marina had been moved by Johann's indecision and anguish. It was not a move she could take back now, so she did what she always did after acting impulsively: she sat down to consider the situation more carefully. Luckily, Rosie and Sofia had run off somewhere and were not in the house. And Pilzer, Marina realized, had not asked her how many children she had. That was fortunate. Perhaps, if there was a haphazard influx of adults and children into the house at various entrances, it would confuse the soldiers enough that they would lose track of numbers. Rosie and Sofia would most likely come back by way of the porch door. If Marina brought the refugees in through the front, past Pilzer and his colleague, it might not be obvious how many people were already in the house. She took a deep breath. "Right under their noses" was going to be very literal.

By 2:30, Edith's baking and tidying frenzy was complete, and she headed upstairs to rest. Now was the time, Marina thought, hurrying to the kitchen. She would have no better opportunity to sneak over to the East Blumental station. Assuming the refugees would be hungry, she grabbed a few leftover *brötchen*, a wedge of cheese, and a handful of berries. She kept her head down as she exited the front door, nodding only briefly to the two guards flanking it. "You will be returning soon, yes?" Pilzer demanded.

"Oh, yes," Marina assured him. "Just going to pick up the children." Pilzer's disinterested nod confirmed her hope that he did not consider children subjects worthy of his attention.

The two little girls were asleep under Johann's coat on one of the long wooden benches. They were curled end to end, feet touching just enough for one to notice when the other stirred. Marina had been poised to hurry the refugees back to the house as quickly as possible, but their tranquillity, and the fact that they were alone, made her pause. Until this moment, she had been so worried about the logistics of getting them from one location to another, so fearful of discovery, that she hadn't let herself think of them as anything other than packages—precious and delicate, but packages nevertheless. Things that needed careful hiding and quick transportation. She had pushed back thoughts about what they'd been through, what horrors they had seen and experienced, for fear that her own maternal instincts might somehow compromise the entire enterprise. Johann had warned her against that at the very beginning, when she first joined his group. Now, as the two sisters lay in sinuous unity, their breathing synchronized in sleep, Marina took a moment to look at them. They did not appear all that different from her own girls. Marina guessed, from the older girl's length and development, that she was about Lara's age. Still so young. What inner reserves of strength and courage must this girl have drawn upon for her little sister's sake? Any mother would be proud of such a daughter. But of course, this girl would not know that. Her mother was probably dead, or else she'd be with them right now. Marina's heart crept upward into her throat as she imagined the girls' mother—the despair of her last instant before darkness, knowing that her two girls would forever be without her, that she would never again be able to braid their hair, or wipe stray marmalade from the corners of their lips, or hold them close during a thunderstorm.

Marina stopped herself. These girls were not her daughters.

Her daughters were safe and cared for. Whatever these girls felt about their mother's disappearance, however heart-wrenching, her own daughters hadn't experienced. At least not so far. And if she met with Erich tonight? He had hinted yesterday that he might have to return to Berlin suddenly. Would she go with him? Last night she had been convinced she would, because she told herself that her girls would be all right without her for a short time. Erich had said the war would be over very soon. He had said it with conviction, as if he knew something. As soon as the war was over, the children could join them. But there would be that short period during which she would be gone. What would her girls think and feel then? What was the cost to a child in losing a mother, however briefly? What would happen to a child's world-view if her mother, whom she had always been able to count on, whose ubiquity was a given, suddenly vanished? The loss these Polish girls knew was vast; their entire family had been obliterated. Marina couldn't let herself imagine it.

The older girl's eyelids fluttered intermittently, and she suddenly shot up on the bench and looked around the station, blinking herself awake. Seeing Marina, she immediately slid over and put her arms around her sister protectively. Marina knelt and smiled, speaking as gently as she could. She opened the bag to show the girls the food she had brought. "Hello, sweet girls, you must be hungry, yes?" She extended both hands, a *brötchen* in each. The younger girl immediately grabbed the bread and started ripping pieces off with her teeth. Her older sister waited until Marina pulled out the cheese and berries. Then she too ate. Marina wished she had more to give them. Perhaps she could sneak into the cellar later and bring them some Linzer torte.

While the girls ate, Marina bundled Johann's coat into her bag. Then she assessed the girls' physical similarities to her own daughters. The younger girl had a wild crop of brown curls, like Rosie. The other's hair was too dark to pass for Lara's, so when they were done eating, Marina wrapped her own scarf around the older girl's head to mask the difference. She didn't have to tell the girls to keep their heads down as she herded them out of the train station: they did so instinctively. The three of them passed right by the large boulder at the side of the building, oblivious to the two pairs of eyes watching them.

– Twenty-Eight –

If Max hadn't asked Willie to help him wash Pastor Johann's church windows, promising to take him on a secret mission afterward, it would have taken him all day. Working together, the two of them finished early in the afternoon, and Willie immediately reminded Max of his promise, which was how they both ended up on the boulder staring into the East Blumental station. After twenty-four hours of lone surveillance, Max had decided that it would be more fun to look for spies with a buddy. Then, if you didn't find anything, as Max hadn't so far, your friend could help you fabricate an imaginary scenario. This afternoon, when Max climbed on top of the boulder and peered through the station window, he expected to see absolutely nothing. Instead, to his great surprise, there was someone on the bench! Max shrieked in disbelief and huddled under the window. "What? What is it?" Willie asked, scrambling up next to him. "What do you see?"

"Shhh!" Max cautioned. "But look, Willie, look!"

Willie looked. He inhaled sharply and crouched down beside Max.

"Max! Is there someone underneath that coat? Who is it, Max? Is it a spy?"

Max clapped a hand over Willie's mouth. "I don't know," he whispered. "But it's a big coat, so it must be a big man."

"We should go tell someone, Max. We should go now and tell someone, right away!"

"No, Willie, wait a moment," Max urged. "Let's just wait a little bit and see if he wakes up."

"But what if he sees us?" Willie whimpered. Max pressed his hand against Willie's mouth. The front door to the station was opening. In their excitement, neither Max nor Willie had noticed anyone approaching the building. The boys cowered under the windowsill, their eyes barely peeking over it. They watched in amazement as Marina Thiessen walked over to the large form under the coat and took a seat on the bench. To their further astonishment, she sat there as if nothing was the matter, as if she didn't care that there was a spy sleeping right next to her.

After a little while, Frau Thiessen touched the coat. And then Max and Willie were truly bewildered, as the large man under the coat, the person they thought was a spy, sat up and turned out to be two little girls! They looked harmless and slight. Max felt a pang of disappointment. He highly doubted that girls could be spies. Still, he and Willie watched, mesmerized and mute, as Frau Thiessen gave the girls some food. They didn't appear to be talking, just eating. Then Frau Thiessen wrapped one of the girls' heads in her scarf and they all left the station, the boys still hiding behind their large rock. When they were gone, Max and Willie stared at each other, too stunned and confused to speak. Eventually Willie broke the silence. "We have to tell someone."

"No, we don't," Max objected. "Besides, what do we tell them?"

"I don't know," Willie said, insistent. "But something is going on. And the Führer is coming today. That makes everything important."

"But it's Frau Thiessen," Max said. "And those are little girls, how could they be dangerous?"

"I'm not saying it makes any sense, but this is big, Max. It's too big to keep to ourselves. We need to find someone who can tell us what to do."

"Pastor Johann," Max said. Willie nodded emphatically, grateful for a plan of any kind. The boys raced back to town, back to the church. Max rushed across the cobblestones of the Mün-sterplatz, with Willie only a few steps behind, and rounded the corner into Hauptstrasse. In that instant, he slammed into Gisela Mecklen as she was leaving the bakery. Fortunately for Gisela, her frame was large enough to withstand the impact of Max's slight skeleton flung against her. Max, however, stumbled back and fell to the ground, disoriented for a moment.

"Careful, boys, careful!" Gisela scolded. "Where are you going in such a hurry?"

"Frau Thiessen just picked up two strange girls at the East Blumental station!" Willie blurted out as he ran up. Gulping for breath, Max struggled to find his voice.

Gisela Mecklen's attention immediately zeroed in on Willie. "I'm sorry, what did you say about Frau Thiessen, Willie?" Still coughing, Max waved his arms to keep Willie from saying any-thing more. But Gisela Mecklen placed her body between the two boys and clamped her hands on Willie, forcing him to look up at her. "Now, Willie, please repeat what you just said."

"Well, I—I—" Willie stammered, trying to look around Gise-la's hips to find Max.

"You saw Frau Thiessen at the East Blumental station?"

"Yes, that's right. That's all." Willie's upper body shifted back and forth, as he tried to catch Max's eye, but Gisela shifted her ample bottom to block his line of sight.

"And there was someone with her. Who was it?"

"I don't know," Willie admitted. And then he gave up. Be-cause he did want to tell someone. He needed to tell. "Two little girls. Very little. I've never seen them before. They're not from around here."

"And what did Frau Thiessen do?" Gisela asked.

"Nothing. She gave them some food. And then they left."

"They left? Where did they go? Did you see where they went?"

"No," Willie said. "They went around the other side of the sta-tion and down the path to the lake."

"Hmm," Gisela mused.

Max took the moment of Gisela's hesitation to step around her body and grab Willie's hand. "Willie and I really need to go now, Frau Mecklen. Really." Before she could stop them, the boys ran off.

Gisela Mecklen stood still, deep in thought. Marina Thiessen was far too close to Johann Wiessmeyer. Frau Thiessen needed a warning; she needed to back off so that Sabine could claim the bachelor for herself. The Liaison for the Enforcement of National Socialism was good at warning people. The LENS had, in the end, done slightly more than warn the Rosenberg family about the dangers that Jews faced in being too prominent in society. But at least the Mecklens now had the bakery location they'd coveted. And Gisela felt certain that, whenever the Rosenbergs were released from whatever detention camp they were being held at, they would not return to Blumental to disturb her family. As for Marina Thiessen, well, her father could protect her from any real consequences of her reckless behavior, whatever it was. But at least she would be warned, and she might stop all these kaffee-klatsches with Pastor Wiessmeyer. Gisela went back into the bakery and opened the cash drawer, where she kept a list of important telephone numbers. Then she headed over to the post office.

– Twenty-Nine –

All day long, Edith tried not to think about the Führer and his imminent arrival. The day's agenda hung over her like the prediction of an afternoon storm: dark skies and low-hanging clouds, visible if she looked but best ignored until absolutely necessary. Edith had focused on each task at hand, or perhaps the task immediately thereafter, deliberately looking no farther into the future than that. Upon awakening, breakfast for the girls: *brötchen*, marmalade, the leftover berries from yesterday's coulis, milk. Then on to the baking with Marina: dough for the strudel, latticework for the Linzer torte. Flowers from the garden: a few sprigs of floribunda roses for the entrance hall; daisies for the table on the patio, in case he chose to sit outside. But probably not, he was an indoor man, preferred artificial lighting. So a large bouquet for the coffee table. Recycle what she could from yesterday's luncheon arrangement, add some delphinium, more roses. Then it was lunchtime. Set out more food. Send Lara for cream from Gunther. Girls gone. Oskar useless, smoking his pipe outside or working upstairs at his desk, sending messages from his field telegraph. Final tidying; she only hoped she could remember tomorrow where she was stashing all these extraneous bits—unattended pieces of mail, forgotten keys, one of the children's books, a hairbrush, ponytail holders. Something important was certain to go missing, but she could not worry about it now.

And suddenly it was time to dress. Thankfully, even the dressing allowed her to maintain distance from the occasion, for it required no thought. Edith had only one suit, the Chanel crepe that Oskar had brought back from Paris more than a decade ago. For Edith, its advantages were twofold: it fit, and it was comfortable, though she had a brief moment of concern about wearing wool in the summer. The collar of her mother's Belgian lace blouse was a complement to its narrow lapels. If it got too warm, she could take off her jacket. Quick brush-through of the hair. Pat the curls and waves in place and hope for the best.

Dressing the girls was far less simple. Checking on their progress in the other bedroom, Edith found Marina deep in conflict with both Lara and Rosie. Lara wanted her hair down, while Marina insisted on flipped braids, *affenschaukel*. "So the monkeys can swing in your hair," Rosie called from her corner of the bedroom, where she was pressing her arms against her sides to avoid the dress Marina was pulling over her head. Marina seemed more short-tempered than usual, so Edith took over Rosie. Tickling was the key to this child: success in just under two minutes, and Rosie went off to parade herself before Opa. Edith hoped he knew his role was to gush and praise. Lara glowered from a chair beneath Marina's quick-braiding fingers. Edith flashed a reassuring smile and returned to her own mirror. Picked up her lipstick. And, for the first time all morning, she allowed herself to think. She froze.

Would the Führer approve or disapprove of lipstick? Was lipstick consistent with the honesty and purity of a German *hausfrau*? Would he interpret it as licentiousness in her character? Or would he consider bare lips an affront, disrespectful? Edith didn't want to appear disrespectful of the Führer. If he perceived her as insolent in her outward appearance, he might begin to suspect the contempt she really felt for him.

Even as she acknowledged the insanity of engaging in this kind of second-guessing—about *lipstick*, for heaven's sake!—Edith could not shake her fear. She was terrified of the Führer and his power, a power that crouched over her country like a malevolent demon, strangling its people and culture. Even more alarming was the Führer's power over her family, over Oskar in particular.

Oskar was, Edith knew, quintessentially Prussian in his adherence to rules and laws, a man who did as he was told. That line-toeing mentality made him a dependable subordinate, someone the Führer could count on to carry out his dictates. He had sworn an oath of loyalty to the Führer early in the administration, but so much had changed since then.

When the Führer had been unknown, when he had been just one of many candidates pontificating and ranting on the political stage, she and Oskar had laughingly dismissed him as a right-wing demagogue. But once he had achieved political power and enacted the fiscal and commercial reforms that Germany so desperately needed, Oskar's view shifted. Coming home from work, Oskar had optimistic reports about the economic programs he was implementing. Mandatory public works projects that assigned men to specific jobs and eliminated unemployment. Corollary compulsory entertainment and leisure plans that organized workers' free time and gave families short vacations to the Baltic Sea at affordable prices. Incentives for working families to save money for a Volkswagen, the car of the people. Oskar applauded such initiatives for restoring economic prosperity to their wounded and downtrodden country. Like so many of his countrymen, he was ready to give political allegiance to a man who could raise the German phoenix from its ashes. And as a former military man, Oskar knew that stability and control required some relinquishment of individual liberties.

Looking back, Edith realized how cunning the Führer had been: as he gradually dictated and corralled every aspect of citizens' lives, he expanded the authority of his secret police. They took over local law enforcement, infiltrating every city and town, keeping lists of all the inhabitants—names, relatives, occupations, movements, and, most important, political affiliations.

They encouraged people to watch their neighbors and report any transgressions, offering incentives like extra ration cards and easier access to travel permits. By the time people realized they were being told not just how to live but what to *think*, they were far too afraid to do anything about it. Because thinking, speaking, or doing anything contrary to proscribed ordinance led to sudden disappearances. Everyone knew that if you did anything wrong, the police would take away not just you, but your children or parents, even if they were completely innocent of any wrongdoing. This threat, more than any other, kept people in line.

Had Oskar realized what was happening? Was he complicit? Edith couldn't say, for as the state increasingly extended its reach, her husband turned inward, keeping his own counsel. Edith knew she was culpable. She allowed herself to be occupied by domestic concerns—helping Marina establish her new household, supporting her and Franz and their new babies, keeping everyone fed and everything organized. And by the time she raised her head and looked around, Oskar had stopped communicating. Now the Führer was inviting him for personal tête-à-têtes at Fürchtesgaden, and she realized that she no longer knew what Oskar believed. Perhaps her husband had crossed the line from approval of the Führer's economic initiatives to affirmative endorsement of his entire vision. Perhaps years of being in the Führer's company, years of being surrounded by others of like small-mindedness, had changed Oskar's convictions. If so, she couldn't fault him, though she devoutly wished for the opportunity to persuade him back to her—*their*—way of thinking.

Because that was it, wasn't it? Edith and Oskar had been of a similar mind on almost every subject throughout their married years, on questions as important as what to name their daughter (they both loved Shakespeare's *Pericles, Prince of Tyre*) and whether there was a God (they were undecided, but tended toward pantheism), and as trivial as how long to cook a soft-boiled egg (three minutes and forty seconds). It was evidence of their compatibility, but to Edith it was also a testimony to their bond, a rare and cherished fusion of mind and heart. They completed each other's sentences, understood each other's thoughts. It was not uncommon, when they were together, for Oskar to voice an idea that was, at that very moment, also going through Edith's mind. So if Oskar had changed his beliefs about the Führer, about something so fundamental—if Oskar now supported the policies that had sent her beloved Hilde and Martin Stern and the entire Rosenberg family to some ghetto for who knew what purpose— well, to Edith, that would be far more than a tear in the fabric of their relationship. It would be a chasm.

For today, she decided, she would be patient. She would watch. She would observe Oskar's interactions with his leader, his demeanor when talking and listening, his responses to the Führer. She knew her husband. She knew, or at least was fairly certain she would know by the end of this tea, where his loyalties truly lay.

Edith applied the pale coral tint to her lips. Better, she thought, stepping back to look at herself critically. She definitely looked more proper, more polished, and that was the image she wanted to convey. When she got downstairs, she found Marina nervously assembling the girls in the entrance hall, positioning them in line from tallest to shortest, giving Rosie's curls one last smooth-ing before she took up her spot next to Lara. "The car is just a few kilometers away," Marina updated her mother. "The security posse is checking the outside perimeter of the house one last time, making certain everything is safe, that there aren't snipers hiding in the cherry tree or positioning themselves atop the neighbors' roofs." Marina rolled her eyes, but Edith felt her daughter's anxi-ety lying beneath the sarcasm.

Edith nodded, adding a plea that she knew was likely to be futile: "You know, my dear, you should be careful with the facial expressions. I'm told nothing escapes him."

"I know, I *know*, Mutti." Marina grimaced and covered her

face with her hands. Edith saw that they were trembling slightly. "It's involuntary. I just wish this were all over already."

Edith sighed. "It will be soon, Marina. Think of the girls, if that is helpful, to get you through this."

As if on cue, at that moment, Lara sought her mother's intervention. "Mutti, will you please tell Sofia to stop bumping me?"

"I can't help it," Sofia said. "Rosie keeps fluffing her skirt and knocking me off balance."

"Enough, Rosie," Marina said. "Stand still."

Edith stepped forward to close the front door, which was still ajar, but Oskar appeared on the threshold, pipe in hand. With some surprise, she noticed that he wasn't wearing his uniform but rather a suit. Civilian attire. She wondered whether there was some meaning to that, an indication to the Führer that Oskar was, in his home at least, more than just a minion. Or was that wishful thinking? "A handsome family," Oskar said approvingly. He looked from Lara, who was smoothing a reluctant ringlet to its spot behind her ear, to Sofia, beaming at him, to Rosie. "Absolutely *beautiful*, you are all breathtaking in your loveliness. No wonder the soldiers dispersed so quickly. The sight of all of you together is unnerving. Makes a man forget his assignment." He stepped inside and took Edith's hand from the knob of the front door. "Leave it open, my dear, his entourage is at the front gate."

The processional arrived. Four years earlier, at the Führer's insistence, his hand-picked legislative council had proclaimed him emperor. Thus, as befitted such a grand personage, a parade of personal guards and officers preceded him in all public appearances. Edith watched one young man after another file past her, each seemingly more blond and blue-eyed than his predecessor, each stopping briefly before her and Oskar, pausing only to jerk his arm up straight in salute in a manner so sudden and violent that it was a wonder to her that shoulders were not dislocated. After the eighth young soldier passed by, Edith noticed a sudden leap in age, for the next set of men looked older and more experienced, more like Erich. These were the *Erleuchtete*, or "enlightened ones," the Führer's elite inner circle of guards, so named because their close proximity to the Führer's person supposedly enhanced their mental and spiritual acuity. The twelve coveted positions coincided in number with the disciples of Jesus Christ. That the Führer embraced such Christian symbols while simultaneously denouncing organized religion was a hypocrisy not mentioned in public. These men were Erich's colleagues. He had been invited to join this personal security force after his graduation from the Military Academy and, except for his detail to Poland at the beginning of the war, had remained there ever since. Like Erich, these men were distinguished officers. Their demeanors, though serious, appeared more relaxed than the youngsters' before them, and their salutes, while strong, lacked the youths' intensity. Probably they had attended countless teas of this sort, Edith thought. All sported the khaki uniform trimmed with deep purple that the Führer insisted upon for its royal effect.

After the last *Erleuchtete* marched by, there was a gap, a space deliberately incorporated into the retinue, Edith suspected, to heighten expectation. The next person who would cross the threshold of Edith's home, she realized, would be the Führer himself. She imagined the timbers that framed her open door straining against the pull of a dark gravity that pulsed with each step the Führer took toward them. For the next few moments, she fought a powerful urge to run forward and slam the door shut to protect her beloved home from intrusion, the contamination of his presence.

But suddenly there he was, standing regally in the open doorway, arms stretched upward and outward—in greeting? to receive adoration?—his petite shape backlit in a full-body halo by the midafternoon sunlight while his face remained in shadow. Everything he had achieved, from political power to military victories to public support, was so vast, so staggering, that it was hard to reconcile the mental image conjured by those successes with the physically diminutive person standing before her. This man was pasty and thin, with a head hunched into his shoulders like a turtle's, and his limbs were almost spindly. In the retelling of his history, the Führer attributed his weak musculature to the atrophy he had suffered from years of wrongful imprisonment for trying to end the debilitating payment of unreasonable German war reparations. Another marvelous reconstruction of the truth, Edith thought, this self-portraiture as a martyr for the cause of German honor. Yes, it was true that the Führer had been in prison as a young man, but he had been jailed for bombing a government building that housed only postal services.

Regardless, the Führer had presence. He had a way of annexing the very physical space surrounding him, commanding and seizing the attention of everything nearby. People on the street stopped and stood immobile, fixed in salute; the sparrows sitting atop the fence ceased chattering, silenced. Even the air seemed to freeze in its movement. The power he wielded was palpable. Long ago, upon seeing him in Berlin, Edith had learned the origin of that power—his eyes. Like everything else about the man, they were, at first glance, unremarkable: small, jet black, and heavily lidded. But their stare, when turned upon someone, was compelling, piercing, and inescapable. Oskar said that the Führer's gaze could penetrate not only a man's soul, but his intestines, and that the lavatory located just outside the Führer's office in Berlin required more toilet paper than any other in government.

Now the man stood in her house, fixing those eyes on her family. "Ah, what beautiful girls! Yes, beautiful. Each more beautiful than the last." The Führer made his way down their small receiving line, his voice wheedling its way around her granddaughters, making Edith bristle protectively. Without looking, she knew Marina was doing the same. She tried to exhale both audibly and inconspicuously so that Marina would remember to breathe. "You never told me, dear General Eberhardt, that you had so many jewels in your possession." The Führer stopped in front of Marina, taking a moment to appraise her, raising his chin and lowering it slowly, his eyes sweeping over her from head to toe and back up again, resting finally upon her face. Edith's quick sideways glance at her daughter revealed that Marina's jaw was tightly clenched, and her eyes, thankfully, were cast downward, lids sheltering the mixture of defiance and fear they undoubtedly would have radiated. While the Führer lingered in front of Marina, staring at the top of her bowed head, Edith felt him willing her daughter to look up, daring her to challenge him directly. But Marina didn't move. The tension between them pulsed until Oskar stepped forward and saluted his superior.

"*Mein Führer*." Oskar's clear, steady voice echoed. "Let me present my family. From youngest to wisest: my granddaughters Rose, Sofia, and Lara; my daughter, Marina Thiessen; and my wife, Edith." With Edith's name, Oskar gave a small flourish of his hand in her direction, and Edith gathered herself enough to curtsy slightly.

The Führer broke off his trance and turned to Edith. His puffy fingers reached for her hand, and his bloodless lips kissed the air above it. "Such a pleasure, Frau Eberhardt, *such* a pleasure to see you." The sour smell of partially digested pickled herring and horseradish drifted from his mouth, making Edith's stomach turn.

Some response was expected of her, but she struggled to find her voice. She was overpowered by her visceral response to his presence. Finally she managed to utter, "Herr Führer, it is my honor to welcome you to our home."

"My dear Frau Eberhardt, I would not miss this opportunity for the *world*! And I may be the only person who honestly has that alternative." The Führer squeezed Edith's hand conspiratorially and winked at her. "Actually, I am here for the strudel and Linzer torte. Your husband cannot stop raving about them. It is quite the distraction when we are trying to get work done up in Berlin and we take a break for coffee and cake. You should hear him gloat about the excellence of his own personal pastry chef." He leaned in toward her cheek, the acidic cloud of his breath polluting the air. "He says your strudel dough is so thin that he can read the front page of the newspaper through it."

Edith felt a cough rising in her chest. Best to escape by moving everyone over into the other room. "Well, Oskar can be prone to exaggeration, but perhaps you would like to try it yourself? My daughter and I did a bit of baking this morning, and I would be grateful for your opinion." Oskar took her cue and opened the door to the living room, motioning the Führer in. The entourage had already dispersed, the younger soldiers taking up position on the outdoor patio, while the *Erleuchtete* stood around the room's perimeter, inconspicuously stationing themselves at doors and windows. The Führer entered the room slowly and deliberately, approaching the sitting area like a bride walking down the aisle of a church: first extending one foot, then bringing the other up to meet it, pausing and looking around, then stepping out again with the second foot to repeat the entire cycle. The halting gait gave his eyes time to dart around the room like small daggers, piercing the shadow of each piece of furniture for hidden foes. This man knew he was hated, and trusted no one, not even his beloved *Erleuchtete*, to protect him fully.

"A lovely room," the Führer concluded, finally standing next to the large upholstered chair Oskar held for him. "Undoubtedly the nicest garage I have ever seen." He chuckled and stared at the seat before him. "Yours, General?"

Oskar looked confused. "The chair? No, *mein Führer*, I generally sit over there." Oskar pointed at a mahogany chair covered in maroon velvet that flanked the window. "But that one, I am sorry to say, has a tear in the seat that we have not had time to repair. This one will be more comfortable."

The Führer frowned. "Comfort is irrelevant, General." He went to the maroon chair and ran a finger over the armrest. "Interesting style. I'm not familiar with it."

"It is American," Oskar said.

"A William and Mary, from Boston," Edith added. "But originally inspired by the Dutch, I believe."

"Ah, American!" A broad smile stretched the Führer's thin lips, revealing overlapping teeth with distinct coffee stains. He patted the seat cushion and settled into Oskar's chair. A moment later, Edith became aware of a soft clicking noise in the room. Although muted, the sound was steady and precise, like a muffled metronome or ticking timer. After several seconds, she realized it was emanating from the Führer. His mouth was slightly open, and he appeared to be tapping its roof with his tongue. A strange habit, Edith thought, and highly unnerving. She wished Oskar had mentioned it to her. But even if he had, she wasn't sure she could have prepared herself for the sense of impending doom that the incessant clicking aroused in her. At least when the man spoke, the noise stopped. "America, America," the Führer mused aloud. "Yes, there is much to learn from that country."

"Really, *mein Führer?*" Oskar had taken a seat in the chair he had been holding. "I did not know you were such a fan of the Americans."

"Oh, certainly. In many ways, an admirable nation. Hacking their way through wilderness to establish a civilization. Pioneers in a wild land. Impressive forefathers." The tempo of his tongue quickened to a minuet. The Führer's eyes sparkled with energy, animated by the imagined life of adventure in a new world. In the next instant, they narrowed. "Of course, they were all criminals and thugs to begin with, so they are tainted, racially. Those kinds of impurities in the blood are impossible to erase."

"Were they really all criminals?" Edith asked, relatively certain that the Führer was incorrect in this assumption but not daring to correct him.

"Oh, yes. Actual prisoners or people the law had not caught up with yet. Crimes waiting to happen. Societal riffraff, panhandlers, paupers. And religious zealots too. Imagine the nightmare! To cross the ocean on a ship with such people, knowing they would be your neighbors forever once you landed." Faster, louder clicks. Edith felt the need to silence them. She leaned forward toward the coffee table, laden with pots of coffee and tea, cups and saucers, a creamer, and a small bowl of sugar cube remnants. Someone had already picked out all the intact cubes. Edith suspected Rosie.

"Tea or coffee, Herr Führer?" she asked.

"Coffee, coffee, my dear. No tea. The English have entirely ruined my appetite for tea." Edith poured two cups from the coffeepot, handing one to the Führer and one to Oskar. She knew Oskar took his coffee black. So, apparently, did his commander, who sniffed the brew before taking a loud slurp. At that moment, Marina entered from the kitchen, bearing a platter of strudel and Linzer torte, both warm from the oven. The Führer watched her approach the coffee table. Like a wildcat watching a gazelle, Edith thought. Marina again averted her eyes, pausing only long enough to deliver the tray of baked goods. She started heading back to the kitchen, but the Führer's words stopped her. "Won't you join us, Frau Thiessen?" His words slithered through the air. His tone made clear it was not a request.

Marina turned slowly and curtsied stiffly in the Führer's direction. "I'm sorry, Herr Führer, but I must decline the invitation. The children—"

He interrupted her. "Surely . . ." He closed his mouth deliberately, his tongue clicking steadily. A purposeful, unhurried clicking, like small nails being hammered into a coffin. "*Surely* the children can take care of themselves. Or you could put the eldest—Lara, is it? You could put Lara in charge," he said with a smug smile.

"Ordinarily, Herr Führer, you would be absolutely correct, Lara is certainly capable of watching her younger sisters. But today—"

Another interruption, the tone more imperious. "*Today* I would like to get to know you, Frau Thiessen. Learn about life here in Blumental. Your interests. Your . . . *activities*." He hissed the last word with vehemence. Oskar shifted in his chair and looked at Marina. Edith had no idea what insinuation lay beneath the Führer's words, but whatever it was had raised Oskar's guard. Marina didn't flinch. For the first time, she met the Führer's eyes. Her look was cold, hard, and distant.

Edith had had that look directed at herself only once and hoped never to experience it again. It was the day Rosie was born. Edith had made the mistake of asking Marina whether she should send a telegram to Franz, who had been ordered to a military training camp near Stuttgart. Propped up in bed with pillows, Marina had been cooing at her new baby, gently stroking the dark damp curls on her head. Her gaze was rapturous and enthralled. It was as if she had never given birth before, as if she were witnessing the miracle of life for the first time. And for just a moment, for the first and only time since Marina admitted her pregnancy to Edith, Edith had felt angry. She was not sure what directed her anger; perhaps it was a sense of injury on behalf of Lara and Sofia or, more likely, Franz. Still, the resentment had asserted itself, molded the question she was formulating in her head about how to inform Franz. When that question finally came out, she could not conceal the tone of judgment her anger demanded.

"Should we let Franz know that *you* have another daughter?"

Marina's eyes that afternoon had pierced Edith with the same steely scrutiny that was now directed at the Führer. Now too Marina remained still, eyes completely focused on him for ten silent, interminable seconds. She stepped carefully over to the sofa, put down the tray, and took a seat next to her mother. Her back was rigid, and Edith felt the stiffness of her body, each muscle poised in readiness for flight. Edith wanted to break the tension yet dared not say a word. She looked to Oskar, hoping his diplomatic skills could aid them. But Oskar appeared stunned—the unexpected suggestion of unspoken suspicions completely silenced his usually facile tongue. The Führer leaned over the coffee table and picked up a large serving knife. "I simply must try these pastries, Frau Eberhardt," he said, holding the knife aloft. He hesitated, twisting it slowly in the air while deciding which baked good to try first.

Watching the knifepoint writhe around and around in tiny circles made Edith increasingly uncomfortable. She tried to take over serving. "Oh, Herr Führer, please let me help," she apologized, reaching for the knife.

Deftly, he held it away from her. "No, no, quite all right, I'm perfectly capable of serving myself." Settling on the strudel, he slashed into it and deposited an enormous piece onto the topmost plate. "This way, I can take as large a portion as I like." Taking the plate onto his lap, the Führer settled back in his chair and grasped his fork sideways. With quick cutting motions, he hacked the strudel into four sections. The metal tines screeched against the china plate, making Edith wince. "I am looking forward to this first bite," he said, holding the fork in front of his face. "The first bite is always the best, don't you think? The anticipation of the unknown conquest, with all of its imagined pleasures and wonders, before its assimilation into the known and familiar. Perhaps that is why I have such an appetite." The Führer brought the strudel up to his mouth and opened it wide. His jaws appeared to dislocate slightly as they accommodated the offering of food. Then, closing his eyes in unison with his lips, he swallowed without chewing and let out a long, contented sigh. "Perfect, absolutely perfect, Frau Eberhardt! Exquisite!" In quick succession, he wolfed down the other three pieces before him. His plate was clean. Remembering his coffee, he picked up the cup and gulped down its contents. Hoping to keep him focused on food, Edith took the pastry knife to cut the Linzer torte and placed a large piece on his plate. But this time the Führer ignored the pastry and turned to Marina. "General Eberhardt, I realize I have been keeping you too much in Berlin," he said without breaking his gaze. "Not only have I been depriving you of the company of these beautiful ladies, but I have put your family in the position of remaining . . ." He paused as if searching for the right word, but

Edith suspected he knew exactly what it was. "*Unsupervised*. And for extended periods of time. That is not good."

Oskar cleared his throat. "Herr Führer, we must all make sacrifices for the Reich. I am lucky in having a wife and daughter who are level-headed and resourceful."

"Resourceful? *Resourceful?*" The Fuhrer repeated the word as if he were learning a foreign vocabulary. "Yes, I imagine they are. Able to tap into *resources*. Frau Thiessen, would you say the *resources* here in Blumental are sufficient for your needs?"

Marina's eyes tightened. "Yes, Herr Führer, on the whole, I cannot say that we are deprived of anything necessary for our well-being. There are, as you know, many farmers in the area, and that gives us a great advantage over our fellow citizens in the north, where we hear of so many food shortages."

"Food, yes, food," the Führer mused. "Of course, food is important. But then, food feeds only the body." The clicking sound, which had subsided while the Führer was licking the remnants of strudel out of his molars with his tongue, now returned. "Are there sufficient resources here in the south for your mind, Frau Thiessen? For your spirit? For your cultural and civic interests?"

Edith had been listening attentively, trying to discern what precisely he was suggesting in the hope that she might be able to deflect him. She saw her opportunity. "Oh, *culture*, Herr Führer! Well, it is true that Blumental is no Berlin, but there are ample cultural opportunities in the area. Especially in music. Why, Marina has even joined a local choir—she has a lovely singing voice, and the choir has quite a reputation in these parts."

Now it was the Führer's turn to narrow his eyes. His lips tightened into a smirk. "A choir. Interesting, a choir. I believe I have heard of this choir. Is that the same choir that is led by the Protestant minister? Pastor Wasserman?"

"Wiessmeyer," Edith offered cautiously. From the voracious look that had come over the Führer, she was no longer certain that this was a good subject. Marina had, at the mention of the choir, lowered her chin and averted her gaze. She was gripping her coffee cup so fiercely that Edith thought the china might break.

"Wiessmeyer, that's right." The Führer lingered on the *ss*, hissing softly. "Yes, yes, I have heard of this choir. Did I tell you, General?"

Oskar was looking intently at his commander. Was he as confused or worried as Edith was? She couldn't tell. His back was stiff and straight, as if he were at full attention in his chair. "No, sir, I don't believe you did."

"Ah, perhaps not. I thought I had. I certainly intended to." The Führer turned to Edith. "Yes, Frau Eberhardt, on occasion, I get reports up in Berlin about activities this far south, even regarding—what did you call them, Frau Eberhardt? Ah, yes, *cultural* activities. And Pastor Wiessmeyer's *activities* have recently been brought to my attention." With this statement, the Führer's eyes fixed on Marina. Oskar's eyes remained on the Führer, while Edith's gaze shifted back and forth between the three of them. Something very dangerous had entered the room and was now lying in wait. Edith dared not speak, but she desperately wished Oskar would say something.

"Mutti, Mutti!" Rosie came running through the French doors from the porch, slamming the glass panels into the two men flanking that entry. Her brown hair had freed itself from the ribbon Marina had woven into it a few hours earlier, and her knees and shins were caked in mud. Oblivious to the company around her, she stopped in front of her mother and thrust forward two dirt-encrusted hands, which she cupped tightly together.

"Look, Mutti, look! I found my snail!" Rosie lifted the hand on top to reveal a fat slug with brown spots. "At first, I couldn't find him and I thought he had disappeared, but I guess he just got hungry because I didn't feed him breakfast this morning." Edith had never been more grateful to see one of her grandchildren, even one as covered in filth as Rosie was. The small girl stood panting before Edith and Marina, beaming with joy. Seeing Marina's eyes focused on the Führer, Rosie turned in his direction. "I usually take very good care of him," she explained, shifting the snail to one hand and petting it with the other. "But this morning, I was too busy helping Sofia look for our old clothes in the train station, and—"

Rosie looked up at the Führer and stopped in midsentence. The delight she had radiated the moment before was extinguished in an instant, and she stepped backward quickly, toward the safety of her mother's arms. Marina wrapped herself around her daughter protectively. "Rosie, your dress is completely covered in dirt," she said in a tone devoid of rebuke. "Let's go find you something clean to wear. You'll excuse me, Herr Führer?" Without glancing in his direction, she stood up and grabbed Rosie's hand.

"Careful, Mutti, don't disturb my snail!" Rosie cried in a small voice. "Don't let it fall."

"Here, Rosie, let me help." Edith grabbed one of the coffee cups and whisked the snail from Rosie's hands into the china. Then she inverted a saucer and placed it on top. "I'll keep it safe for you until you're ready to bring it back to its home in the garden." She looked over to the Führer and was relieved to see a small smile playing across his upper lip. "I can remove this to the other room, if you like, Herr Führer."

He clicked persistently and shook his head. "No, no, it does not disturb me at all. Not at all. But I will admit that the habits of you southerners with respect to the domestication of animals are a revelation." The Führer leaned forward in his chair, addressing Oskar with feigned concern. "Did you know, General Eberhardt, that your grandchild was keeping a snail as a pet? And apparently too she is searching for discarded apparel in train stations?"

Oskar laughed, shaking his head. "No, sir, I must admit quite candidly that I had no idea such creatures were being harbored under my roof." He winked at Edith, a reassurance that balance had been restored. Whatever menace had hovered over the coffee table five minutes ago had disappeared. Edith marveled at the suddenness of the transformation in the Führer's demeanor. In a split second, he had become lighthearted and easygoing, as affable as he had been threatening moments before. Oskar had told her of the unpredictability of the Führer's moods, but the extremity of this shift, Edith thought, was highly unnerving.

"A delightful child, nonetheless," the Führer said, extending his coffee cup for a refill. "Quite a lovely little sprite. Though she might require some taming in the future."

"Well, sir, we are in complete agreement there," Oskar replied, still smiling. He motioned at Edith to sit back while he poured coffee for his commander.

"That is good, General, quite good. Our agreement on things, that is." The Führer took a loud sip of coffee. "Wouldn't you agree?"

"To what, sir?"

"That it is good to be in agreement."

"Why, yes, of course. I agree that it is good to be in agreement." Oskar looked bemused.

"Especially with your commanding officer, wouldn't you say?"

Another slight shift in the atmosphere. Edith felt Oskar's renewed wariness. She saw the tendons in his neck tense up. "*Mein Kommandant*, I would say that whether or not one agrees with one's commander is irrelevant. One does what the officer commands without question."

"A good answer, General. You see, Frau Eberhardt"—the Führer flashed Edith a well-rehearsed smile—"that is why I ask your husband to oversee my agenda. He understands obedience and loyalty. More importantly—*most* importantly—he knows how to instill them in others. But at the same time, I do wonder. Because of course, we are all human, are we not? We do have opinions about things, beliefs, certain *inclinations of conscience*, shall I call them? Yes?" He gave Oskar a piercing look. Oskar said nothing. "Every good general knows that he must be able to command such respect, such unerring allegiance, from his soldiers that their loyalty to him becomes instinctual. Their sense of duty must be honed to such a degree that it overrides, *quashes* really, any contrary inclinations of conscience. Because otherwise they might fester." The Führer paused, and Edith heard a quiet click, but it was a different sound from the one that his tongue had been making all afternoon. From the sudden appearance of one of the *Erleuchtete* at the Führer's chair, she realized he had snapped his fingers. The guard, a heavily muscled man with graying temples, carried a small pouch, which he now opened and held out to his commander.

The Führer reached in and withdrew a small wooden figurine. Slightly larger than the span of his hand, the carving was pale mustard in color and adorned with feathers and shells. It looked like a combination of man and wildcat. It had two pointed ears, accented with stiff yellow and white feathers, and appeared to have a catlike snout painted with sharp teeth. Its chest was bare-skinned and crisscrossed with tiny shells, and between its crouching legs, a long tail curved from its posterior up over its head. The Führer set the figurine down on the coffee table and leaned back in his chair.

"Do you remember, General Eberhardt, the occasion of my coronation as emperor?" The Führer leaned over to explain to Edith. "It was a private ceremony a few years back, Frau Eberhardt; you may remember it. Then, as now, we were engaged in such extensive warfare against our enemies that a more public celebration was just impossible. But when we do finally achieve our military initiatives—and it will happen, fear not, madam—much grander public festivities will be arranged." He turned to Oskar, obviously awaiting a response.

Oskar cleared his throat. "Yes, sir, that was a memorable day."

"Indeed it was, indeed it was." The Führer reclined his head and sighed, momentarily lost in his own recollection. "Did you know, General, that as emperor I received hundreds of letters from foreign heads of state? Yes, many letters, most of them completely unexpected. You see, Frau Eberhardt, I studied geography and history in school, as of course we all did, but my geographic knowledge simply did not include some of these small nation-states. The Te Au Togo tribe in the Pacific, for example. I believe they offered me greetings and congratulations by telegram. It is possible they also sent me a coconut. Or was it the choice of a wife from among their eligible females? I cannot remember."

The tongue clicking returned. It made Edith feel as if time was running out. She took the chance of looking over at Oskar. He was staring at the wooden statuette with curiosity, his brows furrowed. "One of the most fascinating gifts I received," the Füh-rer continued, "was this kachina doll from the chief of the Hopi tribe in northern Arizona. Chief Tinga-Tewa, I believe his name was, though quite honestly, all these native syllables are so in-terchangeable, it hardly matters what we call them." He chuck-led and picked up the kachina doll, fingering the feathers atop its head. "This is Toho, the hunter kachina. The most powerful hunter of the tribe, I am told, and a guardian of the north too. Quite an appropriate gift for a military genius like myself, don't you think?" Edith was grateful that the Führer did not seem to require a response to this statement. "I had stored it away until recently. In truth, I had quite forgotten about it, but my secretary found it the other day while cleaning out some old files, and she asked me whether or not to toss it out." He held the doll close to his face and scrutinized it, tilting his head. "Do you know what I admire most about the Americans, General?"

"No, sir, I don't believe you have ever told me."

"They are, of course, descended from liars and thieves and reb-els, but perhaps that is what gives them their greatest strength as a people," the Führer mused. He was silent, waiting to be urged on.

Oskar appeased him. "And what is that strength?"

"Their survival instinct. It is indomitable, really, their will to survive. It allows them to accomplish extraordinary feats with re-markable efficiency." He paused, petting the kachina's feathers, again waiting.

"What feats, *mein Führer?*"

"The annihilation of another race."

Without warning, images of dead bodies heaped into side alleys flooded Edith's mind. Berlin citizens, dead from shell fire or bombs or collapsed buildings, and later, starvation or disease. There were so many different ways to die near the end of the first war that the gravediggers couldn't keep up. Masses of lifeless humans shoveled into mounds. Was that also what was now happening out east? Had Edith been shutting her eyes to that reality, as she had averted her gaze all those years ago back in Berlin? Because the horror was too great to acknowledge? She looked out the window. Dusk was falling. The chestnut tree cast a gloom over the side yard. Edith felt cold, though all her morning baking had made the interior of the house quite warm.

Oskar sat up straight, his shoulders rigid as if bracing for an assault. It was the same posture he had assumed when sitting for his formal portrait for the Military Academy years earlier: alert, prepared, unyielding. He looked at the Führer deliberately, unwilling now to let any move by his commander escape his notice. The Führer, by contrast, reclined in his seat and continued to scrutinize the doll, as if he were expecting it to give him some sort of answer to an unspoken question. Finally he placed the doll on the table.

"I want you to have this kachina, General Eberhardt. I want you to keep it where you can see it every day. I want you to be reminded of the Native Americans." He pushed the doll across the stained oak toward Oskar. "I want you to remember that you are a hunter, and that hunters do not trouble themselves with conscience. They hunt." Oskar didn't look at the doll. He remained as before, inert and composed.

The Führer rose from his chair. Both Oskar and Edith began to rise, but the Führer held up his palm. "No, stay, stay seated. I will leave through the garden, if I may, Frau Eberhardt." He crossed the room toward the French doors, his gait now more of a shuffle than the majestic step he had assumed upon his entrance. His entourage had reassembled outside on the stone patio, and upon his approach, one of the guards pressed down on the door latch, permitting the door to swing open and allowing the garden's perfume to sweep in. Edith breathed it in gratefully.

"General, I will see you tonight," the Führer announced, his back to both of them. Without turning, he raised his right arm in salute to himself. "Adieu." The glass doors slammed shut behind him.

Edith began gathering the plates and cups and putting them on the tray next to the remaining pastries. To her surprise, the Führer's plate was empty. She didn't remember seeing him eat the Linzer torte. When had he done that? Edith started to ask Oskar if he'd noticed it, but he looked deep in thought. He was still staring at the kachina. "Oskar?" she began.

"Leave them, my dear, I will clear them later," he answered, his voice remote and flat. He did not move. Ignoring his instruction, Edith carried the tray through the swinging door and placed it on the kitchen counter next to the stove. She would put everything away later, she thought. Now she wanted to ask Oskar about the Führer's strange interest in Marina and his comment about the Native Americans. But when she returned to the living room, Oskar had disappeared. Again.

– Thirty –

The floor in the room with the coal pile was very cold. From the rhythmic way her older sister's stomach moved in and out against Pola's head, she knew Nadzia had fallen asleep. Pola wished she could go to sleep again too. She wanted to stop thinking about the past week, what had happened to Papa and her baby brother. One minute they were all packing up to leave. Mama and Papa said they were going to a new home in secret. Then before they could go, the soldiers came and took Mama. And the next day the whole town was marched to the marketplace. When they passed the alley where the grocer piled his empty crates, Nadzia had grabbed Pola's hand and pulled her out of line. She pushed Pola behind the stacks of wood and told her to keep her head down. But Pola heard baby Jakusz crying, and she wanted to go soothe him. Nobody could quiet him like Pola, not even Nadzia, except when she had his bottle. Papa didn't know how to calm Jakusz.

The crying got louder and louder, and Pola began to move, but her older sister held her back and shook her head. Angry voices began yelling at Papa in German and Papa said something she couldn't hear and Jakusz just kept crying and crying and Papa was shouting "Nie! *Nie!*" and then there was a loud smack, as if someone had thrown a heavy rock against a wall, and Nadzia gave a short stifled cry. After that, everything was very quiet, and Pola tried to peer out to see what was happening, but Nadzia pushed her back and held her down. They stayed there until long after everyone disappeared and darkness fell, and then they ran.

That day was the last time she heard Papa's voice. Ever since then, she and Nadzia had been hiding and moving. First they went to the farm that Mama and Papa had said they were going to. The old lady there gave them soup and apologized for how watery it was, but it tasted like a rich stew to Pola. Two nights later, a man came and took them a very long distance in a cart. They had to crouch between chicken cages, and Pola quickly learned to stay away from those beaks. Then there was the woman in the city, and two more men, and lots of walking at night. Pola had been so tired, and scared too, because she and Nadzia had never been alone without Mama and Papa. But she didn't say anything, she just started sucking on her thumb again. It had been more than a year since she quit, but it didn't matter because Mama and Papa weren't there anymore. And Nadzia didn't stop her either; she kissed Pola on the head when she noticed and said nothing. Finally there was the woman in the royal red hat, and a train. The train ride was long, but Pola didn't care because she'd never been on a train before, and they had seats. Then a quiet man with wire glasses and a round face picked them up from the train and brought them over to the empty station, and he told them that they could sleep on the benches if they wanted to. His Polish was not very good, but Pola liked him anyway because he asked her the name of her doll. Most people ignored Daiya, but this man looked closely and told her what a good friend she was. Daiya was Pola's best friend; she could tell her anything and Daiya would listen and understand.

Pola lifted her head slightly from her sister's lap and looked at Daiya sitting at the side of the black coal mountain. She was keeping watch for them. Somehow, Daiya's striped skirt had gotten torn. Pola didn't remember that happening, but Nadzia knew how to sew and would fix it. Perhaps the lady who had brought them to this house had a sewing kit.

This new lady was nice, nicer than the lady on the train with
the hat. And prettier. This lady had very beautiful hair, very soft-
and silky-looking. Like Pola's *mamusia's*. When they'd headed
over to this house, the new lady had taken Pola's hand, and they
had walked fast, so fast that at one point Pola could not keep up
and the lady picked her up and carried her. Pola felt the lady's
heart beating faster as they approached the house. When they
reached the front gate, the lady put her finger to her lips and said
something Pola didn't understand, but she knew she should be
quiet. They had walked very slowly then. As they got closer to
the front door, the lady kept turning her head from one side to
the other. Pola thought she was looking for someone. But no one
was there. Instead, Pola smelled cigarette smoke. She thought it
was coming from the big bushes to the right of the front door.
The lady must have smelled it too, and she smiled. Pola would
have liked to stay with the lady, but after they hurried into the
house and down to a cellar, she made it clear that Pola and Nadzia
should wait behind the coal pile until she came back. The lady
seemed sad about leaving them, though. Maybe that meant she
would come back soon.

A door opened and Pola heard someone flip a switch at the top
of the stairs. Nothing happened. The person mumbled something
and came down the stairs and rummaged around somewhere in
the other room in the darkness. A few minutes later, the lightbulb
at the far side of the room suddenly blinked on. For a moment,
everything shimmered as Pola's eyes adjusted to the brightness.
Nadzia jolted up and pulled Pola toward her so quickly, she had
no time to grab Daiya. She tried to say something, but Nadzia
clamped a hand over Pola's mouth and shook her head. Pola
heard heavy footsteps cross the stone floor toward them. She
couldn't tell if Daiya was visible from the other side of the coal
pile. Someone put a tin bucket down on the floor and picked up a
shovel. Pola heard the steel blade scrape against the stone and felt
the echo of the coal pieces as they clattered against the bucket.

Scrape, pause, clatter, pause. Scrape, pause, clatter, pause. The sounds went on for a few moments. Then they stopped.

Nadzia wrapped her arms more tightly around Pola when a hand reached for Daiya and picked her up. The silence in the cellar felt colder than the air. The person on the other side of the coal pile did nothing for a long time. Then the person took three steps and looked around the side of the coal. It was an old man with grayish-white hair, a grayish-white mustache, and thin lips. He peered down at them through small square eyeglasses as though he had difficulty seeing them. He wasn't smiling, but he didn't do anything that made Pola scared. He simply stared at them for a long time. Then he knelt down slowly and looked directly at her. He looked at her as if he knew her, as if he were trying to remember whose family she belonged to, and then he extended his right arm, holding Daiya out in front of him. Cautiously, Pola took Daiya from his hand. The slightest of smiles crossed his mouth. Then he stood, turned to pick up the tin bucket, and ascended the stairs. When he reached the top, he stopped. Pola did not know why he was waiting, but it seemed like an eternity. Then the lightbulb switched off and the cellar was once again dark.

– Thirty-One –

In retrospect, allowing the girls to eat Linzer torte in lieu of dinner was probably a mistake, but Edith hadn't had the energy to prepare anything else. Lara ate two and a half squares of the walnut-and-jam delicacy before retreating to her room, complaining that she would get fat. Sofia and Rosie, on the other hand, managed only two before they began chasing each other around the living room while Edith watched from the sofa, exhausted. After half an hour, Marina corralled them and took them up to bed. Edith promised to join her shortly. She wanted to talk to Oskar before he left for the concert. He was in the cellar getting coal. She waited for him in the kitchen. Last night, she had been too happy to be with him again, too eager to feel his familiar shape against hers in bed, to engage in any serious conversation. She'd luxuriated in the smell of his skin and the weight of his arms around her. Neither of them had wanted to speak.

But now the need to talk was more urgent. The Führer's visit had unleashed a maelstrom of troubling questions. What was this kachina doll that the Führer had given her husband? Was the statuette a reward for Oskar's service and devotion to his commander? If so, what was the point of the Führer's little speech about loyalty? Oskar was the most loyal person Edith knew. Or did the Führer suspect something? Yesterday, she had been afraid that perhaps Oskar truly believed in the ideals of the Third Reich. Now she found herself terrified that perhaps he didn't. And the

Führer's interest in Marina chilled her heart. It felt predatory, rapacious. She had no idea what had prompted it, but she was desperate to quell it.

Oskar entered the kitchen with the coal pail. Edith saw that it wasn't full. Oskar put the pail down next to the stove and stood still for a moment. He looked like a stunned animal. "Oskar?" He did not answer. "Why did the Führer give you a wooden doll?" Again, no answer. "Oskar!"

He blinked his eyes and gazed at her distractedly. "Edith, my love, where is Marina?" His voice was edged with panic.

"Upstairs, putting the girls to bed, remember?" The look of confusion on Oskar's face was real. She realized that Oskar must also have been affected by the afternoon's events. Perhaps he too had been unnerved, even excessively. "Oskar, are you all right?"

"Upstairs, of course," Oskar said. He turned to the staircase but did not move forward. "I must speak with her immediately."

"But you'll be late for the concert if you don't leave right away," Edith said. "You wouldn't want to give the Führer any reason to question—" She stopped midsentence. Oskar wasn't listening to her, clearly. He was caught up in some kind of internal turmoil; she could feel his mind churning wildly, but she had no idea why. She rose from the bench and intercepted her husband's path to the upstairs, blocking his way with her small frame. Oskar blinked a few more times. She gripped his face to make him look at her. Everything collapsed into a single question in her mind, repeating itself over and over. "Oskar, tell me, are you all right?" That brought him back. The touch, the question. He tapped his heels on the floor and straightened his back.

"The concert," he said decisively. "Edith, I must go to the concert. But I will be back as quickly as possible. Tell Marina to stay here, I must talk to her." He grabbed his hat from the coatrack near the front door and placed it on his head as he reached for the latch. "Don't worry, my dear. You will all be safe. I will do everything necessary to keep you safe." He gave her a kiss and walked out the door.

– Thirty-Two –

Hans Munter hated Klaus Weber's music. It was pompous, grandiose, and far too loud. All that timpani and reverberating brass was disruptive to digestive flow. Hans much preferred the quiet predictability of Bach or, if he was feeling emotional, perhaps a smattering of Vivaldi. But attending the Weber concert tonight had nothing to do with enjoying the music. Had he been asked about his attendance, Hans would have said, in a small voice, that he had been invited. Then, more loudly, he would have proclaimed his fervent belief that a *bürgermeister* must faithfully perform his civic duties.

The soldier who had pounded on his front door early that morning to deliver what Hans chose to think of as an oral invitation to the event had imparted the message through the violence of his knocking and the anger in his voice. A debilitating sense of dread had kept Hans in his pajamas up until two hours ago. He had not expected to attend the concert. He had seen Max Fuchs running around town yesterday morning, dropping off fat envelopes. Later, when he stopped by the Mecklens' bakery for his afternoon *streuselkuchen*, he had heard the town magpies gossiping about what Regina should wear. Putting those facts together with comments he'd overheard, Hans realized, as he pulled off his slippers and crawled under his bedcovers last night, that there was a concert, a *big* concert, and that he had not been invited.

He wasn't surprised by the omission. He was, after all, a mere *bürgermeister*. In the great universe that orbited the Führer, Hans was an insignificant speck of dust hovering at an extreme outer ellipse. He was not unhappy with this remote position. He was perfectly content to maintain his distance from the Führer and went to sleep that night greatly relieved by his exclusion.

But overnight, his fortune must have corkscrewed, because that battering ram of a soldier made it quite clear that the presence of the *bürgermeister* at the Weber estate this evening was mandatory. One could not turn down an invitation to a concert in the Führer's honor, however questionably delivered, without unpleasant repercussions. Nevertheless, all day long Hans desperately wished he could. Fortunately, two hours before the concert, his infallible epicurean instincts came to his rescue and mobilized him out of his house slippers. All it took was one thought to successfully vanquish his fear, or at least allow him to banish it for a time. Food. The realization descended upon him suddenly and unexpectedly, like divine grace: the food at this concert would be exquisite and bounteous. An event celebrating the Great Leader of the Realm (or whatever the Führer called himself these days) would undoubtedly have delicacies that were unavailable elsewhere. It was known, for example, that the Führer adored French cuisine. That meant French butter, French cheese, French liqueur. Hans wondered if there would be any French cognac. Thus did his gastronomic fantasies propel him into a three-piece suit and bow tie and launch him from his home toward the Weber estate. His normal Sunday-evening routine—the drafting of congratulatory letters to local octogenarians who were celebrating birthdays in the upcoming week—would have to wait. With his grandfather's ivory-capped walking stick firmly in hand, Hans made his way lakeward, pausing now and then only to swallow the anticipatory saliva that accumulated with each step.

By the time he reached the perimeter of the Weber estate, he had convinced himself that he was famished. The dirt driveway leading up to the house was lined with rifle-wielding sentinels who gave no indication that they recognized or even noticed Hans as he strode by, though he had no doubt they were watching every step. He did not intend to test their response times. His plan was to act in an entirely usual manner this evening, to fit in seamlessly with all the other guests, particularly those at the buffet table.

Arriving in the garden, still thinking of the buffet, Hans scanned the yard for signs of it. A rather large makeshift platform had been set up about fifty meters beyond the French doors that led into the house. On top of this deck, a small orchestra of musicians were tuning their instruments and practicing snatches of the music set before them on iron stands. Successive arcs of chairs for the audience curved around the platform, and on its far side, closer to the lake than to the house, stood a gazebo draped in the Nazi flag and sheltering three more chairs, which were larger and significantly more upholstered than all the others. From the red velvet cushion on the centermost of these seats, Hans guessed that was be where the Führer would be sitting.

Guests were scattered, some already seated and perusing the printed program, others standing within protective distance of chairs they had claimed with jackets or sweaters. Hans recognized very few of the attendees—just Regina and Gisela Mecklen and their husbands. He had imagined this event to be a kind of town gathering, somewhat like the summer musical events in the marketplace before the war, an occasion for the Blumental men to polish their shoes and the Blumental ladies to curl their hair. But such thoughts failed to take into account the misanthropy of this host. Not only would Klaus Weber not recognize most of his neighbors, he would probably deliberately avoid them if he passed them on the street. Most of the guests for this concert would be guests of the Führer, Berlin cultural luminaries chosen from his social secretary's address book, members of Berlin's high society who had fled to their summer homes when bombs began falling on the capital. Gowns and long gloves, parasols and hats dusty with disuse paraded across the lawn. Hans could only hope that none of the women balancing a wide-brimmed hat decided to sit in front of him. To his great disappointment, no one appeared to be holding a beverage or nibbling on a snack. For a moment, Hans had a flicker of panic that there might be *no* food at all, but he quickly dismissed it as preposterous. The food portion of the event, he reassured himself, must be taking place postconcert. A pity. Well, perhaps it would be best, then, to take care of a quick need of nature before settling down. Hans stepped through the French doors in search of the bathroom.

A series of elegantly calligraphed signs led Hans to a closed door near the kitchen. He tried the brass knob. It was locked. He stood against the wall opposite the bathroom, contentedly inhaling the air and congratulating himself for having made this short journey, for in this small spot, heavenly aromas emanated from the kitchen. His nose detected roast meat, tarragon, and a pungent sautéed onion, or possibly shallots. Béarnaise sauce, he hoped.

Propped against the hallway wall deep in olfactory reverie, Hans did not hear the bathroom door open. A deep voice recalled him: "Herr Bürgermeister, the bathroom is all yours." Hans's eyes opened upon a man in uniform, and from the gold arabesque stitched onto the gentleman's scarlet collar patch, Hans realized that he was staring at a general. A tall general with wavy dark hair who looked vaguely familiar, but Hans could not place him. Yet the general was extending his hand in greeting. Did they already know each other, or was this an introductory gesture? Hans canvassed his memory for some clue, but it was blank. He used to pride himself on not forgetting a face, but the events of the past two days had shaken that faith. That moment of betrayal by his bladder, for example, with everyone watching. Shameful. Was his brain now also beginning to fail him?

"Allow me to introduce myself," the general said. So they did not know each other! What a relief. Hans eagerly shook the proffered hand. "General Erich Wolf. I was at Birnau the other day when Captain Rodemann—" The general cut himself off as Hans colored. Of course. That was why the man looked familiar. Overcome with embarrassment, Hans quickly released the general's hand. But the man's authoritative throat-clearing commanded Hans to look up into a pair of probing and serious brown eyes. "I commend you on your courage the other day. In an extraordinarily fearful situation, you demonstrated great dignity." General Wolf put a large hand on Hans's shoulder. "You are a great role model for the people of Blumental." In an instant, Hans's self-respect was restored. Here was a decorated soldier of the highest order congratulating him for his bearing. Perhaps the general was right. The situation *had* been difficult, quite fearful. And perhaps, if the general had not noticed the small impertinence of Hans's bladder, no one else had either. Buoyed by this hope, Hans straightened his shoulders a bit.

"Thank you, General Wolf, I—" He was interrupted by the call of a solo trumpet outside. That could mean only one thing in the Führer's world of annexed emblems of royalty: the great man was arriving with his entourage. The footsteps of other guests who had been idling in the house, investigating Herr Weber's decorations and displays, now clattered hurriedly over the marble floors. Suddenly the general looked uncomfortable, and he gripped the briefcase he was holding in his left hand more tightly.

"I'm sorry, Herr Munter, I must attend the Führer," General Wolf said curtly.

"Of course, of course," Hans said as the officer quickly strode down the hallway toward the French doors. Hans took one final inhalation of the blissful aromatic cloud from the kitchen and went into the bathroom to contemplate the delicacies that awaited.

Johann could hear the orchestra tuning up as he was trying to extricate his arm from Sabine Mecklen's viselike grasp. The moment they had left her house for a "sunset perambulation," as she called it, she had wrapped her right upper arm around his left biceps and aligned her lower arm with his so that she could grab onto his wrist. If he was going to get away from her, which he knew he had to do at some point very soon, it would take a prodigious effort. The walk was her idea. Having successfully enticed Johann Wiessmeyer to her home, Sabine was not about to release him without first maximizing their chance of being seen together publicly. Using the leverage she had over his one limb, she steered him expertly toward the Blumental promenade. Uncomfortable though he was, Johann did not object. He needed to see what was going on outside.

He was also grateful to breathe the fresh open air, for he desperately needed to clear his head. The atmosphere in Sabine's parlor had been suffocating. There was a smell of rosewater that permeated everything: pillows, upholstery, and curtains too. The scent assaulted him every time a breeze blew through the open window. When Sabine went to the kitchen shortly after bidding him to take a seat, Johann had taken a quick sniff of the china and silverware and could have sworn that these too had been washed in eau de cologne. And the baked goods she brought back with her were so thoroughly suffused with the scent that it did not matter whether he was biting into an apple dumpling or a chocolate macaroon: everything tasted like decaying rose petals that had been liquefied, mixed with corn syrup, and left to ferment in a closet full of mothballs.

Equally suffocating was Sabine herself, trying far too hard to be deferential. She asked him questions in a tone two pitches higher than her normal speaking voice, then leaned in toward him on the sofa, head tilted to one side, eyes bright and bulging, neck tendons and cheeks taut with the strain of holding her tongue. He could never answer quickly enough. Sabine's natural proclivity to chatter led her to fill any silence that lasted longer than half a second, and once she got started, it was impossible to interrupt her. She prattled on and on, her body bent close to his, a steady and uncomfortable encroachment on his physical space. He found himself sliding farther and farther toward the end of the sofa. Very belatedly, he'd realized what a terrible mistake it had been to accept Sabine's invitation. But he needed an alibi. And he had naively hoped that this social encounter would distract him from events transpiring elsewhere that evening. Instead, he was now on the edge of panic, wondering about the Polish girls and Marina and whether they had been safely concealed, whether Fritz had remembered to fill the truck with gas, and whether he would be able to get out of town before roadblocks were set up.

At least the briefcase no longer bothered him. The telegram he'd received in the chapel yesterday from his cousin Gottfried had directed him to deposit the case next to the fountain in the marketplace by two o'clock today. When Johann arrived, the plaza had been empty. He had walked over to the stone basin, found a dry spot beyond the splashing range of the fountain, and placed the briefcase on the ground. Afterward, he stood under an elm, staring at the fountain from a distance. He searched his mind for some remnant of the doubt he had felt for weeks, expecting to reengage in the silent debate he knew so well: the propriety of taking one evil life to save innocent thousands. With great relief, he found neither hesitation nor misgiving. His conscience was entirely clear. Was this an indication that he had done God's will? Or that at least he hadn't contradicted it? Or was it a kind of shock, a short-term absence of emotion after a pivotal undertaking? As these thoughts clamored for audience in his head, Johann consciously tried to quiet them, reluctant to dissect his peace of mind lest it slip away from him.

One final idea presented itself, just as the young Thiessen girls skipped their way into his line of sight near the fountain. Faith. Perhaps all of his doubts were being reconciled by faith. Perhaps the serenity he was feeling was a confirmation of the message he had received yesterday. That God could forgive the action Johann was taking, that in fact He might forgive Johann as He had forgiven Jesus. The guilt that Johann bore for leaving the briefcase would be a very light burden. And the appearance of the girls was a sign that he could now leave.

An hour and a half later, Johann could not resist the temptation to check whether the briefcase was still there. It was not. Thus had he done his part. He had taken the step that he had struggled with for so long: he had actively assisted in a murder. A murder that was necessary to prevent other murders. Johann felt an overwhelming desire to retreat into prayer and contemplation. But he had not yet been able to return to his church. Late in the afternoon, he had run over to check on Fritz Nagel's truck. And now the rendezvous with Sabine. Silence was not something he was going to find with her. "Oh, dear me," Sabine chattered. "I completely forgot to ask you earlier, dear Johann—did the boys ever find you today?"

Sabine was leaning into his left side as they walked, and Johann felt himself being thrown off balance. "The boys?" he asked, trying to push back against her.

"Max and Willie," Sabine said. Her large hips bumped him over to the right, and he shifted his gait to accommodate her. "They came to the house looking for you, because Max remembered that you might be here. They were looking for you at the rectory, it seems."

"Ah." Johann breathed out, trying to anticipate her next bodily advance. "No, I didn't see them. But I wasn't at the rectory this afternoon." He briefly wondered why the boys might have sought him, but his thoughts were interrupted by their arrival at the east end of the promenade. Many of Blumental's citizens were already gathered at the steamboat pier to listen to the Weber concert. The orchestra's tuning sounds were just now being transmitted over the water by a light breeze. Sabine was pushing Johann in the direction of the crowd. He didn't try to resist. The crowd would be a blessing. If it happened while they were among other people, he might be able to slip away. Not unnoticed, not by Sabine, but all he needed was a minute or two of commotion to dis-engage himself from her grasp. Perhaps, too, something to prime her confusion, something he could initiate now.

When they reached the perimeter of the crowd, Johann stopped and grabbed Sabine's left hand. Not expecting this move, she loosened her grip on his arm. This was just what he had hoped for. "My dear Fräulein Mecklen." Johann had decided to address her formally, as it might limit any subsequent interpretations of intimacy, and to keep his declaration simple. "I would like to thank you for a lovely evening." Then, before she could wonder what he meant, he leaned forward and kissed her lightly, as lightly as he could, on her open, startled lips. Thankfully, the concert then began. "Shall we go listen?" Johann asked. Sabine stood before him in a daze, completely immobilized by shock. He put his arm around her waist and moved her toward the pier.

Lara had spent most of the afternoon languishing in her own loveliness. She had made herself as attractive and desirable as she knew how, in anticipation of the Führer's arrival, and felt thwarted by the inattention of his entourage. So many dreamy-looking men, and not a single one cast her a second glance. When the tea came to an end and they all marched off, she assuaged her disappointment with sugar, which turned out to be an ineffective consolation. But Lara was not one to give up easily. By the time her mother came upstairs to put Rosie and Sofia to bed, Lara had resolved that her beauty should not go to waste.

Sneaking out of the house while Marina and Edith tended to her sisters was remarkably easy. As Marina was pulling Rosie's nightgown over her head and Edith was helping Sofia choose a storybook, Lara headed down the stairs and through the living room, softly closing the French doors behind her. She ran down the hill to the lake. She would go to the Weber estate, she de-cided. She would get as close as she could, and at some point, she would be stopped by a soldier. She hoped he would be young and handsome. Just as she was smoothing the skirt of her dress, checking for jam stains, Lara heard a familiar voice. "Lara Thiessen." She turned around but could see no one following her, nor was anyone ahead of her on the path. Confused, she stopped, and in that moment, Max Fuchs dropped down in front of her from the hazelnut limb that he had been perched on.

"Max!" Lara gave a tiny shriek of surprise. "You scared me!"

Max's beaming smile disappeared in an instant. "I'm so sorry! I really didn't mean to."

"No, it's okay, it was just unexpected." Lara put her hand on her chest to slow her heart. "Having you appear like that from above."

Cautiously, Max's grin reasserted itself. "Well, I couldn't let you pass by without saying something." He took a step forward. "You are a vision of . . . of . . . of dazzlingness."

"Dazzlingness?" Lara knew that Max was not the smartest boy in town, but she didn't care. She was thrilled by the way he looked at her. "Is that a word?"

"It may not be," Max said defensively, though he appeared unabashed. "But 'beauty' is not powerful enough to describe you."

Lara's smile widened. "Is that so?"

"Yes." Max stepped toward her again. "It's so." Thinking she should appear shy, even if she didn't really feel it, Lara looked down, and Max moved to her side. "Where are you going?"

"The Weber concert. I wanted to listen."

"Me too!" Max said. "I was trying to find Pastor Johann, but he's disappeared somewhere. So instead I decided to climb the hazelnut to get a good view, but there are too many other trees in the way. Could I maybe . . . Could I walk with you for a bit?"

Lara looked at him. Max Fuchs was actually quite handsome, if you could see past the layers of dirt. He had nice thick brownish-blond hair that would probably be very soft if it were washed and combed, she thought, and his eyes were very friendly. The best part of his eyes was the way they were looking at her now. "Of course you may. You can even . . ." Lara pretended to falter, trying again to feign a modesty she didn't feel. "You can even hold my hand. If you want."

"Oh, yes!" Max grabbed Lara's hand immediately. It was a mildly sweaty grip, but Lara didn't mind. They began walking toward the music, which had just started playing. For a few minutes, they said nothing, each of them caught up in this unexpected development. All thoughts of encounters with soldiers had vanished completely from Lara's mind, erased by the warmth of physical contact with this boy who so clearly adored her.

They were about halfway to the Weber estate when the music they had been listening to ended. Lara had heard enough classical music to know that it would begin again soon, but Max took the interlude to pull her around to face him.

"Lara Thiessen." He said her name in such a dreamy way, as if she were some fantastical, magical creature. In that moment, she felt that she was. "Lara, I have a present for you, a present that I've been making for a while, because . . . Because I have admired you for so long."

"A present?"

"Yes, a piece of jewelry. Kind of. But I don't have it with me, it's at home. I can go get it."

"No, don't go." Lara surprised herself by grabbing his hand tightly. She did love jewelry, but right now, the only thing she wanted was for Max not to leave. "Don't go."

"Okay," Max said, staring at her. "I won't."

Erich Wolf returned to his position at the southwest pillar of the gazebo. One of his colleagues saluted him from the northwest corner. They had worked out their stations earlier that afternoon, and Erich had willingly ceded the northwest spot to the other man, who, as a Weber fanatic, wanted an unobstructed view of the composer as he conducted the debut of his piece. Erich placed the briefcase on the edge of the platform a few meters away from the wooden support column. There was nothing now to impede its explosive force except, God forgive him, the bodyguard seated at the left hand of the Führer. Erich positioned himself next to the case to deflect attention from it until absolutely necessary.

He had waited in the bathroom as long as possible before breaking the vial of acid in the pencil detonator. Once the acid was released, he knew, it would begin dissolving the wire that held back the striker-loaded spring. The moment the spring released the striker, it would fly against the percussion cap in the detonator, setting off the plastic explosives that surrounded it. Gottfried Schrumm had estimated that Erich would have no more than thirty minutes after starting the reaction to get out of its way.

Erich looked at his watch. It had taken the Führer a full fifteen minutes to make his entrance and sit down in his red velvet chair, but he was now finally settled. Erich had timed the first movement this afternoon when the orchestra practiced, and knew that it was approximately eight minutes long. He was hoping to leave between the first and second movements, so it might look as if he were taking another bathroom break. If that was going to happen, the music would have to begin soon.

As he was mentally tallying the minutes remaining, Erich heard a familiar voice. "Erich, I'm so glad to see you." It was Oskar. Erich had assumed that Oskar would be exempted from attendance at the concert so he could spend time with his family. Feeling the beginning of panic, Erich desperately wondered how he might get Oskar away. But Oskar himself provided the answer. "I need to talk to you about Marina. As soon as possible."

Erich snapped to attention. "What is it? Is she ill?" If something was wrong with Marina, if she was somehow in danger, Erich would abandon this venture. Somehow, he would find a way to stop the acid.

"No, no, nothing like that. She is fine, putting the girls to bed right now, I believe." Oskar adjusted his glasses slightly and looked over to where the Führer was sitting. "But the Führer said something this afternoon that has me worried. And then I found something in the house. I wonder if you know anything about it. I know she thinks highly of you, so she might have said something." Erich was grateful that Oskar did not know the extent of his relationship with Marina. Although Edith had guessed the truth years ago, he was fairly certain she'd kept the secret from her husband. Nothing in Oskar's demeanor or attitude toward him had changed in these past five years, as it certainly would have had he known.

Now Erich saw his opportunity to keep Oskar safe. "Oskar, if it concerns Marina, we cannot wait. Let's leave together after the first movement. If anyone asks, you can say you need a smoke."

Oskar patted his coat pocket to confirm that he had brought his pipe. Then he nodded. "All right. I'll look for you after the first movement." He went over and took a reserved seat in the front row. Erich looked at his watch. Ten minutes remained.

Captain Heinrich Rodemann didn't enjoy music. It disrupted his focus. Especially music like this, attention-grabbing and clamorous, insistent upon being heard. This kind of music was dangerous to Captain Rodemann's mission, which was to secure the Weber premises and ensure the safety of the Führer. Obviously, Berlin was going to make use of all the military resources available in the area to protect the Führer, and he himself was quite prepared, even eager, to lay down his life for the Supreme Commander. When the concert began, Rodemann took up position a short distance from the gazebo, on a small hill where he could survey the entire property and notice anomalous movements. His troops patrolled the estate in organized circuits around him, like electrons around a nucleus, Rodemann liked to think, drawing upon the little bit of chemistry that he had retained from Sister Monika's ruler rapping his knuckles. In his afternoon briefing to the men, Rodemann had made it very clear that this commission was more serious than any they had undertaken so far, and that any breach in responsibility would have dire consequences. He had stressed the word *dire* by pausing and tapping his rifle on the ground. The look on his men's faces was, he decided, one of unalloyed fear, and he had been pleased.

Of course, there were multiple layers of security around the Führer, but not all of them were impregnable, Captain Rodemann noticed. Those blond, purple-trimmed fellows, for example, the *Erleuchtete*. Twelve of them had marched in with the Führer, but eight had dispersed to other locations, and now only four remained, standing at the four corners of the gazebo. Rodemann knew the reputation of these men as well as anyone. He had watched their grand entrance in advance of the Führer this afternoon with fascination and envy. Fascination, because it was one of Rodemann's many ambitions to catapult himself through superior performance to these elite ranks. Envy, because he coveted their uniforms; he knew he looked particularly handsome in purple.

Of the four *Erleuchtete* who now flanked the Führer, three of them were, in Rodemann's opinion, listening to the music far too intently, with a kind of rapturous look on their faces. The Führer too seemed unduly transported, though of all the listeners, Rodemann supposed, the Supreme Commander was most entitled to be moved. Only one man appeared to be appropriately disengaged from the concert, the officer at the southwest corner of the gazebo. This officer had his back to Rodemann but kept shifting his gaze from his watch to the briefcase sitting next to him on the ground. The presence of a briefcase at an outdoor concert did not surprise Captain Rodemann. It was rumored that the Führer never took a break from official business, that he was always ready to sign a military order or issue a sovereign dispatch at a moment's notice. No doubt the papers in that briefcase were top secret, and the officer in charge of them had been ordered to guard them with his life. Just as he was beginning to admire this officer's single-mindedness of purpose, the man turned and Captain

Rodemann saw his face. General Wolf. A mixture of anger and embarrassment made Rodemann direct his attention elsewhere. He looked out past the civilian audience to the estate entrance and was reassured to see two of his own men flanking the statues at the main driveway. With pride and satisfaction, he saw that they were standing at attention, as he had ordered them to do. By contrast, Rodemann noticed with disgust, the police retinue not under his command were haphazardly scattered around the lawn, clearly at ease. One of them was even smoking a cigarette! Rodemann determined to find out the man's name and report him to his superior.

The orchestra fell silent. It must be the end of the first movement, Rodemann guessed, turning his attention back to the gazebo. An older gentleman sitting in the front row stood up and pulled out a pipe. Then he went off in the direction of the front gate to have a smoke. But his was not the only vacant spot near the gazebo. General Wolf too had disappeared, yet the briefcase that had stood next to him remained, unattended, sitting on the ground where Wolf had been a moment earlier. Most likely, Wolf had gone to use the facilities, but if so, why not carry the briefcase with him? Perhaps Wolf thought the environment safe enough to leave it alone for a time? If so, here was another example of how disgracefully the Führer was served by his subordinates. Had Rodemann been given charge of the valise, he would have guarded it properly. The Führer deserved no less.

It was an opportunity Captain Rodemann could not pass up: a top-secret briefcase abandoned by the high-level officer charged with protecting it, the very same officer who had ridiculed and embarrassed Rodemann in front of his men. If Rodemann were to go to the briefcase and pick it up, keep it under close watch until the Führer might need its contents, he would be doing his country and his Supreme Commander a critical service. And if, at some appropriate time, the Führer were to learn that Rodemann had stepped in to perform this service because General Wolf had failed him, and if he thereupon dismissed said general for inattention and laziness . . . Well, that would be the kind of divine justice that Captain Rodemann could appreciate.

He walked over to the gazebo just as the orchestra began the second movement. No one paid attention to him. He grabbed the handle of the briefcase, picked it up, and went back to the hill he had been standing on earlier. No need to be immediately visible to Wolf, wherever he might be. Let him wonder what had happened; the man deserved to sweat a little.

The briefcase was heavier than Rodemann had expected. He brought it up against his chest to give his biceps a rest. As he was imagining the look of dismay on Wolf's face, as he saw himself being decorated with a medal of honor by the Führer himself, in front of the Brandenburg Gate of Berlin, with his mother looking on, tears of pride streaming down her face—just then, the acid inside the briefcase dissolved the final millimeter of copper wire that led to the blasting cap, setting off the plastic explosive. The gases exploded outward with such fury that they ripped torso from narrow hips, shattered thick skull, and scattered tiny bits and pieces of Captain Heinrich Rodemann all across the well-manicured lawn.

For Max Fuchs, it was now or never. While the music was starting up. He put his hands on Lara's waist, pulled her forward, and kissed her just as the bomb exploded.

The crowd on the steamboat pier gasped, almost as one. Sabine Mecklen screamed. She was too stunned to notice Johann sink into the crowd and disappear.

Rosie jolted upright from her pillow. "What was that, Oma? What was that?" Startled, Edith dropped the book she had been reading and looked toward the window. For a moment, she didn't answer. Marina stiffened. She stood up from the chair next to Rosie and Sofia's bed, where she had been listening to Edith, and gently eased Rosie back down onto the mattress, smoothed the cotton blanket over her, and briefly rested her hand on her daughter's chest. Next to Rosie, Sofia had burrowed under the covers, careful, however, to leave her right ear exposed so her grandmother's voice could transport her into sleep. Marina stroked the top of Sofia's head, the only part of the girl still visible.

"Sofia? *Liebling?*" Marina whispered.

"Leave her alone, Mutti, she's trying to sleep," Rosie said, squirming. "What was that big boom?"

Edith looked at Marina, who shrugged her shoulders. "It sounded like very loud thunder, didn't it? Perhaps there is a storm coming, Rosie." Edith bent down to pick the book up from the floor. "But just as it is the clouds' job to deliver rain to the grass and the flowers so they can grow, it is your job now to lie back and listen, and then go to sleep so *you* can grow. Right?"

"Right, I'm going to grow taller than everybody," Rosie insisted.

"It's possible," Edith said, smoothing down a page. "Now listen." Marina tiptoed out of the room and headed for the cellar.

Fritz Nagel had done an extraordinary job. The Volvo truck was in the barn with its hood open, and immediately Marina could see that this would work. Fritz had managed to reposition the engine and its many leads and wires to the right side of the engine bay, and he had installed a piece of sheet metal as a barrier between that and the remaining open space to the left. Covering the metal was a sheet of asbestos, to insulate the left bay from excessive heat—an indication, Marina realized, that Fritz had a better idea of what they were up to than they had given him credit for. A perfect space for the girls to hide. And now was the time to put it to the test. When Marina heard the explosion, she'd known immediately that this was the sign Johann had meant. She had no time to wonder what had caused it. She'd rushed to the cellar and hurried the Polish girls out of the house and up to the Nagel barn as quickly as possible. The streets were deserted, but she doubted they would remain so for long.

In the barn, Marina retrieved two heavy woolen blankets that she had hidden that morning and spread them out in the empty engine bay. She motioned the girls to come close. She picked up the younger one to give her a better view, but the older one was tall enough to peer in on her own. "This is where you will hide while my friend drives you to safety," Marina explained. "It will be loud, and it may also get a bit warm, because the engine is right next to you, on the other side of this metal wall. But you will be safe here, so you mustn't let the noise or heat worry you, all right? Perhaps you will even be able to sleep a bit. That would be good." The girls stared into the maw of the bay.

The older one looked at her sister. "*Dobra*," she said, nodding. To Marina's surprise, she quickly hoisted herself up and climbed into the open space. She patted the blanket next to her. "*Chodź, Pola*," she said, beckoning to the younger girl. "*No chodź moja mała*." Pola hesitated and looked up at Marina for reassurance.

"Yes, go ahead," Marina said. "It's all right." She kissed Pola on her forehead and lifted her up onto the blanket. The older girl wrapped her arms around her sister protectively. For a moment, Pola relaxed, even pulled a piece of the blanket up around her as if she was settling in, but then she gave a small shriek and looked all around.

"*Daiya!*" she whimpered. "*Nadzia, Nadzia, gdzie jest Daiya?*" She began to cry. Marina had no idea who or what Daiya was, but she knew the crying had to be quieted immediately. The older girl, Nadzia, understood this too, and began shushing her sister softly. She murmured something to the little girl, who buried her face in Nadzia's chest and continued to sob, but her crying was now muffled. Nadzia kept up a low running monologue, then gradually shifted to a lullaby that she alternately sang and hummed while rocking Pola back and forth.

Marina stood mesmerized. For the second time that day, she was struck by how much these girls reminded her of her daughters. Would Lara comfort Rosie in such a way? She had never seen Lara exhibit maternal instincts—but then, why should she, at thirteen? There had always been someone else to look after Rosie and Sofia, and Lara too. And soon, she reminded herself, there would be someone to take care of these Polish girls as well. Johann would make sure of that before he left them, she knew. As if to confirm her thought, the pastor suddenly yanked the barn door open. He approached the truck with determined strides.

"Is everything ready here? Everything loaded?" Johann inspected the bed of the truck, which Fritz had loaded with crates of fresh tomatoes, cucumbers, young potatoes, and kohlrabi. Canisters of milk and cream from Fritz's dairy operation stood wedged like sentinels between the boxed vegetables. Satisfied, Johann turned to the open engine hood. "And the girls?"

"They're ready." Marina saw Nadzia open her eyes wide upon Johann's approach, then relax when she recognized the minister. He returned to the truck bed and beckoned Marina to come closer while he secured a heavy canvas tarp over the goods.

"There has been an attempt on the Führer's life," he whispered urgently, yanking at one of the ropes. "A bomb. At the Weber concert."

Marina exhaled. She knew that what she'd heard must have been some sort of explosive. She had a thousand questions, but only one mattered. Her tongue felt thick. "And? Is he dead?"

"I don't know," Johann admitted, moving to the other side of the truck bed. "I was at the pier when it happened and ran all the way here. I can't wait around to find out, I need to get these girls out while there's still chaos and confusion." He secured the last knot and moved to the side of the barn, where Fritz had stacked hay bales in an unused cow stall. Maneuvering his hand underneath the top bale, Johann smiled when his fingers felt the metal ridges of the key to the truck. "If I leave now, I should have no trouble." He walked back to the open hood, took two small apples out of his pocket, and gave them both to Nadzia.

If the Führer had been killed, Marina thought, Johann was correct—he would have no trouble. But if the Führer had survived? She remembered his words at tea and grabbed Johann's wrist. "Johann, listen, I have to tell you something. Something from this afternoon. I think . . . I think the Führer knows."

"Knows?" He did not try to wrest his hand away from her. "Knows what?"

Marina let out a small cry. "I don't know!" She recalled the predatory stare, the overwhelming sense of calamity that had pressed upon her. "But he knows *something*. He knows your name. He said he has gotten reports about you. He knows about your 'activities,' though I don't know what he meant." She stopped short, silencing her next words: *And he knows about me.* She didn't want Johann to worry about her, because he had enough to worry about already. And she didn't want to give life to this fearful possibility by uttering it aloud.

"What? What else?"

"Nothing else important." Johann looked at her doubtfully, but Marina shifted her focus back to him. "What is important, Johann, is that you are in danger. If the Führer is still alive, if he's survived this bomb, you're not safe here anymore."

Johann took in this information stoically, his face betraying no emotion as he considered its implications. Gently, he pried Marina's fingers from his wrist. "Well, if what you say is true, it's not just here. It's not just Blumental. I must leave too."

Marina felt tears welling up. "But where? Where will you go?"

Johann gently placed his hands on her shoulders. There was resolution in those hands, and belief. Marina knew that he was well acquainted with the brutalities inflicted by this regime and

its war. At various points, she had questioned him about what he
knew, but he had always deflected her. "Believe me, it is better
not to know," he'd always said. "Better not to have the images
in your head, because once they are there, you can never erase
them." He probably even knew what had happened to these girls'
family. Yet, despite everything he had seen and heard in this war,
despite everything he suspected and everything he knew, he still
had such faith in the world, in the innate goodness of humanity.
That faith was attractive. It drew people. It had drawn her. For a
long time, Marina had been envious of it, knowing that she would
never feel that kind of trust in anything. But she could borrow
that feeling from him, and she did now, absorbing his steadiness
through his fingertips. His palms resting on her shoulders soothed
her for the moment. The feeling wouldn't last, she knew, but perhaps it would see her through until tomorrow.

He was looking at her. His gaze was calm, as always, calm and
determined. Yet there was something else in his eyes, something
that hesitated. Was he waiting for her to say something? When
she did finally speak, her voice was a whisper. "Go."

Johann nodded. He bent his head and kissed Marina on the
cheek. Then he stepped over to the engine. "Now, my dear girls,
are you ready? It is time to begin."

Pola was asleep, but Nadzia looked at Johann and smiled shyly.
Marina leaned into the engine bay and gave the older girl one last
hug. She put her forefinger on her lips. "*Bądź cicho*." Nadzia nodded and lay down, curling her body around Pola's. Marina tucked
the blanket around them. Johann closed the hood. He stepped
into the truck, started the engine, and pulled out of the barn. He
did not look back.

For the second time in seventy-two hours, Hans Munter lay on
the ground, not quite certain whether he was dead or alive. He
was vaguely conscious of women shrieking and of voices barking

out orders, but it was difficult to make out specific words because of the intense ringing in his ears. After lying still under the remnants of wooden chairs that covered him, wiggling his extremities to confirm they were still attached, he looked up.

All he could see was a blanket of smoke and soot and bits and pieces of cloth and paper floating through the air. Most of the concertgoers near Hans were sitting up gingerly, checking themselves or one another for injuries, some of them wiping blood off surface wounds and sobbing softly. Far to his left, Regina Mecklen was leaning over the body of her sister Gisela, crying and slapping her cheeks in an effort to rouse her. Soldiers and policemen hurried around, as seemingly aimless in their movements as ants near an anthill.

Up front, where the gazebo used to stand, there was nothing but rubble and splintered beams of wood. A tuba was wedged beneath one of its collapsed pillars and a few orchestra members were busy clearing away the debris around it, as intent on freeing the instrument as if it were a cherished colleague. There was a body sprawled underneath another pile of gazebo wreckage, but it was ignored by the small group of soldiers who came rushing up to the platform. They were focused on a different figure lying motionless nearby. Hans couldn't see who it was. The soldiers lifted that other body and carried it over to the grass, laying it on top of a blanket. Hans watched as a medic came hurrying over, a stethoscope dangling from his neck. The medic knelt on the ground, and for the next few minutes, Hans saw nothing but the doctor's back as he worked to resuscitate the patient. By this time, Hans felt recovered enough himself to wonder if it would be highly inappropriate for him to take a few morsels home from the buffet. Although the Weber garden was a shambles, the house itself had survived this enemy attack—for Hans was certain that's what it was—completely intact. And it would be such a shame if all that food went to waste.

His thoughts were interrupted by a shout from the medic. The patient was sitting up, spluttering and coughing and calling for a glass of water. One of the soldiers pulled out his canteen and offered it. The patient drank greedily, then tossed the canteen aside. He stood up slowly, arms extending outward, pushing back the surrounding air to reclaim his space. When he turned, Hans recognized him. The Führer.

Marina wasted no time in leaving the Nagel property. When the taillights of the truck disappeared from view, it felt like something important had just been ripped from her. But she had no time to wonder about that feeling; Erich was waiting for her up by the Birnau forest, and she had to meet him, to understand what was happening now and what would happen next. So much of what he had said last night was becoming clear: that he might have to leave suddenly, that everything might change soon. Marina headed north on the road, desperate to see him.

It was only when she got to the Fuchs house that she became aware of the light beams. Stopping for a moment, Marina looked over Blumental. Across the town, bright beams of flashlights and headlights crisscrossed the roads, making their way north and east from the lake. They had already reached the eastern boundary of the city at the foot of the hill below her. Where her family lived.

How long had it been since the explosion? Half an hour? Longer? Marina watched the flickering lights approach her neighborhood and felt nauseous. If soldiers or policemen were going house to house searching for assassins, they would be rough. They would wake the children. Edith was there to reassure them, but . . . Sofia was so fragile. Marina turned around and began sprinting down the hill. Erich was waiting for her, she knew, but this would take only a few minutes. She would stay home only until the soldiers left. Then she would go to him.

Someone was furiously pounding on the front door. The oak panels shook with the urgency and impatience of someone desperate to breach them. Edith was startled awake in her bed. She had no idea how late it was, but the skylight above her revealed an inky gray darkness, not yet the pitch-black of settled night. She had changed into a nightgown and lain down for just a minute after putting the girls to bed. Later, she would tell herself that was a critical error. She never should have put herself in a position to doze off. She should have kept watch.

The battering continued. Edith stepped into the slippers beside her bed and reached for her robe. She opened the bedroom door to find Sofia huddled against it. The girl's eyes were wide open and completely black. The moment she saw Edith, she grabbed on to her body, and Edith winced slightly as Sofia's nails dug through the robe's fabric and into her skin. "Is Rosie still asleep with all this racket?" Edith tried to make her voice sound light. Sofia nodded solemnly. "Amazing." With some effort, Edith picked Sofia up. She untied her robe and rewrapped it, cocooning Sofia against her own nightgown. Then she headed to the stairs. Passing the girls' room, she saw Rosie wrapped around Hans-Jürg in the bed she shared with Sofia. Lara was slumped across the double bed she shared with Marina, in her underclothes, asleep. Marina was nowhere to be seen.

Arriving at the staircase, Edith hesitated on the top step. She had no desire to confront whoever was perpetrating this violence against her front door. It was aggressive, invasive, a continuation of the assault from that afternoon. How gratefully she had bolted the front door this evening before heading upstairs, tightly latching those thick iron bars like the braces of a fortress, keeping the dangers of the world at bay from her family. Every fiber of her being now urged her to run back to bed with Sofia, pull the blanket over both their heads, and wait out the siege. Although she could not say why, Edith felt certain something catastrophic was hammering for entry, and she was determined to keep it out. If an assault was imminent, the house could withstand it. It would protect them. Everyone simply needed to stay still, inside, and together. But now someone inside the house was striding over to the door. Someone was giving up. She heard the bolts slide open. The brass hinges groaned, giving way. Edith peered down into the foyer.

It was Oskar. He must have used his key to come into the house through the porch doors after she fell asleep. With his right hand clenching the thick oak jamb of the door, Oskar's body blocked her view of whoever was outside. She noticed that he was dressed in his military uniform. That was not what he'd worn to the concert. But why would he have changed?

"Stand back! In the name of the Führer, we demand entrance to this house! It must be searched!"

Oskar stood still. The demand that this unseen soldier hurled at him slowly diffused upward into the high ceiling of the entranceway. Now Edith understood why Oskar was wearing his uniform, and she was instantly grateful for his foresight. The uniform conveyed his rank. As a general, Oskar outranked almost everyone. He could deny entry to any other soldier. Edith almost chuckled with relief. She fervently hoped Oskar would send the man away as quickly as possible.

When Oskar finally spoke, he did so calmly and deliberately. "Lieutenant Dietz, good evening to you. Normally it is Captain Rodemann from your regiment who is sent to communicate with me."

"General . . . Sir, I . . . I apologize for disturbing you." Edith was pleased to hear the soldier reduced to stammering. "But I have my orders directly from the Führer, sir." As Oskar appeared unimpressed by this authority, the man's speech disintegrated into sentence fragments and yapping exclamations. Edith's hope grew with his verbal dissolution. "The Führer, sir! Who has just survived a terrible attack on his life! Thanks to the intervention of our captain! Who lost his own in sacrifice, sir!" The soldier took a deep breath and continued. "Which is why I am here. Sir! The new captain. Of the regiment . . ." The last statement trailed off, as if now-Captain Dietz himself could not quite believe all the events of the evening.

Edith listened with shock. *Assassination?* Here in Blumental? Suddenly, she understood the thunderous sound they had heard earlier. An attempt on the Führer's life was nothing new; the man had already survived more than a handful of plots to kill him. Of course, he used each failed effort to his advantage. He was immortal, he insisted. Or divinely protected. God wanted him to carry out his mission, he declared. The aftermath of such failed attempts was always grisly.

"Captain Rodemann, what a shame." Oskar's tone was indifferent. "The Führer is well served by such heroes. Tell me, was anyone else harmed?"

"One additional military casualty, sir, but other than that, no, sir, nothing serious. The bomb was quite powerful, but it detonated some distance from the crowd. But, sir." Captain Dietz took a step forward, and Edith saw a brief flash of blond hair before Oskar extended his arm to push him back and prevent him from coming in.

"Captain." Edith had always marveled at the way Oskar could use his voice to enhance his stature. Her husband was not a big man, but when he spoke authoritatively, as he was doing now, his words seemed to emanate from a much larger, invincible being that was not to be crossed.

Captain Dietz stared at Oskar, trying to evaluate what he was up against. "Sir, there are witnesses who saw you with General Wolf shortly before the explosion."

By his silence, Edith could tell that Oskar did not expect this statement. After a moment, he answered. "That is true, we went to have a quick smoke together between movements and were caught by surprise when the explosion took place."

"Is General Wolf with you now?"

"No, I came home as quickly as I could, to check on my family, and he, well, I believe he must have returned to attend to the Führer."

"He did not," Captain Dietz announced. "He has disappeared."

Edith was stunned. This soldier spoke as if he suspected Erich in some way. But surely Erich was somewhere on the Weber premises, attending to the wounded or ensuring that the Führer was transported to a safer location. Erich would not run away if his help was needed. That was not who he was.

"The Führer has ordered every house in the area to be searched until we find him," Captain Dietz announced.

Oskar sucked in his cheeks thoughtfully, as if tasting this possibility and finding it unpalatable. "No."

"Sir?" It was Captain Dietz's turn to be surprised. His voice squeaked slightly.

Oskar remained impassive but resolute. "I will not let you search this house."

Edith felt her heart pounding as joy and fear competed for space. She had no idea why Oskar was taking this stance, but she was ecstatic that he was defending their home—this sanctuary that they had created together and peopled with children and grandchildren more precious to her than anyone else in the world. Still, she could not ignore the clattering of weapons she now heard in the darkness behind Captain Dietz, which indicated that he might not back down so easily. Instinctively, she grabbed Sofia more tightly. By now, Lara too had been woken by the loud voices, and she stood next to her grandmother, cautiously tugging on her sleeve. Edith put a protective and consoling arm around her.

Downstairs, Captain Dietz was clearing his throat. "Sir, you must let us search this house." When Oskar made no move to step aside, he switched to a pleading tone. "If you do not, how can I explain it to the Führer?" Oskar inhaled slowly. Edith watched him, her breath suspended. Now was the moment, she thought, to close the door. No, slam it. Slam the door, Oskar. She waited, every muscle of her body tense.

Oskar did not slam the door. Instead, he let out a long sigh. "Ah yes, the Führer. He does not like disobedience. Don't worry,

Captain. I would not put you in that unenviable position. I will explain things to the Führer in person. I will come with you."

Edith's thoughts instantly backtracked. As vehemently as she had wanted to keep the soldiers out of her house a moment ago, she was now willing to let them in, if it meant that Oskar would stay. "No, Oskar, stay! You don't have to go with them. Let them search the house. Erich isn't here."

Oskar looked up at his wife, his face filled with sad determination. "Edith, I must go. Erich may not be here, but neither is Marina. I must go until we know Marina is safe. They will search everywhere. *Everywhere.*"

Her husband was making no sense. "Let them search!" Edith felt panic rising in her voice. "Let them search the house. It's all right. They'll search the house and then go. They will find nothing. And we can all go back to sleep."

"They cannot come into the house, Edith." Oskar spoke quietly. "I will not let them come in. I've said no. They must respect that."

"But, Oskar . . ." Edith unwrapped Sofia's arms from her body and quickly placed her on the floor next to Lara, who was grasping the banister with white knuckles. From Sofia's blank stare, Edith knew the girl had slipped into one of her states. But she could not attend to Sofia right now.

Edith hurried down the staircase. She needed to get closer to Oskar to convince him to stay. She needed to touch him. When she reached the threshold, she stopped. Oskar was staring at her intently, and then suddenly he seemed to be looking past her, toward the cellar door. He was trying to tell her something, but again she did not understand.

"Edith," Oskar pleaded, "please tell Marina I love her and that she is not to blame herself. But now I must go. Trust me on this." He stepped toward her, reached for both of her hands, and squeezed them tightly. Edith was dizzy with confusion. Why would Marina blame herself? What was Oskar trying to tell her? Then, as Oskar continued to clasp her hands, Edith began to feel what her husband was feeling: resolution, courage, exhaustion, sadness. No fear, not even an ounce of fear. But love—the love Oskar was communicating to her at that moment was overwhelming.

"I must stay with the Führer until Marina safely returns," Oskar continued. "And someone must stay with the children. Someone must stay in the house." He leaned forward and kissed Edith gently, softly, on her lips, then stepped back again and looked at her. "You are my life, Edith."

Edith was paralyzed. Oskar was giving her secret messages that she could not comprehend, about Erich and Marina, and something too about the cellar, and now he was leaving without explaining. Everything was disintegrating quickly and inexplicably, and she was powerless. She could only watch mutely as the group of soldiers parted to let Oskar pass by. He got into a car that had been idling outside, and Captain Dietz closed the door behind him and got in front, and they drove off into the darkness.

Ten minutes later, Marina ran into the house.

The cell that Erich Wolf was placed in prior to his execution had long been abandoned by the Franciscan monk who used to sleep there. Most of the land surrounding the Kreuzbach Abbey below Birnau had been converted into vineyards, but the thick stone walls of the dormitory and chapter house stood unaltered. These now served Captain Dietz very well, as his soldiers rounded up suspected conspirators and accomplices by the dozens to satisfy the Führer's outrage. Not only did the individual monastic cells make excellent detention facilities, but the courtyard of Kreuzbach within the cloisters was well suited for a firing squad. Executions were being carried out every hour on the hour, as quickly as suspects could be rounded up and summarily tried. There had been no pretense of a trial for General Wolf, at his request. When Erich saw Captain Dietz's posse of soldiers heading up the hill toward the Birnau forest where he waited, he knew at once that the assassination had failed. His surrender was immediate. It was pointless to continue, and Erich had never been one to avoid the consequences of his actions.

So that was why Marina did not come to meet him. If the Führer was alive, he had undoubtedly imposed a curfew. Or perhaps Oskar had refused to let her leave the house. Running away from the explosion that evening, Erich had looked back only once, and he saw Oskar trying to reassure a hysterical woman in a large red hat. Oskar would have headed home immediately after that, Erich reasoned, to his family. Erich trusted that they were all safe. They were his family too. He knew that now.

Erich sat on the cold stone bench, waiting. The bells of Birnau had just tolled three quarters of the hour. He was grateful to be left alone for these last few minutes. He looked down at his jacket, covered in dust from the road, and he methodically brushed the dirt from the gold piping that edged its lapels. Gold, for the cavalry. Earlier tonight, when he was dressing for the concert, he should have chosen the purple-trimmed jacket, which would have identified him as a member of the Führer's personal staff, but he knew he would go with the gold. His allegiance had always been to the horses. He had no regrets with respect to his actions. The only remorse he felt was toward the Eberhardts. Erich would have liked to embrace Edith one last time, give her that last apology for leaving. And he would have liked to speak with Oskar, not to explain himself but to make certain things clear. His gratitude for everything Oskar had taught him: how to be an excellent soldier and an even better man. His admiration, his *reverence* for Oskar's principles and priorities, intelligence and wit. And most important (though Erich was not certain how Oskar might react to such a declaration), his deep, unequivocal love for the man he now realized he thought of as a father. That love overshadowed any questions Erich might have had about Oskar's morals, given Oskar's position in the Führer's cabinet. Erich had never asked those questions, because, quite simply, he could not afford to lose another father in his lifetime.

Would Oskar be disappointed in Erich? It did not matter now, he realized with relief. Whatever Oskar's reaction, Erich would not be there to experience it.

And Marina. Erich could not say when he had fallen in love with her. He knew he had been drawn to her from the first day they met. Somehow, even when Marina was a child, her spirit reached out to his and claimed him for her own. He did not know that at the time, of course; he had been disturbed by his feelings for her as she grew into womanhood. That was why he had made himself leave the house. Tried to divert his heart with other perfumes. He did not succeed.

Distractedly, Erich began refastening his jacket, starting at the bottom hem, as had Marina, that first afternoon in the barn. His fingers, like hers, tracing the outline of each round brass clasp. Slowly massaging the edges of each buttonhole with thumb and forefinger. A wave of her perfume washing over his memory as he sank his face into her hair. The pearl translucence of her skin, offered without reservation to the touch of his fingers, which he skimmed slowly, carefully over her body, as though she might dissolve if he pressed too hard. That afternoon, like every moment with her, outside time and space and reality, yet so constrained by all three. Giving him the two greatest gifts in his life: the experience of her love, and Rosie.

Thus it was that Erich Wolf relinquished his memory of Marina and laid it to rest, finally and tenderly, beside Oskar and Edith, beside the horses of Niebiosa Podlaski, beside the brown curls and beautiful brown eyes of his daughter. As the bells of Birnau struck the midnight hour, he brushed the lapels of his jacket one last time. There was a knock at his cell door. Erich turned to face the soldiers as they entered.

The Volvo truck arrived early at the rendezvous point near the east edge of the Stierenwald, just inside Switzerland. The driver shut off the engine and left its hood open while he went back to check something under the tarp. He opened several milk canisters until he located the one that was filled with diesel fuel. Then he shut the engine hood, got into the cab, and shifted into first gear. The truck continued west toward Basel.

By the time the orphanage master and his nurse arrived at Stierenwald, shortly before dawn, the diesel fumes from the truck's exhaust had merged into the mist of the old logging trail and disappeared. By then, the truck was well out of Basel, heading southwest toward the ports of Lisbon.

– Epilogue –

1966

Marina stood on the porch and scanned the garden for some sign of Edith. Her mother's rubber garden boots stood on the flagstones next to the table, but that didn't necessarily mean anything, since the sun had warmed the lawn all day. Marina knew her mother; if she was in the garden, she'd have gone barefoot.

Seeing nothing but islands of flowers rising from the sea of grass, Marina decided to check the arbor. She made her way past the waving crowds of anemones and hollyhocks, newly freed from the overgrowth that had confined them days before. They really needed to hire someone to mow and trim more regularly. The yard was so much more accessible when properly manicured. Marina had to admire Lara's efficiency. When she arrived last week, Lara had taken one look outside and immediately hired a team of gardeners. "Rosie can't get married in this thicket of weeds!" she'd said. "We'll have to hand out machetes just so people can get to their seats." The next day, four men were mowing and whacking and trimming their way around the yard, under Lara's watchful eye.

Marina passed underneath the arms of the apple tree, now quite gnarled, its gray bark deeply furrowed. But it still bore fruit reliably. Today Marina could see small apples pushing aside the jade leaves of one of the lower branches, the one hanging over the defunct sandbox. If Rosie had had her way, all the guests would be roasting sausages over a fire in that sandbox for dinner tonight. "Sebastian loves grilling," she'd said. "He can tend the fire."

"Over my dead body," Lara had challenged. "His only job will be to dress nicely and help me choose a caterer." It was generous of Lara to pay for everything, Marina thought. Her fashion business must be doing very well. Marina was proud of her eldest daughter, living alone in Düsseldorf, traveling to the catwalks of Paris and Milan and New York, hobnobbing with international designers. Success suited Lara without going too much to her head, for which Marina was grateful. In recent years, Lara had become very solicitous of Rosie, eager to develop the sibling relationship that she had spurned for years.

This wedding, for example. Lara wanted to be a part of all of Rosie's decisions. In practice, of course, that meant that this wedding—at least the spectacle aspect of it—was more Lara's than Rosie's. But neither Rosie nor Marina minded ceding that responsibility. Rosie hadn't even wanted to get married. Sebastian had asked her so often, it had almost become a joke between them. This time, however, he was able to point out the health insurance benefits of legalizing their relationship.

Stepping into the arbor, Marina found her mother standing next to the fountain of Daphne, veiled in a fine spray of mist, shoes in hand. Edith's gaze was fixed on a pool of tiny blue flowers that was slowly spreading along the garden path toward the lake. Forget-me-nots. Marina put her arm around Edith's shoulders. They stood next to each other, looking at the flowers in silence.

Edith had, over the years, made a more solid peace with her losses than had Marina. When the news reports and photographs of the death camps appeared, when the truth of the Führer's genocide was revealed, Edith finally understood Oskar's disappearance. She saw it as her punishment, she told Marina. Her penalty for silence and acquiescence. Not that she knew what she would or should have done had she known the truth back then, but that was no excuse. Deep down, Edith knew that she had been afraid: afraid of the Führer, afraid to confront the possibility that such horrors were happening in her backyard, afraid that the man she loved most in the world might somehow be involved. She had chosen ignorance. And Oskar was taken from her. As so many souls were taken from so many others. All Edith could do now was accept, she said, and try to remember him, them, everyone who was lost, with love and apology.

Marina, on the other hand, had spent years trying to learn her father's fate. Of course, Marina bore a more direct burden of guilt for Oskar's disappearance. For she had realized—when Edith remembered and told her about the half-filled pail of coal Oskar had brought up from the cellar that day—that her father must have seen the Polish girls. That he had offered to go with Captain Dietz that night because he feared the refugees would be discovered by the soldiers. That he went in order to protect Marina and the rest of their family.

It was a heart-wrenching realization. She longed to explain herself to her father in person, to persuade him that she had had no real choice in bringing danger to their home. Would she also have apologized to him for putting him in such a difficult position? Perhaps. Certainly she would have thanked him for protecting all of them. But she never had the opportunity.

Marina did not understand why the Führer never released her father, if in fact he had been imprisoned, as she and Edith assumed. When Johann left for America, when the refugee operation in Blumental shut down altogether, and especially when Marina herself was not arrested, why did Oskar not return? Days turned into weeks and then months, without any sign of him. Marina's love for her father, fueled into a frenzy by her guilt, demanded some sort of answer. Even after the war ended and the Führer committed suicide, and his entire dark regime dissolved, there was no information. No sign of Oskar in any of the jails or detention camps. All of Marina's inquiries, through both unofficial and official channels, led nowhere.

Out of desperation one day, Marina ransacked Oskar's old Biedermeier desk. She pulled apart its cabinets and dismantled its shelves, even pressed on panels of wood looking for secret compartments. Yet she discovered nothing new or extraordinary. Only piles of official papers, and various notebooks that she'd scoured and been unable to decipher.

She did, that day, find one small black binder that had somehow wedged itself into the runners beneath one of the middle drawers. But it turned out to be nothing more than a log, in Oskar's handwriting, of all the telegrams he had sent from the field telegraph machine he kept at home. The log covered the year 1944. Flipping through it, Marina saw numerous entries for Oskar's last two days, July 19 and 20. But, as with all of the correspondence logs he kept, Oskar had recorded only the initials of the recipient in Berlin to whom the telegrams were sent. G.S. She had no idea who that person was; nor did Edith, when Marina showed the log to her. And there were no public records of Third Reich personnel that they could consult. The log book was, like everything else, a dead end.

Erich's fate, on the other hand, was certain. So was Franz's. The Führer issued a public statement the day after the assassination attempt, reassuring the public of his own safety and well-being and daring anyone with information about the conspiracy to remain silent. The statement closed with a list of names, all the conspirators who had been tried and executed. Erich's name headed that list. A week later, Marina received a letter informing her of Franz's death on the beaches of Normandy.

Marina was better able to accept the loss of Franz, perhaps because she had, ever since Stalingrad, been mourning the gentle naturalist whom she had first loved. That beautiful, quiet man had really died in the snows of a Russian winter, and the soldier who went to Normandy was nothing more than his ghost, awaiting the bullet that would free him to fly with his birds.

Erich's death was different. Initially, she simply could not grasp the reality of a world without Erich Wolf in it. His disappearance was too abrupt, and swept away with it were all her dreams for the future. She was also angry with him, angry that he would have taken part in an assassination attempt at a time when the war was so close to ending. That he would have chosen to put his life, and by extension their life together, in jeopardy by engaging in such a foolhardy task. She was angry that he had left her alone. For solace, and because she knew Erich would have wanted it, Marina had his horse, Arrakis, shipped south and boarded in a nearby barn. For many years, she rode Arrakis daily, and for hours at a time. To her, the dark Arabian was an extension of his former master. Sitting on his back was as close as she could come to having Erich right there with her, arms encircling her waist and holding her tight.

Marina trembled involuntarily at that memory. "So many more flowers this year than last," Edith said with a sigh. Marina did not remember how many of the small blue flowers there had been the previous spring. Edith extended her arm and stretched out her fingers, measuring the expanse of blue with her hand. "Last year they were just up to my middle finger," she said. "Now they're past my pinkie."

"I wish memories were that tenacious," Marina said. Because the memories she had of her father were fading. Only isolated snapshots remained: the way Oskar pursed his lips and sucked in his cheeks when he first lit his pipe; how he used his finger to follow the type as he read a newspaper; how his forehead wrinkled when he laughed. Perhaps that was why she kept returning to her memories of Erich. She didn't want to lose him, as she feared she was losing her father.

Edith kept gazing at the flowers. "They spread themselves like souls," she said quietly.

Marina did not understand. "Memories?"

Edith continued as if she had not heard the question. "You see the one flower, which blooms and then disappears. Its roots creep underground, this way and that. Eventually, those roots send up stems from which countless other flowers bloom." She reached for Marina's hand. "Our memories of the people we love fade over time, and we fear it means that we are forgetting them." Marina nodded, teardrops forming at the corners of her eyes. Edith's voice was tranquil and subdued. "But what is really happening is that their souls are becoming more and more a part of us, and of everyone else who loved them." She turned and looked at Marina, wiped her daughter's eyes. "They continue blooming through us. We can no more forget them than we can forget ourselves."

Marina dropped her head against her mother's frail shoulders. She had not wanted to cry today. But it was impossible not to feel the loss. "I still miss them all so much," she said. "On a day like today, they should all be here. Especially Sofia."

It would be three years this September since they found Sofia's note on the kitchen table: *I cannot bear being outside the blue anymore. I love all of you so much.* Weeks later, her body was found in the lake. The pockets of her skirt were filled with the heaviest stones that could fit. She must have just walked into the water, kept walking as it reached her knees, her thighs, her waist. Continued even as it touched her chin, entered her mouth, covered her eyes. Would she have gagged then? For months, Marina had nightmares of drowning. She hoped Sofia had been in some sort of trance, that she had not really felt the water wash over her scalp and take her, finally, for its own.

Sofia would have loved celebrating the changes in Rosie's life. Perhaps Rosie could even have pulled her sister away from the maelstrom of internal pain and calamity that she had endured ever since Oskar's disappearance. The promise of life fighting the seduction of darkness. But Sofia had never been a fighter. That was Rosie. Sofia's defense had been withdrawal. The blue space that she gave herself to was her only solace. "Sofia would have liked these flowers," Edith said finally.

"I think that's why Johann suggested them," Marina said.

"Oh, Johann! That reminds me, my dear. You have a letter

from him in the hallway. That is, what? The fifth letter this week,
I believe."

Unexpectedly, Marina blushed. Johann's letters had been a
godsend. For years, the family had received an occasional letter from Brooklyn, but when he heard about Sofia's death from
Edith, Johann wrote to Marina daily. His letters were filled with
thoughts on life and death and God and the human spirit and hu-
morous anecdotes about the oddities of his church members. He
shared tales of his exploits as an uncle to his sister's rambunctious
children, and proclaimed the advantages of leading a choir in a
nursing home, where no one could hear well enough to know that
they could not sing. He told Marina about Pola and Nadzia, both
of whom had settled in New York and married, and both of whom
subsequently sent Marina their own letters of gratitude. In short,
he bombarded Marina with hope and love. Almost three years of
daily letters. Lately, Marina was responding as frequently. It was
much cheaper than telephoning, and she found herself wanting
to talk to him every day.

"Mutti! Oma!" Rosie's voice carried clearly across the garden.

"Ah," said Edith, turning around. "We are being hailed by the
queen."

Marina laughed, grateful to be pulled out of her reverie. "Actually, I think Lara is probably the queen. Rosie is only a princess,
even if it is *her* wedding day."

"No, of course, you're absolutely right. Lara is, was, and always
will be the queen."

The two women left the arbor just in time to see Rosie running
down the hill in search of them. She was wearing her wedding
dress, which she had put on the moment she woke up that morning, so that she would not have to change later in the day. Marina
had not seen Rosie in the dress since they'd chosen it months earlier. She was glad that the tailor had been able to accommodate
Rosie's seven-months-pregnant belly.

"Stop running! Stop running before you fall, you crazy goose!"

Lara cried, appearing on the porch. "They're right there, Rosie! Look, they're coming up from the arbor."

Rosie slowed and looked in their direction. "Oh, hello, you two!" She stopped and stood beaming at them. "How's the garden?"

"Oh, my goodness, what a question!" Lara ran over to Rosie and draped her arms over her sister's shoulders. "Don't distract them with questions, Rosie. If you get Oma started on the garden and how her flowers are, we'll never get her dressed."

"I'm coming, I'm coming," Edith said, leaning on Marina. "Anyway, who cares if I'm dressed? No one will be looking at me."

"So you think, Oma," Rosie said. "But you need to look your best anyway, for my sake at least. And Lara has a surprise. She found a minister!"

"Really?" Marina had given up hope of finding anyone affiliated with any religion to officiate at the wedding. Rosie's pregnancy was too visible at this point. And this part of the country was too Catholic. "Who is it?"

Lara ignored her mother's question. "Oma, let me help you upstairs." She took Edith's hand.

"Thank you, Lara. You are my queen." Edith winked at Marina as she was led inside.

"I'm so happy the sun came out," Rosie said, looking up at the sky. "Do you think it will stay?"

"Sweetheart, you are your own sun today." Truly, Marina thought, Rosie's beauty was transcendent. Lara had pulled Rosie's hair back loosely, into a low, slightly tousled bun, and had woven Edith's beloved *gänseblümchen* into her curls. A few free tendrils framed Rosie's face, which was radiant with joy.

Rosie laughed. "You're right, you're right. If it rains, we'll tell the guests to share towels." She put her hands on her stomach. "Oof! Somebody's waking up."

Marina reached out and felt the skin under Rosie's dress distend as the baby repositioned itself. "What is that? An elbow or a foot?"

"Who knows? As long as there's two of each." Rosie suddenly looked up. "Aha, here he is."

"Who?" Marina asked, following Rosie's gaze.

"The minister." A man was approaching them from the garden. He had entered the yard from the lakeside gate. But he was not walking along the path next to the cherry tree, which would have been the most direct route. Instead, he was making his way out of the arbor, where Marina and Edith had stood a few minutes earlier. Marina squinted, but he was still too far away for her to see him clearly. "Well," Rosie said, turning toward the house. "I'm going to go check on Sebastian. See if he's put on his trousers yet. No groom should go without trousers, right?"

"At least not until nighttime." Marina smiled. "But, Rosie, tell me before you go—who is this man? Where did you find this minister?"

"Oh, we had to go far afield to find him. He's come a long way." Rosie gave her mother a quick hug and a kiss on the cheek. "But if you're nice to him, he might stay."

Marina watched the stranger draw nearer. There was something familiar about his walk, slightly lumbering because of his large frame, and his face too, its shape so round, with wire-rimmed glasses . . . and then she knew.

– Acknowledgments –

This book would not be what it is without the support and insight of so many friends and colleagues over the past decade. Working backward in time, I begin with enormous gratitude to Trish Todd, who embraced a fledgling story and, together with an extraordinary team at Touchstone, crafted it into a work of art. Equally heartfelt thanks to Leigh Feldman, for her early faith in the manuscript, her expert guidance, and her unfailing humor. And to Ilana Masad, for plucking me out of a mountain of pages and opening a new door. I feel blessed to have such skillful and enthusiastic champions.

I am indebted also to the sure and skillful pen of my beautiful friend and mentor Pamela Toutant, who spent innumerable hours helping me shape the final draft. Her creative insights were absolutely critical, and I will be forever thankful for her help and friendship.

Along the way, numerous friends, colleagues, and family members read early versions of the book, and I thank them all for their constructive comments and steadfast support: Benson Forman, Kendall Guthrie, Judy Austin, Marianne Green, Katinka Werner, Rudolf Werner, Beth Werner, Dan Simon, Anne-Louise Oliphant, Bill Wescott, Bob Zachariasiewicz, and Terri Lewis. Also many thanks to the wonderful Susan Chehak Taylor and all the inspirational writers of her 2013 Advanced Novel class, and to the Iowa Summer Writers' Workshop program.

To my immediate family—Geoffrey, Julia, Anna, and Emily—there really are no words that can convey what my heart feels for, and owes to, each of you. Every day, I live in your miraculous web of love and encouragement. You are my world.

Ursula Werner is a writer and attorney currently living in Washington, DC, with her family. Throughout her legal career, Werner has pursued creative writing, publishing two books of poetry, *In the Silence of the Woodruff* (2006) and *Rapunzel Revisited* (2010). This is her first novel.

The Good at Heart

For Discussion

1. *The Good at Heart* opens with a famous epigraph from *The Diary of Anne Frank*: "In spite of everything I still believe that people are really good at heart. . . . If I look up into the heavens, I think that it will all come right, that this cruelty too will end, and that peace and tranquillity will return again." How does this epigraph work as a lens through which to read the novel? To which character(s) do you think "good at heart" refers?

2. In chapter 1, the narrator tells us that "for the Eberhardt family . . . the house was enough." Why do you think Edith and Oskar spent so much of their marriage fantasizing about the house in Blumental? What symbolism does the small house hold for the couple? For the family?

3. Discuss the relationship between Oskar and Marina. Would you call their relationship strained? Typical? Prob-

lematic? Do you think the two are truly at odds in terms of ideology? Why or why not?

4. A possible theme emerges in chapter 2 when Rosie notes, after Hans Munter's narrow escape from death, that the rope was still tied to the tree, "swinging slowly back and forth, a reminder of how suddenly things could change." Do you think the swiftness of change is a theme in the novel? Why or why not?

5. What do you think is Marina's goal in joining Johann's underground group? Does she want simply to help right the wrongs of the regime, or is it something more? Do you think helping refugee children assuages her guilt about her crumbling marriage and her affair?

6. In chapter 10, Marina says that walking through her mother's garden and breathing in the scent of roses are "pockets of comfort." Where else does Marina find comfort? What about Edith? Johann? Lara? Sofia? Rosie?

7. Revisit the scene in chapter 13 when Edith and Sofia get trapped underground during the bombing of Berlin. Why do you think Sofia escapes to her "reveries" of blue as a result of this traumatic event? What is the connection between being trapped in the basement and the desire for blue? Do other characters in the novel "escape" in their own way? How so?

8. For Johann, the question of participating in an assassination attempt on the Führer is inherently complicated because of his vocation. He wonders, "Would a God who gave Moses the Ten Commandments condone assassination" (see chapter 14)? Ultimately, how does Johann conclude

that delivering the suitcase is part of God's will? Do you think he abandons his faith temporarily in order to fulfill this obligation, or is he acting in accordance with it?

9. Discuss the three-part structure of the novel. What symbolism can you glean from this structure? How does the compression of time in the novel influence the characters' decisions? Consider Marina, Johann, Erich, and Oskar in your response.

10. What do you think of Erich Wolf? Is he a sympathetic character? How does his sudden arrival in town prefigure his sudden death?

11. Were you surprised to discover that Rosie is Erich's daughter? How does Rosie seem distinct from her older sisters? Do you have the sense that in the end Rosie and Lara know the truth about Rosie's father?

12. How does the tension between Marina's decision about whom to love—Franz or Erich—mirror the tension in the house as it prepares for the Führer's visit? Are both equally doomed enterprises? Is there any way that Marina could have changed the outcome and not lost both loves? Is there any way the family could have avoided losing Oskar?

13. In chapter 22, Edith ponders the notion that "perhaps the only way to forgiveness was through pain." What pain(s) do you think Edith is referring to in this moment? Does she ultimately find a way to forgive in the end? Who or what does she forgive?

A Conversation with Ursula Werner

The Good at Heart is your debut novel. Can you share with us what it was like to write this story? How much is inspired by true events in your family? How much is fictionalized?

The basic questions of *The Good at Heart*—what might be the stresses and difficulties facing a German family living in the midst of World War II if the patriarch of that family was a high-ranking official in the totalitarian government—came directly from my own family. My great-grandfather, Hans Ernst Posse, was a cabinet secretary under Hitler. That fact, along with the silence of my family surrounding his activities during the war, weighed heavily on my psyche for many years. I wondered what he knew and didn't know, what he did or didn't do, and I was equally curious about what he told his wife and children—whether they asked him about his activities, or whether they were too afraid to do so. Writing *The Good at Heart* allowed me to examine, imaginatively, not only those questions, but also the larger question of the collective or cultural guilt that settles upon a nation ruled by a dictator like Hitler.

I also grew up with stories from my parents about what it was like to live in southern Germany during the war. To a large degree, these stories conflicted with the images of Germany and German civilians during the war that I had seen on television and in film. So my secondary imaginative endeavor in writing the book was to present a snapshot of a small southern German town during wartime—where people might try to live their lives as normally as possible, given the police state surrounding them, and the circumstances of war.

The town of Blumental, though completely fictional, is based upon a real German town in which my mother currently lives, and many of the physical locations—including Birnau, the pink church on the lake—are real. And there is a real historical truth underlying some of the events described in the book: for example, Hitler really did visit a composer who lived in that town, and the mayor of the town was almost murdered by a sadistic SS officer. But the vast majority of the plot details are fictional.

Why did you choose to structure the book around the three days leading up to the assassination attempt on the Führer? Is there an argument to be made that this novel has a clear beginning, middle, and end?
Because I wanted to tell my story from multiple points of view and because there were a number of different, possibly confusing plot lines, I decided to limit the time frame of the novel to three days. Structurally, that kept the story from becoming too unwieldy. Also, by focusing on just three days, I was able to present a more detailed picture of day-to-day life in Blumental—what might market day have looked like during the war? What kinds of games might the kids have played?

In my mind, there is a distinct structure to the book, beginning with Erich's arrival in town (quickly followed by Oskar's arrival), leading up to the tea with the Führer, and culminating in the assassination attempt at the concert and its aftermath.

It is noteworthy that you have many different narrators throughout the course of the novel, from Rosie to Marina to Johann to Erich. Why did you decide to tell the story from so many points of view? Ultimately, whose story is this?
My hope in using a multitude of points of view was to present a realistic picture of the different attitudes and perspectives of

different Germans toward the war, and toward the regime that governed them. In particular, I wanted to focus on the complex questions confronting people who opposed Hitler's policies in principle, but found themselves constrained by the deadly threats of his police state. Marina, Johann, Erich (and even Edith) all oppose the Führer, but they face different obstacles in deciding what to do to voice their opposition, or whether to voice it at all. The only character whose viewpoint we never hear—and I knew from the beginning that he would remain silent—is Oskar. By not giving voice to Oskar's thoughts, I wanted to put the reader in the position of myself and countless other Germans who never really knew what people like Oskar were up to. I wanted to make Oskar as likable as I knew my great-grandfather was, someone who was loved and respected by his family members and neighbors. What does it do to your image of such a person when you learn that they *might* have been involved in a reprehensible and horrendous crime? And do you temper any censure you might feel when you remember the context of Hitler's police state, and the fact that people during that time weren't really *free* to make decisions as we are today?

Ultimately, although *The Good at Heart* tells the story of the Eberhardt family, I hope it tells a larger story as well: that of the average German person living under the Nazis during World War II and confronted with harrowing rumors about the activities of that regime; the story of someone who may have wanted to help the oppressed, but might not have known how to do so effectively, or how to do so without bringing danger to herself or her family. And beyond that story lurks, for me, an even bigger principle, applicable to so many other situations—that we really can't judge the actions of other people without imagining what it is like to be in their place, considering the totality of all the influences surrounding them. Even then, we can't judge others, I think, because everyone has different instincts, values, and priorities.

Do you relate most to one character? If so, who is it and why?

I probably relate most to Marina, though I can identify with aspects of all the characters. I know what it is like to raise three daughters and to experience the intense fear that some of the decisions you make might cause them pain. I also believe, like Marina, that it is possible to love deeply more than one person in a lifetime, even at the same time. I'm not sure that I would have had the courage—or bravado—that Marina has, in bringing refugees to her house at the same time as the Führer is coming to tea, especially where that action puts the lives of her entire family in danger. But I admire her for it.

Author Susan Meissner wrote that *The Good at Heart* offers a "fresh perspective on what we are willing to surrender for the greater good." What are the characters in your novel asked to surrender? In the end, does good triumph over evil?

In the end, two of the characters, Erich and Oskar, surrender their lives for what they see as the greater good. Erich risks his life in order to try to kill the Führer. Although the assassination attempt fails, and Erich is executed, the fact that there even *existed* an internal resistance group trying to remove the Führer is a triumph of good over evil, in my mind. Ultimately, too, Erich has to act in accordance with his conscience. As a single man, he has a certain freedom to engage in risky activities, without implicating family members. His participation in the resistance is an internal moral triumph; he can go to his death knowing that he was true to certain principles he believed in.

As for Oskar, he ultimately sacrifices his life so that his family can remain safe. (As a sidenote, my mother was very angry with me for killing off Oskar. She kept asking me to find a way to let him live.) At the time Oskar goes with Captain Dietz, he does not know that Marina has already removed the refugees, so he is trying to avoid a house search. In that sense, Oskar's sacrifice is more heartbreaking, because the reader knows it was unnecessary. Nevertheless, I consider it a triumph, because it's a demonstration of a father's overwhelming love for his daughter, and his willingness to do anything to protect her, his wife, and his grandchildren.

Although I love Erich and Oskar, and I love dear, gentle Sofia, and they all die, I cannot say that evil triumphs. What triumphs, in my mind, is life. That was the revelation of Rosie's pregnancy in the epilogue: life goes on, life endures. War takes its victims, but there are survivors, and they can be strengthened through their suffering, and they can march forward to create something new.

Discuss the title. Would you say that all the characters—and maybe by extension, all of us—are truly good at heart?
I have to say that I am in awe of Anne Frank's ability to believe that people were basically good at heart, in light of everything she had experienced in her life up to the time she made that statement. Every time I reread her diary, I am struck by how beautiful and insightful the writing is for a girl only thirteen years old. I can only imagine—and mourn the loss of—the extraordinary writer Anne would have become, had she not been murdered.

Yes, like Anne, I do think people are basically good at heart. As a Quaker, I believe there is "that of God in every one," and it is relatively easy for me to equate the concept of a God with goodness and love. Of course, it is difficult to reconcile this belief with the historical reality of a person like Adolf Hitler, who truly seems to have been evil incarnate. With respect to Hitler and other people who sow fear and hatred, I think that the inherent goodness of a person can be overwhelmed or shackled by negative human instincts, developmental circumstances, and/or societal forces. The light of goodness in such people has been extinguished, in some cases permanently, in others, hopefully not.

Because this novel was inspired by events in your own family, did you encounter any particular challenges in telling this story? Or, did the personal aspect of the novel give you better access and insight into the lives of ordinary Germans during World War II?

My mother was very concerned about factual accuracy in the book. Her family, the Posses, was the model for the Eberhardts, and she still lives in the town that Blumental was based upon. I kept trying to remind her that the book was fiction and that Oskar was *not* really Hans Ernst Posse, Edith was *not* Margaret Posse, etc. But it was hard for her to embrace that fictionalization, particularly when she was worried about the reactions of people who might see themselves as characters.

I recently visited my mother in Germany, and we were invited to have coffee with a family in the neighborhood. At one point, we began talking about the novel, and our discussion evolved into a rich and fascinating recitation of events in the town during the war. It was there that I learned for the first time about a rumor that Hitler had visited the town several times, because he was friends with the wife of a composer who lived just down the street. I thought that I had completely fabricated the Führer's visit to Blumental, but apparently, there might be some truth to that story! I also learned that our neighbors hid a Jewish family in their house overnight so that they could be smuggled over the border to Switzerland. These were stories I had never heard, and I hope that this novel will foster similar discussions, especially as the generation of people with first-hand knowledge of World War II is growing older.

If Franz and Erich had not died, what do you think Marina would have done? Would she have stayed married to Franz or run away with Erich? Along similar lines, does the end of the novel imply that Marina and Johann are together?

Ah, well, in my mind, this question touches on the much bigger topic of whether authors create and control their stories, or whether the stories and characters take on lives of their own. A few years ago, I had the privilege of hearing Kazuo Ishiguro speak about his writing, and he said at one point that nothing any of his characters did was a surprise to him, that in his experience, the author was always firmly in control of the story and its details.

That, however, is not my experience at all. There were several points during the writing of this novel when I had absolutely no idea what was going to happen. I had to step away from the writing for a time and let the story reveal itself to me. And it always did, usually while I was on a walk or running through the forest with my dogs.

So I can't really say whom Marina would have chosen, because only she can know that. But I like to think that Edith's statement to Marina in chapter 18—that Franz deserved to be married to someone who wanted to be married to him—might have allowed Marina to leave her marriage without too much guilt.

Similarly, I can't say for sure that Marina and Johann end up together. In fact, the ending came as a *complete* surprise to me. I had no idea Johann was going to pop up again in the epilogue. I had just put Edith and Marina in the garden, talking about forget-me-nots, when Rosie came out of the house, and lo and behold, there she was, pregnant! And next thing I knew, Johann was heading through the grass to officiate at her wedding.

There is a subtle kind of feminism in the novel as Edith and Marina—and Marina's three daughters—form the central focus of the story and represent the stronghold of the family dynamic. Was it your aim to offer a female perspective on the war? How do you think their gender contributes to the choices the characters made—or do you?

One of the reasons the novel is dominated by female characters is because the Eberhardt family is based upon my mother's family. The Posse family is predominantly female: my maternal great-grandparents had two girls and a boy; my maternal grandmother had three girls; my mother had two girls; my sister and I each have three girls. There are very few boys or men in that family tree, and those who marry into it usually divorce, back out, or die off relatively young. There was a moment during one of my family visits to my mother's house when my husband was getting a bad cold and my mother brought him some echinacea oil, claiming it would minimize his symptoms. He took one look at the dark brown fluid in the tiny vial and pushed it away, shaking his head and saying, "This is how the men in this family disappear, isn't it?"

So I don't think I consciously set out to present a female perspective on the war, but in retrospect, there may have been some unconscious instincts toward that end. While I have read enough memoirs by male (and more recently, female) soldiers to know that the reality of fighting in any kind of war is horrendous, I think that there are unique hardships in being left behind on the home front while your loved ones are off at war. I wanted to give voice to some of those difficulties—maintaining a facade of hope and cheer for your children, even as fear and anxiety over the safety of your loved one gnaws at you day and night; offering your loved one unequivocal support by phone or telegram or mail, even as you yourself might desperately need comfort or reassurance; struggling to keep a household running during a time of rationing or shortages so that life seems as normal as possible.

I think the women of *The Good at Heart* make some of their choices not so much because they are *women* but because they are *mothers*. It is the nurturing instinct to take care of another human being, to put his or her well-being ahead of their own, that informs many of their actions. I don't believe that kind of instinct is necessarily limited to women. But I do believe that if ninety percent or more of the earth's leaders had the instincts of mothers, we would live in a vastly different world.

What would you name as the major theme(s) of the novel?
I have no doubt there are many more themes in the novel than the ones I might identify, but one of the major themes in

my mind is the strength of family. All the adult Eberhardts—Edith, Marina, and Oskar—cherish their family and prioritize its cohesion and safety. Edith focuses on maintaining domestic stability during wartime. Marina struggles mightily with the passion she feels for Erich, which pulls her away from Franz, her parents, and her children. And Oskar offers his life as the ultimate sacrifice to keep everyone else in the family safe. The importance of family ties during war is, of course, nothing new. But I do think that keeping that theme in mind gives us some insight into the conflict many Germans faced when they considered what actions, if any, they might take to oppose Hitler and his policies.

Which brings me to another concept that I hoped to express in the novel: the shortsightedness of a black-and-white approach to history. When you really look at historical situations closely, trying to consider all the circumstances surrounding difficult questions, I think it's almost impossible to view them in sharp contrast. From the distant perspective of the future, looking backward, historical questions always appear more black-and-white than they actually were at the time. I don't mean to deny that terrible incidents of hatred and violence—by both actors and onlookers, Nazis and ordinary Germans—took place in Nazi Germany. Undoubtedly and tragically, they did. But I think we should be careful before we assume that all Germans were complicit in and sympathetic to such incidents.

My novel suggests that history's truth, if it can ever be determined, is more gray. That's one of the reasons I love visiting my mother's home in southern Germany in the winter: gray is the predominant color over the Bodensee in November and December, and there are countless shades of it. The gray reminds me to keep my judgment in check; to temper my preconceptions about other people; to slow down, look, and listen to everyone and everything, because in fact we all know so little.

Anne Frank's quote provides a lens through which the reader can come to understand the characters and their motivation to do good. Was the *Diary of Anne Frank* an inspiration for you in writing this novel? Can you tell us other novels or memoirs that inspired you as you wrote?

I had read the *Diary of Anne Frank* long before I wrote the novel, but what I am struck by, each time I read it, is what I suppose I would call its relative "ordinariness." Here is a young girl, forced during wartime into hiding in a relatively cramped space with seven other people, under constant threat of discovery and either execution or deportation to a work camp—and she still fills her diary with humor, complaints about the foibles of others, and run-of-the-mill adolescent angst and self-analysis. That human ability to create normalcy, even in the context of an ongoing fearful and uncertain situation, shaped how I wanted to present my story. Because in the midst of the war—Captain Rodemann's haphazard firing of machine guns through the streets, an underground effort to smuggle refugees into Switzerland, and a plot to assassinate the Führer—the people of Blumental are living their lives as normally as possible. They are going to market, they are inviting each other for coffee, they are gossiping, they are going to choir practice. I consider that instinct to establish normalcy part of our survival instinct, and it is an amazing demonstration of the adaptability of the human spirit.

There were many books and memoirs that informed and inspired *The Good at Heart*. I read numerous biographies of Hitler, which so cluttered the bookshelves next to my front door that I began to fear what people would think of my politics when they entered my home. More inspiring were the biographies and writings of Dietrich Bonhoeffer (upon whom Johann is very roughly modeled), whom I consider one of the most admirable men in history. And I was fascinated to learn about the activities of the German resistance, especially as recounted by Joachim Fest in *Plotting Hitler's Death* and Peter Hoffmann in *Stauffenberg: A Family History*. Also, Barbara Demick's book *Nothing to Envy* about life in

North Korea, was an invaluable resource for understanding the reality of life in a police state.

Are you working on a second novel? Can you share any plans with us for future projects?
The project I am currently working on is a mixture of memoir and history, a story of growing up in South Florida in the 1970s—a tale fraught with backyard alligators and flying cockroaches and sudden thunderstorms spawning waterspouts around a small family sailboat. One future project I am particularly excited about, but for which I have yet to do an enormous amount of research, is a historical biography of a well-known biblical figure.

Enhance Your Book Club

1. For the characters in *The Good at Heart*, choices between right and wrong are never clear-cut. In many ways, all the characters had to make tough decisions about what was right in the moment—sometimes with terrible consequences. "Our choices are not always what they seem to others," Oskar tells Marina in chapter 15. With your book club, discuss this quote in light of Oskar's job. To what "choices" do you think he is referring? Does this quote act as an omen for the ultimate choice he has to make to disappear from his family—or do you think that disappearing was not his choice? Consider all the tough choices the characters in the novel have to make, and share a time when you faced a dilemma in which you had to make a choice that could have seemed wrong from another point of view. How did you manage to make the decision? Did you gain any hindsight after the choice was made? If you had the chance to do it all over again, would you?

2. Edith's statue of Daphne in her garden becomes a kind of sanctuary for the women in the house, a place to sit and contemplate difficult decisions or the unlikely roads that led the family to have the Führer in their living room. With your book club, read the myth of Daphne: www.greekmythology.com/Other_Gods/Minor_Gods/Daphne/daphne.html.

3. Afterward, discuss the myth as a group. Why do you think Edith—and later Marina—feel drawn to the statue? Can you note any connection between Daphne's story and the story of these women?

4. Despite the turmoil aroused by the Führer coming to the Eberhardts' home, much care and attention is given to preparing the best desserts to accompany coffee and tea. Host an afternoon tea for your book club, and prepare some of the same treats Edith and Mariana made, including a Linzer torte (www.joyofbaking.com/LinzerTorte.html) and a strudel (www.quick-german-recipes.com/german-apple -strudel-recipe.html). Over tea and coffee and the desserts, discuss what it must have been like to have Hitler sit at your table. How do you think Edith, Oskar, Marina, and the others managed? Share a time when you felt distressed about a guest arriving in your home.

5. The work Johann and Marina do to offer safe harbor to Jews during the war is difficult in part because of Oskar's prominent position in the Führer's cabinet. Difficult— even impossible—decisions are often the focus of Holocaust narratives. Host a movie get-together with your book club and watch Sophie's Choice (1982). Discuss how Sophie's Choice parallels the choices the characters in the novel have to make. What do you think you would do if faced with such impossible decisions?